LEXI HODGES

Break Her Heart

First edition

ISBN: 979-8-9920172-2-9

This book was professionally typeset on Reedsy.
Find out more at reedsy.com

I never meant to let you in. But then, I should not have kissed you.
-Klaus Mikaelson

Contents

Content Warning

The contents of this book may be triggering and disturbing to some readers.

A complete list of content warnings for this book can be found on the author's website at www.lexihodges.com

ALENTARA
ICE REALM
NIGHT REALM
MOUNTAIN REALM
LAND OF THE HEALERS
QUEEN MOTHER'S LANDS
FOREST REALM
SUN REALM
FLOWER REALM
OCEAN REALM
SEA OF MAVROLA
JOVERYN
ERYNDOR
SERANTHIA

1

Bronwen

You made me king. I'll make you my queen.

The words rang in my head—too loud, too real. My stomach twisted. I had expected his hatred, his rage. I had been ready to die for what I had done. But this? This wasn't vengeance.

This was a claim.

And somehow, that terrified me more.

"N-no."

August's laugh tore through the woods, echoing off the trees like thunder. Snow swirled through the air, flakes catching in my hair and melting against my flushed cheeks.

"No?" His voice was a blade. "Do you expect me to listen? Like you listened to me when I told you not to kill him? I am your king now, remember? And as your king, you will do as I say."

I recoiled at his words. His *command.*

"I will not marry you."

In an instant, he was standing above me, pressing my back against a tree. His eyes glowed red, a wicked brightness against the midnight shadows.

"Say that again," he whispered, edged with madness. His breathing was uneven, his fists clenching and unclenching as if he couldn't decide whether to strike me or pull me closer. He pressed forward, pushing me harder against the tree, his movements sharp and jerky, like his own body was fighting against him. "You think you can just walk away from me? After everything?"

My hands trembled as rage burned beneath my skin. He was not going to tell me what to do.

But the August standing in front of me wasn't the one I had come to know. Not the one who made me feel... *something*. Dark webs pulsed beneath his red eyes. That playful smirk he always wore was long gone. His hair was in disarray—the hair that I had clenched in my hands only hours earlier. He was so vulnerable then, worried about me, begging me to trust him. And I did. Then I used his trust to do the one thing that I knew he despised. I pulled his magic, sending him through what I could only imagine to be unbearable pain, and I used that to kill his father. When I did that, something inside him had shifted, like I'd broken a part of his soul that he could never get back.

The way something inside me broke when my parents died.

The guilt twisted through me like thorns, sharp and relentless. I had used him. Manipulated him. And now I stood here trying to pretend I was the righteous one.

But hadn't he been manipulating me, too? Keeping secrets, holding back the truth until it suited him? Trying to control me even now? My thoughts tangled, torn between anger and guilt, between the anguish in his eyes and the cruelty in his words.

No. Carrow deserved to die. I was willing to sacrifice my

relationship with August for that. That was a truth that didn't change. No emotion burned brighter than the pain I felt from seeing my parents' lifeless bodies. Nothing mattered more than getting revenge.

"But you hated your father," I snapped, pushing him off of me as I moved out of his reach. My breath spilled out in frantic clouds, the chill scraping against my lungs.

"This has nothing to do with my father," he said coldly. "This is about Carrow."

"What?" Why did he say things like this? Things that never made sense. "Your father is Carrow!"

August glanced to the left as if he'd heard something that I couldn't. His shoulders tensed, jaw clenched. His gaze flickered through the darkness, searching for whatever threat he sensed.

"Your brother is looking for you. Let's go."

He stepped forward, but I matched the distance with a step back. Fear threaded through me, each breath a struggle against the cold that seeped into my bones.

"I'm not going anywhere with you."

His eyes locked onto mine. "You will."

My fists clenched at my sides, the heat of the magic I stole from Carrow rising like a fever against the winter chill. Flames itched beneath my skin, desperate to be released.

"Tell me, *Winnie*," he said, cruelly calm. "Has your... curse been broken? Do you feel the magic pulsing through you? Are you fixed? Or are you still a hollow shell of a witch?"

His words cut deep, but the truth remained. Nothing had changed. No surge of magic when I killed Carrow. No divine awakening. Just the magic I had stolen from him, still burning beneath my skin like an echo of what I could never truly have.

I didn't answer.

He laughed, bitter and full of venom. "I thought so."

Again, he looked to the side, his body coiled like a beast ready to lunge. "Now come on."

"No!" My voice cracked. "I will not go with you. I will not be your queen! I never want to see you again."

"Winnie—"

"Don't call me that!" I hissed. "You kept things from me this entire time. You knew who Carrow was from the beginning. You let him meet me, *feed* on me—and you let him kill my parents. I told you I would kill Carrow, and I did."

"You didn't," he said.

"What is wrong with you? Did you not see me kill him? Are you truly that insane?"

He ran his hands through his hair before letting out a grunt, the frustration in him boiling over. "You killed his host body."

"What are you talking about?"

"On the next Blood Moon, his soul will take over my body. It's his loophole—his way to gain true immortality. You can't kill him. He will always be here, controlling everyone around him."

The air vanished from my lungs. "No," I said, barely above a whisper. Fire flickered in my hands, heat rolling down my arms, defiant against the frigid air. "He—he can't. That's not possible."

"It is. He left his fae form and took the body of the Joveryn King. When that body gave out, he moved to the son, and then the next son. Now?" August's eyes met mine, cold and calculating. "Now it's my turn."

I shook my head slowly, the world tilting beneath my feet.

"No," I whispered, but the word tasted wrong—empty

and thin. I stumbled back a step, needing distance, needing something to hold onto. But there was nothing. Only the jagged ruins of what I thought I'd won.

"You're lying," I said, but even I could hear the desperation bleeding through the words. August didn't move. He didn't blink. He just stared at me like he was waiting for the rest of me to shatter.

He's dead, I wanted to scream. *I killed him! I killed him!*

But deep down, in the place I couldn't protect, the truth had already started to root itself. I knew it. I had felt it even then—that killing Carrow hadn't been enough. That it was all wrong.

I wrapped my arms around myself, trying to hold in the panic clawing at my ribs.

"I burned him," I said, as if saying it out loud could make it true. Could make it real. "I burned him to nothing. There was nothing left."

August's mouth twisted. "Ashes can still speak. You just weren't listening."

The floor seemed to shift beneath me, and I squeezed my eyes shut.

This wasn't just my failure. It was everyone's loss.

And it was mine to carry.

I dug my nails into my palms, welcoming the sting. *You did this. You trusted the wrong person. You let the wrong man close.*

When I opened my eyes again, August was still there. Waiting. Watching me fall apart and daring me to stand back up.

"What do you want from me?" I rasped.

"I want you to fix it," he said simply, as if it were the easiest thing in the world. As if it hadn't already broken me.

He looked like a caged animal, every muscle pulled taut,

his breath uneven and raw. Fury swirled within him, but something else too—something frantic and helpless.

I shook my head as he stepped closer.

"So you can either kill me now," he said, "or you'll marry me and find a way to stop it."

Snow crunched behind me.

"Bronwen."

My name, spoken in a voice so familiar, cut through the icy darkness like a blade. I turned sharply, my body still shaking from the fight with August. Adar stood just a few steps away, his chest heaving, eyes wide with panic. His gaze darted between August and me, confusion twisting his features into something close to horror.

I had kept so much from him this entire time. *You have to trust me*, I had said when I formed the plan.

And he did, without a second thought. But he didn't know that everything that happened was my fault. He didn't know that the man I told him I was sparring with was a monster. One who dragged us all into this nightmare.

But it was all coming together for him now.

"What did you do?" The words scraped out of his throat like broken glass. His eyes searched mine, pleading for an explanation that I didn't have.

August's voice sliced through the air like a knife. "You haven't told him?" He laughed, the sound splintering against the silence. "You didn't warn him that he was killing the king?" Each word flung like a poisoned dart. "Or that you were fucking a vampire?"

Adar recoiled, his shoulders jerking as if the words had struck him physically. I saw the betrayal flicker across his face, raw and bleeding. His fists clenched at his sides, knuckles white from the force of it.

August smiled. "Or that you are the reason your parents are dead?"

Fire exploded from my hands.

I wanted to make it all stop. The madness, the pain, the twisted threads of truth and lies that bound us all together. The fire lashed out of me, uncontrollable and savage. I was ready to end it. To move on from the games that had consumed me. To finally kill August.

But instead, I ran toward Adar, grabbing his arm with fingers that trembled with both fury and desperation.

And then we were gone.

2

Bronwen

I watched the fire dance in the hearth. The feeling of victory I felt when I killed Carrow left as quickly as it came. August said I didn't kill him, but he could have lied. He always kept things from me and this could just be another one of his games because he was mad that I went behind his back and did something.

He *had* to be lying.

Because the truth was too hard to bear.

I reached into the fire, waiting to feel something—anything. The flames danced around my hand, wrapping between my fingers as they nipped viciously at my flesh, but my skin stayed clean, and all I could feel was a little heat.

What did it feel like to burn? I'd watched a man at Market stand too close to a pit where they were roasting a pig. The tail of his coat caught immediately, trailing up his back, but he ripped it off and was left unscathed other than a few burn marks. But a vampire... it was as if they were made entirely of kindling. A candle could burn them in a matter of seconds. Did it feel the same as it did when a human burned? I'd never know.

The fire didn't hurt me, but part of me wanted it to. Maybe if I burned, it would feel like penance. Like proof that I could still feel anything at all. I thought pain would bring me clarity. Or punishment. Or something other than this numbness pressing down on me like a weight I couldn't shake.

I felt nothing. Just heat and silence.

My thoughts were fragmented, slipping away as fast as they came. Everything felt foggy. I couldn't remember how long I'd been sitting here. Minutes? Hours? The flames blurred in front of my eyes, and for a moment I forgot where I was.

What I would give to have Shadow with me right now. Was he okay? Did the townspeople make him pay because he was the property of a witch? Or was he still in the barn waiting for us to return? Alone and starving.

The thought punched the breath from my lungs. I blinked slowly, a sick heaviness pressing down on my chest.

I needed to know.

The scar on my neck pulsed, faint and steady, like it was listening. A soft reminder that August would always be tied to me in a way I couldn't shake. I pressed my fingers against it, but it only throbbed harder, like it was mocking me.

Is this what Papa meant when he said darkness would consume me? The darkness that was left in my soul after losing him and Mama?

"Bronwen!" I jumped at the sound of my name, ripping my hand away from the hearth. I was so lost in my thoughts that I hadn't realized that the flames had crept up my arm, searing the fabric of my sleeve. Adar's voice had never sounded so much like Papa's.

He sat in a small wooden chair behind me, daylight peeking

behind him through the windows. I had brought us to the coven's cabin and immediately sank to the floor in front of the fire. Now I realized I had been sitting here for hours. Had he been talking to me?

He stared at me, unmoving. His eyes looked glassy, like he couldn't believe what he was seeing. He dragged a hand through his hair once, then again, before his knuckles whitened against the armrest. Then he erupted.

"You told me nothing! Trust you? I did. I followed you blindly and we killed the fucking king! But that wasn't the worst part. Your little *boyfriend* is one of them! Bronwen, what did you do?"

Tears pooled in my eyes.

Adar took a breath, but I flinched as he shifted forward. My whole body tensed, instinctively pulling back like I expected him to lash out. He froze, his brow furrowing at my reaction, and that made the shame hit even harder.

"Tell me what you've done," he said, steadier now, but with an edge that scraped like ice.

And I did.

I told him everything. I watched his face shift with every detail, and with each passing second, the distance between us grew. I hated how hollow I sounded. Like I was narrating someone else's story, not mine.

I told him about the night I was marked—how I let it happen, how I convinced myself I could handle it. I told him about the nightmares and how real they felt, how they tore pieces of me away one at a time. I told him how many times August and I tried to kill each other, and how I started to forget why we stopped.

I couldn't meet Adar's eyes when I told him about the

journal. About the witches. About Lowen and his friend. I saw something shift in him when I got to the part about the Legion soldiers. His mouth opened slightly, maybe to interrupt, but he didn't say a word. He just listened.

And when I finally told him about meeting the king—about how I didn't know it was Carrow, how I let myself get close—I felt the final crack split wide open inside me.

"I didn't know his father was Carrow," I said, barely above a whisper. "I should have. All the signs were there, but I was too blinded to see them. Too stupid. And now they are dead."

I waited for him to say something. My pulse pounded in my ears, drowning out the crackle of the fire. I braced for him to yell again, to walk out, to tell me I was as twisted as August. The silence felt like standing at the edge of a cliff, waiting for the wind to shove me over.

"Please. Say something."

He didn't look at me. Instead, he kept his eyes on the ground. I thought this was it. That he had shut me out. I wouldn't blame him if he did.

And still, a part of me feared it so deeply I couldn't breathe.

He pushed himself out of the chair and knelt in front of me. "You went through all of that. Alone." He grabbed my face, pain painted across his own. "No more secrets. No more lies. We only have each other, and I—I can't lose you."

I nodded, wishing this was it. That we could move past it all, run away and start over. But it wasn't.

The numbness hadn't lifted. The guilt still dug into my bones.

"He said I didn't really kill him."

"What?"

"He wasn't making sense, but he said that on the next Blood

Moon, Carrow will take over his body."

Adar closed his eyes and took a deep breath. "He could be lying."

I nodded. "I know. But I need to see him. To see if he's telling the truth."

"Then I am going with you."

"No. He won't hurt me." Not physically at least. Emotionally, probably. "He had the chance, and he didn't."

"Do not keep me in the dark anymore. Let me take this burden on with you. Please, B." His voice cracked, his eyes searching mine with desperation.

"He won't talk if you're with me."

"Oh, he's going to talk," Adar growled. "If he wants to fucking live, he's going to talk. Besides, I have something that will make him talk."

* * *

We had formed a shell of a plan, but Adar wanted to wait until sunset to ensure no one in town saw us. We had a giant target on our backs now that everyone knew we were witches. I was fine with waiting, because something else had been bothering me for days now.

I needed to see Shadow.

The sun hung high in the sky now, but it did nothing to chase cold away as I slipped through the pines. I wanted to come alone. And I almost convinced myself to slip out when Adar wasn't looking, but if he found me gone, the little bit of progress we had made would have been for nothing. With him came Jonah, one of Papa's oldest friends, who used his magic to get us here faster. It was the logical choice. I would have been miserable riding for hours from the coven's safe house to our home in the middle of winter. But still, I'd rather be alone.

Jonah brought us to the woods. He worried that if we spelled ourselves straight to our home, someone would be on the road and see us. He decided to let us visit our home alone and wait in the woods to take us back.

As we walked, my mind constantly replayed what had happened last night—tricking August, the trap we formed with our witches hiding under a cloaking spell, and August almost stopping me.

"How many witches died last night?" I asked, breaking the long silence between me and Adar.

"Three. None if your lover hadn't shown up."

I tensed at those words. There was no love in those eyes. Not anymore.

Adar sighed. "I'm sorry. I shouldn't have said that."

But it wasn't like he was wrong.

"I went to him before," I admitted. "Planned to kill him for what he let happen. But I couldn't."

Adar nodded, and I was sure he had something he wanted to say, but he stopped himself.

The smell of smoke hit me before I saw it, curling in the back of my throat like a scream I couldn't swallow. Our home was a pile of ashes. Where once there were windows glowing with candlelight, now only scorched timbers jutted like broken bones from the earth. And the barn—*oh gods*.

I ran through the yard. My breath came fast, shallow, and panicked, clouding the freezing air like smoke. The world blurred, grief coating it in static. I could still see Papa on the porch, laughing at something Mama said. I could still hear the creak of the barn doors, the soft huff of Shadow greeting me. Gone. All of it was gone.

"B! Wait!"

Smoke still filled the air, clinging to my clothes, my hair, my skin. How could someone do this? Did they leave the horses to burn? I dropped to my knees on the far end where Shadow's stall once stood, my fingers digging through the blackened debris like I could uncover a miracle. Ash clung to my hands, and sparks flickered with every desperate movement. Would I find anything to know if he was in here? Bones? Hair?

"No, no, no, no, no." The word was barely a whisper, ripped from the hollow pit in my chest as I clawed through the rubble. My fingers closed around something half-buried beneath the ash—a warped metal halter buckle, still warm from the smoldering ground.

My breath hitched. I pushed deeper into the rubble, my heart thudding in my ears. What if he had been trapped? What if he had cried out for me while I was off chasing vengeance?

I could feel the panic clawing at my throat, my vision swimming with tears and smoke. The silence around me was unbearable. The absence of hoofbeats, of familiar snorts, of the quiet sounds that had always told me I wasn't alone.

He couldn't be gone. Not Shadow. Not him.

Hands grabbed my shoulders.

"B, we need to go. There is nothing left."

"How could someone do this? This—this is beyond cruel!"

A twig snapped to my right. I jumped to my feet. It had to be him. He never stayed away. He knew I would come for him. I saw nothing through the trees but took a step forward. Before

I could move again, Adar jerked me back toward him.

"What are you doing? It's got to be him! I have to go to him!"

"Shh!" Adar scanned the woods.

A figure stepped out from behind a tree, draped in a deep green cloak that blended with the forest shadows. My heart leapt into my throat.

August.

I stumbled back instinctively, but Adar stepped in front of me, his arm across my chest as he reached for his sword. The tension in his body was rigid, every muscle ready to strike.

I couldn't see their face, only the outline of their body—a woman—and the wild black curls peeking beneath the hood. Not August.

The figure raised both hands slowly. "I'm not here to hurt you."

Still, neither of us moved. My fingers itched at the hilt of my blade. With a cautious motion, the figure pulled the hood back.

"Talia," Adar whispered with disbelief as his arms fell away from me.

I scanned the woods around her. No one could be trusted.

"I'm alone."

"What are you doing here?" I stepped forward. "Is there a bounty on our heads now? Have you come to slay the witches? Because I promise you that this won't end well for you."

She frowned at me. "I would never hurt the two of you."

"Then what do you want?"

"I came for the horses."

I froze, unsure if I'd heard her right. My pulse stuttered, lungs locking. "What... what about them?"

She paused, watching me carefully. The silence stretched too long, and my stomach twisted into knots. My grip on my blade tightened.

"My father came home from Market and told me what happened. He questioned me about you, asking if I knew." She hesitated, twisting the edge of her cloak between her fingers. "Then he told me that he and several other men were going to your home to see if that was where you fled."

Her eyes flickered with guilt. "I followed and watched from the woods as they broke into your home. And when they couldn't find you, they torched it. Then they headed for the barn. I could hear the horses in there, pounding the ground, snorting as if they knew what was coming. I'd hoped my father was better than leaving innocent animals to die... but I was wrong."

I felt the bile rise to my throat.

"After they didn't see you inside, they set it ablaze. I waited until they left and then ran in. The fire had already climbed the walls, the hay fueling the flames even faster. I went to Shadow first and then continued down the line. The last one bolted so quickly that he knocked me into the wall, and I burned myself."

She raised the sleeve of her cloak to show us the blistered skin underneath. Adar and I both stared in silence for a breath too long.

"Why... why are you here now?" Adar asked cautiously.

"I've come every day since. Just in case the horses found their way back."

My heart twisted. "You've been waiting?"

Talia nodded slowly. "They scattered when I got them out. I wasn't sure if they'd survive the cold—or if they'd remember how to find their way home. But I couldn't leave it to chance."

Shadow might be alone in the woods, but there was still hope. He could be safe.

I studied her face, waiting for the catch—the lie. "Then why didn't you run when you saw us here?"

She met my eyes without flinching. "Because I don't care what you are. What anyone says you are. You're still Bronwen. And Adar is still Adar. That's enough for me."

Adar exhaled slowly, tension leaking from his posture, but I couldn't find the words. My throat felt too tight. I turned to look at Adar, to see if he trusted her.

His eyes weren't on me—they were on her. There was a softness there, one I hadn't seen in so long it almost startled me. A longing that ran deep and unspoken. I knew that look. Because I knew him.

He still loved her.

Maybe he always had.

He had let her go once, saying it was to protect her. That being with a witch would only put her in danger. But she still came back. She still risked herself to save what was ours.

They weren't together anymore, but the ache in his eyes said he never stopped thinking about her.

It was like watching a wound he'd long buried begin to bleed again.

I turned my gaze to Talia and noticed the way her lips parted like she wanted to say something that had been sitting on her tongue for years. But before she could speak, Adar blinked and looked away. The vulnerability in his face vanished like it had never been there.

"We need to go," he said. "It's not safe here."

I wanted to protest, to give Adar a chance to be happy, but he was right. We still weren't safe. We had to deal with August.

3

August

I stared at the fire for longer than I ever had. Letting it sear into my memory. The way the heat licked at the stone. The way the shadows danced like taunts. Every flicker branded into my brain. Because I didn't know if I'd ever see fire again—real, wild, roaring fire. Not the kind in nightmares or hallucinations, but the kind that crackles in a hearth and smells like burning wood and old safety. I didn't even know if I'd see the light of day again, for that matter.

It had only been one day.

Just *one*.

That was all it took for the walls of my mind to fracture, for time to stretch and warp and gnaw at itself. It felt like years had passed since she left. A lifetime.

But it had only been one day.

And it was only a matter of time before they realized he was dead. A matter of time before they came through that door and took every bit of freedom that I had away from me. I just hoped she would come first.

I *prayed* she would come first.

And for a moment, I let myself imagine her there—out on the hills, beneath the pale sky where the snow had just begun to fall. The first snow of the season, soft as ash, blanketing the world in quiet.

I had taken her there.

The place my mother used to bring me when I was a boy. Where the wind never seemed to bite, and the grass grew even in winter's grasp. Where I'd felt human once. Alive.

I told her about my mother. About the lullabies I only remembered in pieces. About how we'd lie in the grass until the stars came out, and the world felt far away. No one else knew that. No one else *got* that piece of me.

And I gave it to her.

I saw her again in the memory—laughing, her black hair catching flakes of snow, her cheeks flushed from the cold. She lay back and pulled me down beside her. We stayed like that for hours. Just us. Just warmth. And I let myself believe it was real.

But the memory twisted.

Her smile sharpened. Her eyes filled with something cruel. She stood over me now in the vision, her boots pressing into my chest, voice cold as the snow falling around us.

"I used you."

I blinked. The room snapped back into place.

Gods. I had *let her in*. Let her see me. Let her dig around in my ribs and take whatever she wanted. And she smiled the whole time.

I wanted to throw up.

I had given her something pure, and she turned it into a weapon.

The one who made me *beg.* The one who looked at me like I

mattered. Who said my name like a promise. And then lied.

She should've been different.

I despised her for what she did. Lied to me. Used me. Played me like a fool. But gods help me, I wasn't letting her go. She was mine.

And she would fix this. Even if I had to chain her to the damn wall.

The silence filled the room. Something I usually despised as it let the dark thoughts take hold of my mind a little tighter, but for now, I let it happen. There wouldn't be any more silence once they came for me. Someone would always be watching me. *Protecting* me.

I stood. My body barely remembered how. The wreckage around me wasn't new—I'd done it hours ago. Glass shards sparkled in the corners like fallen stars. Books with their spines ripped open. Blood smeared across the stone like art. My own, I thought. I didn't feel it anymore. I'd destroyed everything. Except the fury.

No pain. No bruises. Just the ghost of rage crawling under my skin like worms.

I walked the room like a ghost. The wind outside howled, but it was nothing compared to what screamed inside me.

She said she loved me.

Or maybe she didn't. Maybe I made that part up.

But gods, I felt it. Every moment with her was etched into my skin like scripture. I remembered the way her breath caught when I touched her wrist. The way she looked at me when she thought I wasn't watching. The way she whispered my name like it meant something sacred.

She was in my blood. My bones. I couldn't find the edges of myself anymore without finding her too. She wasn't just a memory.

She was a hunger.

I turned in the ruin, chest heaving. The wind hissed through broken panes and dragged the curtains like specters across the floor. It all looked how I felt. Shattered. She had made me beg. *Me.* August. And I did it. I would've given her my fucking heart if she asked for it. And all along, she was twisting the knife.

I hated her. Hated the way I still thought about her. The way I still wanted her.

I reached for the bottle—empty. I crushed it against the wall, watching it explode like a star dying. Beautiful and pointless. The rage pulsed in my bones. But below it, darker and crueler, throbbed something else.

Need.

And I hated her for that most of all.

The journal lay open like a wound. I'd read every damn line, searching for answers. Nothing but ink and emptiness. Confusion. Madness. Carrow was fucking insane from the beginning. The kind of madness that hides in genius. That masquerades as brilliance until it's too late to run.

He wrote in circles—pages full of half-sentences and loops. Names scratched out. Symbols I didn't recognize. I didn't know what they meant. But I read it anyway.

Again. And again.

I wondered if he was already in me. Waiting. Watching. Laughing at how I had been fooled. Sometimes I swore I heard him. A whisper when no one was near. A voice in my own head that wasn't mine. Telling me to hurt. To destroy. To *burn.*

I caught my reflection in the glass and my eyes seemed darker. My smile a little too wide. Maybe I did inherit something from him. Maybe I was never supposed to survive him. Maybe I was only ever meant to become him.

I slammed the journal shut. My hands were trembling.

A creak. My head snapped toward the door.

No scent.

The cloak. Fucking magic.

Don't be insane, I warned myself. Not now. Not yet. She needed charm and control. Not teeth and claws.

The door cracked open just a sliver, and for a moment, I thought I was hallucinating again. My body locked up. The shadows shifted, but they didn't move like ghosts. They moved like her.

Her hood slipped back slowly. Those eyes—gods, those eyes—met mine.

I didn't believe it was real until the scent hit me, warm and sharp, soaked in jasmine and memory. For a breath, I just stared. Silent. Staggered. If I blinked, she might vanish.

And I said nothing. I couldn't. If I opened my mouth, I might confess everything. Or tear her throat out. The words clawed up, burning. I swallowed them.

Then I smelled something too late. Something wild and *male* behind me.

The blade tore through me.

I dropped, breath knocked out, pain like lightning caging my ribs. Her fucking twin. He knew exactly where to strike. Precise. Just like her.

It wasn't wood, and yet the pain was excruciating. Fire raced through me. It was poisoned and completely wrong. I could barely breathe. My limbs betrayed me, folding as shadows closed in. My mind scrambled to hold onto anything.

Her face. Her scent. Her name.

Her face. Her scent. Her name.

Gods, I would kill for her.

I *did* kill for her.

And still she betrayed me.

I laughed, even as the world unraveled.

The pain flared, impossibly bright, like someone had poured molten iron through my veins.

"So you're not here to apologize, I see."

Darkness took me.

4

Bronwen

He woke slowly, his eyelids fluttering like a bird struggling against the wind. His chest rose and fell in shallow, uneven breaths. Sweat beaded along his forehead, darkening his hair at the temples. It took far longer than I expected for him to open his eyes—too long.

And part of me hated that I'd worried about him.

He was alive. Or whatever a vampire's version of alive was. But the way he slumped in the chair, the lines of strain etched across his face, made me wonder just how close Adar's blade had come to truly ending him. My stomach twisted.

The spelled chains clinked softly as he stirred, his wrists and ankles bound to the chair. We'd reinforced them just as Papa had done for every vampire he caught. Nothing too aggressive, but enough to keep him from tearing us apart the second he woke.

Because I knew August's strength. And his temper.

I glanced at Adar, who stood near the door, arms crossed over his chest, eyes fixed on August like he expected him to break free at any moment. There was tension in his shoulders—wary and waiting. But there was satisfaction, too. His fingers traced the dagger's hilt, itching to use it again.

"What did you stab him with?" I asked warily. Adar's methods were often... thorough.

"Something Jonah brewed," he replied, his tone clipped. "Works well enough on humans. Makes them spill their secrets like wine over a cracked glass."

"But he's not human."

"No. But it will work."

I swallowed, my gaze returning to August. His head lolled forward before jerking up, his eyes flickering open at last. They looked different. Still red like they were when he seemed to lose control over himself, but also glassy and unfocused. As if he were struggling to recognize where he was.

"What...?" His voice was rough, shredded from the sound that was a mix of a laugh and a scream I'd heard before he went under. His gaze snapped between me and Adar, the tension in his body growing even as the chains held him tight. A shudder ran through him, the kind that rippled beneath his skin like it hurt to breathe.

The drug was supposed to make him tell the truth. That was what Adar claimed. But it had been made for humans, not vampires. And part of me wondered if we'd just poisoned him instead. It was usually given orally because humans are much easier to force to take it, but with August's strength, we knew we had to do it a different way.

A sound tore from August's throat. Not a groan, not a snarl—*laughter*. Broken and wild. His head tipped back, the spelled chains rattling as his shoulders shook.

"Is this it?" he choked between laughs. "This is your plan, Winnie? Tie me down and dose me like some lowly prisoner? I expected something... *cleverer-er?* No, that's not right. Cleverer! Cunning. But this?" Another round of laughter spilled out, breathless and sharp.

The sound of it settled something inside me. It was familiar, even if it was maddening. Proof that he was still himself and not hollowed out. Definitely drugged. But still himself. Actually, more like the August I knew before I killed Carrow. I released a breath I hadn't realized I was holding.

But when I glanced at Adar, his expression was different. Uneasy. The way his fingers tightened around the dagger at his side told me he was closer to lunging at August than laughing along. His lips curled in disgust.

Had I really grown so used to August's madness? The realization tightened something in my chest. Maybe I was blind to what he was. Or worse—what I'd let myself accept.

Still, I couldn't help but stare at him. The man who laughed while in chains. The man who, even now, seemed untouchable.

"Or is this your way of telling me a regular fuck just doesn't do it for you anymore?" August sneered, his eyes locking onto mine with a hunger that made my stomach twist. "Chains I can get on board with, but your brother watching? That might take some getting used to."

"Enough!" Adar pushed himself off of the wall and barreled toward August. Before I could stop him, he held the dagger against his throat, pushing hard enough that blood tainted the silver blade.

"We are here for the truth," Adar spat. "If you can't give me that, I'll take great pride in killing you."

The look in August's eyes shifted, fury coiling behind them. His muscles strained against the spelled chains, the sound of metal creaking as if it might give way. He leaned forward, pushing the dagger in more.

"Let me go and I'll show you exactly what the truth looks like," August snarled. "Or are you too much of a coward to face me without hiding behind your little spells and daggers?"

"Stop," I said quickly, stepping between them before Adar could drive the blade any deeper. "How is this going to work?"

Adar's eyes flicked to me, his jaw clenched so tightly I thought his teeth might crack. "He won't be able to lie or stay silent. The truth will come out whether he wants it to or not."

"But he's a vampire. It could be different. It could be—" I stumbled over the words, the urgency making my voice crack.

"It will work," Adar snapped. "It has to."

August smirked, the darkness in his eyes glittering with amusement. "Why don't you find out?" he challenged. "Ask your questions, Winnie. Let's see if your precious truth serum holds up."

I took a breath, trying to calm myself. This had to work.

"What's your name?" *Why did I choose that?*

His lips curved into a smirk.

"Augustus Andra Vael." August's voice was steady, his gaze unwavering. "Prince—well, no, *the Joveryn King* now, thanks to you. I mean, if you wanted title, too."

Chills ran down my spine. August. The Joveryn King.

"Did I kill your father?" I pressed, forcing myself to remain calm.

"You destroyed his body, but he's been gone for much longer than that."

I scrunched my eyebrows. *What does that even mean?*

"Did I kill Carrow?"

"I guess for a little while you killed him, but he will be back."

This wasn't working. He was the same infuriating August that loved to confuse me.

"Is your father Carrow?"

"No."

I threw my hands up and walked away, pacing to keep myself from screaming. "Nothing you say makes sense. Make sense, August! Please!" I said, the desperation bleeding through.

Something came across his face. Like the August I had grown so used to, but it left just as fast as it came. "Carrow came to Joveryn in his fae body, but he couldn't reverse the age his body had endured, so he needed a host body to inhabit. He went to the Joveryn King spewing his charismatic, magical charm—tales of strength, speed, and immortality. He left out the part where the king's body would be immortal but his soul would be lost when the spell was completed. And Carrow took over his body."

I watched him closely, trying to read the truth in his expression. His shoulders slumped against the chains, but his words were deliberate, precise.

"But I destroyed his body."

August shook his head. "Carrow is smart. He knew there were always loopholes, just like how he lost immortality the first time. So he found a way to jump to new bodies. His newfound immortality was tied to the original king's bloodline so he couldn't jump into other bodies—only his descendants. He just didn't know his weakness until he lit a match too close to his body and it set him aflame."

Adar's gaze flickered toward me, his jaw clenched. I could see the skepticism in his eyes.

August continued, his eyes never leaving mine. "I didn't know the entire story at first. Everyone is so secretive. That's why I had you find Carrow's journal. He had always written everything down, and I thought if I could find the one from when the spell happened, it would give me answers. I was trying to find a way to truly kill him so this wouldn't happen to me. I could have had *centuries* to figure it out, but you cut that short. So now I am in a race to find a way to stop it before the next Blood Moon. And you are going to help me."

"Why would I help you?" I asked as my hands trembled at my sides.

"Who do you think he is going to come after first?"

A shudder ran down my spine, my breath catching. August's eyes gleamed, sensing my fear. Adar shifted beside me, his presence a rigid wall of fury and protectiveness.

"I could just kill you now before Carrow is in your body," I snapped, more to hear myself speak than anything else.

August's smirk widened. "Then do it."

I stood still, seeing the test in his eyes. "If I did, would it stop Carrow?"

"No. I am his first option, but not his only one."

If he had to be in the king's bloodline, did that mean—

"You have siblings?"

He made a face at that word. "Yes. So kill me if you want, but that won't stop Carrow from coming after you in a few months."

A few months.

Twelve weeks to find answers.

Twelve weeks until the Blood Moon rose again and Carrow came back to finish what he started.

Adar's fingers dug into my arm, pulling me back from August. "We can run. You don't need to do this."

I nodded, though leaving the only place I'd ever known felt

like breaking the last intact piece of my heart. There was nothing left for us here; the coven would be safer without us anyway.

"If you help me stop Carrow, witches will be free to practice."

I stopped breathing. The words struck me harder than any blade. The room felt smaller, the air thinning.

"What?" Adar trembled with disbelief.

"No more persecution," August continued, eyes locked on me as if my brother didn't exist. "Witches will be safe, and if anyone tries to harm them, they will be going against the crown. And they will be dealt with."

"No, B. It's not worth—"

"Okay." The word slipped from my lips before I could stop it. My chest tightened, my pulse a wild, frenzied beat.

"Bronwen! Have you lost your mind?" Adar shouted, his eyes wide and furious.

"This is what Papa would have wanted. It was what he lived his life for." I forced the words out, each one feeling like it cost me something. "All he wanted was to protect the coven."

"Not at the sacrifice of you!" Adar's voice cracked.

I knew the risk. August had brought more chaos and pain into my life than I had ever experienced.

"Let me handle this." I looked at my brother. "No more secrets, but this is my choice."

He looked as if he wanted to argue, but he knew my mind was made up. Because August knew exactly what to say to get to me. Adar walked back to the corner of the room, making his expression unreadable, but his rigid posture told another story.

"I will help you stop Carrow. For the coven."

August's gaze remained locked on me. The chains binding him seemed insignificant—nothing more than a slight inconvenience to a creature like him. His smile curled at the edges, sharp and hungry. "Good. But you will marry me first."

I stared at him, willing the words to twist into a joke. A bluff. I had hoped I imagined the first time he said he wanted to marry me, but here it was again—real, undeniable.

"You're insane," I said, the disgust curling sharp in my throat. "You think you can chain me to you like this? After everything?" My fists clenched as I tried to keep myself calm. I took a step back, needing space I wasn't allowed.

"You knew I was insane from the moment we met," he cooed. "And yet here you are."

"Why would you even want to marry me?" I forced myself to meet his eyes, even though looking at him felt like staring into something wild and dangerous. "I can help you without being your wife."

August's eyes flickered, something feral flashing in their depths. "Because I've said it before. Even though I'd love nothing more than to kill you right now for what you've done." He leaned forward, the chains groaning in protest. "You're mine, Winnie. The blood that runs through your veins is mine. Every hair on your head is mine. Every word that comes out of your pretty little mouth is mine. You *belong* to me."

"I am not yours." My words trembled, but the defiance in them remained. My heart pounded so hard it felt like it might tear itself free from my chest.

August's smile deepened, all sharpness and cruelty. "You marry me, or no deal."

My mind reeled, struggling to wrap itself around it.

I stared at him—at the vampire chained in front of me,

smiling like he already owned me. Like this was inevitable.

You marry me, or no deal.

The weight of it pressed down, suffocating. I thought of Papa, of Mama, of the coven hiding in their homes, waiting for a world that might never come. I thought of Adar, still bleeding from the wounds I couldn't heal.

And I thought of myself—what little of me was still left.

Could I really do this? Could I give myself to him?

A hundred memories crashed through me at once. August's hands wrapped around my wrists. August's laugh breaking against the darkness. The way he'd smiled at me before I'd betrayed him. The way he'd begged me to trust him.

The way he'd looked at me after I thought I killed Carrow.

Anger flared in my chest. He wasn't supposed to have this power over me. He wasn't supposed to be the one to offer me salvation—or damnation. I could say no. I could spit in his face. I could walk away right now and take my chances in a world that wanted me dead.

But if I did... Carrow would win.

I dug my nails into my palms so hard I felt the skin break.

You have to be strong, I told myself. *You have to be stronger than your fear.*

Slowly, I lifted my gaze to his. His smile deepened—as if he'd known all along what my answer would be. That made me hate him even more. And yet I still couldn't seem to stop him. Even after everything.

But it wasn't just about him.

It was about the coven. About Papa. About the life we had fought so hard to preserve. If I didn't do this, I would be turning my back on all of it. And I couldn't.

I forced the word out. "Fine."

The chains rattled slightly as August leaned forward, his red eyes gleaming. "Louder."

I bared my teeth in something that wasn't quite a smile. "I said fine," I snapped. "But don't ever think for a second you own me."

Something flew past me, striking August's stomach.

I turned to see Adar barreling toward him. He held another piece of a broken chair leg, fury in his eyes. "I will not let this happen!"

I stepped in front of him, practically falling into August's lap as I used my body as a shield. "Adar, no!"

He stopped inches from us, the wood nearly in my neck. A piece of wood stuck out of his stomach, yet August burst into laughter.

I grabbed the wood from Adar's grip and slowly lowered it. "I have to do this. You have to let me."

For a heartbeat, he just stared at me, frozen. Then he stood. But I saw a little piece of him shatter.

I felt August lean forward beneath me. His lips were inches from my ear. "Good girl," he murmured.

I jumped up.

His gaze devoured me, inch by inch, as if seeing me surrender had lit something savage inside him. Without a second thought, I slammed the piece of wood in my hand into his thigh.

He jerked back, but the smirk never left his face. "So others can't hurt me. Only you, Winnie? Good to know."

"I hate you."

"You should."

I grabbed the wood sticking out of his stomach and pulled it out, making sure to pull upward as I did. He groaned.

"I am going to kill them all," I whispered.

"I hope you do."

"I am going to be your worst nightmare." I forced the words out, but it was a promise. For him to force me into this. To force me into submission was the worst thing he could do. He was going to regret it.

A grin curled over his mouth. "Gods, I can't wait."

5

Adar

She said yes.

Not to escape. Not even to buy us time. She said yes like it was the only option left. And I couldn't breathe.

I stood there, frozen in place, watching my sister agree to marry a monster. My fists clenched so tightly my nails dug half-moons into my palms. I didn't even feel it. I was too focused on her voice—steady, resolute, and completely wrong.

What the hell is she thinking?

My heart hammered behind my ribs, each beat like a warning I couldn't ignore. The way August looked at her made my skin crawl. Not with lust, not with rage—something else. Something darker. Like he owned her already. Like he had since the moment she stepped into his world.

She thought this was what Papa would've wanted. That sacrificing herself was worth protecting the coven.

But Papa wouldn't have asked this of her.

He would have fought tooth and nail to keep her free. To keep her safe.

I turned away before I said something I couldn't take back. I couldn't look at her right now, not when every part of me wanted to rip August apart and drag Bronwen out of here.

But she'd made her choice.

And the worst part? I could see why. The promise of safety. Freedom for witches. No more hiding. No more fear. It was everything we'd ever wanted.

And now it came with a price.

Her.

I forced a breath through my teeth and stared at the wall, at anything that wasn't the chains or the vampire grinning behind them. If this was the deal she was making, then I was going to make damn sure she survived it.

Even if it killed me.

"I'm coming with you," I said, turning to face them both. I was barely holding it together. "To the castle. I'll live there too."

Bronwen looked at me, her brows pulling together in silent protest, but it was August who responded first.

He tilted his head slightly, that ever-present smugness tugging at the corner of his mouth. "That won't work."

"Why not?" I snapped. "She's my sister. I'm not leaving her there alone."

August's smile didn't reach his eyes. "Because that's where most of the vampires live. Hundreds of them. I will have my hands full keeping them in line as it is. I can't protect both of you."

He said it like it was a kindness. Like he was doing *me* a favor.

My jaw tightened. "Then don't. I'll protect myself."

"Adar—" Bronwen pleaded.

"No," I said. "If this is happening, then I'm staying close. You don't get to shut me out again."

Bronwen stepped closer, her eyes wide. "Adar, listen to me—you can't be there. You need to be with the coven. They need a leader now more than ever."

I blinked at her, stunned. "Why do you even care about the coven?" I asked, the bitterness slipping out before I could stop it. "You've spent your whole life hating them! Hating how they treated us."

Her jaw clenched. "Because it's what Papa would have wanted," she said, her voice cracking at the edges. "He spent his life trying to keep them safe. Trying to keep us safe. If I can do that now—if *we* can give them a future without fear—then I won't turn my back on that. Not now."

I stayed quiet, the silence stretching. There was so much I wanted to say, so much I didn't know how to. I saw the guilt she had for what happened to them, and I knew there was nothing I could say to help her. She was going to drown in her own guilt if she didn't find a way to honor Papa and Mama.

Bronwen shifted closer. "You can move into town. It'll be safer, and closer. We can meet for breakfast every morning. You won't be far."

"Every morning won't work. Weekly—maybe."

She glanced at August. I waited for her to argue, but instead she nodded. She fucking *agreed* with him. I had never seen her so submissive with someone.

"Weekly breakfast." She leaned in to whisper as if he still couldn't hear everything she said, "unless I can sneak away more."

Her words tugged at something inside me—something fragile and tired. I didn't want to let her go. But I knew where she was going wasn't just some grand hall with velvet curtains and royal guards. The castle wasn't just a building. It was a prison filled with bloodthirsty monsters.

I saw it written all over her: she was scared. But she was still walking in anyway. Because she thought it was the only way forward.

And gods help me, I wanted to scream. To beg. To fight her on this. But I didn't.

Because the truth was, Papa would've seen it too. The logic behind it. The sacrifice. The strength it took to offer yourself up like that.

So instead, I nodded.

"You won't be far," she said again. "It'll be different now."

A pointed cough cut through the fragile quiet. August shifted in his chair, the chains binding him rattling faintly. "Now that we've all had our heartfelt little moment, can someone take these off?"

I turned to him slowly, jaw tight. He looked too calm. Like he hadn't just sat here and dismantled everything we believed in. Like he wasn't enjoying every second of this.

But Bronwen's gaze was already on him.

There was something in the way she looked at him now— not affection, not exactly. But familiarity. Like she'd accepted something about him I couldn't. Maybe didn't want to.

My stomach twisted.

Bronwen reached out and grabbed the chains, pulling the magic out of them. They unclasped one by one and fell to the floor with a dull clatter. August rose slowly, flexing his fingers and rubbing at his wrists, the skin there slightly raw.

"That stuff is good." He stretched, neck rolling with a few satisfying cracks before flashing a crooked grin. "Other than the truth part, it made me feel better than wine ever has."

How was he so casual? Last night, he was no different from any other vampire. Rage consumed him. And yet now, he acted as if he didn't have a care in the world. As if there wasn't a good chance that he would be dead in a matter of months.

Bronwen glanced at him again, seeming to notice the same thing I did.

"Well," he said, casually dusting off his shoulders, "our ride is here."

I frowned. "What—"

The door burst open with a bang, cold wind whipping into the room. I spun, hands instinctively going to the hilt of my dagger. Four vampires stormed inside, their red eyes immediately locking on August, then snapping to Bronwen and me.

"He's not safe," one of them growled.

They lunged before anyone could speak. One went straight for Bronwen, another closing in on me.

I didn't hesitate. Dropping my blade, I grabbed the vampire and incapacitated him before pulling a wooden stake from my side and driving it into his heart. Bronwen's flames roared to life, engulfing her attacker in a searing burst of fire. The vampire shrieked and collapsed.

"Enough!" August's voice cracked through the air like a whip.

The remaining vampires froze mid-lunge, their fangs bared, eyes flicking nervously between us and August's furious expression.

August's eyes burned with fury. He was different now— commanding. Like a switch had flipped, and I realized I barely knew anything about the monster that my sister was leaving with. He was far more dangerous.

"She is your future queen."

They looked at each other in confusion.

August smiled. "Bow."

Without objection, they lowered themselves and bowed before Bronwen.

But the part that worried me the most was the spark in Bronwen's eyes. The same look that burst to life when she pulled magic, bested me in a sword fight, or left a rude person speechless. She'd always craved power in any form that she could get.

And this was something completely in itself.

August's demeanor shifted once again, back way too casual. "Are you ready to go?"

"Now?" I asked.

She had just agreed. I had barely had time to be with her.

"We're on a deadline. The sooner, the better."

Bronwen came to me and hugged me. Something she didn't do often.

"B—"

"I won't let him in this time." I saw it in her eyes this time. The rage behind the submission. She may have agreed, but she was fucking pissed. Good. "But I have to finish this. For Papa."

August looked at me. "As soon as we wed, I will make the decree. Until then, I suggest you keep to yourself. I don't think the Legion would be gentle if they see a traitor walking through town."

I tensed. The Legion that I had given years of my life to wouldn't hesitate to kill me now.

A vampire glanced at August before taking an uneasy step

toward Bronwen. She matched his step, keeping distance between them and raised her arms in defense.

The vampire bowed his head. "My—my lady."

"My *queen*."

He glanced at August again, but I could see the rage and the humiliation written all over the vampire's face. "My queen, I am only trying to escort you out."

"I do not need you touching me."

He nodded and gestured to the door.

Bronwen placed her hand on my arm. "I'll see you soon."

I didn't know if she said that more to convince herself or me.

"Actually." August turned to the vampire and plunged his hand into his chest. "I don't want anyone to know she's a witch." He pulled his hand out along with the heart of the vampire.

The other hesitated, torn between fear and duty, his eyes flicking from August's bloody hand to the open doorway. Then he turned to run.

August blurred forward, so fast I didn't even see his hand move. One second, the stake was clenched in my grip, and then it wasn't.

I turned, confused, just in time to see it already embedded in the vampire's chest. The creature looked down, stunned, as blood poured over his hands.

Only then did I realize August had taken it from me. Not just taken it—*calculated* it. Measured the distance. The angle. The moment.

He hadn't hesitated. Not for a second. He killed them to protect her secret, and he did it with terrifying precision.

He was going to protect her—of that, I was certain now. But

gods help us, I wasn't sure what that protection would cost. The vampire collapsed, crumpling to the floor.

August straightened slowly, wiping his bloody fingers on his coat as if it were a napkin. As if none of it mattered.

Then he gestured to the door. "Let's go."

6

Bronwen

The cold pressed in around me, but I barely noticed. My hands were clenched at my sides, fingers stiff from the cold and the tension that refused to ease. The kind that had been building since the moment we went to August.

We had been walking through the town—quiet, snow-covered, shuttered up tight. The full moon glowed brightly, casting just enough light to make the world easier to see. I hadn't even realized where we were headed until it was almost too late. Until the gate loomed ahead and my boots slowed.

August stopped a few steps ahead, his back rigid. He didn't turn right away, but I saw the way his shoulders squared like he felt it too: the weight of what waited for me next to that gate. When he finally looked over his shoulder, his eyes flicked to mine. I tried to say something. To form the words.

Please. Don't make me walk past them.

But they stuck in my throat like thorns.

"Keep walking, Winnie."

"August."

He turned to me. "Unless you want me to carry you, either

keep your head down or walk with your eyes fucking closed. There is no other way to the castle."

I gritted my teeth as I fought the urge to take him to the ground.

Now isn't the time, Bronwen. You can kill him after you stop Carrow.

Keeping my head down, I forced one foot to go in front of the other. I just had a little farther to go, but I looked up before I could stop myself. That was when I saw it. Or rather—what wasn't there.

The stage was gone.

I froze.

Their bodies should've been hanging. I had braced for that. Had tried to prepare myself for what it would feel like to look Mama and Papa in the face, frozen in death. But instead, the square was empty. A pile of charred wood and ash sat where the gallows had stood, blackened snow scattered around it like soot-stained petals.

Someone had destroyed it.

A part of me reeled with relief. Another part tensed with confusion. Who would've done it—and why?

My parents' bodies wouldn't have burned. What did they do with them?

I turned to August, but he didn't offer anything. His gaze was set ahead, jaw tight. When I lingered a beat too long, his hand came to my back.

"Keep walking," he said.

That was all.

No explanation. No acknowledgment of what had or hadn't been done. He just pushed me forward, ushering me through the open gate as if none of it mattered. But it did. It mattered to me.

And to Adar.

I had left him behind in that small, suffocating room, and every part of me ached with guilt for it. We'd only just spoken, only just started to see one another again, to rebuild the quiet bond that had always lingered between us. And then I left. Vanished into the snow with August, like I hadn't just promised I would stay.

He would be safer without me. That was the truth I kept repeating to myself.

But it didn't stop the ache. Didn't stop me from wondering if he'd waited at the door, watching the road. If he thought I'd lied to him. The wind bit against my cheeks. My body felt too heavy to move, but I knew I couldn't stay here forever. August wouldn't let me. And neither would the cold.

Once we reached the large gates, they swung open, their hinges creaking under the weight of disuse. A carriage waited on the other side, sleek and dark, with more vampires standing nearby, each dressed in dark uniforms marked with the royal insignia. One of them sat at the front, reins in hand. The horses shifted restlessly in the snow, their dark coats gleaming in the moonlight. They reminded me so much of Shadow that my chest tightened, but I quickly pushed that memory away. I couldn't be distracted by anything anymore.

"A carriage? You could run faster to the castle."

He turned to me, emotionless. "Then come here."

I huffed and walked past him toward the carriage.

"Your escorts, Your Grace?" One of the vampires asked.

"They're dead," was all he said. None of the vampires reacted, as if it were the most normal thing in the world.

The carriage door opened with a slow creak, and August

gestured for me to go first. I hesitated, glancing one last time at the place where the stage had been. The silence of the square stretched out like a shadow, wrapping around the town in something colder than winter. I looked at the coachman again, his eyes locked straight ahead. I wondered how he could be so close to the horses considering Shadow threw me off the second August got close. Maybe it was just August.

I climbed in without a word.

The interior was stiflingly quiet. Neither of us spoke for a while. The only sounds were the crunch of wheels over snow and the occasional creak of wood shifting beneath us. The road curved up toward the mountains, winding like a ribbon of ash through frostbitten trees. The deeper we went, the more the world fell away.

I nearly jumped when August finally spoke. "There are some things you need to know before we get to the castle. When you are above ground, you will be free to move around."

"Do not talk to me."

He nodded, completely ignoring what I said. "Since all vampires except for Carrow's golden line can't walk in day-light, they needed a way to ensure they were safe. The castle is as deep in the ground as it is tall. Most vampires stay underground at all times unless they leave to feed, and there are only a few who are allowed to come to the upper floors of the castle during the night. The best, most controlled. Some guards, my... *siblings* as you called them, Carrow's favorites."

I couldn't help but laugh. "Controlled? Any vampire I've encountered seemed to have no free will or ability to stop themselves from feeding."

"It's because of your smell."

I recoiled. "My *smell*?"

"Your blood, Winnie," August corrected, his eyes narrowing on me. "They are trained to control themselves around humans. But your smell… it's nothing like I've ever smelled and I have been around more humans than probably anyone you'll come across. I am not sure how much they will be able to control themselves, so you can only be alone when you are above ground. You will be around vampires up there, but they are much older and much more controlled than the lower levels. Still, I wouldn't provoke them."

I crossed my arms, forcing my gaze out the window, struggling to keep myself composed. The longer we rode, the more I realized how far from town the castle really was. The gates, the people, the streets—they all belonged to a different world. This one belonged to August.

And now, so did I.

I couldn't hold out any longer. "So you're giving me rules?"

"I am protecting you."

"I can protect myself," I snapped.

"No, Winnie, you can't," he answered, his jaw tightening. "No one can know you are—" He stopped himself, glancing toward the front of the carriage where he knew the coachman sat. He leaned in closer and whispered, "*what* you are. Vampires can control themselves, but they won't care to if they know what you are. Carrow has taught everyone to loathe them."

I rolled my eyes. "He hates the thing that gave him immortality."

August glanced out the window and his demeanor immediately changed. "I don't understand most of his reasoning."

I followed his gaze and my breath caught. The castle loomed out of the mist. Its black spires cut through the dark sky like daggers, jagged and unwelcoming. Gothic and immense, it rose from the mountainside like it had clawed its way out of the stone, more beast than building. It didn't just stand apart—it ruled the landscape, brooding and vengeful.

"It's the beginning of the end," August whispered, his voice carrying like a prayer meant for the night itself—not for me.

By the time the carriage rolled to a stop, I realized that the thin protection those gates had offered was gone now, and my entire body tensed as I stepped down. The air felt different here—colder, heavier. Even the silence was suffocating, like the mountain itself was holding its breath.

A man stepped forward from the shadows, dressed in dark livery. He extended a hand to help me down. I hesitated.

When I finally placed my fingers in his, I realized with a jolt—he was human. Not because of his eyes or the way he smiled. It was subtler than that. It was the absence of magic under his skin. The absence of that humming energy that pulsed through the vampires like a second heartbeat. He was quiet. Still. Familiar in a way that almost undid me. A human was living here among them.

Human, and standing here like he had always belonged.

I stepped down and glanced back at the coachman. His gaze remained fixed ahead, unblinking. I edged closer until I was near enough to see the glassy sheen over his eyes. He sat rigid, more statue than man—but human.

"You're not the only human here."

I jumped when I heard August, spinning to find him standing so close I could feel the tension radiating off him. I hadn't even heard him move, hadn't realized he had followed me. I looked past him, toward the castle doors. A tall figure stood beneath the archway, cloaked in shadow. At first, I thought it was another servant—but then she shifted, and the flicker of torchlight caught her face and the red eyes staring down at me.

She saw me.

A wicked smile formed before she turned on her heel and disappeared inside, her movements quick and graceful and gone before I could blink.

"Inside," August said softly, hand pressing lightly against my back.

It took every ounce of self-restraint I had not to dig my heels into the ground. I followed him up the steps, and the moment we crossed the threshold, the heavy doors shut behind us with a deep, echoing thud.

The foyer was vast and dim, lit only by flickering candles in iron sconces along the walls. Shadows danced along every surface, yet the space still managed to feel extravagant. The floor beneath my boots was polished stone, dark and veined with silver. Two massive staircases curved upward on either side, their banisters carved in intricate detail—serpents, roses, and things I didn't recognize winding through the wood. A second-floor balcony overlooked the entryway, empty now, but I could feel the eyes.

Watching. Waiting.

I could sense more magic than I ever had.

August glanced around as if he too could feel the presence of others. He took a deep breath before he said, "Come out."

Almost instantly, several vampires stepped out from the shadows. Some stood on the balcony above, others only feet from me. I gripped my cloak. Red eyes surrounded us. I knew this was what I would be walking into, but now living in it, I considered grabbing August and setting the entire place on fire.

Some bore the royal insignia like the guards outside, while others were dressed extravagantly—velvet cloaks lined with fur, jeweled pins fastening their collars, and silken fabrics. One stepped forward with the quiet elegance of someone used to being obeyed. He was tall and thin, with skin like old ivory and hair slicked back in an inky black wave. His clothing was richly tailored, embroidered with silver thread that glinted faintly in the candlelight.

"Halston," August acknowledged.

"Augustus," he said, bowing with theatrical grace. "What have you brought home?"

"I need a human wife to continue the line, don't I? Well, I've made it easier on everyone and chosen one myself."

Halston stepped forward and I tried to back away but August's hand was firmly on my back. The vampire brought his face close to mine, assessing—*sniffing*. Then he leaned down further to my neck. "I can smell why you've chosen her."

"Get the fuck away from me."

He stood. "Oh my king, this one is marvelous."

August laughed. "You have no idea."

Halston ran his hand down my arm. His head tilted slightly, like a dog hearing a strange sound. "So soft and delicate."

I'd like to show him just how delicate he would be in my grip.

"Your name, dear?"

"Bronwen."

"And how did our king get so lucky?"

I smiled. "Manipulation."

Halston let out a wicked laugh. "Carrow is going to love

her."

August's eyes flashed. Just for a second, but enough.

I saw the way his hand twitched at his side and his body shifted forward, like a beast coiled and ready to strike. Halston saw it too. His grin slipped for half a heartbeat. He dropped his gaze with the kind of instinct only something lesser had when confronted with a predator. But he recovered quickly, straightening and schooling his face into something smooth again.

"Enjoy her while she's yours."

I waited for August to react, but instead he shifted his gaze to the balcony. "Where are they?"

"You know how they are. I am sure I can round them up later for you. They are going to barely contain themselves with this one."

August stepped forward, putting himself subtly between me and the rest. "If you'll excuse us, I'd like to show her around."

Halston bowed again, slower this time. "Of course, Your Grace. We only hoped to welcome your bride properly."

There was nothing welcoming in his tone.

August didn't move. "You will have plenty of time tonight."

He nodded, a new spark forming in his eyes before he raised his hand. And then, slowly, the red eyes began to fade back into the dark.

August grabbed me and pulled me through the hall, his grip tight around my wrist like he didn't trust me to follow otherwise. We climbed one of the sweeping staircases, the velvet runner muffling our steps, then turned down corridor after corridor. The walls here were tall and narrow, lined with paintings whose eyes seemed to follow me as I passed. Most I didn't recognize, but then my gaze caught on Carrow, unmistakable even in paint, and only a few portraits later, August stared back at me from the canvas.

I tried to trace each turn, count the doors, mark the windows—anything that might help me later if I had to run.

It was still a very strong possibility.

At the end of one particularly long hallway, he shoved open a set of double doors, revealing a chamber bathed in soft, flickering candlelight. I stepped inside and stilled.

The room was massive. Ornate crown molding swept across the ceiling, and heavy drapes pooled against the floor on either side of tall windows that looked out into the dark. A grand bed, larger than anything I'd ever seen, sat in the center beneath a carved canopy. A small dressing table stood in one corner, with a desk positioned in the other. A door on the left stood open, revealing a washroom, while two armoires faced it from across the room. Everything was symmetrical. Clean. Controlled. Perfectly placed, like no one had ever actually lived here.

"This is our room," he said.

My heart nearly stopped. "Our room? There isn't anywhere else I could stay in this giant castle?"

"And what would that look like if the queen wasn't sleeping in the same bed as the king?"

"You don't know how badly I'd like to take that smile off your face. Your magic is begging for me to take it."

He leaned in close. "And we know just how much you love to use me."

I caught it. It was barely there, but I heard the snap in his words. As if I didn't already feel guilty for using him the way I did.

But he had done far worse.

"A handmaiden will be here shortly to dress you," August said.

"Dress me for what?"

This time he smiled. "To meet the family."

* * *

I was going to meet August's *family.*

Until today, I had never once considered that there was more than just him. He told me about his mother, loving but ripped away from him far too soon and his father—who now I knew was Carrow—had shown him nothing but disdain.

But he had siblings. Knowing August had kept far more from me than he'd told me just angered me more. He had forced me into this arrangement and yet he had the audacity to keep things like this from me.

I had felt bad for what I had done to him. But after today, that guilt was entirely gone.

So here I was, sitting on the edge of the bed and waiting. The handmaiden had already come and gone—a young, blonde-haired, blue-eyed girl who seemed more than content with her place in this strange world. She had smiled easily, moved with purpose, and insisted on handling every detail herself. She bathed me, braided the top half of my hair into intricate knots, and painted my lips red. Then she dressed me in a gown that clung to my shape like it had been made for me.

The dress was made of some thin, silky fabric that clung to every curve like a second skin. Thin straps wrapped over my shoulders and tied in a delicate knot behind my neck, leaving most of my back bare. The neckline plunged scandalously low, barely containing my breasts, and the sides dipped enough to reveal the edge of my ribs. The skirt fell fluid and sheer around my legs, slit high on one side to reveal too much thigh with every step. It shimmered faintly with every breath I took, catching the firelight like it was meant to be watched.

It was beautiful. Seductive. Dangerous.

And of course it was red.

I hated how much I liked it.

I had tried to tell her that August—to which she quickly corrected me: *King Augustus*—didn't care what I looked like. That he wouldn't notice. But she only smiled and said, "He will tonight."

She wouldn't take no for an answer.

And, truthfully, I hadn't minded the warmth of the bath or the gentle tug of the brush through my hair. It reminded me, distantly, of something soft. Something normal.

Now, the quiet pressed in around me as I sat, waiting to be summoned.

Like a prize. Like an offering.

August stepped in, quickly closing the door behind him. He was dressed in black from throat to boots—an embroidered high-collared coat with silver filigree that shimmered faintly in the candlelight, tight gloves tucked into a wide belt at his waist, and polished boots that made no sound against the stone floor. His icy blonde hair was swept back from his forehead, just slightly tousled, like he'd run a hand through it in frustration or distraction. The starkness of his pale skin only made the deep brown of his eyes more unnerving— ancient, unreadable, and locked entirely on me. I stood and tried my best not to show him anything other than indifference, though the pounding of my heart betrayed me. He slowly dragged his eyes up my body like he was memorizing every inch of it. My skin prickled beneath the weight of his stare, heat curling low in my belly no matter how tightly I clenched my jaw. And then he smiled. Like nothing had changed. Like he hadn't ruined me and I hadn't let him.

"Can we go?" I asked, anything to keep from saying something I'd regret.

"No." He stepped closer, nostrils flaring slightly. "You have no idea what you smell like to them. To *me*."

"Like food?" I taunted.

"Like temptation and sex and everything I was never supposed to touch." His voice dropped. "But I did. Didn't I?"

His words only made my blood heat hotter, fury clawing up my throat. I snapped my arms across my chest, glaring at him. "Unfortunately."

He laughed. "I've already heard enough whispers since we arrived. I'd hoped that knowing you were mine would be enough for them to control themselves. But it seems they need... reminders."

"I do not *belong* to you."

"Debatable."

My jaw clenched. Now wasn't the time to fight him. I needed to see the castle, meet everyone I possibly could to ensure I knew what I was living around. So I took a deep breath. "And how do you plan to remind them?"

"You need to smell like me."

I blinked. "Excuse me?"

"You need to have my scent on you. *All* over you."

My breath caught. The way he said it made the words feel

heavier than they should have. I hated that my mind twisted them into something else. Something that made my stomach flip. "And how do you plan to do that?"

He stepped forward slowly. His hand brushed my arm, then glided up with a possessive kind of patience until he reached my hair, threading his fingers through the loose curls. His other hand found the back of my neck. I could feel the warm press of his palm, the weight of his intention. He leaned down, his breath ghosting over my neck, and I felt my knees weaken.

I didn't breathe. Couldn't.

Because if I did, I would smell him—smoke and cedar. His fascination with fires was something I never understood, especially since a stray spark could have killed him. Maybe that was why he was fascinated with me.

He brought his face to mine and rested his forehead against mine, thumb stroking my jaw as his fingers slid deeper into my hair. I kept my eyes locked on his, refusing to flinch, even when he leaned in and kissed me.

Soft. Controlled. Measured.

I ignored the heat it stirred. Ignored the tremble in my hands.

Bronwen. Get a hold of yourself. You hate him.

You hate him! You hate him! You hate him!

He knelt before me, his head nearly resting against my chest, his breath teasing across my skin. I stared down at him, at the way he moved like this was a ceremony, not a game. One hand rested on my bare ribs while the other moved the slit of my dress before gliding slowly, shamelessly, up my thigh. He leaned down, pressing his lips against my hip where he had shifted the fabric aside, his eyes never leaving mine.

I shivered. Not from cold.

He inched closer to my center, but I grabbed him by the hair and yanked him back before he could do what I knew he intended. He stood with an ease that made my heart stumble, adjusting his coat like nothing had happened. Like he hadn't just branded me with his touch.

"You're a vampire," I hissed. "You could've used your speed and done all of that before I even realized what you were doing."

"Yes." He smirked. "But then I wouldn't have seen just what I could still do to you, Winnie."

7

Bronwen

"Dinner? Am I going to sit and watch all of you just feed?" I asked as I followed him down another corridor.

Our footsteps echoed off the stone, each one swallowed quickly by thick walls and heavier silence. The halls twisted and turned like a maze, lit by sconces spaced just far enough apart to keep everything in a half-shadow. The air smelled like wax and stone and something older. Something wrong.

"No. It's an actual meal prepared by humans. I told you vampires can eat." August turned down another hall as if he had the entire place memorized. But of course he did. This was the real him. Not the one I had grown so used to.

"But you do not need to eat."

August let out a breath.

"My sister planned this as soon as she heard of your arrival. To welcome you, or assess you to determine the best way to hurt me. I never know with her. Besides, you need to eat."

I didn't argue. I hadn't eaten since before Adar and I questioned August, and that felt like another lifetime. My stomach tightened, but not just from hunger. The dread was growing stronger the closer we got.

August stopped and turned to me. "Do not provoke them."

I scrunched my nose. "Why?"

"Because I do not wish to kill them on my first day back," he said. "It will already be hard enough as it is without you doing something to piss them off."

I crossed my arms. "So you *do* care about them. They were never important enough to tell me about before. No—I guess *I* was just never important enough for you to tell me about them."

He flinched. Barely. But it was there.

"Has it never occurred to you that everything I kept from you, including them, was for your safety?"

"And yet here I am with two dead parents, a brother being hunted, and vampires fighting the urge to kill me around every corner."

His jaw ticked. "Get through this meal. Be as indifferent as you can. They will be bored enough that hopefully we will see as little of them as possible."

"I don't need your protection."

"You do."

There it was again. That simple, absolute certainty that made my blood boil. He spoke like he owned me, like I was a stupid girl who didn't know what she was walking into.

We stepped into the dining hall, a vaulted chamber lined with dark stone and towering archways that seemed to swallow the light. The only illumination came from tall candelabras pushed to the far corners of the room, their wax-dripped arms casting long, twitching shadows across the cold floor. None of the flames were allowed near the table—too dangerous, I realized, for a room full of vampires whose very skin could catch fire.

The table groaned under the weight of food—glistening fruits not yet in season in Joveryn, exotic meats whose scents curled into the air like perfume, pastries that looked too delicate to be real. It all shimmered with wealth and presentation, but it felt wrong. Like it had all been arranged for a show, not a meal.

Halston shooed the servants through a set of double doors when he saw us, before stepping to the dining table adjusting the vase of roses in the middle and admiring his work.

Four other vampires stood together: three men and a woman. They turned toward us in eerie unison. Though their eyes were shades of brown or blue, I felt the familiar thrumming of magic that told me they were nothing close to human. They were just different, like August.

"Long time no see, brother." One stepped forward with a languid elegance, lifting a silver goblet of wine with fingers that sparkled with rings. He had dark hair that curled at the edges, tousled like he had no care for his appearance. His striking blue eyes gleamed with mischief and something sharper underneath, and his smile looked more suited to a dance floor than a throne room. He wore a deep crimson jacket, open at the collar, exposing just a little too much skin in a way that felt deliberate. Every movement was theatrical, exaggerated, as though life was just one long performance to him.

"But here you are in the same form I left you in."

Then he glanced at me, tilting his head in the same animalistic way August always had. "We are honored," he said, bowing just slightly. "Though I admit, I never expected our dear brother to bring a human when he would only be here for a few months."

August didn't blink. No matter how much fear he had for Carrow taking over his body, he never showed it to anyone, which was probably smart. "This is Simon."

"Of course," Simon said, with a smile that didn't touch his eyes. "Your ways have always been... unconventional."

The silence that followed was thick with unspoken insult.

"Bronwen." I nodded, cutting through the tension. I refused to be called the human for the rest of my life.

He opened his mouth to speak, but someone grabbed him and pulled him to the side. Just as he stepped aside, a woman swept in with loose golden curls that glimmered like sunlight against the candlelight. Her lips curled into a wide, wolfish smile that didn't reach her bright eyes. She moved with a predatory grace, like she was always circling someone, waiting to strike. It was the woman I had seen when we first arrived, and up close, her presence felt even more dangerous. She was stunning. And she knew it.

"You're prettier than I imagined," she said to me, tilting her head. "So soft. So pink. I wonder what you'd taste like if someone bit you right *here*." She reached out and traced a finger along the line of my throat.

Her eyes widened when her fingers grazed the mark. "Oh but it seems someone already has. Now Auggie, don't you know the dangers of marking someone?"

I didn't move. I wouldn't give her the satisfaction though every natural instinct in me told me to set her on fire.

"I guess all your time away has caused you to forget what happened to your dear mo-"

"Speak of her again and I will have your tongue cut out, Lavina. Do not forget who your king is."

August's mother was marked?

She straightened. "For a few months. It is a shame we lost our father, but at least we have you to bring him back to us."

She tossed her hair over her shoulder as she stepped back.

Then a third vampire stepped forward—his deep brown skin smooth and unblemished, a striking contrast to the golden embroidery of his dark velvet coat. His hair, a rich chestnut, was perfectly styled and tucked back behind his ears with the kind of precision that screamed vanity rather than habit. His deep blue eyes were sharp and assessing, and he carried himself with the confident ease of someone who assumed everyone in the room should already be watching him.

"We're all very... curious, of course," he said, swirling the dark wine in his glass. "We never see our brother and when he is forced back, he brings a woman with him." He looked up at August. "You must really despise her to leave her for Carrow when he returns."

"Careful, Corwin," August warned.

Simon gave Corwin a sidelong glance, amused. Lavina, on the other hand, looked vaguely annoyed—like she hadn't been the one to land the insult first.

"You can say that to my face, you know. I don't need a man to defend me. Least of all him."

Corwin inclined his head, and August placed his hand on my back as if silently reminding me of our earlier discussion. I took a deep breath as I tried to push my emotions back down.

August gestured to the last man, who sat slightly apart from the others, his posture withdrawn but not unsure. "That is Benedict."

Benedict had dark, shoulder-length hair that fell like a curtain, half-concealing his sharp, pale features. His eyes were shadowed, as though he was always somewhere else in his mind. He didn't radiate menace the way the others did. Instead, he carried the quiet presence of someone who had never quite belonged here but stayed anyway. Where the others wore their roles like finely tailored clothes, Benedict seemed untouched by it all. Like he existed on the edges of their world, always observing, never partaking.

August grabbed my hand, his grip firm, and led me down the long stretch of table. We passed his siblings, who parted only just enough to let us through, their eyes following us like hawks tracking prey. Then, in a blur of motion, they vanished from our path—appearing at their seats in flashes of movement too fast for human eyes to follow. The sudden shift made the candle flames tremble.

As August took the head of the table, the room seemed to settle, the tension strung tight like a bow. It was clear that this was his place, whether they liked it or not. And by the stiff posture of his siblings, they didn't.

"What? You might as well get used to seeing your brother here. If Carrow's lucky, he will be in this body for a millennia."

They exchanged glances, but August ignored them. Halston lingered near the kitchen doors, his posture careful, his gaze fixed uncomfortably on me.

"You are dismissed, Halston," August said, draping a napkin across his lap.

Halston's eyes snapped away from me as if waking from a trance, darting to August instead. Flustered, he dipped his head quickly. "Yes, Your Grace," he muttered before hurrying out.

August grabbed a plate of meat and started piling it on my plate. "You need to eat," he muttered.

"How endearing." Simon glanced toward us, smiling as he studied me.

August shot him a glare, and Simon only chuckled under his breath before shaking his head and dropping his gaze to the food in front of him. The other siblings had already started eating—forks and knives cutting silently through rare, barely cooked meats. Their conversation flowed easily now, fluid and dismissive, like we weren't even at the table.

Lavina was telling some sordid story about her latest hunt, her laughter sharp and glittering like broken glass. Simon interrupted with a crude joke that made Corwin roll his eyes and mutter something under his breath about decorum. Benedict sat silent, methodically dissecting his food with surgical precision, occasionally glancing at the rest of them with thinly veiled disdain.

At one point, Lavina snapped at Corwin for correcting her. Simon mocked them both with a lazy toast, while Benedict kept his head down, clearly tired of it all.

For the longest time, none of them looked at August. None of them acknowledged him—or me.

It was like we were ghosts at their feast.

Then, Lavina leaned forward. "Did you live in town?"

There was a long moment of silence before I realized everyone was looking at me.

I straightened. "A little outside of it."

"Siblings?"

"A brother."

"And your parents?"

I paused for a moment, trying my best to not show the despair that wanted to desperately come out at the mention of them. "Dead."

"Oh, a poor orphan girl. How sweet of Augustus to bring you in."

I clenched my fists under the table. *Breathe.*

"You know," Simon cut through the conversation. "You smell oddly familiar."

"Maybe it's because your brother had his hands all over me right before we came in here."

He let out a loud laugh. "Do you enjoy that? Having something so dangerous be so... *obsessed* with you?"

"Not as much as I enjoy having my hand wrapped around his throat," I said before I could stop myself, but I didn't regret it. I was tired of being quiet. Tired of being told to behave. The look of frustration that twitched across August's face only made me smile. If it made his life harder, good. I wasn't here to make things easy for him.

The room stilled for a beat, and then something like amusement flickered across Lavina's sharp smile. Corwin raised an eyebrow, clearly intrigued, while Benedict actually glanced up from his plate for the first time.

Simon gave a delighted laugh, clapping his hands once.

"Oh, Bronwen," he purred, leaning forward. "I think we are going to get along splendidly."

August leaned back in his chair and closed his eyes. I guess I wasn't boring them like he wanted.

The siblings talked more as servants brought in towers of decadent sweets.

August leaned closer, his voice low enough to be mistaken for a breath. "You never listen, do you?"

I turned to face him, ready to snap something back—and froze. His face was so close, our lips nearly brushed. I hated how I still noticed things like that. How the heat rolled off him despite everything.

"Listening to you has gotten me nowhere."

8

Bronwen

We walked down the stairs, and more stairs, spiraling deeper and deeper into the belly of the castle. The staircase wound tightly in a corkscrew of cold stone, open at the center so you could look over the edge and see nothing but darkness below. On each landing, a hallway branched out, lined with doors on either side. I could feel the pull of magic behind every one of them. There was no doubt in my mind that vampires waited just beyond, listening, breathing, existing in the silence. The deeper we descended, the louder the sound of drums became. Low, pulsing beats that echoed off the stone, ancient and primal.

The hairs on the back of my neck rose as unease crawled through me. After dinner, August's siblings had risen and slipped out of the dining hall without a word. When August finally stood and gestured for me to follow, the only thing he'd said was, "The night is far from over."

He offered me no other answers as we descended. By the time we reached the bottom, I bent forward, struggling to catch my breath.

"Are you okay?"

I glanced up to see August staring at me with wide eyes.

"No, August, I'm not. No human should ever have to walk down that many stairs. And in heels! Is this why you really brought me here? To torture me?"

He scoffed. "Yes, this was my plan all along. To have you doubled over, heaving. I can't believe you figured it out."

I straightened. "What are we even doing down here?"

He took a slow breath, eyes flicking toward the massive doors before us. "You're about to see what it's really like here."

Then he nodded once to a nearby guard who stepped forward to open the doors. "Here we go," he muttered, more to himself than to me.

As we stepped forward, I realized we had entered a chamber that felt larger than the entire town itself. Hundreds of vampires filled the space, their laughter and music crashing together in a cacophony of indulgence. Some wore extravagant finery that shimmered like woven starlight, their coats embroidered with gold thread, corsets boned with jet-black metal, and sweeping garments that moved like water. Others wore almost nothing at all—bare skin glinting under candlelight, jewelry resting in places clothes never touched, and a few not wearing anything at all. It wasn't shameful. It was pride.

Chandeliers of black iron and dripping wax hung from the vaulted ceiling, casting erratic shadows across the marble floors. Silk banners with the royal crest waved gently from invisible breezes, and candlelight shimmered off bodies that twisted and writhed to the beat.

Some danced—elegant, slow, intoxicated on the sound.

Others lounged on velvet pillows, sipping from goblets so dark I doubted it was wine. In the corners, fangs gleamed. Bodies pressed. Some kissed. Some were wrapped so tightly around each other that I wasn't sure exactly what they were doing. It was beautiful and terrible.

Above ground was a show. Something that seemed almost human.

But down here, everyone looked like they were having the time of their immortal lives.

And all of them turned to watch us enter.

The drums slowed, some bowed, while others stared at me with sick smiles.

"King Augustus!" The guard introduced him.

As if on cue, the crowd parted. Vampires stepped aside in synchronized motion, giving us a clear path through the center of the room. The scent of blood, perfume, and power thickened as we walked, and every step echoed louder than it should have.

This was for Mama and Papa, I told myself. *Their deaths wouldn't be for nothing.*

Whispers followed us. Curious eyes clung to my every movement. The fabric of my dress shimmered like flame in the dark, catching the light with every movement.

Some of the vampires looked fascinated, their gazes lingering with something like awe—or hunger masked as interest. But others seemed to tense the closer I passed. I caught the faint pulsing of veins beneath their eyes, and I knew they were fighting to stay in control.

It was my scent.

I was their prey.

Several figures offered nods or brief bows to August as we

passed, murmuring greetings I couldn't make out over the whispers. He returned none of them. His hand hovered near mine, not touching, but close enough to herd me forward.

At the far end of the room, a grand staircase rose in a sweeping curve up to a high platform that overlooked the entire chamber. At the top, two thrones waited—one carved from obsidian and trimmed in blood-red velvet, the other smaller but no less imposing, silver laced with dark engravings. More guards stood at the bottom and the top of the staircase.

That was ridiculous.

We climbed the stairs slowly, every eye still on us.

The music never stopped. The revelry never paused. But I could feel their hunger shifting. It was less toward blood, and more toward what August and I represented now.

Power.

A union that was never meant to happen.

I sat in the smaller throne, feeling like an impostor cloaked in silk and resentment. The silver markings curled cold and unfamiliar beneath my fingertips, and my gown pooled around me like a shroud. I was meant to be their queen, but all I felt was trapped.

"What is this?" I asked, the edge to my tone impossible to miss.

"I told you they indulge. This is the great room, and they do this every night. And we have to be here," August replied without looking at me. His tone was flat, almost bored, like he'd explained it before and didn't care to again.

From here, the details were even starker: bodies intertwined on cushions, bare skin flashing in the candlelight; the glint of fangs as one vampire sank teeth into a throat; the way the music surged when blood spilled.

Laughter erupted from somewhere below, wild and unrestrained.

I saw a vampire dancing alone, covered in fresh blood, twirling as if in a trance. Another fed from someone who looked all too willing, their hands tangled in each other's hair. In a far corner, a group lounged on a velvet circle of cushions, their limbs tangled lazily as they passed a silver chalice from mouth to mouth. A low, musical hum drifted from their circle, hypnotic and strange, as if they existed in a dream separate from the chaos around them.

I leaned forward, narrowing my eyes through the candlelit haze. Halston stood with a woman with dark hair. She had her hand on his arm as she whispered something in his ear. He smiled, not like the malicious smiles he had given me... it seemed genuine.

Movement below caught my attention. One of the men being passed between vampires looked familiar. Light brown hair, tousled from too many hands. Pale skin, growing paler with every greedy bite. Then I recognized him.

It was the man who helped me out of the carriage only hours ago.

He had looked so content then. Proud, even. Had he known what awaited him?

Another vampire gripped his jaw gently, almost affectionately, petting his face like one would calm a trembling animal. He leaned in close, whispered something I couldn't make out.

Then, without hesitation, he bit into his own wrist. Thick blood welled instantly, and he pressed it against the man's lips.

My heart dropped.

"What—"

The gasp tore out of me as the vampire snapped the man's neck with an audible crack.

I shot to my feet, the throne scraping against the stone floor behind me. My hands trembled as I walked toward the edge of the perch, breath catching in my throat.

In an instant, August was beside me.

"What is it?"

I pointed to the broken body lying in a heap on the marble below.

"Oh, that?" August said, unfazed. "Give him a moment."

"A moment? What do you mea—"

Then I saw it. The body convulsed. The man sucked in a sharp breath, his chest rising like something had clawed its way back into it. When his eyes opened, they glowed crimson.

No longer a human.

A vampire.

I stared down at the sight. Vampires cheered as one came forward, pulling a pale woman along with him. She looked as if she was seeing through everyone around her with a smile shining on her face. When brought to the new vampire, she extended her neck to him. I blinked and he was on her feeding with such force that she went limp almost immediately.

"He wanted that," August said.

I turned to him. "No one would want that."

His jaw tensed, only for a moment before his cool composure returned. "You'd be surprised. Many of the servants here are working for one thing—immortality. The better they serve, the faster they get turned. But most of them are just here, stolen in the night."

"And the woman that just lost her life?"

August laughed. "Don't start acting like that bothers you,

Winnie."

I stared at him as he scanned over the crowd, the candlelight catching the sharp lines of his face. He looked more at home here than anywhere else I'd seen him—regal, detached, a king in his kingdom of horrors. But I saw the tension in his jaw, the stiffness in his posture. He didn't smile here like he used to, not like before everything happened. This wasn't ease. It was control.

I wanted to tell him he was wrong about me, but he knew me better than most.

August turned to me slowly, his eyes drifting up my frame before meeting mine. He tilted his head just slightly, then gave a single, deliberate gesture back toward the thrones.

I rolled my eyes and moved back to my seat.

As August sat beside me, a pale servant glided forward, offering him a goblet of deep crimson. Without hesitation, he took it.

I watched as he raised it to his lips. The liquid inside moved thickly, almost syrupy, and I knew instantly it wasn't wine. My stomach turned as I watched him drink. His eyes slipped shut, the smallest sigh leaving his lips.

"It calms the hunger," he said softly, catching my gaze before I could look away. "Helps me think."

"But it doesn't stop it?"

He glanced down my throat. "No, Winnie, it doesn't."

I hated the way the thought of him feeding on me sent heat curling low in my belly.

My gaze dipped downward, sweeping over the great room below. Amid the chaos, I caught sight of Corwin, lounging on a velvet chaise and deep in conversation with another vampire. But his eyes weren't on them—they were on me. A wicked smile pulled at his mouth when he noticed me watching.

A chill crawled down my spine. There was something in the way he looked at me that set every instinct I had on edge.

I turned back toward August—and found him already watching Corwin. His face was a mask, completely unreadable, but his knuckles were white where they gripped the arm of the throne.

"Is this where you were on the nights you weren't with me?"

He turned his head just slightly, but his eyes stayed locked on his brother. "Why do you think that?"

"Everyone seemed so comfortable at dinner, and then at the end, you all got up like this was second nature. I had just assumed you needed a break from harassing me, but now I'm not so sure." I pointed to a particularly happy woman spinning herself dizzy on the dance floor. "I just don't understand. Your siblings are here, and yet you had a home in town."

August was quiet for a moment, as if he was sorting through his thoughts. "When I lived here, I made it as difficult for everyone as possible. I pushed every limit Carrow tried to place. He punished me, locked me up, starved me. But I never stopped. Eventually, we came to an agreement. I didn't have to live here if I attended a weekly dinner to let him live out his fantasy and comp—" He stopped mid-sentence but quickly recovered. "*perform* my duties that he expected of me. It let him pretend he still had power over me."

It wasn't always once a week that he disappeared. It was random, leaving me wondering what took his attention away from me. I shouldn't have cared. "And the other nights?"

He sipped again, the red staining his mouth like a bruise. "Some of those nights were my designated time to hunt."

I frowned. "Your what?"

"Carrow scheduled when we were allowed to feed. Another one of his rules. The night we met, it was my night to hunt. He sent the other vampire to watch me, for 'protection.' I told you that."

"I wasn't sure what I could believe of the things you told me," I muttered, watching as another vampire laughed with a mouth full of blood.

"I kept things from you," he said, turning back to the room, "but only because I thought it was best."

Guilt surged up again, churning my stomach and battering against every wall I had so carefully rebuilt.

No. I couldn't feel bad for him.

Not after everything he had decided to take from me.

"When is the wedding?"

He tilted his head to the side and smiled at me. But it didn't quite reach his eyes. His hair fell loose across his forehead, a pale curtain in the flickering light. I had to fight the ridiculous urge to reach up and smooth it back. To touch him like I used to. Like nothing had changed.

But everything had.

"So eager to marry me, Winnie?" he asked, amused, but there was something frayed at the edges. Something brittle.

I didn't flinch. "Eager to know my brother is safe."

He rolled his shoulders, a slow shrug that seemed more like a show of strength than anything else. "In a couple of days. It takes time to plan these things. But I told them to be as quick as they can."

I narrowed my eyes. "Plan what exactly?"

He turned his face fully toward me, the candlelight catching the glint in his deep brown eyes. "Do you think this is going to be a hidden wedding? *Me?*"

My stomach tightened. "And until then, I'm supposed to just sit here and let everyone stare at me?"

He leaned closer, and I could feel the chill radiating off him despite the warmth of the room. His voice dropped to a rasp meant only for me. "No. You know what we'll be doing until then."

A thrill of heat curled low in my traitorous stomach. I hated the way he looked at me and that I still wanted him to.

But it was nothing but my body betraying me.

I may be playing this game with him now, but I had already made up my mind. After we stopped Carrow—after I knew that my brother was safe—I was going to kill him and every vampire in this castle.

9

Bronwen

I glanced down the road, nerves coiled tight beneath my skin as I waited for someone—anyone—to spend the night with. I was on edge, but I kept reminding myself no women had gone missing in several months. I just had to find someone and get back inside before the sun disappeared completely below the horizon. I never imagined I would become one of those women waiting on the street for a man. My mother had always kept me far from this part of town and yet, here I was.

It was easy, though. Bat my lashes, fake a giggle when they flirted poorly, and count down the minutes until sunrise. I waited a while, until a man with several missing teeth zeroed in on me. I quickly spun around and pretended to be interested in the crumbling brickwork of a nearby building,

Gods, was I really being picky?

I glanced at the sky again, nerves grinding tighter, and I was just about to give up when I laid eyes on one of the most beautiful men I had ever seen.

His hair was white and tousled, like snow that had never settled. It framed a face that was both sharp and unfairly perfect, his skin pale and smooth, his lips full. His eyes were dark—depthless, endless—and locked onto mine like they could swallow every thought I'd ever had. He was tall, easily over a head above the crowd, and dressed in a long, tailored coat that shimmered like starlight. Everything about him screamed wealth, power, and danger.

What was he doing on this side of town? Surely it was for the parties or the extra strong wine. There was no way he was here looking for someone like me. But he was coming straight to me.

He stopped just in front of me, his smile lingering as his dark eyes swept over me with far too much interest. "What's your name?"

"Elira," I answered, lifting my chin slightly.

He repeated it, letting the syllables stretch over his tongue. "Elira. Funny. I think that means to be free."

I raised an eyebrow, unsure whether to be flattered or alarmed. "What are you looking for?"

He tilted his head, grin widening until the tips of his fangs glinted in the dim light, just as his eyes bled into crimson. "I'm hungry."

I woke with a start, my breath catching in my throat.

The room was dark, save for the yellow glow slipping in through the curtains. My heart pounded against my ribs, the nightmare already slipping away like mist. I reached instinctively to the other side of the bed.

Empty.

My fingers brushed over the cool sheets where he should've been. I sat up slowly, rubbing at my eyes, and that's when I saw him.

August was hunched over the desk across the room, his back to me, illuminated only by the dying flicker of a candle. His shoulders were tense, unmoving. Whatever he was reading or writing, he hadn't noticed I'd woken.

Or maybe he had.

After the party last night, August brought me to our chambers and told me he had things to attend to. I didn't bother staying up to wait for him. I welcomed the time away, and after being out nearly all night, sleep came easily. Thankfully, the nights I spent in the woods had already trained my body for this strange new schedule.

I walked over to him to see the journal open before him. Empty goblets and discarded scraps of parchment surrounded him. He had been at this for hours.

He didn't look up. "You're awake."

The word scraped against my skin, but I ignored it. "So are you."

He grunted, flipping a page with more force than necessary. I drifted closer, drawn despite myself.

The journal looked worse than I remembered. The ink was faded, the language twisted and ancient, half the margins filled with frantic notes in a hand that must have been August's.

"Anything useful?" I asked, nodding toward the mess.

August finally glanced at me, his eyes rimmed in red from lack of sleep. "If it was useful, don't you think I'd have done something by now?"

The bitterness in his voice landed hard.

I bristled. "I'm not standing here for fun, August."

"No, of course not." He dragged his thumb along a margin. "You're just waiting to see what kind of monster I'll be next."

Snappy.

I crossed my arms.

"Half the journal's written in dead tongues. It's not just translating—it's interpreting. Guessing. Hoping."

I leaned in, frowning at the unfamiliar script, my arm brushing his where he hunched over the page.

The contact was brief, barely a graze, but it burned hotter than a brand.

I jerked back instinctively, nearly knocking over an ink pot. August didn't move.

He just stared at the journal, jaw tightening, a muscle ticking in his cheek.

I swallowed, glancing over to the notes he had written on a scrap sheet of paper. "You found something."

I hated how aware of him I was. How even now, my body recognized the ghost of what used to be between us.

His eyes flicked to mine before he dropped them back to the journal.

"*At the dying of the blood, he will rise not by voice, but by hand. The blade calls him home.* It doesn't make any sense."

I stared down at the brittle pages. "You know, I've been thinking about how the... transfer works. Does Carrow have witches hidden somewhere in this castle to use?"

"No, of course not."

"Well unless vampires can perform magic and you haven't told me, something has to hold the magic to use on the Blood Moon. A celestial event could be the activator but a magical object would need to be used. Something my ancestor would have created to use every time it's needed."

"So a blade like this says?"

I shrugged my shoulders. "Maybe."

August glanced up at me and I noticed how his eyes shifted to my lips before he cleared his throat.

"Get ready. You have a dress fitting soon."

He stood abruptly, the chair scraping against the stone as he pushed away from the desk. Without another word, he strode across the room and disappeared through the door, slamming it shut behind him.

I rolled my eyes and exhaled sharply. The tension still clung to the air like smoke.

Alone now, I wandered the room, taking in the heavy furnishings and dim candlelight. One of the wardrobes caught my attention. It was tall, carved with roses and twisted vines. I opened it cautiously.

Clothes. All his. The scent hit me immediately—sharp, smoky, and unmistakably August. My breath caught before I could stop it. I slammed the door shut.

Another armoire stood to the side. I stepped to it, pulled it open, and found a collection of gowns. Each one was as stunning as the one I wore last night and clearly chosen with care. Silks and velvets in shades of midnight, blood, and gold shimmered in the low light.

I ran my fingers along the fabrics when the door creaked open behind me.

My heart leapt into my throat. I froze, already picturing August catching me snooping. No—I wasn't snooping. I was doing exactly what he told me to: finding something to wear. The only reason he'd think otherwise was if I looked guilty.

I took a steadying breath and crossed my arms. "That wasn't nearly enough time to get dressed, August. Trying to catch a glimpse of me naked?"

But when I turned, it wasn't him.

Corwin leaned casually against the doorframe, his eyes glinting with quiet interest.

"Can I help you?"

His eyes raked over me. "I've barely slept since meeting you yesterday."

I arched a brow. "Yeah, well, I have that effect on men."

He chuckled once, low and soft. "No, I mean it. I can't stop thinking about it. About *you*. Why you're here. Why *he* brought you here."

I said nothing, but my spine straightened.

Corwin took a step into the room. "He's damning you to a fate worse than death—and yet, his scent is all over you. His eyes never leave you. *Gods*, he even worried about you eating."

"It's to keep my strength up," I said flatly. "So he can feed on me."

"And yet... there isn't a mark on you," he murmured, his eyes narrowing slightly. "Not one. Just that scar. That's not what feeding looks like. You should be a bloody mess with bruises and bite marks all over you."

"He likes to bite me where you can't see." I shrugged, even as my pulse quickened.

I was only in a night slip—thin, nearly translucent. There wasn't much it hid, and I knew exactly what he saw. Perfect, untouched skin.

Corwin's expression didn't change. He didn't look convinced. If anything, he looked more curious than before, like he knew I was lying and wanted to know why.

I blinked and he was suddenly in front of me, so close I could feel the air shift.

"He doesn't care about me," I snapped, more to convince myself than him.

Corwin's lips curled, not quite a smile. "Then let's test that theory."

Before I could react, he grabbed me. One arm hooked behind my back, the other beneath my knees, and then we were moving. The room blurred around us.

I gasped, my hands flying to his chest, one gripping his coat as the other sparked with the instinct to pull magic. But I held it back, teeth clenched, heart hammering.

I squeezed my eyes shut, forcing the rising bile back down my throat as fear twisted through me. "Where are we going?"

"We're going to see if Augustus gets to you before you hit the bottom of the stairs."

Fuck. That.

I reached for the power inside of him and yanked.

Corwin's knees buckled. He gasped, collapsing forward and dropping me hard onto the floor.

I stifled a scream as my shoulder connected with the floor. I crawled over to him as he writhed, fingers clawing at the carpet.

"He doesn't care about me," I hissed as I gripped his hair in my hand. I pulled more from him, the power flowing into me like wildfire, mending the dull ache in my shoulder. Dragging his face close to mine, I whispered, "He *fears* me."

My palm sparked, a ball of fire swirling to life in my hand. But the sliver of logic left in my head—small, stubborn, and annoying—forced itself forward.

Someone would smell him burning. Someone would come. There would be questions.

With a hiss of frustration, I extinguished the flame.

Instead, I lifted my hand and summoned whatever wood I could find nearby. A door creaked open down the hall, and a chair snapped through the air, whistling toward us.

The chair slammed into Corwin with a brutal crack—one

leg spearing through his heart, another tearing into his stomach, the remaining legs pinning his body to the floor like a grotesque marionette.

That was a little more than I meant. I winced. "Whoops."

Footsteps thundered down the hall.

August appeared a second later, breath ragged, eyes flashing. He looked around sharply, making sure no one else had followed, then turned to me with a look that was somewhere between fury and disbelief.

"Gods alive, Winnie!" he hissed. "You couldn't wait twenty-four hours?"

My mouth fell open. "He was going to throw me over the balcony!"

"Shh!" August snapped, glancing down the hall again. "Do you want the entire castle in here? We have to clean this up before someone sees."

I looked at Corwin's body—gray, still, pierced through the chest and stomach. August didn't even hesitate. He grabbed the shattered remains of the chair, yanked it free from the corpse, and hurled it over the balcony like it was trash.

"They won't know whose blood this is," he muttered. "But we need to get rid of the body. I am not dealing with this right now."

"Get rid of the body? You're not upset that I just killed your brother?"

"Upset?" He turned to me with a scowl. "No. Inconvenienced? Absolutely."

August slung Corwin's body over his shoulder with a grunt, blood still dripping from the chair splinters embedded in the corpse.

He made it a few steps before glancing back over his shoulder, catching me still kneeling on the blood-slick floor, my breath uneven.

"Do I need to carry you, too?"

* * *

A wedding dress.

It was beautiful.

Too beautiful.

Silk and lace, soft against my skin, with delicate beading that shimmered like frost in the candlelight. The bodice clung to me like it had always known my shape, while the train billowed behind in heavy waves, so long and so luxurious it seemed made for another life.

But the weight of it—it didn't feel like a gown. It felt like a warning.

Earlier, August had taken Corwin's body back to our chambers. He ripped it apart piece by piece and burned each limb in the hearth. He did it slowly, methodically, because a large fire would have summoned questions—too many servants, too many vampires with too keen a sense of smell.

I sat and watched.

And the worst part was, I wasn't horrified. I was more concerned he'd accidentally set himself on fire than I was by the sight of him covered in blood and gore, reducing his brother to ash.

Now I stood in a room surrounded by fabrics worth more than the house I grew up in, being pinned into a dress that felt like a cage stitched in ivory. A vow I never made. A surrender.

I had never worn anything so exquisite.

The seamstresses worked with swift, practiced hands, whispering to each other in a language I didn't understand. They circled me like vultures, pinning and tucking and smoothing as though sculpting me into someone else entirely.

August lounged in a tall velvet chair near the door, head resting on his hand. He didn't speak. But his eyes never left me. They followed every brush of a hand, every adjustment, every inch of lace that was pulled taut over my skin.

I glanced at his hands—broad, steady, deceptively gentle. I could still feel them on me from earlier, right after the bath I took to rid myself of Corwin's blood. He hadn't said a word as I emerged clean and quiet, but he'd touched me anyway. Hands over my skin, lips on my neck, smoothing nothing, adjusting nothing. Just placing his scent over mine like a brand.

There was a possessiveness in his gaze that made my cheeks flush, though I fought not to show it.

I looked back at myself in the mirror, at the way the dress hugged my ribs. It was easier to focus on fabric and posture than the memory of his hands on me, of how he'd touched every inch of skin just to coat me in his scent. I tried to push it down, to pretend it hadn't happened. But my body remembered even if I didn't want it to.

"There is no way they made this dress in a day," I muttered, watching my reflection.

"Well, they did," he said lazily, but his tone didn't match the slouch of his body. There was something too careful in it. A quiet tension behind the ease.

I turned toward him, careful not to twist too much with the pins still in place. "August, I was raised by the most skilled seamstress in Joveryn." I glanced down at the women in front of me. "No offense, but this would have taken her months."

He opened his mouth—maybe to lie, maybe to explain—but before he could speak, Halston stepped into the room like a shadow slipping in under the door.

"Excuse my interruption, but I would like your opinion on some things, Your Grace."

August stood without argument, adjusting the cuff of his shirt. "I will be back."

He glanced at me once more before following Halston out. I let out a slow breath and turned back to the mirror.

"It was his mother's dress," one of the seamstresses whispered, too softly for anyone but me to hear.

"Nadia!" the other hissed.

I blinked. "His mother's?"

The younger seamstress nodded, eyes wide. "I heard that she wore it on her wedding day. Before she—" She stopped herself, suddenly interested in the hem.

I swallowed hard, staring at myself again. Draped in history. In legacy. In the ruin of a woman who birthed a monster.

It fit perfectly. As if it had been waiting.

The door creaked open.

"August, why didn't you—"

I stopped short. It wasn't August.

Simon stepped inside, the scent of expensive cologne wafting in ahead of him. He gave me a dramatic once-over, eyes sparkling. "Beautiful, Bronwen."

Not another one.

I didn't return the compliment. "I know."

He circled the pedestal slowly, taking care not to step on the train. His gaze was curious, glittering, too knowing.

"It's strange," he mused. "To see Augustus with someone.

But then, who could resist you?"

I didn't respond, waiting for his attack.

He smirked, sensing the tension. "Relax. I prefer my lovers taller and broader, and my heart belongs to someone else." He paused, inhaling deeply—too deeply. His eyes widened. "I knew it."

I frowned. "Knew what?"

"I smelled you. Months ago, in the woods. It was… overwhelming." His smile faded. "I almost came to find you. But Augustus found me first."

I narrowed my eyes. "Convenient."

"He was strange that night. Wanted to spend time with his brother. Took me away from the scent, acted like he couldn't smell it." Simon tilted his head. "Which now I know was a lie."

I crossed my arms. "So you followed him instead."

"I did." He looked almost embarrassed. "I watched him feed. Six people, maybe more. It wasn't hunger. It was frenzy. Like something inside him had snapped. It was sweet of him, protecting you from me."

I kept my expression neutral. "Maybe he was protecting you from me."

Simon blinked, caught off guard. For the first time, he looked unsure—his tongue stilled behind parted lips, as if realizing just how much he didn't know about me after all.

"What are you doing in here?"

August's voice cut through the room like a whip. He stood in the doorway, one hand braced against the frame, his eyes fixed on Simon with a look that could gut a man.

His gaze flicked to me, then dropped lower—to the lace clinging to my waist, the bare slope of my shoulders. When he looked back at Simon, the rage was quiet but unmistakable.

Simon stepped back instinctively. "I just came to let you know that Lavina wants to do another dinner tonight."

August didn't move. "Does she."

Simon swallowed and tried a smile, but it faltered under the weight of August's stare.

August finally pushed off the frame and walked into the room. "Why does she wish to make my life more difficult?"

"It's Lavina," Simon said quickly. "That's why the gods gifted us with a sister."

August stepped up to me, his eyes sweeping over the front of my dress with quiet deliberation before finally meeting mine. The pedestal I stood on brought me level with him—eye to eye, breath to breath. I fought the urge to step down, to retreat from the heat of his gaze and the closeness that made the air feel too thin.

"Very well," August mumbled.

"You haven't seen Corwin today, have you?"

I knew questions would come, but not this fast. They couldn't know what I did. Eventually, they'd all know what I was capable of—when they were screaming and burning. But not now. Not yet. I forced my breath to stay steady, my spine stiff.

"No." August rolled his neck, a muscle twitching in his jaw, but his eyes stayed locked on mine. "Is that all?"

Simon hesitated a beat longer than necessary, gaze flitting between us like he sensed something was off. "I'll see the two of you tonight, then."

As if silently instructed, Simon left in a blur, the air practically hissing in his wake.

"Why not tell them no? You're the king."

He exhaled through his nose, the edge of a bitter smile tugging at his mouth. "Because being king doesn't mean they'll stop trying to gut me when I'm not looking. Appeasing them with dinner is a lot easier than having to watch my back around every corner."

I rolled my eyes as I looked back at myself in the mirror.

I knew I was going to be miserable at dinner.

10

Bronwen

I lied. I loved this dinner.

The smell of the decadent food alone was enough to make my mouth water—roasted meats glazed in dark, rich sauces, platters of steaming vegetables dressed in butter and herbs, soft breads still warm from the ovens. But it was the desserts that made me dizzy with happiness: sugared tarts filled with spiced apples and golden honey, delicate pastries dusted with powdered sugar, thick slices of velvet cake layered with cream.

I thought nothing could compare to grape jelly. I was wrong.

My plate was already piled shamefully high, and I had no intention of stopping.

And I couldn't forget my dress. It was deep purple, silk with a plunging neckline and gold stitching that caught the candlelight every time I moved. It cinched at the waist, dramatic and sharp, and flared at the hips with just enough volume to make a statement. I looked powerful in it. Dangerous.

Lavina kept glancing at me from across the table, her smile too sharp. She didn't hide her displeasure well, which only made the food taste sweeter.

Hearing the gossip, even though I had no idea who they were talking about, was oddly comforting. The voices overlapped in quick, vicious bursts—scandal, innuendo, half-truths passed between them. Their cruelty was effortless, elegant even. In a twisted way, it felt like a family. Not the kind you trusted, but the kind that made you feel alive, seen, part of something dangerous and dazzling. I was the stranger at their table, but they didn't ignore me. They looked. They whispered. And I smiled.

My eyes drifted to Corwin's empty seat. None of the siblings mentioned him. There were no questions. No concern. If they noticed his absence, they hid it well. Their indifference was either calculated or careless. I didn't know which was worse.

"Did you see the man Lavina took to her chambers last night?" Simon asked with a wicked grin, swirling the wine in his glass. "I tried to get her to share, but you know how she is, especially when she likes the way someone screams."

Lavina leaned back in her chair, her jeweled fingers resting delicately on her goblet. "He was divine. Just a taste and I was half drunk. But I'm not ready to toss him aside yet. Maybe if you're on your best behavior, I'll let you watch."

"You marked him?" I asked. I had heard the stories. I had experienced it myself, but I had never seen it happen to someone else.

Benedict, ever the quiet one, kept his gaze on the surface of his drink. "It's one of her favorite pastimes," he murmured.

Lavina's eyes glittered. She tilted her head and let out a peal of laughter that echoed down the long dining hall. "Oh, it makes their blood sing. So much more flavor when they know they're owned." Her eyes slid to August with mock affection. "Augustus knows what I mean—don't you, brother?"

August didn't respond.

"I'm just shocked he's kept you this long," she said, directing it at me with a syrupy smile. "The longest I ever lasted was a few weeks. The hunger always wins. You either feed or you fracture."

I leaned forward just enough for her to see the glint in my eyes. "I am not owned."

"Oh but aren't you? He dresses you up, pulls you around to dinner and the parties, and then after you spread those legs for him and give him the one thing he des–"

"Lavina," August warned.

I gritted my teeth as August placed his hand on my thigh. *I could be mature. I could do what was necessary.*

"You may have some strange hold over Augustus, but it won't matter soon enough. All you'll be needed for is to bear Carrow some sons."

No, I couldn't.

"And what are you needed for?"

She looked at me, a mix of shock and intrigue etched on her face. I lasted a day being quiet. That in itself was a victory.

"I mean I'm sure you realize that you were a mistake. A *woman.* What did Carrow want with a daughter?" I twirled the fork between my fingers. August tensed beside me, but I could see the smile he was fighting back.

"At least your other brothers know they are the back up plans for Carrow's attempt to be truly immortal, but you?" I took a sip of wine, dragging this out for as long as I could. Everyone stared at me and I relished in it. "All you seem to be here for is to be the castle bitch."

Simon spit his drink out.

I started to turn toward August, lips twitching from Simon's reaction, when I caught the faint glimmer of something metallic in the candlelight. My breath hitched a second before the pain struck.

August moved, a blur of motion—but not fast enough.

The knife sank into my stomach with sickening precision.

The world tilted.

I gasped, pushing myself from the table. Pain bloomed through my middle like fire, and I didn't know whether to pull the knife free or leave it. My hand hovered uselessly near the hilt.

"Forgive me," Lavina said. "It just slipped."

August was already moving—shoving the table aside, reaching me in an instant. His body blocked mine, his arm stretched protectively as he faced her. "You—"

He didn't finish. He launched at her, and she didn't even have time to brace herself.

She hit the stone wall with a dull thud, a low grunt escaping her lips as she slid halfway down. But she laughed. She laughed as if this were a joke. "So protective," she purred. "It's almost romantic."

"Touch her again," August growled, "and I'll make sure you never touch anything again."

Lavina's gaze swept lazily to the blood now soaking the front of my dress. "You don't have to worry," she said with a cruel smile. "I think I nicked something important. You always did have a weakness for fragile things."

I whimpered. I hadn't meant to, but the pain was too much.

August snapped, and this time even Lavina flinched. He seized her by the throat and slammed her into the stone with enough force to crack it.

"You think this is a game?" He roared through the dining

hall. "You think I won't rip your throat out?" His fangs bared, his eyes glowed like coals. "Come near her again and you'll crawl away—if you're lucky."

Lavina tried to step away, but August grabbed her again, this time by the back of the neck.

"Oh no. You break it," he hissed as he hurled her toward me. "You fix it."

I didn't wait. I gripped her wrist, letting the magic flow. She screamed.

The knife slid free of my body with a squelch, and the pain drained with it. The hole in my stomach closed before my eyes, leaving only blood and torn silk.

"I really liked this dress," I muttered. I held her longer than necessary. Just enough to make her squirm.

But even with her withering away under my touch and every vampire in this room wide-eyed, it wasn't enough. This fucking bitch thought she could hurt me. I placed the knife in front of her face so she could watch as it turned into a wooden stake.

"Augustus!" one of the brothers shouted.

He turned, fangs gleaming. "Move and I'll rip your heart out."

I shoved the stake right next to Lavina's heart.

"You shouldn't worry about his threats. My favorite thing to do is kill vampires." I brushed her hair aside, fisting it tightly in my hand. "And now you've made it personal."

I released her, watching her crumple. She was pale and trembling as she weakly fumbled with the stake.

"Maybe he was protecting me after all," Simon whispered.

August glanced at him.

And I smiled.

Simon cleared his throat, setting his goblet down with exaggerated care. "Well, that escalated."

No one laughed.

Benedict stared at Lavina. "She's a witch," he said quietly. Not with disgust. Not with dread... but curiosity?

"This doesn't leave this room," August commanded. "If I hear a whisper of this—if any of you breathe a word—I will kill every last one of you. Carrow needs you. I don't."

Simon gave him a slow, tense salute before tossing back his wine. Lavina was only just starting to rise, her limbs sluggish, drained. And Benedict—he hadn't taken his eyes off me once as if he was reassessing everything he thought he knew about me.

August grabbed my arm and pulled me from the hall. Every step I took echoed with the pulse of stolen power surging through my veins. I felt weightless, unshakable. Moments ago, I'd been dying. Now, I moved like a storm in human skin. One sibling dead. Another trembling from my threat. And now they all knew: I was no fragile girl.

August turned to me, a flicker of alarm flashing in his eyes as he frantically glanced past my shoulder, like he could hear something I couldn't. "We need to get you changed. Get the blood off of you."

I clutched the ruined fabric and felt as it stitched itself back together, and the blood disappeared. "There. All better."

August didn't respond at first. His eyes stayed fixed on the spot where the blood had just been, his chest rising and falling faster than it should've. For a moment, he looked like he was somewhere else entirely—like something inside him was unraveling.

He blinked slowly, as if he was trying to pull himself back

into his body. Something was fraying in him. A thread pulled too tight. If I touched it, I didn't know if he'd snap or bleed.

Then, he scowled, which only infuriated me. He was trying to hide every true emotion from me.

"Oh, I'm sorry." I crossed my arms. "Did I ruin your chance to get your hands all over me again?"

His eyes raked over me. My breath hitched, and I felt the heat crawl up my throat, blooming over my chest like a fever. I swore I could still feel the imprint of his hands on me from earlier, the ghost of his grip, the heat of his palm.

I shivered, but not from the cold.

"I've only done what's necessary."

"Right." I knew he was lying. I saw the pure hunger every time he touched me, putting his scent all over me. He had to force himself to hold back. But how was that possible? If what Lavina said was true, how was I still alive?

"How did you stop yourself? Every time you have bitten me—how did you not drain me dry?"

His eyes darkened. "What?"

"Lavina said the mark drives you mad with need. So why haven't I done that to you?"

His stare locked on mine, and something unspoken roared beneath the surface. "You've done far worse to me, Winnie."

My breath caught in my throat. "But how do you control it?"

His jaw clenched, and his hand rose with hesitation. He brushed his fingers across the raised scars on my neck like he was punishing himself for putting them there.

"Because if I ever gave in and killed you," he said quietly, "I'd follow right after. I wouldn't survive it."

The words sliced through the space between us like a blade,

far too vulnerable for either of us to handle.

For a moment, I saw him. Truly saw him. Not the king. Not the vampire. Just the man who had fallen so completely into whatever this was with me, he didn't know how to climb out.

But then his shutters came down.

"We won't cross that line again," he said, voice rough, retreating behind the mask. "You're only here to stop him from coming back."

The words landed like a slap across my cheek, burning with quiet cruelty. They didn't just draw a line between us… they carved a chasm between us.

He'd been pulling away, slowly, subtly. I saw it. I felt it. But part of me had hoped he wouldn't say the words out loud.

Now he had.

And something cracked deep inside me. Not like the sting of a wound, but like the soft, sickening break of something once whole finally giving way.

It hurt more than the knife ever could.

* * *

The great room was alive again.

Music swelled beneath the chandeliers, every note laced with menace. The vampires twirled across the marble floor like predators in silk, laughing too loudly, moving too smoothly. Everything shimmered with opulence and violence.

We sat on the thrones overlooking it all. I adjusted my posture, spine straight, chin high, pretending the conversation we'd just had hadn't gutted me.

August sat beside me, a statue of tension. His gaze swept the room with precision, but his hand gripped the throne's arm like it might splinter beneath his fingers.

"I am not letting you out of my sight now," he said under his breath.

"That happened with you sitting right next to me, August."

His jaw flexed. No comeback.

"I've learned my lesson. I will not be unarmed here."

He turned, slowly, his eyes scanning my face. "How much did you pull from Lavina?"

I tilted my head, letting the candlelight catch the wicked glint in my eyes. I said nothing. Instead, every candle in the room flickered—flames dancing in unison.

His voice dipped into something darker. "Winnie. It is for your best interest that no one else finds out."

"They won't." My lips curved. "Unless I am provoked."

His eyes lingered on me for a long moment.

I turned back to the dancers, catching a glimpse of Lavina and Simon tucked in the corner, their eyes on me. Let them look. Let them wonder what I was capable of.

Let them be afraid.

11

Bronwen

August and I spent the next few days looking further into the journal, but the deeper we went in, the less we understood. And the words he could decipher didn't align with what we had already learned.

August had taken me to Carrow's old chambers, and the moment I stepped inside, I felt the weight of it—everything was spotless and perfectly in place, as if Carrow had only stepped out for a moment. The curtains were neatly drawn back to let in slivers of light, illuminating polished furniture and immaculate floors. I scoured the room for anything that felt magical, hoping I could find the blade—or whatever object was used in the ritual.

The only thing that called to me was August.

August had given me nothing but mixed signals since we had gotten here. One minute he was rubbing his hands on me to put his scent on me, and the next he ignored me for hours. He would lean in a little too close or stare a little too long and then his expression would shift into something close to disgust.

He had always been confusing, but now I wasn't sure if he was fighting himself or had finally shown how he truly was.

Like what he had been before was all an act.

But I knew better.

I almost wanted to try to talk it out with him, to push past the way we both betrayed each other, but then the wedding would come up and anger overpowered every other emotion I had.

He knew this was the last thing I would want, and he was going to do it anyway.

But that was tomorrow.

Today, we needed to work on the journal more. But we had combed through every page over and over again and found nothing.

So now we were walking through the castle because August had an idea.

We walked up several flights of stairs, passing only servants until we came to a large set of double doors, and I paused just beyond the threshold. The room was massive, lit with soft golden light spilling from the daylight that streamed through large, arched windows high on the walls. The beams of sun caught the dust in the air and painted the room in soft, hazy gold. Seeing so much sunlight eased something in my chest. I knew then that any vampire lurking nearby would think twice before stepping inside. Shelves stretched high above my head, filled with old leather-bound books, scrolls, and strange artifacts.

Then I heard it—a quiet shuffle off to the side.

I turned quickly, pulse spiking, only to see a man stepping out from between the rows of towering shelves.

"Forgive me, Bronwen. I didn't mean to startle you." It was

Benedict.

I had only caught glimpses of the siblings in the great room since Lavina tried to kill me. Dinners with them had stopped, and they seemed to avoid us entirely.

"What are we doing?" I whispered to August even though I knew Benedict could still hear me.

"I told you I had an idea."

My mouth fell open. "You told him what we're doing?"

August nodded. "I trust him more than the others."

I wasn't sure if that was comforting or terrifying.

I crossed my arms. "So you think he can help us?"

"Benedict has never left," August said. "He's lived here all along. He knows the castle. He knows Carrow. I'm hoping he'll help."

My gaze flicked back to Benedict.

As if sensing the doubt still clinging to me, his eyes softened. "Carrow has terrorized us all. Some more than others." He glanced at August. "If there's any way to stop him, I want to be part of it."

This Benedict and the one at dinner every night felt like two entirely different people.

August reached into his coat pocket and pulled out the journal that had given me more truth than he ever had. I wondered if I could have read it myself, if I could have prevented all of this.

He handed it to Benedict who opened it and stilled when he realized what it was.

"I see you have been doing your own research already," he mumbled as he flipped through the pages.

"What did you think I was doing all this time?"

Benedict glanced at me, his gaze flickering down, and he

snorted.

"Benedict," August warned.

"I knew you were planning something. But bringing her into this mess made no sense—until our last dinner." Benedict's eyes flicked to me and he smiled before he turned back to August. The amusement didn't carry. He looked down at the journal again, fingers brushing the page. "Where did you find this?"

August shrugged. "Near where the first spell was completed. I can't read it all, though."

"Of course you can't. That is what happens when you leave before your schooling is finished." Benedict's tone was stern, one similar to the one I had heard from Papa countless times. My heart lurched at the thought of him, but now wasn't the time. I pushed the thought to the back of my mind as I tried to focus on the conversation before me.

"Schooling?" I asked.

"I told you that vampires are more civilized than you think."

I rolled my eyes and looked back at Benedict. "You were here during the last Blood Moon ritual?"

"Yes, but I wasn't at the ritual. Only a select few that Carrow trusts the most are allowed at that."

August nodded toward the table in the center of the room. "Let's get started. Time isn't exactly on our side."

The long table was covered in tomes and scraps of parchment, the battered journal lying open like a wound at its center. August stood at one end, arms crossed, and I took the farthest chair from him that I could.

The silence stretched as August stared at me.

"Where are we stuck?" Benedict asked, finally moving toward the table.

August gestured to the journal and rested his hands on the back of a chair. "Everywhere."

Benedict slid into a chair beside me without waiting for permission.

August's hands flexed.

"I was around when some of the old tongues were still spoken, and I've studied the others," Benedict said to me. "August thought I might be of some use."

August gave a grunt that could have meant anything.

I offered him a small, guarded smile, still uneasy with how different Benedict was acting from the silent observer I thought I knew.

He began scanning August's notes.

"Close enough," he muttered. He flipped the page and looked closer.

Time passed slowly.

I sat for a while, watching Benedict's face tighten in concentration, his fingers tracing the faded script. Every so often he'd grunt or mutter something under his breath. It was clear this would take hours.

My attention drifted. I glanced at August again—only to find him already looking at me. There was something unreadable in his expression, something almost soft, and that unnerved me more than any glare ever had. I looked away.

I stood and began to move quietly around the room. Shelves lined the walls, cluttered with relics from centuries past— tarnished crowns, weapons too fragile to wield, boxes inscribed with runes that pulsed faintly. The air near some of them hummed, like the magic inside hadn't settled, or didn't want to. There were more magical objects in this room than I expected a vampire that persecuted witches to have, which only worried me. If I was right about the ritual using a magical object, how could I figure out which one was what we were looking for?

I trailed my fingers along a blade with a split hilt and immediately recoiled—the energy that burst through my skin was wrong. Not dark like Carrow's, not consuming like August's. Just... off. Like the echo of a scream caught in metal.

Other objects felt different. A pendant throbbed with heat when I brushed it. A scroll crumbled at the edges but still hummed with purpose. It was as if the room remembered what it was meant to protect.

And I wasn't sure if I was meant to be here at all.

I jumped when August slammed his fist against the table, the sharp crack of it breaking through the stillness. Benedict had just said, "You had most of the translations right and the ones you didn't weren't important," and I didn't even have time to process the words before August snapped.

"So there is nothing in there? I've spent years looking for this and it's useless?"

Benedict shook his head, fingers drumming the edge of the journal. "There are plenty of things in the archives that may be of use. More journals. Logs of all the artifacts Carrow has collected."

August ran his hand through his hair as he glanced at me. "Tell him what you think."

I hesitated, choosing my words carefully, not wanting to sound foolish but knowing I had to say something. "Since vampires don't have magic and can't perform a spell, it has to be an object that brings forth Carrow. A blade maybe. "

"Do you think Carrow's soul is already in Augustus and a blade brings him forward?"

I glanced at August. It would explain *a lot.* "Maybe."

Benedict leaned forward slightly, eyes gleaming with a spark of curiosity and unease. "Maybe there's documentation of a blade that can do such a thing."

Behind him, August whispered something under his breath—too soft to catch, but it didn't sound like words meant for us. I turned toward him, but his gaze was blank, distant. He didn't even seem to realize he'd spoken. A chill threaded through me.

It would explain *that.*

August took a breath, rubbing a hand across his mouth. "Start with that, Benedict."

"We aren't helping?"

He shook his head. "Not today. Halston needs to speak with us about tomorrow."

"What—" And then I remembered. Tomorrow was the wedding. My stomach dropped like a stone.

* * *

We sat in a room on the main floor of the castle. The chairs were plush, velvet-backed things that were dulled with age. A hearth flickered low in the corner of the room, the fire inside barely more than a whisper of flame, caged behind glass to keep all embers from escaping.

August sat across from me, drumming his fingers on the arm of his chair with a glint in his eyes. But it wasn't amusement— it was something sharper. Restless. Like his body was here, but his thoughts were pacing somewhere far darker.

Halston waltzed into the room. "Your Grace." He bowed and glanced at me as he stood back up, a flicker of disapproval tightening the corners of his eyes. "I didn't realize you were bringing the human with you."

I stared daggers at him.

"I want her here to understand what will happen tomorrow," August said, his tone clipped.

Halston's hesitation was noticeable. "As you wish. I just wanted to go over the ceremony one last time. It will be quite simple. I will speak the traditional words. The two of you will be crowned, and I will announce you as King and Queen."

"No."

Halston blinked. "No?"

"I want to do it like the humans do. The rings. The kiss. Even the silly practice that has been lost in time. What is it? Ah, yes." August smiled. "Binding."

I shot out of my chair, the legs scraping loudly against the stone floor. "Are you fucking serious?"

The weight of everything came crashing down at once, settling in my chest like stone. Binding two souls together wasn't some romantic tradition—it was sacred. A ritual where you called to the gods and asked to be tethered together not just in this life, but in the peace found after. It was a promise for eternity.

And it wasn't lost to time. The humans stopped doing it, because they believed it was witchcraft. Dangerous. But our witches still did it. And only with the deepest love. The most unshakable trust.

How did he even know about that?

"I will not bind myself to you," I said, the words sharp enough to cut.

August didn't even look at me.

"Your Grace, I do not think that is a good idea," Halston said carefully.

"Why not? It doesn't concern Carrow. It is soul to soul. Mine to hers. Forever."

Halston faltered. "Well, I suppose—"

"You suppose nothing. You'll do it because I command it."

I stepped forward, fists clenched. "Are you deaf? I said I will not bind myself to you!"

August waved me off like I was a child throwing a fit.

"I'm sure you remember how they used to do the bindings. Prepare for it."

"August—"

He moved before I could finish, cradling me against his chest. And then we were blurring through the halls of the castle, faster than I could process, his grip unrelenting.

I hated when he moved like this—inhumanly fast, air whipped past my ears, the ground vanished beneath my feet. Every time, it made me nauseous.

He stopped in our room, and I shoved out of his grip.

"I feel like this conversation would be better if it was private," he said, brushing his shirt where it had wrinkled from holding me, as if that inconvenience mattered more than my fury.

"Binding? Are you serious? I would never bind myself to you!"

"Well, you are." August lifted a brow, the corners of his mouth twitching like this was all mildly amusing to him.

"No, August. I'm not."

"It's already been decided."

He waved his fucking hand again, that same dismissive flick

that made my blood boil.

I lunged, grabbing his arm and pulling on his magic, forcing him to his knees with a satisfying thud. "Do not ever wave your hand at me like that again," I hissed, magic still thrumming at my fingertips.

His gaze landed squarely on my chest—which I could only blame myself for considering it was only inches from his eyes given his current position—and I scowled, ready to snap at him. But then he looked up slowly, amusement flickering behind his dark eyes, and gave me a real, unguarded smile.

As if he liked that I fought back.

"What's worth more to you, Winnie?" He tilted his head. "You or your brother's freedom?"

He knew the answer to that. My stomach twisted as I turned away from him, dragging my hands through my hair in frustration.

"That's why you haven't made the decree yet." I spun back around to face him—only to find him already on his feet. "You were planning this."

"No. I actually just came up with it. Pretty good, right?"

"You're horrible."

"Consider it another... *incentive* to ensure we find a way to stop Carrow. He doesn't take over my body, I'll live forever and you'll never see me in the afterlife."

"I will haunt you."

He shrugged nonchalantly. "You'd just add to the voices I already hear. It won't make a difference."

He turned and began walking slowly toward the doors, speaking as casually as if he were discussing the weather. "I have several things to take care of before the ceremony so I will have food sent to you. Relax. Take a long bath. Sleep as long as you can before a nightmare wakes you." He reached the doorway, paused, then glanced back over his shoulder and winked. "I'll see you tomorrow."

12

Bronwen

"Oops," I mumbled to myself, taking in the wreckage I'd left in my wake. August's clothes were strewn haphazardly across the floor, torn from his armoires. The once-elegant curtains now lay in shreds, dangling limply from their rods. I had screamed, hurled objects until they shattered, torn down everything within reach. Then, I had stood in the middle of the wreckage, breathing hard, weighing my options: storm through the castle and track down whatever crypt August had buried himself in to finish our fight? Scale the towering window—which, I now realized, was far too high—and run for my life? Or use the magic I'd hoarded from Lavina and August and reduce this castle to a smoldering ruin? I'd conjured twin flames in my hands, ready to start with the bed. One spark, and it would all burn.

But I stopped myself.

Because it wouldn't stop Carrow.

So here I waited, numb and motionless, for Jane and the seamstresses to arrive and prepare me. My hands sat folded in my lap like they belonged to someone else.

I had been as calm and submissive as I possibly could since we arrived. Only defending myself. I wasn't sure why. Maybe I hoped August would change his mind if he saw how we could work together. Maybe I wanted to believe the version of him I saw in fleeting moments—the one who spoke gently, the one who looked at me like I was more than a weapon or a pawn.

But he didn't change.

He went off the fucking deep end.

I heard the door handle twist before I saw him. A gust of cold air swept in ahead of him, curling around me like a warning. My breath caught. Somehow, I already knew it would be him.

Then, the doors swung open, slamming against the walls with a force that made me flinch. I jumped to my feet, my fingers instinctively trying to smooth the folds of my dress, even as my heart began to hammer in my chest.

August stepped in, the dark fabric of his coat catching the candlelight as he fumbled with something in his hand. His expression was unreadable as he glanced around at the mess until his eyes met mine—and then, for the briefest breath, something shifted. The cold mask slipped. He looked like the August who had shown me where his mother used to take him. He looked as if he might say something.

This was it. He regretted it—he was changing his mind.

I waited.

But whatever war was being waged inside him ended just as quickly. The emptiness returned to his gaze, and he adjusted his coat, jaw tight, eyes averted.

Like he had done every time.

He started to walk out the door again. Maybe I could stay calm and reason with him.

"August, I really don't know if I can do this. The binding.

It's irreversible which means I could never bind myself to another."

He stilled and turned back to me.

"You think this changes anything?" he asked, voice low and dangerous. "You were mine the moment you let me mark you. The moment you let me touch you. There will be no one else."

My hands curled into fists, nails biting into my palms. *Don't show him anything. Not fear. Not anger. Not even hate.*

And still, I met his gaze, steady and unyielding. "If you think that, then you don't know me at all."

August laughed—a soft, broken thing that sounded almost like pain.

"Oh, I know you," he said. "Better than anyone ever *wanted* to."

For half a second, I let myself believe he meant to fix it. That he'd come to tell me none of this would happen—that we could still find a way out. That he still felt what I felt.

But then he opened his mouth, and I remembered who I was dealing with.

I couldn't hold it in any longer. I didn't like how he thought he had something over me.

I hesitated, searching for the cruelest truth I could wield. "I thought the mark meant something. That it meant something about us. But it was just a trick. I see that now."

His expression didn't move, so I pushed harder.

"I hate you for letting me believe it could've been real. And I hate myself for wanting it to be. You ruined my life!"

Then something inside him snapped. The veins around his eyes pulsed with anger, his face twisted with rage.

"Ask me how I felt about you."

His voice didn't sound like a command this time. It sounded

like a man dangling off a ledge who needed me to let go. Like he needed to say it out loud so he could stop feeling it.

"What? Why?"

"Ask me."

I swallowed hard. My fingers curled tightly around the fabric at my sides. "How did you feel about me?"

"At first, there was a part of me that woke up thinking about you," he said. "And no matter how hard I tried to fight it, I couldn't get you out of my mind. I thought it was just bloodlust. That's what I told myself. But then I'd think about your eyes, your hair, the way your nose scrunched when I aggravated you. Or how you would tap your thumb and fingers together when you were about to break. I don't think you even know you do it. But you were doing it a moment ago. That's how I knew to keep pushing."

He let out a bitter, broken kind of laugh.

"But when I was trying to get to you before you saw your parents—I realized it wasn't just that. The panic I felt... the way I thought I might shatter if you saw what they'd done. All I wanted to do was protect you. I l—"

"Don't say it."

He stared at me, a storm raging behind his eyes. "I loved you."

He said it like it hurt. Like the words had to be torn out of him. For a man who had lived hundreds of years, I wondered if I was the first person he'd ever said that to. And now it would never be said again.

The words hit like a blade through my ribs. My breath hitched. I had tried not to think about my feelings toward August—how tangled and impossible they were. But I'd seen it in him before, in the way he started to look at me. And maybe, just maybe, I'd felt it too.

Maybe I still did.

How else could I explain why I never killed him? Why I stepped between him and Adar?

Because I did. I loved him too.

He stepped closer. "Ask me how I feel about you now."

His voice had changed. Flat. Dead.

I could see it in his eyes. The warmth that had been there was gone.

"No," I whispered, backing away.

He advanced, closing the distance between us in a single, quiet step. He leaned in, his breath cold at my ear.

"I feel nothing."

He pulled back just enough to look into my eyes, his gaze sharp as glass.

"It's crazy. In my three hundred years, I never felt anything close to love for someone other than my mother. And I knew you for what? A month? And you ripped that away in a night."

My vision blurred.

"So do what you want here. I do not care. Fuck the whole lot of them if that's what it takes to fill the empty void you have. But you will be at every dinner, every party, and everything else I must endure—because you chose my fate." He stepped closer again, his eyes hard as obsidian. "And now you'll live in it with me. Not because I love you. But because I *don't*."

A tear slipped down my cheek.

"You're mine, forever. And I'll never touch you again. So keep hating me, and never stop."

Jane and the seamstresses stepped in and August smiled as he looked down at me.

"Time to get ready, Winnie." His tone was flat, almost

mocking, before he turned on his heel and strode out the door.

* * *

I stood at the doors that I was escorted to, a veil covering me. I was too stunned by August to process how I felt.

My feet barely moved. My body floated, disconnected. I felt like a ghost in a gown. Like something already buried, now being paraded back to the surface to wed the thing that had killed it.

The doors swung open and my breath caught.

The cathedral hidden deep in the castle stretched upward like the inside of a stone throat, vast and cold. Soaring buttresses loomed overhead, ribs of blackened bone reaching toward a vaulted ceiling lost in shadow. Candlelight flickered along massive stone columns carved with grotesques— vampires feeding, witches burning, saints with hollow eyes.

A guard nudged me forward, and my legs obeyed before my mind did, carrying me slowly down the aisle. The aisle was lined with blood-red roses, petals dark and wilting. The scent of them mingled with wax and incense, hanging like fog in the air.

At the far end stood August, savoring every eye upon him. He wore black from throat to boots. His coat was tailored close, sharp at the shoulders and adorned with thin silver thread that curled like ash down his sleeves. A high collar framed his pale throat, and around his neck hung a single onyx pendant. Atop his head sat a dark iron crown, thorned and cruel.

He looked like something out of a nightmare—beautiful in

the way wildfires are beautiful. Devastating. Consuming. This spectacle was crafted for him, and he basked in it—relishing the attention, savoring the power—as if to prove every fear I had ever tried to bury was true.

He didn't want me.

He *needed* me.

Halston stood next to him, cloaked in black, a leather-bound tome resting in his hands. The siblings stood on either side. Lavina's gaze flicked to me like a blade. If she remembered the last time I nearly burned her alive—and I knew she did—she gave no sign of it. But her posture was too rigid, too poised. She was ready for a show. Simon, as always, looked amused. His lips curved into the faintest smirk, eyes dancing as if he'd been waiting for this moment just to see how much I would unravel. And Benedict's hands were folded neatly in front of him, his gaze fixed somewhere in the distance, jaw tight.

Candles burned in rusted sconces along the walls, casting trembling shadows that made it feel more like a crypt than a chapel. The light barely reflected off the faces surrounding me, but the glowing red eyes didn't need much to see. Vampires filled the pews that lined both sides of the aisle. Some I'd seen in the great room, others I hadn't seen before.

Each step was harder to take.

When I reached the end, August extended his hand to help me up, but I denied it. He didn't glance at me. Didn't smile. His face was stone.

Halston began to speak. Each word echoed off the stone and seemed to seep into my bones, heavy and inescapable. He spoke of power. Of duty. Of binding. His tone was solemn, ceremonial, but I could feel the hunger behind it. The pride. As if what he was doing was sacred.

"This union," he said, "binds not only flesh and name, but soul to soul. Not just for this life, but for every life to come. In shadow and ash, in flame and blood, you are tethered now, beyond the grave. Forever."

Forever. The word rang in my ears like a death knell.

The veil suddenly felt too tight, like a shroud. My dress, too heavy. Forever with the monster I created.

My hands trembled at my sides. Rage built in my throat, thick and hot. My body craved to grab the magic that practically floated in the air. I wanted to tear the walls down. To scream until the castle cracked apart.

I hadn't chosen this. I wasn't some bride. And if he thought binding me meant taming me, he was wrong.

I would make this place bleed before I let him own me. Let them all feel what it was to burn.

August turned to me then. Halston's words still echoed in the chamber, but all I could hear was the roar of my own heartbeat. He reached for my hand, and I barely noticed the cool pressure of the ring as he slid it onto my finger. My eyes stayed locked on his the entire time, unblinking. Unyielding. If he expected softness, if he expected surrender—he would get neither.

He gripped me tightly. I was unsure whether he was trying to keep me from running or hurt me. He handed me a second ring. I took it with fingers that trembled from fury, not nerves. Then I shoved it onto his finger with enough force to twist his hand. A few startled gasps broke the silence. Whispers rippled through the room like smoke.

August didn't flinch.

Then, the knife came to bind our souls. August held it up between us. The room seemed to exhale all at once, a breathless hush descending as he turned it toward me. His fingers brushing mine as I gripped the hilt of the blade. Slowly, I pressed the blade to my palm and dragged it across the skin. The sting didn't even register. Only the blood dripping to the ground did.

The reaction was immediate and sharp. Gasps echoed from the pews—sharp, startled, and hungry. Some vampires recoiled, red eyes flaring as they struggled to control themselves. A few clutched the edges of the benches, knuckles bone-white with restraint. Others hissed and turned away entirely, storming from the room in sudden, silent retreat. The scent of my blood had filled the air like perfume laced with danger. They weren't just curious now. They were tempted. On the edge of losing control.

A low growl echoed as several vampire guards rose from the edges of the cathedral. They stepped forward, hands hovering near their weapons. It wasn't a threat—it was a warning. A command to the crowd not to move closer, not to test their control.

August took the knife next. He didn't hesitate. Didn't even blink. He cut himself clean and deep, blood welling instantly. His eyes never left mine.

He extended his hand and whispered, "Soul to soul."

You or your brother's freedom?

"Soul to soul," I said through gritted teeth. I pressed my hand to his with more force than necessary. Our blood mingled. Magic sparked at the edges of my vision—silver light that arced and curled like smoke through water. My knees almost buckled.

Halston closed the book and stepped back with a bow of his head.

August reached for my veil. He pulled it away completely, letting it fall in a whisper to the stone floor. His eyes swept over my face before he turned and picked up the crown resting on a velvet cushion beside us.

It was dark iron, forged in sharp lines and delicate arches, a cruel and beautiful thing. Etched with symbols I couldn't read and crowned with subtle thorns, it shimmered like obsidian laced with shadow. Red jewels glimmered faintly among the iron, catching the light like drops of blood. It looked like something stolen from a fallen star—both sacred and savage.

August placed the crown on my head, and it was not a gesture of affection.

It was a claiming.

He leaned in to kiss me, and I turned my head, allowing his lips to only brush my cheek.

The room fell silent again, this time with the weight of insult. Someone hissed through their teeth. Another growled low in their throat. Even the air seemed to recoil. I could feel the way their red eyes bore into me like I'd just desecrated something holy. My jaw clenched, my spine stiff.

If they wanted a queen, they would get one.

But she would not be kind.

13

Bronwen

"King Augustus and Queen Bronwen!"

The sound hit me like a wave, all thundering applause and sharp whistles. The great room was wilder than it had ever been. More vampires filled the room, dancing, kissing, drinking. They were chaos in motion, an unholy sea of movement and sound. But the moment we entered, their attention snapped toward us.

My hand was still bandaged from the ceremony, wrapped in fine linen now spotted faintly with blood. Some vampires noticed. I caught the way their eyes drifted toward it—how their nostrils flared and their pupils dilated. August had told me I couldn't heal it because it would raise questions.

A few stepped forward to offer congratulations. I ignored them. I didn't bow my head, didn't offer a smile. One brushed my arm, murmuring something about sacrifice. Another dipped into a low, theatrical bow, their movements too exaggerated to be sincere. I said nothing. I didn't even blink. My gaze was locked forward, past them all.

August said nothing either. He merely walked beside me

as if we were a matched pair. But I felt every inch of distance between us. Every step echoed with the tension we didn't speak aloud.

We ascended the platform together, and the eyes of the court followed us like tethered ropes. When we reached our thrones, we sat in unison, two carved statues in a sea of living shadows.

The music resumed—strings and drums, frenzied and sharp—but it felt distant, disconnected. The vampires spun and twirled like shadows, elegant and careless, but I didn't move. I didn't breathe. I just simmered.

The weight of the crown on my head grew heavier with each passing second. The gold band on my finger sat like a shackle. My hand throbbed beneath the bandage, the ache syncing with the pulse behind my eyes. My teeth ached from how hard I was clenching my jaw. My spine was so stiff I thought it might snap.

The rage crept higher, inch by inch, like hot wax filling my veins. My thoughts spiraled—burning, blistering, sharp. I wanted to scream. I wanted to tear every candle from the wall, rip my dress down the center, set the whole fucking castle on fire.

He had taken *everything*.

And now he expected me to sit still and smile like a well-fed pet?

Not a chance.

I would make him bleed for every second he made me sit beside him like this.

I stood up, feeling the sudden shift in the room. Eyes flicked toward me. I half-expected August to stop me, to grip my wrist or say my name. But he stayed silent.

"Move," I said to the guard that stepped in front of me when

I made it to the stairs.

He hesitated, glancing over my shoulder to August.

"Do not look at him. I told you to move." My voice cut through the music like a blade. "So move."

He looked again, this time meeting August's gaze. I turned to see August give him a single, slight nod. Permission. That infuriated me more than anything.

I descended the dais, each step echoing across the marble floor like a challenge. I didn't glance back at August. Marrying him had not been my choice, and his smug stillness beside me as the ceremony ended had only made it worse.

Especially after he ripped my heart out.

The tables were covered in blood-red wine—no, just blood— and plates of half-eaten meat, steam still curling in the air. A few of them whispered as I passed. One dared to bow. I didn't acknowledge him.

I moved toward the dance floor. The vampires spun and laughed, a haunting mix of beauty and malice. The music pounded like a second heartbeat. I was still in my wedding gown. I, dressed in white, stood out in the sea of darkness. I was their sacrifice. I tilted my chin higher, heart hammering from more than just the rhythm. I would not sit and be looked at like a doll. I would not be silent beside August like some prize he'd won.

Someone caught my hand.

A vampire—tall, pale, handsome in that ageless way they all were—grinned and pulled me into the dance. I let him. His hand was cold and strong, and he twirled me easily, as if I weighed nothing.

"So this is the little queen," he said as we spun. "I thought you'd be taller."

My brow twitched, but I said nothing.

"You know," he sneered, "usually the human queen is kept locked away, used only for the ability to bear a child for Carrow's bloodline to continue. But here you are. In the den where in one quick motion, you could become my next meal. What makes you so special?"

I smiled, but it didn't reach my eyes. "Would you like to find out?"

He laughed, low and cruel. "Oh, but I think I already know. Your scent is not just your own. Our dear King Augustus has marked you. You know, I might feel a little pity for you now. It was all just a game to him. A spectacle. And I think he is just waiting for someone to toss you around like the nothingness that you are."

The words struck like slaps. And maybe that's why I did it.

Maybe I just wanted him to shut up. Maybe I wanted to feel something other than the hollow August left behind. Or maybe—I just wanted to hurt something. Someone. Anyone who dared look at me like I was weak.

I wrapped my fingers around his forearm, sharp and sudden.

His laughter faltered. "What are you—"

I pulled. Magic rushed into my hand, drawn straight from the vampire's body. He screamed. It echoed over the music.

Everything stopped.

Eyes turned. Music died. Conversations ceased mid-word.

A crackling orb of fire bloomed above my palm, pulsing and alive, like it had a will of its own. It cast flickering shadows across my face, painting the great room in shades of terror and awe.

Someone screamed, "Witch!"

The word sliced through the air like a blade. Chairs scraped against the floor. Cloaks whipped. Fangs flashed. Movement swelled at the edges of the room like a tide preparing to crash.

But I didn't run.

My breath was slow, controlled. My body was still, defiant. I turned my head with precision, ignoring the chaos unraveling around me. I sought only one face.

August.

He hadn't moved. He sat sprawled across the throne like a god watching a play, chin resting against his knuckles, elbow propped casually against the armrest. He looked so calm. Too calm.

And then, slowly, deliberately, he smiled.

My stomach turned to lead.

He wasn't angry. He wasn't horrified. He wasn't even surprised.

He was fucking *entertained*.

Like this was exactly what he wanted to see.

My fury rose like a second flame, consuming every thought I had. The magic surged again, wilder this time, clawing through my veins with a hunger I couldn't restrain. I let it feed. I let it consume.

The vampire in my grasp choked, his scream faltering into a rasp. Color leeched from his skin like water draining from cloth. His cheeks sank. His veins turned black beneath his flesh. Bones pressed against skin.

Gasps rang out like cracks of thunder. One vampire clutched the arm of her date. Another fell back into a chair, eyes wide with frozen fear.

The room pulsed with light and heat. For one moment, I felt as if I were floating, as if the power inside me had lifted me above it all. Around me, vampires dropped to their knees. Their skin dulled to a sickly gray, veins standing out like blackened roots. They clutched at their throats, mouths gaping open, gasping for air that wouldn't come, their bodies beginning to wilt under the pressure of my magic.

It felt as though invisible threads had tethered them to me, their strength siphoned without a single touch. I had never managed that before.

Still, I held on.

Then—

I let go.

The fire erupted from my hand in a violent surge, a wave of heat and fury that ignited the vampire's chest. Flames bloomed like twisted roses, engulfing him in seconds. He dropped to his knees, clawing at the fire as it consumed him, but there was no escape. In near unison, the graying vampires around me burst alight, flames spearing through their chests as if their bodies themselves had betrayed them.

Gasps and shrieks tore through the great room. A few vampires backed away in horror, but others stumbled, fangs bared, their instincts slipping free of control. Sparks arced from the magic still crackling in my hand, and where they landed—skin ignited. One vampire yelped as his sleeve caught fire. Another clawed at her throat, flames licking up her collarbone before she vanished in a blur, smoke trailing behind.

Others snarled and surged forward, ready to strike.

I stood my ground, fire still dancing in my palm. I looked up at the throne to see August leaning forward with a wicked grin. As if he was urging me to go further. As if I had done exactly what he was hoping I'd do.

I dropped my hand, letting the fire burn out. Vampires

launched forward, but before they made it to me, August's voice boomed through the room.

"No one touches her."

He descended with deliberate steps, each one echoing against the silent, blood-scented air. No one dared move. Vampires froze, caught in the tension that wrapped around the room like smoke. August stopped in front of me, close enough that I could see the slight shimmer of amusement in his eyes—and something darker beneath it.

He leaned in, too close, and whispered, "You never disappoint, my queen."

I froze.

My stomach twisted, but beneath it throbbed something worse than fury—betrayal. Had any of it been real? The protection, the stares, the way his voice softened when no one else could hear? Or had I always been part of the show?

"But Your Grace, she is a witch!" cried one clinging to Simon's arm, his face pale with panic.

Simon tilted his head slightly, a faint, curious smile curling his lips. He looked less concerned than entertained, as if he were watching a particularly dramatic opera rather than a threat. I guess he had come to terms with this since I almost killed Lavina.

"Do you think I am so dumb that I didn't already know that?"

Whispers rippled through the vampires.

"This changes nothing. She is your queen. You will submit to her. If she chooses to leave you alive, then you *thank* her." Then he turned his head and locked eyes with me again. "And if I even hear of an ill word said about her, you better hope that she gets to you first. Because my methods will be long, drawn out, and excruciating."

He felt nothing and yet he said that.

In an instant, the world blurred, and my stomach dropped like I'd been hurled from a cliff. By the time my vision stopped spinning, we were in our chambers and I was in his arms, cradled like something fragile and breakable.

I shoved out of his grip, stumbling back. Fury flared in me.

August smiled but it didn't touch his eyes. If anything, it looked like it hurt. Like he was smiling just to keep from breaking apart. "Was that your attempt at being my worst nightmare, Winnie?"

"You should be angry!" I screamed.

"Oh I am angry. Angrier than I've been in a long time."

Gods, he was truly insane!

"Then why are you smiling?"

"Because I should have known better. Of course you did the one thing I asked you not to do! You wouldn't be Winnie if you didn't!" Then his eyes widened, as if something had just clicked—some horrifying truth or revelation known only to him. And instead of fear or fury, he laughed. A deep, unhinged sound that spilled from his mouth like a wound torn open.

I shoved him with both hands, hard enough that my palms stung. He didn't stumble. Of course he didn't. "What is so fucking funny?"

He moved closer. "Well, Winnie, before you did that, you still had freedom. Time away from me. But now? Now you'll have to be with me at all times. Every second of every day. Even during your *baths*."

My jaw clenched. "What?"

"You being a witch is going to raise questions. And vampires love gossip. If they find out what you did to Carrow, his supporters will crawl out from under their stones to seek revenge. Just to win favor with him."

I just stared at him.

"So was it worth it?" He spoke coldly. "To spend forever with the person you betrayed?"

"Why would you want that if you felt nothing?"

His voice dropped. "You said you were going to be my worst nightmare. I'm just returning the favor. And you haven't even seen what I'm capable of yet."

He reached out and gently brushed a strand of hair from my face, his touch a mockery of kindness. "And when you scream, when you cry, when you try to claw your way out... I'll still be there. Because that's what you chose when you betrayed me."

14

August

Stupid. Stupid. Stupid.

She just *had* to be the center of attention. Had to make everyone be just as infatuated as I am with her. Of course everyone was looking at her! You had to be blind to not notice Winnie.

Mine.

My Winnie.

The only thing in this cursed world that could ever make me feel anything again—and the only one cruel enough to use it against me.

I paced the room. My hands were fists at my sides. I couldn't sit still. I couldn't fucking breathe.

I was supposed to feel satisfied. I'd won, hadn't I? She was mine. Bound to me by every dark vow that could be sworn under fire and blood. So why did I feel like I'd just carved out my own heart and handed it to her?

I wanted to tear something apart. I wanted to find the vampire she burned and set him on fire all over again just to see if she'd flinch. Just to see if she'd *care.*

I hated her. I wanted her. I wanted to bite her and rip her open and pull her close and make her beg. I wanted to drag her into the dark and drown in her until there was nothing left of me.

That was what she did to me.

And I had no one to blame but myself.

I backed her into a corner. Put her on display. Threw her into a pit of monsters and waited for her to bleed—because I *knew* she'd break.

For what? To chain myself to her more tightly? When I was already hanging on by a thread every time she breathed in my direction? It was fine. I could keep my distance even if I'm in the room with her at all times.

Ha!

What a fucking joke.

I had shackled myself to the only person in this world who could destroy me—and then dared her to do it.

She turned to me again and I could see the wheels turning behind those emerald eyes. What did she see when she looked at me right now? Was I holding it together? Did I look at her like she meant nothing to me? Gods, I hoped so.

"Is that why you said those things to me before the wedding?"

I flinched. Just slightly. Just enough that I prayed she didn't notice. I couldn't remember what I'd said—there were too many voices, too many memories all crashing at once.

I feel nothing—Fuck the whole lot of them.

Fuck no, I didn't mean that! I could barely stand them looking at her. If someone tried to touch her like that, I'd rip their throat out.

"No. I meant them."

Her hands curled into fists at her sides. I didn't know how much power she still held from killing that vampire, but I wouldn't be surprised if she unleashed it on me. In fact, I kind of hoped she did.

But instead, she straightened.

"I need to get out of this dress."

She turned, presenting the laced back to me, and waited.

Gods alive!

I hesitated. The space between us pulsed like a wound. I didn't trust myself to touch her right now, but I stepped forward anyway. My fingers found the ties at her back, trembling with restraint. The fabric resisted me, as if it knew what would happen if it fell too fast.

My knuckles brushed the curve of her spine. My throat burned with the scent of her, and I nearly choked on the desire clawing its way up from my chest.

I wanted to sink my teeth into her shoulder. To claim her again in the only way I understood. To hear her moan my name until it was the only word left in the world.

I wanted her to scream, but not in anger. But I'd take the anger too.

She turned to face me again, shrugged her sleeves down, and let the gown fall. She stood there, bare, unflinching, eyes locked on mine as if daring me to look away.

I didn't have to look down to know exactly what she looked like. It was engraved in my mind. I saw the curve of her breasts, the dips in her hips, and the few freckles that led to her navel every time I closed my eyes.

She glanced at me with hooded eyes. I held my breath, begging to the gods that I wouldn't smell her scent of jasmine that would be my undoing making me forget the little restraint

I was trying to hold on to.

She stepped forward until her breasts nearly touched me, her voice soft and lethal. "Goodnight, husband."

Gods help me. What have I done?

* * *

She slept with her back to me.

I wasn't able to sleep long.

At some point in the early hours—before the castle had begun to stir, before the candles outside our door flickered back to life—I'd woken up gasping for air, throat burning like fire, like I was dying all over again.

The dream had been too familiar. Too real. I kneeled, bound in magical chains on the ground. Then, she reached for it—no, she *ripped* it from me. Drained the power through my veins like it belonged to her. Fire exploded from within, consuming me from the inside out. My skin split, blistered, melted. I tried to scream, but the air burned in my lungs.

She didn't flinch.

She stood over me with her hand still raised, eyes burning with power. She burned me alive, using my own magic to do it.

I woke with the scent of ash still in my nose, the phantom pain of seared flesh clinging to my bones. My skin still itched, like the flames had left a residue under my flesh. I flexed my fingers just to feel them move.

But when I opened my eyes, I was back in this cursed bed, drenched in sweat, the sheets tangled around my legs. And she was still asleep.

I hadn't woken her.

Somehow, I'd kept the scream buried in my throat, where it lived now like a shard of glass.

The quiet was a lie. It pressed against my temples like a vice. The castle hadn't woken yet, but my mind hadn't stopped screaming. Not since she turned her back on me.

I wished I had woken her. Maybe then I wouldn't be lying here, watching her sleep like nothing had changed. Like she hadn't torn the ground out from under me.

The image of her beneath me burned in my mind—her hands wrapped around me just before she did the one thing I begged her not to. I wanted to hate her. I *should* hate her.

But I didn't. I couldn't. So I watched her instead.

The castle was still cast in shadow, though it had to be well into the afternoon. The servants had just begun to stir beyond the chamber door, the distant scrape of footsteps and clink of dishes too faint for human ears. But I heard it all.

I lay still, watching the steady rise and fall of her breath. Her hair fanned around her like ink across the pillow, her face relaxed in sleep—young, almost innocent. Vulnerable.

I hated how peaceful she looked, and yet I couldn't look away.

Part of me still wanted to reach for her. To brush a strand of hair behind her ear. To pull her into me and pretend—just for a moment—that we were still something worth saving.

But another part of me burned with the memory of what she'd done.

She left me. Chose this path. Forced the crown onto my head like it was some kind of salvation. And now she slept like none of it mattered.

My Winnie. My *wife*.

I rolled onto my back and dragged a hand down my face. If she woke now, I didn't know what she'd see. And I didn't know what I wanted her to see.

Had I gone too far yesterday? Had I broken something between us that couldn't be put back together?

No, it had to be done. She had to hate me. She had to let go.

Because no matter how hard I tried to stop it, I still wanted her.

And I didn't know if I could survive wanting her again.

Yet even now, I kept pulling her in. Marrying her. Binding her to me with blood and duty. Tricking her into exposing herself. Forcing her closer under the guise of protection. It was a noose I'd tied for both of us.

I was fucking insane.

She stirred.

A sharp inhale. A twitch of her fingers. Then a sound—soft, broken—slipped from her lips. A sound I'd never heard from her before. She bolted upright, hair wild, chest heaving like she'd clawed her way out of drowning.

Good for her for sleeping longer than I had.

I wondered what I did to her in her dream this time.

Her breathing slowed. Then her eyes found mine. Those eyes—damn them—still had the power to twist something sharp in my chest. Neither of us spoke. Then her gaze dropped. Just for a second. But I saw the shift. The heat behind it. She'd noticed I wasn't wearing a shirt.

The air between us stretched tight like a drawn bow. Before anything else could be said—or done—I threw off the covers and stood.

"I'll send word for Jane," I said, tone clipped and flat.

"We're going to town to make the decree."

"We're going to do it? I thought you'd send word or something."

I turned, just enough for her to see the edge of my expression. "Would you believe me if I said I had someone do it?"

"No."

I nodded once. "This way you'll know it's done. And we can continue our work."

I didn't wait for her to answer. I walked to the wardrobe and yanked it open like it had insulted me, focusing on anything but the burn of her eyes on my back.

She tried to move quietly, but I heard her steps on the floor, soft and deliberate. My senses picked up everything—the shift of her weight, the rhythm of her heartbeat.

For a moment, I saw myself turning. Grabbing her, slamming her against the wardrobe just to feel her gasp. Just to feel something break. I blinked, and the vision passed. Control. I still had control.

I turned just as she stopped behind me. "What?"

She straightened. Close. Too close.

I thought this would be easier. But her scent ruined me. Sweet and infuriating. No matter how many reasons I gave myself to stay away, my body betrayed me.

I couldn't let her pull me under again.

"Your eyes."

I looked across the room to the small mirror at the dressing table to see red eyes looking back at me.

Closing my eyes, I calmed my hunger to bring back the human eyes I fought to wear. It was growing harder by the day. Having her near me without tasting her was torture, but I wouldn't let that happen again.

I'd starve before I gave her that control.

15

Bronwen

August wasn't lying when he said he wouldn't let me out of his sight now. He watched Jane bathe me. He watched Jane dry me. He watched Jane brush my hair. I stared right back at him the entire time.

He sat draped in a high-backed velvet chair, one leg crossed over the other, lounging like he belonged to every dark corner of the room. A perfectly tailored coat of deep charcoal clung to his tall frame, the sharp lines of his shoulders softened only slightly by the luxurious fabric. A high collar framed his pale throat, and dark crimson threading marked subtle patterns along the cuffs. The crown rested on his white-blonde hair like it had always been there, glinting in the candlelight like it had fused with him.

His dark eyes tracked my every movement, unreadable but alert, and his mouth curled into that same infuriating smile. I thought he used to piss me off, but nothing compared to how mad he made me now.

Watching. Always fucking watching.

The nightmare I had the night before hadn't helped anything. I hated him and yet I had to relive another one of his kills through the eyes of his victim. But it wasn't simple this time. He had changed the way he toyed with his prey before the kill. Because he had... *eaten* before he fed. His mouth was all over me—not me, the woman's body I was trapped in—and I felt every sensation that came with it.

Gods! Yesterday, I had finally felt nothing but rage when I saw him and then I shut my eyes and *that* happened.

Jane pulled a dress from the armoire, the soft thud of the door closing snapping me out of my spiraling thoughts. After helping me into the dress, I finally tore my gaze from August and turned to face the mirror. It was beautiful, elegant and expertly tailored, but it itched at the seams and clung too tightly at the ribs. It made me miss the dresses my mother used to sew, soft and simple, stitched with care and familiarity. I wished I still had one. Just one. Something made for me out of love, not obligation.

I stilled when August stood and walked to his armoire, his movements unhurried but certain. My breath caught when he returned with the same crown he'd placed on my head at our wedding.

Yesterday hadn't felt real. It had played out like some grotesque performance, staged for the bloodthirsty creatures lining the castle walls. But now, with the crown gleaming in his hands again, the weight of it all sank into my chest like a stone.

He stepped behind me and gently lowered it onto my head once more. It wasn't *just* a spectacle yesterday.

August, the Joveryn King.

And me... the Joveryn *Queen*.

He leaned in next to me and stared at me through the mirror, his breath brushing the curve of my ear.

"You have to look the part, don't you think?"

I hated the way he made me feel. And yet, when he leaned in, his breath ghosting over my skin, I didn't flinch. Because a part of me—one I hated—wanted him to do more than whisper.

I reached up, running my hand across the cold, sharp jewels. They glinted under the flickering candlelight like blood frozen in time.

"I knew my Winnie liked nice things."

I ripped my hands away. I was not his.

He didn't react. Just turned and grabbed a cloak, his movements smooth and practiced. Then he held it out for me. A silent gesture that made my skin crawl. His hands were so close to me.

Too close.

As we stepped to the castle doors, Halston stood at the end of a dark hall.

"Where are you going?" he asked, folding his arms across his chest.

"To town," August answered, bored.

"No. You can't. Carrow—"

"Carrow isn't here. I'm going to spend these few months how I want to spend them. If you try to stop me, I will throw you out in the sun. Got it?"

The threat was calm, even, and absolute.

I made note of how Halston's expression faltered, how quickly his demeanor shifted. When we made it through this, he would be the first one to go.

The cold bit at my skin the second I stepped outside. After days spent inside the castle's dim corridors and candlelit halls, the snow-glared brightness forced my eyes to squint against it. The sun was blinding, making the ice-crusted ground shimmer like a field of diamonds. I tugged my cloak tighter around me, my fingers already numb, and blinked through the dazzling light, disoriented by how alive the world looked compared to the lifeless chill of the castle.

A new man, I guessed since the old one could burn in the sun now, helped us into the carriage, smiling like a fool. As if the threat of vampires didn't exist behind every corner.

Inside the carriage, I sat as far from August as the space allowed. Plush cushions lined the bench seats, but the air inside felt just as cold as it did outside. My breath fogged in front of me, and the windows were already beginning to frost at the corners. He didn't seem to care about the distance I put between us. He just looked out the window with a half-lidded gaze, like it was any other day. Like he hadn't watched me be stripped and dressed like a doll.

I studied him in the silence. His jaw was tense, the vein in his neck pulsing lightly with each second that passed. Every now and then, his fingers tapped against his knee—a rhythm that betrayed how tightly he was holding himself together.

"I thought the king never left the castle," I mumbled, breaking the stillness.

He turned to me with a smirk. "And lose the chance to have everyone's eyes on me?" He laughed, as if it were obvious.

His words reminded me of the last time we walked through town together during the day. How he'd dropped to his knees in the middle of the square, clutching his hands like a desperate lover, tears in his eyes. Begging for forgiveness.

He was someone completely different now. And yet I could still see the old August slip through sometimes.

"When we get there, keep your hood on until I make the decree."

I glanced at him, eyebrows raised. "Add to the dramatics of it all?"

He said nothing, but I caught the corner of his mouth twitching like he was amused. Or maybe proud. It was always so hard to tell with him.

I rolled my eyes and turned to look out the window again. Frost veined the edges of the glass, blurring the world beyond into pale silhouettes of rooftops and people gathering at the gate. We were almost there. A crowd larger than I had ever seen had already gathered. Most of them were bundled in thick cloaks, boots half-buried in the snow. The cold must have stung their skin just as much as mine, but still, they came. Curious. Starved for distraction.

"I sent word to the Legion to notify every house of this in hopes we would have as big of a crowd as possible," August said.

"So you command a castle of vampires and the Legion now," I said, rolling my eyes. "Oh how far you've come from taking pleasure in watching me kill the things you're in charge of now."

He tilted his head, just slightly, studying me like he didn't quite recognize me. "Have I given you the impression that I don't still enjoy those things, Winnie?"

Shivers ran down my spine, and it wasn't from the heavy snow outside of the carriage.

We came to a stop, and I pulled my hood on, careful not to knock the crown off. But before August could step out, I felt the full weight of the silence outside the carriage.

It wasn't just quiet, it was suspended. Like the moment

before a match strikes. I glanced out the window. Rows of people packed the square, boots buried in snow, eyes locked on the carriage like it might birth a god.

My heart beat louder in my chest. I could almost hear the shift of fabric, the creak of someone leaning forward for a better view. No one spoke. No one dared.

Then August stepped out.

The ripple of whispers broke loose like a sudden gust of wind. Meeting one king only a week ago and now seeing another step out wearing a crown. It was something out of a fable. A dangerous one.

I waited for him to move aside, to let someone else help me down. But instead, he turned back toward me and simply held out his hand. My chest tightened. I bit my tongue before I said something I couldn't take back. Now wasn't the time.

I took his hand, and we walked together, our fingers laced. I took his hand because I had to. Because the crown on my head meant I no longer had the freedom to refuse. But the moment our fingers laced, something ugly twisted in my chest.

His touch still did things to me. And I hated him for it.

I stole a glance at the crowd and quickly scanned it for any sign of Adar, even though I knew it would be useless. Everyone had their hoods drawn tight, faces shadowed. Adar couldn't risk being recognized, couldn't risk someone attacking him. Still, I hoped. I needed to know he was here. That he was safe.

A Legion soldier stepped forward to greet us—the older one I'd first seen with Adar in the woods. He didn't bow, but his stance shifted ever so slightly in deference. A silent nod to August's new title.

August stood beside me like a fallen god, every inch of him regal and dangerous. His crown gleamed in the winter sun, and his pale hair lifted in the breeze. He looked untouchable.

August leaned in close, lips nearly grazing my ear. "Get ready, Winnie. You're about to see the chaos that comes with you getting everything you wanted."

I didn't respond. I didn't trust what I might say.

"My dear father was in a tragic hunting accident last week and is no longer with us," he said, his voice calm and cool, but it carried through town like thunder. "But I am starting a new age. An age of peace, forgiveness, and... *love*."

The word cracked against my ribs like a whip. *Love.* From the same mouth that told me he felt nothing. I clenched my fists inside the folds of my cloak.

I knew he was still angry with me—for the countdown I'd placed on him, for the secrets I'd kept—but he was thriving in this moment. Whether he'd admit it or not, he basked in the weight of every gaze turned toward him. Power radiated from him in waves, and I realized that maybe he had always been this powerful. Maybe he'd just hidden it to make himself more palatable to me.

"And because of that, I have a decree," he continued. "One that I expect everyone to follow immediately."

The crowd froze. A young mother clutched her child tightly, a hand pressed over their mouth like a seal. Even the wind seemed to pause.

"Witches are now free to practice."

A collective gasp broke through the hush like glass shattering.

"You will be welcoming of the witches," August said, raising his voice. "The Legion is now in the service of protecting witches. And if they get word of any unkindness, they will handle you in the way they handle things."

Whispers rippled through the crowd. Cloaked figures leaned into one another, trading hurried words as the weight of the decree sank in.

"But your majesty, they are monsters!"

That voice—I knew it instantly. Lydia Reeves. Lowen's mother.

Slowly, I removed the hood of my cloak, revealing my face and the crown. Her eyes met mine, and she recoiled like she'd seen a ghost.

"Are you calling your queen a monster?" I asked, my voice cutting through the silence like a blade.

August smiled.

"I suggest you choose your next words carefully," he said. "Your queen tends to not be as kind as I am."

Lydia's eyes darted between us, her expression crumpling as she bowed her head and stepped back into the crowd, silence trailing her like a shadow.

And that's when I saw him.

Adar, tucked into the corner of the crowd, his eyes wide. I expected comfort. Instead, I felt sick. What did he see when he looked at me now? His sister? A puppet queen? August's favorite weapon?

August, meanwhile, had stepped forward. His expression was almost serene now, the corner of his mouth lifting like this was all unfolding exactly as he had imagined. "I understand your hesitation," he said to the crowd. "You were taught to fear them. You were told witches bring ruin, that they are unclean, unnatural. But you were wrong."

The crowd held its breath.

August's voice dropped lower, but somehow it carried further. "This is your queen. You will not just accept her. You will *revere* her. You will understand that what runs through her is not something to fear. It is something to kneel for."

He let the silence stretch. Let the words sink in.

"Those who cannot live with this new law," he said, "are welcome to leave. Today. But if you choose to stay and harm a witch, an example will be made out of you. And I promise that example will not be quick."

A sudden movement caught my eye.

Adar.

He stepped forward—no, he surged forward, breaking through the edge of the crowd like something inside him had snapped. His eyes locked on mine, wild with urgency. I could see the moment his restraint crumbled, the moment he stopped caring about being recognized or what might happen.

"Bronwen!"

But he didn't make it far.

Legion soldiers moved fast. Three of them stepped between us, drawing their swords in one unified, metallic hiss. The crowd stumbled back, startled gasps breaking the tension. Adar skidded to a halt, hands raised.

My heart lurched.

"Let him through," I commanded. "He's my brother."

Without any hesitation, the soldiers moved. And I didn't like how much I enjoyed that.

Adar didn't wait. He rushed past them the second their swords lowered, pushing through the final space between us. And then his arms were around me, crushing and warm and desperate.

His familiarity hit me so hard I nearly collapsed. It had been so long. Too long. He didn't speak. He just held me tighter, like he was afraid I'd vanish. My arms moved on their own, curling around him. The burn behind my eyes was sharp, sudden, and I blinked hard against it.

For the first time in days, I let myself feel safe. Just for a moment.

August stepped back, giving us space, though I could still feel the gravity of his presence like a storm held at bay. He didn't interrupt, but I knew he was watching.

The crowd, sensing the shift in energy, began to stir. Slowly at first, like they weren't sure if they were allowed to move. Then one by one, they began to step forward.

The first man dropped to his knee before August, then another, and another. Until a line had formed, each person bowing, murmuring their oaths or keeping their eyes down-cast in reverence or fear—it was hard to tell which.

They were welcoming their new king. Not with cheers, but with submission.

And August, the mad thing that he was, stood at the center of it all like he'd been born for this moment. He looked like divinity wrapped in silk and steel.

I let go of Adar and looked at him. "You're okay," I whispered, more to convince myself than anything.

"You're okay." He glanced over me as if he expected to find something wrong.

"Did you go back to the cabin?"

"I went back to talk to Jonah but I couldn't stay that far, not knowing the next time I'd see you. I've... I've been staying in August's home and leaving only when necessary."

I blinked. "You've been in town? That was too dangerous."

"You've been in a castle of vampires. I don't want to hear it."

I managed a tight smile. He hadn't changed.

A sharp whiff of smoke pulled my attention away. I turned and looked at the blackened remains of the podium, its wood scorched and splintered.

"Do you know what happened?"

I shook my head slowly, still staring at the pile of wood like it might give me answers. My fingers curled tighter around the edge of my cloak. Adar stared at it for a moment longer, his eyes distant and unfocused, as if he were back there in the moment that it happened. His chest rose and fell with a breath so deep it trembled slightly at the top, and then he finally tore his gaze away.

"Well, have you made any progress?" he asked, quieter now.

"We think we are looking for a blade of some sorts." I kicked at a chunk of ice with the toe of my boot. "But that is all we know. Just pieces. Clues that don't make sense yet."

Adar was quiet for a moment. I felt his gaze on me, heavy and thoughtful.

"We can still run," he offered, like it was the last thread of hope he could give.

"I'm not giving up yet," I whispered. "There are so many pieces... I just have to figure out how they go together."

He stepped a little closer, his breath misting the space between us. "If I could help you, I would."

I nodded. I wasn't the smartest, but Adar had always struggled more than I did with schooling. He never let that stop him from trying, though. That stubbornness—it was something we shared.

Behind us, a throat cleared. August.

We turned together, and there he was, standing just close enough to remind us who held the leash. He said nothing. Just lifted a hand and gestured toward the carriage like it was time to move on.

I turned back to Adar, not ready to let go yet. "Let's meet for breakfast at the bakery in a week," I said, squeezing his hand.

He gave a nod, but before I could step away, his grip shifted. He caught my wrist, firm and steady.

"Hey," he said, low. "Be careful. Don't let this go to your head."

"What are you talking about?" I asked, brow furrowed.

"The power, B." His eyes searched mine. "Do not fall for him again because of it."

For a second, I couldn't speak. Then I gave the smallest nod, the kind that said what I couldn't say out loud.

And then I let go.

16

August

"What about this one?" Winnie spun a short-bladed sword in her palm, dancing it through the air like she was testing its hunger. The silver gleamed under the low candlelight, whistling faintly each time she slashed it through an invisible opponent.

I didn't look up. My eyes burned from hours of reading, flipping through yet another leather-bound tome Benedict had hauled out from whatever cursed part of the castle he'd scoured. "That's the fifth one you've asked about. I still do not know."

She let out a breath through her teeth, frustrated. "We could just destroy them all."

I finally glanced up. She was so at ease with the sword, her grip confident and playful, but beneath that was calculation. She didn't mind breaking things.

We were able to sneak to the higher floors of the castle without anyone stopping us. It was one of the only perks that no one other than my siblings could harass me until the sun was no longer in the sky. And considering Benedict was the only one not completely afraid of my wife, nosy Lavina and her sidekick were nowhere in sight when we returned. We changed and went straight to the archives to work.

I watched Winnie longer than I meant to. Her fingers curved around the hilt like it belonged to her, like she was born with it in her hand. The way she moved—it was elegant, almost seductive in its ease, but there was always that edge. A willingness to cut. To hurt. And gods, it drew me in.

There was a line along her collarbone, a faint scar I had memorized long ago, one of many that I could trace in my mind even with my eyes closed. It vanished beneath the fabric of her dress with every tilt of her body, teasing me, even though I already knew exactly where it ended.

It reminded me of how breakable she looked. And how little that meant.

She pivoted, the hem of her gown brushing her ankles, and something inside me twisted. I hated her in that moment. Hated how she could stand there with fire in her blood and a smirk on her lips and not flinch while surrounded by monsters. Hated how much I wanted to sink my teeth into her throat just to see if she'd shiver or smile.

The paper in my hands tore.

I blinked down at it, confused to find my fists clenched tight around the fragile edge of the tome. The page had split, an ugly gash through words I hadn't even read.

I let out a slow breath and forced my grip to loosen. Tried to collect the chaos inside me, to seal it back behind the mask I'd spent centuries perfecting. But it was hard when I let it slip away so easily for her.

"Well?"

I looked back up to see her waving the sword in her hand.

"Carrow wouldn't leave the object that can bring him back just lying around," I said, trying to bring myself back to the task at hand. "Besides, destroying ancient witch-crafted artifacts? You could unleash a soul, rot someone from the inside, or worse—curse *me*."

She narrowed her eyes. "You're deflecting."

"I'm surviving. There's a difference."

Winnie stared at me for a beat, then turned and placed the sword back on the wall. "So what's your brilliant plan?"

"We keep searching," I said, glancing at the rows of objects. "And hope we find it before the Blood Moon."

She trailed a hand along a row of blades, fingers whispering over their hilts like she was listening for one to call to her. There was a hunger in her gaze that startled me. "Have you read anything important yet?"

I caught myself watching her too long. "The Gerotian Sword." I think I said it too quickly.

She turned, eyebrows raised. "The what?"

Yeah, I had said it too quickly.

"The Gerotian Sword," I repeated, slower this time.

She glided over to me and bent over my shoulder, her hair spilling across my cheek, brushing against my skin.

Her blood hit me like a punch to the gut. My throat burned, my fangs ached behind my lips, and I had to grip the edge of the table to stop myself from pulling her into my lap. I hadn't fed in days other than sips from goblets, but that animal blood did nothing to curb my appetite. Not when she was this close. Not when every breath she took stirred the air between us like bait.

I had been able to manage until we went to town. Being surrounded by so many humans had stirred something feral inside me, clawing its way up from the depths. A beast that only ever wanted her.

I stood quickly, faster than I intended to. "It was forged by the leader of a coven on a small island west of here. He spelled it to seek out vampires—to make the hunt easier."

Benedict grunted from the shadows. First sound from him in hours. He watched her with something between awe and fear. Not like the others did, drawn by her scent. He watched her hands. The way they moved. How gracefully she moved with a sword. And yet her bare hands were far more dangerous.

"Carrow heard of it and slaughtered the entire coven to claim it," Benedict said. "It's on the far end of that shelf. That was when he still wore our grandfather's body."

Winnie followed Benedict's direction before stepping onto her toes to reach the blade. I clenched my jaw, resisting the pull to help her.

She'd spent the last hour drifting from artifact to artifact, touching each one like she owned them. Benedict winced every time. He'd spent decades preserving this room like a sacred tomb, and now a young, temperamental witch treated it like a market stall.

Winnie studied the sword in her hand, turning it slowly, watching how the runes shimmered beneath her fingers. She pointed it away from us at first, thoughtful. Then, without a word, she turned it toward Benedict.

The engravings glowed, pulsing like they recognized the blood in his veins.

She smiled. "I could've used this hunting."

Hunting. My vision swam.

The humid night air had clung to her skin, and when she lowered her hood, I remembered how my body reacted.

The moment I caught her scent—sharp, maddening, unlike anything I'd known—I had moved without thinking, standing before her in a blink. She didn't cower. She lifted her chin and met my gaze like she was the threat, not me.

When I brushed her hair back, exposing her neck, I thought she would run. She didn't. I inhaled, trying to place what she was. Human, yes. But there was something ancient in her blood. Something wild.

I bit her.

Her blood hit my tongue like lightning. The world narrowed to just that taste, that moment. But then the pain came, the tearing sensation when she pulled the magic from me, her hand around my throat like a vice. It gutted me. And gods help me, I loved it. She stood looking down at me, victory carved across her face like a crown she thought she'd earned.

Then it shifted. Her arms wrapped around me, kissing me like it was the last time she would. That was the night she tricked me. The night she kissed me to steal from me again. I remembered the feel of her lips on mine, the way she pulled me closer like she needed me, like this was something real. I let myself believe it. I carried her to my bed. I touched her like she was something sacred.

I moved inside her slowly, memorizing every sound she made, every tremble of her breath. I thought I was giving her something. I thought we were sharing something.

Then she pulled the magic from me again.

Her hands in my hair as she ripped the power from me. I saw the tears in her eyes like it hurt *her*. She took my strength and my trust and yet she looked upset.

I looked at her now and all I felt was rage.

Not just rage—something worse. Something festering.

Something alive. It curled inside my ribcage like a living thing, slithering up my spine and coiling tight around my thoughts until they weren't thoughts at all, just noise. White, buzzing, blistering noise.

How dare she stand there, radiant and unbothered, when I was the ruin she made? How dare she look at me with those eyes—green and glinting and full of secrets—and act like she didn't know exactly what she did to me? Like she didn't carve her name into every breath I took?

I wanted to rip the memory of her from my mind. I wanted to strip the want from my bones. But she was in everything. In the way the candlelight moved. In the smell of dust and blood. In the throb behind my eyes.

My jaw ached. I didn't know when I started grinding my teeth.

I hated her. Gods, I hated her. And I wanted her more than I had ever wanted anything in my life.

I blinked hard and forced myself back to the table, lowering into my chair with a stiffness I hadn't noticed settling into my limbs. I grabbed another tome at random, anything to distract myself. But the letters swam before my eyes. The words twisted, refused to make sense. I reread the same paragraph three times before realizing I hadn't retained a single line.

Her scent still clung to the air. Her voice echoed in my skull. Hunger was eroding every thought that wasn't her.

I rubbed at my temple, frustrated, furious with myself. I couldn't afford this. Not now. Not when every second mattered.

* * *

We dined alone that evening.

The dining hall, usually filled with sharp-tongued siblings and sharper glances, sat eerily quiet. Lavina had kept her distance since Winnie nearly set her aflame with a single thought.

Halston was nowhere to be found, which I found to be odd considering he always waited for us at dinner as if he was hoping we would compliment how well he put it together. It was always exquisite, but I'd never tell him that.

Winnie ate like she hadn't been fed in weeks—savoring every bite like it might be her last. I couldn't look away from the way her lips curved around a spoon of honey-glazed figs or the smug glint in her eyes when she caught me staring. She didn't care that she was the only witch in a vampire castle. She owned it.

It made my hunger worse.

After dinner, the castle stirred again. Distant music filtered through the halls, laughter drifting from the great room.

Halston met us as soon as we stepped inside the great room, stepping a little too close. "What have you done?"

I could smell the human blood on him and I pinched the bridge of my nose to stop my eyes from turning red. I needed to feed soon. Desperately. The scraps of animal blood weren't enough.

Not when the one I craved was standing right next to me.

"We had dinner if that's what you're asking."

He scoffed. "No—I am talking about your *visit* to town."

Now I understood why he wasn't in the dining hall. He was upset and wanted an audience. I shrugged my shoulders. "Oh, that."

"You." He pointed a finger at Winnie, his face flushed with

fury. "Have you found a way to spell him into obedience? Just know that Carrow will not be happy with this when he returns."

Who the fuck did he think he was talking to her like that? I considered ripping that finger off of his hand so he could never point at her like that again. But instead I kept my composure, adjusting my coat and trying to look as unbothered as possible.

Winnie wasn't as good at hiding her emotions. Her hand flinched like she was considering grabbing him.

I think I'd let her.

But I didn't know if that was the smartest thing to do right now. We had enough eyes on us as it was. Me bringing a witch home wasn't normal and I could smell the suspicion on some of the vampires.

Halston was one of them.

"Careful, Halston," I said smoothly. "You're speaking to your queen."

He turned to me, disbelief etched across his face. "You made a decree legalizing witches! In front of the humans. In front of the Legion. Are you trying to disobey Carrow?"

Oh yeah, the decree wasn't helping either.

"Did you really expect me to go down easy?" I asked as I stepped closer. "You know me better than that."

He'd been at my birth. Been around me when I disobeyed Carrow constantly. I had run through the halls and destroyed everything in my path even as a child, only caring for my mother. Is he truly so dim that he thought I would let this be an easy transition?

I planned on stopping Carrow, but if I couldn't, I was going to mess up everything that he had done before he came back.

His mouth opened, then closed. He looked at Winnie again,

as if trying to decide whether she was the source of the madness or simply the match that lit it.

A crowd had begun to form.

I started to speak, but Winnie's smile stopped me. She stepped closer to Halston and lifted her chin. Halston tensed. I held my breath.

"I don't need a spell to make him obey."

Her eyes flicked toward me, something sharp and amused passing through them.

Halston scoffed. "You're throwing centuries of order into chaos. Carrow—"

"Carrow is not here. *I* am. And I will not be asking your permission to rule Joveryn."

Halston's jaw tensed. "You're playing with fire."

"Good," I said coldly. "I've always liked fire."

I felt Winnie's heart rate spike.

For a moment, no one spoke. The silence echoed off the walls like a warning.

Halston bowed, stiff and reluctant. "As you wish, Your Grace."

But as he bent forward, his eyes shifted to the guards standing at the entrance. He wasn't bowing in deference. He was checking. Calculating. Gauging whether any of them might stand with him if he made a move.

He was testing the boundaries. Testing me.

So I crossed the distance between us in the blink of an eye and my hand closed around his throat, lifting him an inch off the ground. The guards tensed, but didn't move.

"Are you looking for a fight, Halston?" I hissed through clenched teeth. "Is that what you want? You think they'll side with you?"

His eyes bulged slightly as he clawed at my wrist. I leaned in, close enough that he could see the red bleeding into my gaze. "They're not stupid enough to forget what I can do."

I let go abruptly, and he crumpled forward, coughing, humiliated.

"Now," I said, voice like ice, "let's try that again."

He looked up at me, confusion flickering across his face.

I tilted my head, smiling coldly. "As you wish, Your Grace," I mocked, every syllable dripping with venom.

He stood, slower this time, one hand still rubbing his throat. He didn't meet my eyes. He bowed, deep and stiff, gaze locked on the ground. "As you wish, Your Grace."

He turned and disappeared into the crowd, but I felt no satisfaction in watching him go.

Because Carrow would return if we didn't find a way to stop him.

We sat on the dais. Winnie kept her gaze fixed firmly on the dance floor, but I couldn't look anywhere else. My eyes stayed on her, tracing every subtle movement.

She wore black tonight. Not just any black—something sheer and glimmering, a shadow stitched from sin and silk. It clung to her waist and dipped low along her back, the fabric whispering against her thighs with every step she took like it was just as desperate to touch her as I was. Slits ran up both legs, high enough to make my breath catch, and the sleeves— if they could be called that—were little more than threads of beaded lace hanging off her arms.

It was dangerous letting her wear it now. Dangerous to let her sit beside me like that, eyes glinting with amusement, knowing exactly what she did to me.

And gods, her smell was stronger now than ever.

The scent curled around me. It was enough to make my restraint falter. I could hear her pulse in my skull, feel it echo through my limbs.

I curled my fingers around the throne's armrest hard enough to crack it.

I closed my eyes, trying to breathe through it. To remember who I was and what she was and how dangerously close those two things had become.

But when I opened them again—I was no longer in my seat.

I was kneeling in front of her.

I didn't remember moving.

I was so close I could see the flutter of her pulse beneath her skin. My mouth hovered just inches from her thigh, parted and hungry, drawn to the warmth of her blood like it was the only thing left that mattered. My body leaned toward hers instinctively, helplessly, every muscle coiled with the need to taste. The scent of her, the heat of her, it overwhelmed every rational part of me.

And still, I didn't move. Not yet.

Her skin glowed in the candlelight, flawless and tempting, and I imagined how it would look marred by my teeth. How she would sound if I sank them in. Pleasure or pain—did it matter?

It was the sound of her voice that snapped me back.

"Don't you dare."

17

Bronwen

"What do you mean you haven't fed in over a week? You almost lost control in front of the entire great room, August!"

I paced across our chambers, the hem of my gown swishing around my ankles, my bare feet silent on the cold stone floor. The moment he overcame the animalistic part that had taken him over, we'd left.

"Do not scold me like you are my..." He exhaled, dragging a hand through his hair. "You know what? Never mind."

"Your wife?" I snapped, spinning on him. "I am your wife, and you almost bit me in front of *everyone*. Why haven't you fed?"

"I have been busy," he muttered, jaw clenched.

"Too busy to feed? Too busy to do the one thing that keeps you alive? Wait." I crossed my arms, my anger burning just beneath my skin. "What about the blood in the great room? I've seen you drink that."

"That is animal blood. It is enjoyable in the moment, but it doesn't help long term."

"Animal blood?" I scoffed, eyebrows lifting. "What type of

animals? Deer? Cows?" I gasped. "Horses?"

"You don't want me to answer that."

My eyes widened. "Oh my gods—you didn't."

August stared at me. "That bothers you more than me feeding on humans?"

I crossed my arms. "I grew up knowing vampires fed on humans, but animals? Horses? That seems unnatural." A cold dread bloomed in my chest. I brought a hand to my mouth. "Shadow's missing. If he was stolen in the night like you say humans are, I swear to the gods, August, I will burn this castle to the ground tonight."

He stepped closer to me and shook his head. "There hasn't been any deliveries in weeks."

I exhaled in relief, but only for a second. When I looked up, August's eyes had shifted—crimson bleeding into the brown, veins darkening beneath his skin like cracks in porcelain. My stomach dropped.

"August. You have to go feed."

He turned his face away, jaw clenched so tight I could see the muscle ticking. For a moment, I thought he might argue. But then he closed his eyes. "We are going now," he said quietly. "I can't risk losing control around you again."

August walked ahead of me through the dark streets, his guards trailing a few paces behind us. We both wore cloaks, hoods drawn low to obscure our faces from any curious eyes peering out through the cracks of shuttered windows. I had assumed he would take us below the castle, to some dim corridor where a willing servant awaited their turn. But no— he insisted he had to hunt.

Not just feed. *Hunt.*

There was something primal in the way he said it. Like the

idea of anything less repulsed him. It unsettled me, the way his hunger twisted into something almost sacred. I kept glancing at him as we walked, wondering what kind of predator needed a performance just to survive.

His pace was brisk as he turned down another street.

"Seems like you know exactly where to go," I said, raising an eyebrow.

He didn't answer. Didn't even glance back.

I sped up, falling into step beside him. "I could lead us there, considering I've gotten to the part of your long life where you enjoyed the company of easy women before you fed."

That stopped him cold. He turned his head slowly, his gaze cutting sideways with razor precision. "Are you having sex dreams about me now?"

"Unwanted nightmares."

He smirked, but his eyes shifted to my neck and he turned around.

"Why don't you stay back with the guards? I don't know how my hunger is going to react."

I wanted to argue, to get under his skin a little more because I was still angry with him, but he was right. I let him get well ahead of me before walking further down the cobbled street, past shuttered shops and dimly lit inns. Wild music drifted from somewhere ahead. As we turned a corner, the street opened up into a part of town that felt alive in a very different way. Drunken laughter spilled into the air. A few bodies lay slumped against the stone walls, passed out or too far gone to care. A man sang off-key from the steps of a tavern while another danced in the mud with his coat halfway off. The scent of sweat, ale, and something more acrid clung to the breeze.

But I knew August wouldn't choose from these.

Still, he didn't stop. Just kept walking, gaze cutting through the haze like he was searching for something specific. Until he saw her, a tall brunette smiling like she already knew what he wanted. He stopped in front of her, and she said something, low and teasing, and I couldn't hear the words. But I saw the way he leaned in slightly, the way his head tilted to the side.

He was flirting.

My chest tightened. A slow, hot burn lit behind my ribs—jealousy, sharp and unbidden. It wasn't fair, and I knew it. He wasn't mine. Not really. Not in any way that mattered. But that didn't stop the possessive rage that coiled low in my stomach, the irrational need to tear her away from him.

I hated the way she looked at him like she already knew him, like he was hers. I hated the way he leaned into it, let her touch his arm, let her laugh like it didn't matter that I was right there—watching. Like I was invisible.

I hated that it hurt.

And I hated myself for caring at all.

He said something else—too low for me to hear—and then they vanished into the alley together like they'd done this a hundred times before.

I should've turned away. Should've stayed where I was. But I didn't.

I moved, creeping forward, staying low against the edge of the wall. My heart pounded louder than my footsteps, echoing with every step like betrayal.

"Your Grace," one of the guards whispered, but I waved a dismissive hand, too angry and too determined to care what I might see.

I found them in the alley. Her back was pressed to the stone, her neck arched and her lips parted in ecstasy. His mouth was at her throat, and she moaned as he fed. His hands gripped her waist with reverence, like she was something sacred.

My breath caught, and heat flushed beneath my skin in waves. It was sick—awful—and yet my stomach coiled with need so fierce it nearly dropped me to my knees. My thighs pressed together without meaning to, heart pounding as I stared. I should've looked away. I should've turned and left. But I couldn't.

Because I wanted that.

Not the flirting. Not the alleyway. I would've rather caught him kissing her. At least then it would've meant less. But this? His mouth at her neck? This was worship.

And gods help me, I needed him to bite me like that again.

The jealousy came like fire and ice all at once. My pulse screamed in my ears. My skin buzzed with resentment, shame, and something darker. Something desperate. I hated him for doing it, hated her for enjoying it, and hated myself most of all for wanting it.

I watched the life drain from her, slow and strangely graceful, until her knees buckled and her body slumped to the ground.

August raised his head. Blood on his mouth. Eyes wild. Then he went still. His nostrils flared—and before I could move, he turned.

In the space of a heartbeat, I was pinned against the wall, his body pressed to mine, his breath hot against my cheek. But he was more monster than August right now.

"It's me." I pressed my hands against his chest, ready to stop him if he couldn't stop himself.

"Winnie," he whispered.

His lips brushed my neck, and my skin pebbled. He pulled

back, just enough to look at me. His eyes were still red, glowing like coals beneath stormclouds. He stared—like he didn't trust himself to blink. And then, slowly, deliberately, he closed them. When he opened them again, they were brown.

"No," he said, voice raw. "I can't."

And in that moment, I saw it.

The crack in the mask.

He'd lied. Again. He always lied. At first, it was to protect me. To keep me from knowing too much. Now, it was to keep himself from feeling too much.

But I saw through him.

He hated me, maybe. Maybe he couldn't even look at me without remembering everything I destroyed. But he felt something. Still.

And I was going to make him feel all of it until he shattered.

* * *

Another party. Another show. August had kept his distance since last night, walking a fine line between fury and restraint. I could feel it in every clipped word, every time he looked away too quickly. He was barely holding on to his control. And I wasn't about to make it easy for him.

The dress Jane brought me this time was nearly translucent, a whisper of silver silk that shimmered like starlight and sin. It clung to every curve, sleeveless and scandalously low across my chest, dipping even lower at my back. The fabric pooled at my feet in a way that made each step deliberate, regal. I never would've chosen it for myself.

But I wore it.

And I loved it.

I caught my reflection as we descended the staircase. For a moment, I didn't recognize the woman staring back. She looked like she belonged here. Not a prisoner. Not a pawn. A queen carved from defiance.

When I looked up as we walked through the great room, I saw how they watched me. Not just with wariness.

But with want.

Their eyes clung to me, sliding over bare skin like hands. Fear still lingered—good—but now there was hunger in it too. A shift. A recognition that I was not just dangerous.

I was desirable.

One vampire leaned to another and muttered something with a grin. Another tipped his glass to me, and I didn't look away. August walked beside me like a thundercloud, his silence louder than anything. The tension rolled off him in waves, and every time someone stared too long at me, I felt it spike higher.

That was the part I liked best.

We ascended to the thrones as the great room pulsed beneath us, music rising like a heartbeat. Dancers twirled, laughter cut sharp through the air.

Then Simon appeared.

He was the first of the siblings to approach us during one of these displays. He bowed low in exaggerated fashion, holding a goblet out to me. His grin was too white, too easy.

"For the queen."

I didn't move right away. My eyes slid to August.

He didn't even glance my way. Just sipped his wine and said, "He wouldn't be stupid enough to try something. Drink."

That told me everything I needed to know. He was watching, even if he wasn't looking. And he hated this. I took the goblet. It was chilled and heavy in my hand. The liquid inside caught the light like garnet—deep red wine that smelled of dark berries and spice, rich and heady.

Simon lingered, gaze flicking to August, then back to me. I took a sip. It was good.

"Would you like to dance, my queen?"

August stiffened beside me, his jaw flexing. "I don—"

"Yes, I'd love to," I said quickly, rising before he could finish.

I took Simon's hand. I would've turned him down if it weren't for August trying to answer for me. But now? Now that I knew his indifference was an act? I wanted him to watch.

We danced. And drank. Simon spun me until the room blurred, handed me drink after drink until the edges softened. I laughed once—maybe too loudly—but I didn't care. For a little while, I forgot what surrounded me. Monsters in beautiful clothes. Danger disguised as delight.

And above it all, August watched. Burning.

18

August

Fucking Simon!

I knew he loved to play his games and tonight it was how drunk he could get the queen. And she let him. I'd never seen her so carefree. Ever since we got here, she had been tense, calculating, apprehensive toward everyone. The type that would never let me near her. Just as she needed to be.

But tonight, she wasn't. She danced, her laughter spilling out. She smiled at strangers, let their hands rest too long at her waist, twirled beneath their arms like she didn't feel the weight of what this was. Drink after drink, she let herself slip further from the rigid control she always clung to. And gods, she was beautiful in it—infuriatingly beautiful. I watched her from the throne, every touch she allowed from another man stoking the slow burn of jealousy beneath my skin.

My Winnie.

But not mine.

But still mine.

And here I was carrying her back to our room. I started to run, but she screamed and said she would vomit if I went too fast. So I was fucking walking up this spiraling staircase.

She wouldn't shut up. Talking about everything—how many men she danced with, how good the wine was, how Simon told a joke that made her laugh so hard she cried. On and on, like she didn't even need me to respond. I just kept walking, tightening my hold on her with every word. Part of me wondered if that's what I sounded like when I spiraled—rambling and frantic and pretending I wasn't breaking apart.

She closed her eyes and nuzzled her nose into my chest, taking a deep breath. "Take me to bed, August."

I stilled as I stepped into our chambers.

"Excuse me?"

She glanced up at me as if I had two heads, her eyes wide. "I am tired so take me to bed."

I shook my head, trying to clear the thought of truly taking her to bed out of my mind. "No, you need a bath. I can smell those vampires all over you."

She trailed a single finger up my chest. "Are you jealous?"

I ignored her.

She let out a huff but didn't fight me as I carried her to the washroom. I helped her out of her dress—well, the thin pieces of fabric that barely covered her. These dresses tested my control every time she put one on.

Then I noticed the wooden stake strapped to her thigh. Interesting.

When I tried to help her step over the side of the tub, she snatched her hand from mine. "I am perfectly capable of getting in the bath myself."

I threw my hands up before pulling the stool up that Jane always used and sitting down. Just as she stepped into the bath—steam curling around her limbs like smoke—she slipped. She let out a sharp gasp just as I heard the scrape of flesh against metal. My body stiffened instantly. The scent hit me before I saw it.

Blood. *Her* blood.

She'd caught her hand on the jagged corner of the table. It was a small cut, but potent. My mouth tingled. Hunger flared like a match struck too close to dry paper.

"Oops," she said lightly, easing herself into the water as if nothing had happened. She lifted her hand, staring at it with theatrical curiosity before dragging two fingers through the blood. The motion was slow. Deliberate. Seductive.

She turned her head, eyes gleaming with mischief, innocence painted across her face like a dare. "Want a taste?"

Fuck me!

My throat tightened. I hesitated, wrestling against instinct, against the sharp spike of desire from the scent of her blood. My vision darkened for a beat, pupils stretching wide.

Inhale. Steady. Don't move.

And in the space of that hesitation, memories surged.

Flashes of her standing over the corpses of Legion soldiers, blood dripping from her fingertips, calm as the moon above. She'd killed them so easily—like it meant nothing. Anyone sane would have been repulsed.

But I wasn't.

Another flash—her kissing me in that alley, her lips stained with her own blood. She didn't care. She kissed me anyway.

I leaned forward before I could stop myself.

She smiled as she slipped her fingers into her mouth. Her eyes never left mine as she sucked them clean. A soft, satisfied giggle escaped her lips.

"See?" she whispered. "I knew you still wanted me."

She thought she could control this. Control *me.*

But she didn't know how dangerous this game was.

I couldn't handle this. I had to show her that I was the one in control. Not her. I rose slowly, unbuttoning my shirt. Her bravado faltered—her arms came up, covering herself like I hadn't already memorized every inch of her.

Then my pants hit the floor with a soft thud. Her gaze dropped instinctively. She hadn't meant to look, but she did—and when her eyes found my hard-exposed length, they widened. A pink flush crept up her neck. I couldn't help the slow, wicked smile that pulled at my lips. She quickly looked away, but it was too late. I saw it. She still wanted me. And gods, I wanted her to know it.

I stepped into the bath without a word. She tensed, shifting backward until her spine pressed against the porcelain wall, trying to retreat. But there was nowhere to go. Her pulse thundered in my ears. The scent of her—arousal, defiance, the coppery trace of blood—wrapped around me like a noose.

I leaned back, water lapping up my chest, and draped my arms along the rim of the tub behind her.

Close. Caged.

I tilted my head and let my eyes drag slowly over her face. "Don't think you can win this, Winnie."

I forced my gaze to stay on her face. Her skin glistened, water catching the flicker of candlelight. My voice was low, controlled—but beneath it, the hunger stirred. Not just for her blood. But for her.

She narrowed her eyes, but didn't move. "Then what are we doing here?"

I leaned in, just enough for her to feel the brush of my breath. "You tell me. You drew the blood. You issued the invitation."

"I thought you were trying to stay away from me," she whispered.

"I was." I glanced down at the rippling water between us. "And yet here we are."

She reached out, fingertips brushing my chest. It wasn't gentle. It was a test—measuring just how far I'd let her go.

"Do you feel nothing for me?" she asked.

I closed my eyes, jaw flexing. "Yes."

"Liar."

My eyes snapped open. She was closer now. The distance between us reduced to nothing. I could hear her blood pulsing, feel the heat of her body through the water.

"Actually I do feel something," I said, jaw clenched. "The need to drain you of every drop of blood."

She leaned in until our lips almost touched. "Then do it."

I was a breath away from disaster. "You keep pushing me. You want to see what happens when I stop holding back?"

She tilted her head slowly to the side, exposing the delicate column of her throat. Her black waves spilled off her shoulder, revealing bare, flushed skin. The pulse in her neck fluttered visibly. "Yes."

My restraint shattered.

With a sharp inhale, I grabbed her by the waist and pulled her into my lap. She gasped—whether from surprise or anticipation, I couldn't tell. Her thighs pressed to either side of mine, her hands braced against my chest. I didn't give her time to think. My lips found her throat, brushing the skin where her pulse throbbed like a drum. She arched into me as I sank my fangs in.

It wasn't rough. It wasn't violent. It was *intimate*. Deep and slow. Her fingers dug into my shoulders, not to push me away but to pull me closer. I drank just enough to taste her. To feel her.

When I finally pulled back, her chest was heaving. Her lips parted. Her eyes glazed. She was still in my lap, still holding onto me like she didn't want to let go.

Too far. This was going too far.

My hands lingered on her waist a moment longer than they should have. Her breath ghosted against my cheek, shallow and warm, her pulse still racing from the bite. It would be so easy to stay there. To let her pull me under again.

But I couldn't.

With a sharp breath, I pushed her off me—not harshly, but firm enough to make her stumble slightly in the water. Her eyes widened, shocked, maybe even hurt.

I stood, the bathwater rushing off me in waves that slapped against the porcelain and spilled onto the marble floor.

"We can't." My reply was a choked off whisper.

She didn't respond, just watched me with parted lips and a storm of emotion in her eyes. Lust, confusion, and something close to fury.

I didn't look back again. I reached for a towel and stepped out of the room, leaving behind the ache of her body, the scent of her blood, and the weight of a line I'd already crossed too many times.

But it wasn't enough.

The moment the door shut behind me, I slammed my fist against the stone wall. Pain exploded through my knuckles. I welcomed it. With a guttural sound I couldn't suppress, I seized the edge of the dressing table and cracked it in half. Wood splintered under my grip, fragments flying. Playing with fire always had a price.

And tonight, it almost cost me everything.

19

Bronwen

My head throbbed. I sat on the bed and plucked another grape from the platter Jane had brought me this morning. The only bit of peace I felt was that I didn't have a nightmare last night. I guessed drinking so much that you remembered nothing helped. August sat at the desk, flipping through another tome Benedict found.

"This one is useless," he mumbled. He stood and walked over to me, but would barely look at me. "Get up. We're spending as much time as we can in the archives today."

"No," I lay back on the bed and pulled the blanket over my head. "Let me rest a little longer."

The covers disappeared. "Get ready."

He stepped out and sent word for Jane before he began shoving all of his scratch paper in a drawer in the desk. I rolled my neck, feeling a little sore. I must have slept on it wrong.

"Good morning, Jane."

She just smiled at me, glancing back at August as she stepped to me with a dress draped across her arms. Her pale hair was pinned neatly on the top of her head. She seemed so wary around August that I didn't think she was one of the ones here for the promise of vampirism.

As she helped me into the simple, gray dress, her eyes never left August as he walked to the window and flung the drapes back. I sat at the dressing table as she began to brush my hair. I ran my hands along the smooth stone top. I vaguely remembered it being a dark wood.

"Is this new?" I asked as I glanced at Jane through the mirror.

She only nodded as she pulled my hair back to begin braiding and that was when I noticed it. A fresh bite mark on my neck.

I jumped out of the chair nearly knocking Jane over in the process. "What the fuck did you do?"

August turned from the window, that infuriating smirk on his face. "Jane, leave us."

Jane almost ran out the door.

August came to me, slow, deliberate with his steps as if he knew the longer he took the madder I'd get. "You mean during our bath last night, Winnie?" He tilted his head to the side. "When you practically *begged* me to bite you?"

It all came flooding back. Dancing like a fool with Simon. August carrying me. Me teasing him. And me in his lap just hoping it would go further.

"How did you sleep last night? Because I slept marvelously."

I reared back and punched him. He could've stopped me. He was faster than me. But he didn't. And he still smiled.

"Finish preparing yourself. We have things to do."

* * *

"What is this?" I pointed at a drawing in the tome I had been looking through for an hour. It was dark with only blacks and grays creating the sketch. Tall slender trees lined the page and they looked as if they were leaning in to grab you. Strange beasts peered around some of the trees that looked like they came straight from a nightmare.

Benedict leaned over my shoulder. "Part of Alentara. It's one of the more dangerous areas, but a place where a lot of the artifacts Carrow collected seemed to originate from. The magic there is strong, but the area's overrun with creatures that make vampires look like angels. They call it the Night Realm because it is complete darkness at all times."

"I get why Carrow came here. That is terrifying."

August leaned over too, glancing at the image. He shrugged. "I think he was running from something."

I spun the gold ring on my finger. Since the moment we stepped into the archives, the tension had been unbearable. Neither of us had spoken more than necessary. The events of the night before refused to stay buried, looping through my mind while I tried to focus on the texts. The bite, the bath, the smirk on his face—I couldn't shake any of it. So I had done the only thing I could: I avoided him. I spent the day talking to Benedict instead, keeping a polite smile on my face as I asked him about the tomes, the artifacts, anything to avoid August's gaze.

But that didn't make it any easier. My thoughts were still a tangled mess, and staring through ancient drawings while pretending my insides weren't twisted into knots made my headache worse by the hour. August still leaned over my shoulder looking at the tome, but I knew he was more interested in bothering me than the drawing he was staring at.

I slammed it shut, the sound echoing louder than I meant it to. My hands trembled as I stood. Being this close to him—feeling his body brush against mine when he leaned over my shoulder, the way his scent curled around me and sank its claws into my chest—was too much. I could still feel the phantom pressure of his hands on my waist, the heat of his breath at my ear. It was suffocating.

I stepped over to the shelves and ran my hand across a few of the artifacts in my line of sight. I could feel the magic pulsing inside each of the objects, like a quiet heartbeat.

Benedict straightened behind me, his gaze lingering a beat too long. He gave me a curious look. Like he was trying to solve a puzzle: why his brother, the king, had tied himself to a witch who set vampires on fire without blinking. "They'll never stop talking about you downstairs, you know," he said. "Not every day a pretty witch sets the great room ablaze. And then days later dances as if none of it ever happened."

I stiffened. Out of the corner of my eye, I saw August's fingers flex against the table—a warning without words.

"They'll talk themselves to death," I said coolly, turning back around.

You keep pushing me. You want to see what happens when I stop holding back?

Our conversation echoed in my mind, and I hadn't realized until today just how bad the need for him was. A part of me had never stopped wanting him. I was angry—for the secrets, the marriage, the ruin he'd brought into my life—but that didn't change how badly I still wanted him. Craved him.

We could do things. It could mean nothing. Stopping Carrow and sex. I wondered if that too much to ask.

But I couldn't believe how easy it was for me to push him to the edge. I wanted more. I *needed* more.

I glanced back at August and watched him flip through another tome. He sat with his legs spread, fingers curled around the leather binding. And all I could think of was how those same fingers had felt inside me when he first touched me like that. The look in his eyes when he watched me fall apart.

I looked up. He was already watching me. I spun back around too quickly, catching my arm on a metal statue. Pain flared, and I hissed as I clutched the sore spot.

Before I could move again, August was in front of me, his body pressing mine against the wall. A wall I hadn't even been near.

Benedict was watching us, his eyes now glowing red.

"If you'll excuse me," he mumbled, shifting awkwardly from one foot to the other.

"Go," August said, his voice low and lethal.

Benedict vanished.

And August turned to me, and his eyes dropped to my arm. The fabric of my sleeve had torn slightly, exposing the angry red mark blooming across my skin. Gently—so gently it startled me—he reached for it. His fingers brushed the edge of the mark, but didn't touch it directly, like he didn't trust himself to.

His jaw clenched.

I felt the weight of his restraint. It was in the way his hands hovered, shaking ever so slightly, in the way his pupils dilated as he stared at the spot of blood just beginning to surface. Like he was fighting the worst part of himself.

He swallowed hard.

"It's nothing," I said, but my voice came out softer than I meant it to.

He looked up, and our eyes met. And for a second, I swore he looked terrified of himself. Of what he might do if he didn't walk away.

But he didn't walk away.

He reached out. "You can't walk around here with an open wound."

I almost took his hand—just to feel him again—but I remembered the way he looked so hurt before. The way I hurt him. So instead, I wrapped my fingers around the gash and pulled from the tiny well of stolen magic inside me. It buzzed against my palm as the wound knit together.

August watched it happen, his jaw ticking. "Why do you have magic?"

"I have been taking it from the others. Just a little with each touch. Not enough to notice, but enough to add up. I told you I wouldn't be defenseless again."

I'd purged Lavina's power the moment it became too much—her magic felt like it was unraveling my mind—but I'd figured out how to take without being noticed. Just a sliver here, a flicker there. It wasn't enough to feel the rush I used to get from truly pulling, but it was enough to protect myself.

Enough to avoid needing him.

"Is that why you had a stake strapped to your thigh last night?" His voice was low. "A contingency plan?"

Flashes of him standing above me naked raced through my mind. "August."

He smiled as he looked down at me. He wasn't getting the upper hand. I had to break him.

"Why do I have to be here every day with you? I could find

plenty of other things to keep me busy. This castle needs to come to this century. I could visit Adar." I smiled as his brow furrowed. "Or I could find that vampire that keeps making eyes at me every night. Not eyes like he wants to drain me but eyes like he wants to fu—"

"Because you have to help find a way to stop—"

I cut him off with a wave of my hand. "Stop Carrow. I know. That's what you keep saying. But how? I can't read the language, I don't understand half of the things you and Benedict mutter under your breath. And don't insult me by saying it's for my protection. I'm not helpless anymore. So what's the real reason?"

"Dagger to throat, kiss to the crown, a witch in the palace will burn it all down."

I blinked. "What did you just say?"

He didn't answer. Didn't even seem to realize he'd spoken. His eyes were somewhere far away—distant and haunted—and then, just like that, he was back.

"You're pretty to look at," he said, clearer this time, as if nothing strange had happened at all.

I narrowed my eyes. "So I'm being punished. Spending the rest of my life married to you, always stuck at your side, because I'm pretty?" I sighed. "I knew my looks would ruin me one day."

He laughed. Not cruelly. Not mockingly. Just genuinely laughed—and somehow, that was worse. But he caught it and stepped back, the mask he wore now sliding back over his face.

"Last night didn't mean anything. It was nothing but the mark pulling us together."

Liar.

Still, I smiled.

"I know," I said, stepping forward until my chest brushed him. "It meant nothing. Just instinct. *Hunger*."

A small piece of lint clung to the fabric of his sleeve, and I plucked it off, flicking it away with more satisfaction than the gesture warranted. I didn't look at him. I didn't have to. I could feel him watching me, every muscle wound tight, like a predator unsure whether to pounce or flee.

"Doesn't mean it wasn't good," I added, barely above a whisper.

That got him. I glanced up just in time to see it—the flicker in his eyes, the way his jaw clenched, the breath he had to force through his nose.

He wasn't prepared for me to throw his own indifference back in his face. And it thrilled me. Let him stew in it. Let him remember every second as vividly as I did.

I turned and walked away before he could gather a response. My heart was pounding, my skin flushed with heat, but I didn't let him see that.

20

Bronwen

I didn't sleep that night. I stared at the ceiling, replaying every word, every touch, every lie. He wanted me to believe it meant nothing. That it was the mark. But I knew better.

And if he thought he could push me away and hide on his throne like a coward, he had another thing coming.

Something shifted within him when he fed on me. I saw it— a crack in the wall he kept so carefully constructed—before he shoved it down, buried it like it meant nothing. But it wasn't nothing. Not to me.

It had been days now. Days of near-silence unless we were buried in texts or hunting answers. Days of his eyes skimming past mine like he couldn't bear to look too long. The space between us stretched wider by the hour, each inch lost like a pulled thread unraveling something I wasn't ready to let go of.

I flipped through another tome from the endless stack on the table in the archives, usually only stopping when I found a drawing with a sword, but this tome seemed to be a log of different creatures. One had long tendrils and rows of teeth.

Another looked like a giant cat with wings. I turned to the next page and brushed my fingers over the face staring back at me. She looked human. More beautiful than most. Almost perfect. But she had pointed ears.

"What is this?"

Benedict came to me. "That is a fae. The human-like faeries in Alentara."

I nodded. "That's what Carrow was."

August leaned over the table, brows furrowed as his fist slammed on the table. "I can't just keep digging through things and hope something will lead me in the right direction. Not now that time is limited."

This is your fault, Winnie. That's what he wanted to say.

A long pause passed between the two of them, heavy and uncertain.

Then Benedict said, "There's someone who might know more. One of the old ones. He was locked away in the dungeons decades ago after he went feral. No one sees him. No one speaks to him. But I am certain he was there during the last ritual. He was close to Carrow."

August stiffened. "You're talking about Varric."

The name alone made the room colder.

Benedict nodded once. "He's not entirely sane, but sometimes he speaks in riddles that match pieces of the old texts. It's possible he knows something about the blade."

I looked between them. "Then why hasn't anyone gone to him before?"

"Because he attacks anything that breathes," August answered. "And he speaks madness. And if Carrow had gotten word that I was trying to stop him when he was here, he would've locked me up too."

I bristled at the thought of a feral vampire, but we were out of leads. And madness was better than silence. As we made our way back up through the winding halls, we stayed silent, careful not to alert anyone. But just as we reached the landing that opened up to the main floor of the castle, a figure stepped into view.

Lavina.

She stood at the base of the staircase, her posture tight and uncertain, as if she'd been waiting for us—or perhaps trying to gather the nerve to walk the other direction. We hadn't exchanged a word since the night I almost killed her.

My body tensed instinctively, bracing in case she lunged or tried something. I didn't trust her. Not after everything.

August slowed beside me, his body stiffening like a shield raised out of instinct. He'd never shown her kindness. Not once. From the moment I'd arrived, his disdain for her had been unmistakable—cutting words, cold glances, a constant reminder that she held no favor with him. He didn't like any of his siblings. He tolerated Benedict more than the rest, maybe, but with Lavina, the hostility was unmistakable. It made me wonder why.

Lavina's eyes flicked between August and me, then shot to Benedict as he came into view behind us. Her lips curled with something between amusement and suspicion. "Now, what are the three of you doing together?"

August stepped closer to her, a smile tugging at his mouth as he gave a low chuckle. "Go find something to eat. You're looking a little... *gray.*"

She stiffened, and I couldn't help but smile at the reminder of how she looked days ago.

"Oh, did I strike a nerve?" he mused, flashing her a grin

before glancing sideways at Benedict.

Lavina huffed and turned away, and August watched her retreat with a pleased expression, scanning the corridor once more. Seeming satisfied that we were alone, he let out a low chuckle, but it faded quickly. His smile fell, replaced by something far more grim.

"Let's go," he said, gesturing toward the winding staircase that led below the castle.

The dungeon air was thick and wet, clinging to my skin like rot. The torchlight flickered against stone walls, casting long shadows that danced as we moved deeper. We stopped outside a heavy iron door. The guard posted there looked relieved to have company.

"He hasn't spoken in weeks," he warned.

August stepped forward. "He will now."

The door groaned open, revealing a crumbling cell, and something stirred within the dark. Varric was crouched in the far corner, long limbs curled in on themselves like a corpse half-forgotten. The way he moved—sluggish yet predatory— made the hair rise on the back of my neck. His eyes, milky and unfocused, snapped toward us. His mouth moved first, lips twitching like they were forming words his throat hadn't caught up with.

"Carrow?" Varric said, voice low.

August stood slightly in front of me, like he was trying to protect me. "No. He hasn't gotten to me yet."

Varric grinned. It was all gums and rot. Then he looked at me, his pale eyes seeming to search for something beneath my skin. "I remember you."

I hesitated. "You do?"

"Who could forget those emerald eyes?" he rasped, leaning

forward as if trying to peer deeper into me. His expression twisted, almost lucid for a heartbeat. Then his tone darkened, teeth bared in a grimace. "Those poisoned, *evil* spheres in your head."

I squinted at Varric, trying to place what it was that unsettled me so deeply about him—beyond the rot and the madness. Had he come across me on one of my hunts?

My stomach twisted as I turned to Benedict, who stood behind us. "Why hasn't anyone killed him? Taken him out of this misery?"

"Everyone is afraid to get too close to him," Benedict said. "Afraid they'll catch whatever madness is in him."

I folded my arms. "I could always set the room on fire."

August turned sharply, eyes wide. "Yes, Winnie. Let's burn a room in a castle full of vampires and hope no one else goes up in flames."

I shrugged. "It wouldn't be the worst thing to happen."

Benedict gave a quiet chuckle but stayed where he was, hovering a safe distance back.

"Varric," he said clearly, drawing the vampire's attention. "We've come to ask about the Blood Moon."

Varric twitched, glancing around the room like a bird spooked from its nest.

"Do you know the spell that is used to bring Carrow back?"

He shook his head violently, and for a second I thought he might lunge at us.

Then, with a guttural rasp, he said, "The blade wields the soul. For one to leave, you must sacrifice another."

August sucked in a sharp breath beside me.

"What did you say?" I asked, barely above a whisper.

Varric didn't respond. He just began rocking, clawed fingers scratching rhythmic nonsense into the stone floor.

But August was already turning to me, his expression stricken.

"At the dying of the blood, he will rise not by voice, but by hand. The blade calls him home," he repeated, his voice barely audible.

The words dropped into the space between us, heavy as an iron weight.

"The blade wields the soul. The blade is used as a..." I waved around the room. "A holding cell for him until it is time to take over a body."

He looked at me, something grim flickering behind his eyes.

I dragged in a breath, the dungeon suddenly colder than before. "We need to narrow it down to the blades that can... hold things within it."

Benedict glanced at August, and something unspoken passed between them.

"You might be right," he said quietly.

August said nothing, but his clenched jaw was answer enough.

We were running out of time. But maybe—just maybe—we finally had a chance.

Before either of us could speak, Varric's body tensed like a wire pulled taut. His eyes locked on me again, but this time they burned with hatred.

"It's you! It's all your fault!" he screamed, lunging forward.

August moved faster than I could process. In one blur of motion, he shoved me behind him and slammed Varric back. The feral vampire flew across the cell, crashing against the far wall with a sickening crack.

August didn't even wait for him to rise. He grabbed my arm,

yanked the door open, and we were gone—vanishing from the cell in a gust of cold wind and frayed nerves.

* * *

The music throbbed through the great hall, low and haunting, like it had been conjured from the bones of the castle itself. Crimson and gold light spilled from the chandeliers, dancing off the high vaulted ceilings and across the sea of guests that filled the room. Vampires, draped in silk and shadows, spun their partners with inhuman grace. Laughter echoed through the air—too sharp, too hollow.

I let myself be pulled into another waltz, my gown sweeping across the marble floor like mist. The vampire leading me had sharp features and a pleasant enough smile, but his eyes were always calculating. All of them were. They never truly looked at me—not like I mattered, not like I was more than a game they couldn't quite win.

Except for him.

High above us, August sat draped across his throne like a fallen god. One leg slung over the armrest, a goblet of blood cradled in his hand. His face was carved in stone, unreadable.

But his eyes never left me.

Always watching. But never touching. Never showing me anything.

And I was tired of it.

Tired of the coldness. Tired of the silence. Tired of being on display while the man who once burned for me now acted like I was nothing more than a crown he was forced to wear.

The vampire twirled me again, his hand warm and steady at my back. His grip lingered, fingers brushing just a little too possessively against the fabric of my dress.

"You must be very delicious to have the king so smitten with you," he murmured near my ear, his breath sickly sweet.

I tensed at his words. Smitten wasn't the word I'd use. Obsessed, maybe. Possessive. But love? Affection? Not lately. Not anymore.

Still, his words gave me an idea.

I needed to see something other than joy in my destruction. It seemed like I was always doing exactly what he wanted me to do. He hated this place. These vampires. Of course he didn't care if I killed them. He didn't care at all. I was doing him a favor.

I glanced at August again. He hadn't moved. He just sipped his blood and stared at me from that throne like he was waiting. Testing. Daring me.

That was going to stop. His pouting, his anger, his—his bastardness—was going to stop. It was just a show. It had to be.

I met his gaze, head tilted just slightly in defiance. I promised him his own hell. I was going to give it to him. We had both done things to each other. It had always been this way. But now the clock was ticking.

"I don't know." I turned back to the vampire, my voice lilting as I brushed a lock of hair behind my ear. "Why don't you have a taste for yourself?"

He blinked, surprised. "I don't think the king likes to share."

"I am your queen," I said, letting the authority slip into my tone. "And I am telling you to do it."

I tilted my chin, exposing the delicate line of my throat,

letting my hair fall back. The pulse beneath my skin fluttered like a dare.

His pupils dilated, the veins beneath his eyes blooming with hunger as he hesitated. His lips parted, breath shallow. He leaned closer, slowly, like a man hypnotized.

Then his mouth hovered just above my skin. His breath brushed against my neck. Just as his lips grazed me—

A blur. A crack.

I was no longer in his arms. A gust of wind whipped around me, and in the space between two heartbeats, August was there.

His hand was around the vampire's throat, squeezing tight. With a single, fluid motion, he lifted him from the ground like he weighed nothing and slammed him into the marble floor. The stones shattered. The ground cracked. Shards of marble flew into the air as the impact echoed through the hall like a thunderclap. A table nearby toppled, goblets of blood shattering across the floor in a wash of red.

The music stopped mid-note.

The crowd gasped as one.

August didn't say a word. His face was still—dangerously calm. But his eyes, those eyes, were burning. A feral, possessive fury blazed behind them, locked on me like I was the only thing keeping him tethered to sanity.

And finally, finally, I knew I had his attention.

21

August

What the fuck was she thinking?

I took her out of the great room, ordering everyone to stay where they were. I could kill her. I could kill everyone in that room. That fucking idiot who thought he could touch *my* Winnie?

He'd better fucking run before I get back in there. But then I noticed it. The flush still blooming across her cheeks. The way her chest heaved, shallow breaths slipping through parted lips. How she couldn't stop herself from smiling. She was radiant in that chaos, in the aftermath. And I had done exactly what she wanted me to do.

Which only pissed me off more.

I took a step toward her, fists clenched, and she matched it—like she was daring me to keep coming. Like she wanted to see how far I'd go.

I slammed her against the wall but held the back of her head so my hand took most of the impact, the sound echoing down the corridor. "What are you doing?"

She smiled, damn near glowing in the dim light, and ducked

under my arm to ascend the stairs. Impossible, defiant, *beautiful* woman.

I was in front of her again, my hand wrapping around her throat before I even knew I'd moved. Her skin burned beneath my fingers.

"I thought you said you felt nothing," she whispered.

My hand flexed.

"But it sure looks like you hate me right now. Maybe a little jealous, even."

That smile again. That beautiful, infuriating smile that I wanted to kiss and erase in the same breath.

"What are you trying to do?"

She looked up at me, innocence painted across her face. "What was it you said? Take everything you hate and make it yours."

"Winnie," I warned. I told her we couldn't be together. I thought she understood.

"Well, I'm already yours, remember?"

Her hands trailed down my chest, nails scratching lightly over the fabric, until they reached the waistband of my pants. My whole body responded—tight, aching, furious with want.

No. You don't want this.

"Hurt me. Break me. Show me just how much you hate me."

I pulled her lips to mine, hard, savage. She whimpered into my mouth, and I slammed her against the wall again, needing to hear it again.

"We can't," I whispered against her lips, even as my hands dug into her waist like she was the only real thing I'd ever touched.

She looked up at me with those damn eyes—emerald and endless and shining with the storm we both refused to outrun.

"*Ruin me*, August."

I wanted her to hate me. Hate me to the point that if it came down to it, she would burn this castle down and me along with it if it meant she would be safe. And I thought, even though she wanted me, she did hate me. Just enough.

But then I remembered—

We thrived off hating each other.

There was madness in her eyes. The same kind I saw every time I looked in the mirror. Reckless. Wild. Beautiful in its ruin. She didn't want to be saved—she wanted to burn alongside me.

And maybe, just maybe, I adored her for that.

She was just as twisted. Just as cursed. And she wore it like a crown.

And gods, I needed her.

I kissed her again—wild and desperate—like every moment without her had been oxygen-starved, and I was finally breathing. My hands slid up her sides, fingers skimming the curve of her waist, the line of her ribs, until they tangled in her hair. She moaned into my mouth, her body melting against mine as her hands tugged at my shirt, fumbling with buttons, trying to tear me open.

We didn't move. We couldn't. Not when every part of us screamed for more. Her leg hitched up over my hip, dress bunched around her thighs, and I ground against her. I wanted to devour her. Right there on the stairs. Let everyone hear who she belonged to.

She slid her fingers beneath the hem of my shirt and dragged it up over my skin. My name left her lips in a broken breath, and I swallowed it with another kiss, deeper this time, rougher.

Footsteps.

Shit.

Voices—closer now. A pair of guards, maybe, or servants. I didn't care. I wanted to rip their throats out.

"I told them not to leave," I growled against her skin.

She blinked up at me, dazed and breathless. Beautiful.

Mine.

I didn't wait. I swept her into my arms and carried her through the corridor, past paintings and candles and whatever poor soul happened to catch a glimpse. Let them see. Let them whisper.

She was mine tonight.

Even if it killed me.

I didn't bother setting her down gently. The second the door to our chambers slammed behind us, I had her pinned to it, lips back on hers, our bodies already lost to the fire.

Her fingers clawed at my shirt again, this time more desperate, more demanding, until I tore it off over my head. She made a sound—a low, breathless gasp that only spurred me further. My hands yanked at the back of her dress, finding the fastenings and ripping them apart with a growl. The fabric slipped from her shoulders, revealing inch after inch of flawless skin I'd dreamed about every night.

She didn't shy away. She pushed into me, dragging her nails down my chest as the dress pooled at her feet. Gods, she was beautiful. Untouchable. And yet completely mine.

I kissed down her neck, across her collarbone, my fangs scraping lightly against her skin, and I felt her shiver. My name left her lips again like a plea, and it almost undid me.

I needed to go slow. I needed to have some control.

But I didn't.

She made me lose it. Always had.

I lifted her, and her legs wrapped around me instinctively. Our mouths never broke. My mind was screaming restraint, but my body didn't listen. Every part of me burned for her. Every inch wanted to claim.

"Tell me to stop," I whispered against her lips.

She didn't.

Her fingers slid into my hair, tugging, guiding, her breath warm against my cheek. "Don't hold back this time."

I hated how good she looked asking for it. Hair wild, pupils blown wide, body arching toward me like she knew I was going to lose.

That was all it took.

I stepped toward the bed, but then I hesitated—just long enough to glance at the desk.

Don't hold back.

She wanted it all. She wanted to make me angry so I would give her everything I had tried so hard to stop myself from doing.

So I changed course.

With one arm still wrapped around her, I swept the books, inkpots, and parchment off the heavy desk in a single violent motion, sending them crashing to the floor. Her eyes widened, but not in fear—in anticipation. She loved this. The frenzy. The rawness.

I laid her across the desk like something sacred and sinful all at once.

Her hair spilled over the wood like black ink, her back arching as my hands trailed up her thighs. I kissed my way down her neck, across her collarbone, down to the swell of her breasts. Her fingers gripped the edge of the desk, knuckles white, legs trembling around me as I worshiped every inch.

She moaned—soft at first, then louder, more urgent—and it took every ounce of willpower I had not to lose myself completely. I wanted to take her hard, fast, right there. But gods help me, I needed to feel all of it. To make her feel all of it.

Her hands found my hair again, tugging me closer. I kissed lower, slower, her breath shuddering every time my mouth touched her skin. Her thighs tightened around me as I pressed a hand flat to her stomach, holding her steady.

I was shaking. With need. With hunger.

And with something deeper. Something that clawed its way up my throat and lodged there like a vow.

I dropped to my knees before her, hands gripping her thighs, parting them slowly as I looked up at her—watching the realization dawn in her eyes. She gasped, fingers slipping from my hair to cover her mouth.

Good. I wanted to surprise her. To worship her. To ruin her completely.

I lowered my head between her legs and kissed the inside of her thigh—once, twice—until she was trembling above me. Her body jerked when I finally tasted her, soft and wet and fucking perfect. Her hand flew back to my head, clutching tight, her breath coming in sharp little gasps as my tongue moved with practiced cruelty.

She was already falling apart.

And gods, I loved that I could do this to her. That no one else would ever know this part of her. *Only* me.

She moaned my name—high, broken—and I gripped her hips harder, dragging her closer, burying myself in her until there was nothing but the sound of her falling to pieces on my tongue.

When she came, it was violent. Her legs locked around me, her body arched so high I thought she'd break in half. And I kept going. Just a little longer. Just enough to feel her sob out and try to shove me away, her hands weak and shaking.

I stood then, lips wet, heart thundering, and met her eyes.

"I'm not finished," I said.

And I wasn't.

Not even close.

She was still gasping when I brought my fingers to her entrance, slipping one in slow, curling until she moaned again. Her body clenched, still sensitive, still riding the edge I'd left her on. I added another, thrusting gently at first, then harder.

"You want it all, Winnie?" I murmured, voice dark with promise.

"Yes," she whimpered, her hips rolling against my hand.

I bent over and kissed her stomach as my fingers slowed. "Yes, *August*. Say my name. Say it like I'm the only thing you want."

She bit her lip as she looked down at me, her eyes gleaming with unfiltered need. "You're all I want, August," she whispered as her body trembled with desire.

I let my teeth scrape against her stomach as I dragged them up to her breasts, nipping at the soft swell until she arched into me. The tip of my cock nudged at her entrance, slick and ready, but I held back—barely—as I took in her scent. There was no going back after this. Every instinct screamed at me to pull away, to rebuild the crumbling barriers I'd tried so hard to keep between us.

But I gave in.

I bit her, hard, just above her left breast. The moment her

blood hit my tongue, it was like being struck by lightning—sweet, intoxicating, laced with something only she possessed. My mind blurred, my body caved to instinct as I plunged into her, driven by a need so deep it bordered on madness. The taste of her flooded me, shattering whatever restraint I had left.

She cried out, nails raking down my back, and I gripped her breast with one hand while the other slammed the desk against the wall. The rhythm came fast, rough, relentless. I couldn't stop. Didn't want to.

The desk groaned under us, the thick wood bending with every punishing thrust. I hit it harder, again and again, until it began to splinter, the legs quivering beneath our weight. One final slam and the wood begged to break away, a sharp crack echoing through the room as the surface finally gave out beneath her.

But I caught her. My arm locked around her waist, lifting her as if I'd never broken stride. Still buried inside her. Still moving. I carried her to the bed without pausing. My mouth was on her breast, licking the drops of blood that ran before we landed, and I thrust into her deeper, harder, desperate to have all of her. Each thrust was more punishing than the last, but she didn't break. She met me—stroke for stroke, moan for moan—like she was made for this. *For me.*

Her fingers clawed down my back again, harder this time, and I hissed through my teeth as I felt the sharp sting of her nails breaking skin. The pain only anchored me deeper in the madness, made me feel more alive in her grasp.

"Again," she whispered. "Bite me again."

Gods, she didn't know what she was asking. Or maybe she did.

Her neck was bared, her head thrown back against the pillows. I could see the rapid flutter of her pulse. I hovered above it, panting, lips parted—torn between worship and hunger.

"I can't," I growled. My body trembled. "If I do, I'll take too much."

"Do it," she whispered. "I trust you."

Those three words nearly undid me. She was mine. Trusting me. Offering herself up like a prayer I didn't deserve.

I leaned down and sank my fangs into the curve where her neck met her shoulder. The moment her blood hit my tongue again, it was like I was no longer in control of my body. A low growl escaped my throat as heat surged through every inch of me, drowning thought and reason in one violent flood. I felt the edge of my sanity fray, instincts roaring louder than logic, and I gripped her harder.

My hips slammed into hers. The bedframe cracked.

She gasped, a strangled moan breaking from her throat as I drank, as I fucked her, as I came apart inside her. I pulled back before the line blurred too far, dragging my tongue over the bite and kissing the spot like it was sacred. She was trembling beneath me, breathless and wild and perfect.

"I shouldn't have done that," I whispered against her skin, forehead pressed to her neck.

She laughed, shaky and wrecked. "Then why do I want you to do it again?"

I stared down at her, chest still heaving, sweat cooling on my skin.

Because she was just as mad as I was.

* * *

A low golden light poured through the curtains.

She was warm beside me, tangled up in the sheets, in me. Her leg slung across my hip, her hand pressed flat against my chest like she was trying to anchor herself. Or maybe me.

I stared at her. At the soft line of her jaw, the way her lashes fanned across flushed cheeks, the faint bruise from where I'd gripped her too hard still blooming just above her hip.

Last night. *Gods*, last night.

It hadn't just been sex. Not for me. I could still feel the echo of it—her body around mine, the way she'd said my name, the way I'd finally stopped fighting and let myself have her again. I told myself it was to protect her. That keeping my distance was noble. But it wasn't. It was cowardice.

Because I loved her.

And I was terrified.

She shifted beside me, her brow tightening faintly before her eyes opened. I opened my mouth, but she pressed a finger to my lips before I could speak.

"I know what this was," she said barely above a whisper. "And I know what this is going to be."

I blinked, frozen.

"Just sex," she said, pulling the sheet tighter around her.

Something inside me cracked. Loud and jagged. She wasn't looking at me. Her voice was too even. Too practiced. And before I could speak—before I could tell her she was wrong— my cowardice returned.

"Right," I said. I forced my voice to stay steady. "Just sex."

Her shoulders relaxed, but not in relief.

And I knew then I'd let her believe it.

Because if I told her the truth now, if I admitted that I would rip the world apart to keep her, I didn't know if either of us could survive what came next.

She stood, but I caught her wrist. She turned to me and looked at me with her brows scrunched.

"On your knees, Winnie."

22

Adar

"I'm going to have to get Jonah out here to trade spots with me if you keep coming at me this hard," Darrin said, breathless, sweat running down his temple as he parried my strike.

I stared at the aging man before me, and I couldn't help but wish it was Papa sparring with me instead. Darrin and Jonah had always been more like uncles than simply Papa's friends. Jonah, the worrier, and Darrin, the steady voice of reason, had been constants in my life. And their presence now gave me comfort as I tried to carry the weight of leading the coven. But no matter how grateful I was for them, nothing filled the hole left by Papa.

I shook off the thought before he could take advantage of my distraction and best me.

"If you'd just admit to me that you're old and tired, I might back off," I taunted, circling him.

He smiled. "Never."

He lunged, and I stepped aside just in time, letting his momentum carry him forward before I swung my sword up, catching his blade with a sharp clang. The steel rang out through the clearing, echoing in the still morning air. We moved fast—boots crunching against the softening earth, blades flashing in and out of sunlight that streamed between the branches overhead.

Darrin was better than most gave him credit for. Strong. Precise. But he favored his left side today, and I used it. I twisted, ducked, then came up hard with a swing meant to disarm. He caught it, barely, grunting as our swords locked. We stood close, the tension between us humming through the vibrating metal.

"Trying to make me retire early?" he grunted.

"Trying to see if you've still got it."

With a sharp shove, he broke the bind and swept a kick toward my legs. I jumped back, regaining footing just in time to meet his next swing. We clashed again, sparks flying as the blades kissed.

This wasn't just training. It was therapy. It was survival.

And I needed to stay sharp. Because I had a feeling peace wouldn't last forever.

We both lowered our blades, chest heaving. I wiped sweat from my brow and leaned against a tree, the bark cool against my spine.

My days now were spent traveling across Joveryn to let the coven members know of their newfound freedom. It had been nearly over a month since the decree was made, but there were still parts of the kingdom that hadn't gotten word. If this had happened any other time of the year, the word would have traveled almost instantly, but instead it had to happen in the middle of winter when most of the coven—especially the ones that lived north of town—spent the next couple of months in their homes and only traveled when necessary.

Some days I visited entire villages where witches had never set foot outside their homes for fear of being hunted. I sat with mothers and grandmothers who wept and looked at me like I had brought them the sun.

Others were more hesitant. Some demanded proof. Some watched me warily, years of caution etched into every glance. And I gave them the truth. The pain and the sacrifice. My parents' deaths and the fire Bronwen lit to break the chains holding us all.

"Your parents' sacrifice will not go unnoticed. We will honor them with our commitment to you," they all said, something along those lines after they wept, cheered, hugged me like I had a magical sign floating above me, asking to be embraced.

Their sacrifice.

Their *lives*.

Bronwen's sacrifice.

Bronwen's *freedom*.

Everything I loved had been taken from me, but I couldn't let the weight of it all drown me. I had to bury it deep, hide my emotions, and be the strong leader I was raised to be. But I didn't want any of that. The only reason I continued through the motions was for Bronwen. I had given up a lot, but she had given up more.

This had been the darkest winter we'd endured, and yet it seemed to pass faster than any before. The ground had begun to soften, thick patches of snow were melting, and if you stood in the sun long enough, you could feel a moment of warmth.

Maybe the gods had taken pity on us and thought we'd been through enough this year.

When I wasn't traveling, I trained with Jonah and Darrin, ensuring my skills didn't falter. We might have a weird sense of safety right now, but deep in my gut I knew that something else was lurking out there, waiting to strike.

And then there was the one moment of weakness when I came across Talia in the woods, still searching for Shadow.

For a second, I wanted to reach for her. I wanted to say I was sorry for how we ended, for the truth she never got to hear. And when she stepped closer, when her fingers brushed mine and she looked at me with something almost like forgiveness, I didn't pull away.

We didn't speak. Not with words. Just a quiet desperation that pulled us together beneath the cover of trees and fading light. It wasn't planned. It wasn't wise. But it felt inevitable. I held her like I used to, kissed her like I still meant it. And when I whispered her name against her neck, I felt her shudder like she'd been waiting years to hear it.

She still loved me. I felt it in every touch, every breath she shared with me that night. And I loved her too. I always had. But loving her was dangerous. My life wasn't safe. And no matter how much I wanted to stay in that moment, in her arms, I knew I couldn't let it happen again.

Because the next time, it might kill her.

As the sun rose higher, I forced my thoughts back to the present. I brushed the dirt from my clothes and sheathed my blade before heading down the trail that led to town. The walk wasn't long from Darrin's home, just far enough to separate the quiet of the woods from the low hum of life in the streets.

People were beginning to emerge from their homes, wiping sleep from their eyes, some carrying baskets for Market, others leading sleepy children by the hand. A few stopped to greet me, smiling in that cautious, grateful way I still wasn't used to. I offered nods, a few quiet words. But I kept moving.

The whispers followed me. Not loud. Not obvious. But I'd caught enough to know what they were saying.

"She's a witch, isn't she? The king married a witch!"

"Her parents were burned by his father. Can you believe that? What kind of man marries into the bloodline his father tried to wipe out?"

"I heard she turned one of them to ash with a flick of her wrist."

"He was working with the Legion. Hunting his own kind!"

"And now magic's back? What does that mean for the rest of us?"

Speculation hung in the air like smoke from a hearth fire. Bronwen's name was enough to stir unease. She had become a symbol. Of freedom and of fear. She was the quiet storm that unsettled the entire kingdom.

I kept walking.

Because I savored every fleeting moment I could spend with her now.

23

Bronwen

August tried to fight me on this every week, trying to use every possible reason to keep me from going, or at the very least let him come with me. I wouldn't back down on this. No vampires would be in town in the middle of the day. The only ones capable of it were his siblings and I thought they understood well enough now that I was off limits.

The first time I went for breakfast with Adar, August rode with me to the gate, tried to come with me, but when I threatened to spell him to the carriage bench until I returned, he complied.

I had given August everything he asked, but I wasn't budging on this time with Adar.

We eventually settled on a compromise: one Legion soldier would accompany me into town. It was unnecessary, and we both knew it. I could handle myself. But August insisted, calling it a matter of "appearances." I was the queen now, after all, and it was already strange enough that I chose to walk the streets of town once a week like I was still just a seamstress's daughter.

I walked down the cobblestone street with my head high, even as people around me gawked and whispered, their words brushing against my ears like biting wind. I didn't need a crown for anyone to know who I was. Some bowed, some turned away, and others just stared with wide, uncertain eyes. But I kept walking, spine straight, chin lifted.

Over a month had passed since the night August and I gave in to each other again. In that time, we'd developed a rhythm—if you could call it that. A truce, maybe. During the day, we worked in the archives with Benedict, who served as a buffer more than anything else. The space between us remained tense but manageable as long as we had something to focus on.

We would have dinner together, sitting on opposite ends of the table. Other than the servants bringing in food and Halston waiting until we sat at his decorated table to leave, we were alone. Then we would go downstairs to the parties and act as the model king and queen. No one brought up August slamming the vampire into the ground, but the broken marble reminded everyone to be careful.

But at night—*every night*—we unraveled. We undressed each other with equal parts fury and hunger, like it was the only way we knew how to speak. Each touch burned, every breath was a surrender, and when I thought I couldn't take anymore, August would push me further, drag me over the edge again and again, only to hold me after like I was something precious.

Still, it wasn't a relationship. It wasn't love. Just sex—violent, necessary, addictive sex. It made being around each other easier. We didn't have to talk. We could just release all of our frustration and fear into each other's bodies and collapse, too worn out to keep the war going.

And maybe it helped that the nightmares had stopped. That when I fell asleep tangled in his arms, I didn't wake up screaming. We both slept like the dead now, wrapped in the very thing we pretended didn't mean anything at all.

I stepped into the small bakery, the smells of fresh-baked pastries making my stomach rumble. Adar sat in the same chair he did every week, waiting for me. He always arrived before me, always made sure it was set before I arrived—just like Mama used to. He tried to act like nothing had changed every time I saw him, but he couldn't change his appearance.

The light hit his face in a way that showed the hollows under his eyes. His skin was pale, not from lack of sun, but from worry. The lines around his mouth had deepened, carved by too many responsibilities and too little sleep. He looked thinner, too, like the weight of the coven was eating him alive.

My heart tugged. This wasn't the same Adar who used to drag me into snowball fights or argue with me over the best kind of bread. This was a man holding too many broken things in his hands and trying to keep them from slipping through his fingers.

He tried to smile when he saw me, but it didn't reach his eyes. He had tried too hard to fight his way back to the man he was before, but I knew I wouldn't truly see that part of him again until this was all over—if at all.

We ate in silence for a while. I went for the grape jelly as always and a puffy pastry while Adar barely touched his tea.

"I have a little news."

I glanced up at him, wiping the jelly from the corner of my mouth.

"Talia found Shadow."

I gasped, the pastry falling into my lap. "Is he okay?"

Tears welled up before I could stop them. I had tried convincing myself he was fine—that his instincts had kicked in and he was thriving somewhere wild and free. But a part of me always feared the worst.

"He's okay," Adar said softly. "I took him to Jonah's for the time being. He's safe."

"That's the best news I've heard in a while."

"Apparently, Talia never stopped looking for him."

"She's an angel," I said, shaking my head with a watery smile.

Adar didn't answer, but I caught the subtle twitch of a smile tugging at his lips, the way he looked down into his tea like it suddenly interested him.

I narrowed my eyes. "You've been spending time with her?"

He stiffened, eyes darting away. "Why would I?"

"Adar, you only stopped seeing her because of what we were hiding. You still care about her. Don't lie to me."

He picked at the rim of his mug. "It's not about what I feel. I ended things because it wasn't safe. I couldn't drag her into all this."

"I know that. So I thought—"

"Thought what?" he asked. "Have you stopped Carrow yet?"

My breath caught, jaw tightening at the sharpness of his words. Neither of us usually mentioned August. Or Carrow. We never did when we were together like this. It was as if the weight of everything that haunted our nights didn't belong at this table. Not when time was so limited, and comfort so rare.

"We aren't safe then," he said before I could respond. "I'm not bringing her into this. All I've ever wanted to do is protect her, and that isn't changing now."

He leaned back, rubbing his hands together like he needed to do something with them. The silence between us stretched.

So I just nodded, biting my lip as I reached down to clean the pastry crumbs from my lap. "She makes you happy. Doesn't that count for something?"

He exhaled slowly, the tension in his shoulders softening just a little. "It does. And everybody I love is always taken from me."

With the snow melting, more people had begun to fill the streets. The air was sharp but promising, carrying the scents of fresh bread, dried herbs, and something fried in thick oil that made my mouth water. Someone was selling roasted chestnuts. I could smell the sugar glaze from across the square. A smaller version of Market had been set up at the square, their vendors shouting prices over one another in a chaotic rhythm that almost felt familiar.

I weaved between the booths, the sound of bargaining rising in waves. My fingers trailed across a bolt of deep blue velvet out of habit, and for just a second, I imagined Mama beside me, appraising the quality, arguing for a better price. Papa would've already handed over the coin, just to make her smile.

People stared. Some whispered. A few bowed their heads. I didn't know what any of them truly thought, and I didn't care. But the weight of their eyes always followed me.

I paused at the empty patch where our family's booth used to stand. The space looked smaller than I remembered, but the memories it held were too large to ignore. Mama scolding me for being rude to customers, Papa bringing Mama a bouquet of flowers he bought for her, and August and I arguing because he would never leave me alone.

"Bronwen." It was a whisper but the goosebumps on the back of my neck told me it was sent through a spell and not from someone near me. I scanned the booths around me, craning my neck to look to the buildings surrounding the square.

Jonah.

I stepped to him and he pulled me into the shadows. What was he doing? Witches were free now. We didn't need to slink through alleyways like criminals anymore. But his hands were shaking, his eyes scanning the open square like someone might be following him.

"Jonah? What is it?"

"The—the coven," he said, the words forced like he didn't want to say them.

My stomach twisted. "What about the coven?"

"There are some that are giving your brother a hard time."

A pit opened in my chest. "What do you mean?"

"They're not wanting to submit to him. I've listened in on some of their conversations." He leaned in closer, voice barely a breath. "They plan to overthrow him."

The air around us seemed to still. The noise from Market faded, replaced by the ringing in my ears. After everything, after all we had lost—how could they?

"Do you have names?"

His throat bobbed. "The one leading it is in Bodaira. Alden Gran."

The name didn't mean anything to me, but the location was enough. Bodaira told me where to start my hunt. I let the silence linger for a breath longer than needed, forcing the fury to settle beneath my skin instead of bursting out. "I will handle it."

* * *

I sat in the archives with August and Benedict, looking through another tome of artifacts to find any blades that seemed like they could be used. I finally felt like we had made some progress. We had determined over the last few weeks that the blade must be one that was from Alentara. I told August when we were alone how Carrow felt different when I touched him, that the magic in his veins was darker, stronger than what I felt from any other vampire I had come across.

When Benedict questioned why we thought it was a blade forged in Alentara, August admitted that I had encountered Carrow before, but he didn't go into specifics. So we read. And read. And read. I hated it.

This was what I imagined torture to be like.

We'd come up with nothing other than a few names of blades that we decided were important enough to find more information on. It was nearing dusk, so our time had come to an end, which meant it was time for me to pay some witches a visit.

"I am going out tonight," I said as we stepped into our chambers, already bracing myself for the argument that was sure to follow.

"Out?" He leaned in, smiling like he was teasing, but there was something tight beneath the curve of his mouth. "Does my Winnie have a date?"

The words were meant to be playful, but his eyes betrayed

him. Jealousy simmered there, barely masked.

"A date with some witches that need to remember their place," I said flatly, shrugging off the tension and turning toward the door.

He stepped behind me, close enough that I could feel the heat of his body. I didn't need to look to know his jaw was ticking. He hated this—hated not knowing, not being in control.

"Oh, this sounds delightful. Let's go," he said too casually.

I spun on my heels and pressed a hand against his chest, stopping him mid-step. "I do not need your help."

"You're right," he said. "But I wouldn't miss this."

I narrowed my eyes, folding my arms. "I am going to Bodaira. I don't have time to wait for your guards, my *dear* king."

His lips twitched, not quite a smile. "We can leave and return before they realize I'm gone."

"August," I warned. "They will send an army after us to find you."

"It's beginning to get a little boring around here, don't you think?"

There was something desperate in his tone—like if he didn't do something reckless soon, he might shatter. It unnerved me how often I felt the same.

"Fine. But you will keep your mouth shut and let me handle it."

"As you wish, my queen." He bowed, but the glint in his eyes was pure mischief.

Then, he extended his hand out in front of me, palm up, fingers wiggling like he expected me to take it without question.

I narrowed my gaze. "Really? You've been pouting about me pulling magic this entire time and yet you're so willing to do it now?"

"I have not been *pouting*," he muttered.

"Yes, you have."

"There is a difference between me giving it to you and you taking it."

My breath hitched the moment I looked up at him. He was staring at me like he was trying to memorize my face, like he didn't know if he wanted to kiss me or kill someone just to make me stay.

My own heart stuttered in answer.

He was slipping. And the worst part was—I didn't want to stop him either.

24

August

We walked along the wooden deck that lined the shore of the Sea of Mavrola. The salt-tinged breeze tangled through Winnie's hair, and though the afternoon sun bathed us in gold, unease clung to her like a second skin. She kept glancing at the water like it held ghosts only she could see.

But when she stopped in front of a small apothecary, her spine straightened and her chin lifted. She flipped her hair over one shoulder like armor, masking whatever war she was fighting inside. The moment we stepped inside, the bell above the door gave a startled chime and the woman behind the counter—a middle-aged woman with streaks of gray threading through her dark hair—locked eyes with Winnie and dropped the small glass bottle in her hand.

"Oh, there is no need to worry over me," Winnie said, her voice light but cold. "I just have a question and then you'll hopefully never see me again."

The woman's gaze flicked to me and she paled before dipping into a deep bow. "Y-Your Grace. It is an honor. I can't thank you enough for what you've done for us."

Winnie didn't pause. She waved a dismissive hand as she stepped farther into the shop, her eyes scanning the shelves. "We don't have time for the formalities. I just need the location of someone—Alden Gran."

The woman's posture stiffened. "Why are you looking for him?"

Winnie picked up a bar of soap and sniffed it, as if we had all the time in the world. "Old friends."

"You didn't seem like friends the last time you were here."

"Excuse me?" Winnie's tone sharpened.

"Father may not have seen you terrorizing those poor boys, but I did."

I took a half-step forward, instinct clawing its way through my throat, but Winnie had warned me. Stay back. Let her handle it.

So I did. Barely. My hands curled into fists at my sides. I leaned against the frame of the doorway like I didn't care, but every muscle in my body was tensed, ready to act the second she needed me.

Winnie's eyes glittered with something dangerous. "Which one was Alden?"

"Oh, so you didn't even know who they were? You just *take* from whoever you please?"

"Which one?" Her voice cracked like a whip.

"I do not answer to you. You are not Mother."

Winnie stepped forward, smile slow and cruel. "No. I am your *queen*."

Gods help anyone who forgot that.

"They are traitors to the coven and will be dealt with as such." Winnie's eyes narrowed. "Should I add you to the list of people I need to *deal* with?"

The woman blanched. "I—I had no idea. I swear it! I may not care for you, but your brother... your brother has proven to be just like your father, even with his difficulties with magic. Caring. Honorable. I am loyal."

Winnie took a step forward, letting the silence stretch between them. "Which one was Alden?" she asked.

"The one with the red hair," the woman answered quickly.

Winnie gave a single, decisive nod. "And where can I find him?"

"He lives right outside of town. The blue house with green shutters."

We walked toward the woods as the sun started to set. Silence stretched between us. I couldn't help but replay the conversation in my head as I looked at her. She tried to act like it wasn't bothering her, but I could hear her heart and saw how her fists clenched and unclenched. *You take from whoever you please. Traitors to the coven.* And yet her brother—the one who took responsibility when Winnie came with me—was no where to be found.

"Did Adar ask you to handle this for him?"

She shot me a look. "No. One of Papa's friends stopped me in town and told me. Adar acted like nothing was wrong at breakfast."

I followed closely behind her as she headed down the driveway that led to a nicer home compared to the ones surrounding it. Large windows sat on both sides of a wooden door. Candles illuminated the inside, and though no one was in view, I could hear three heartbeats, one closer than the other two.

So he didn't *know* what she was doing. "He isn't going to be happy about this."

"Since when are you my voice of reason?"

I smiled and gestured to the door. "After you, Winnie."

Every step she took, I felt it like a thread pulling tight in my chest. I wanted to reach for her elbow, to guide her away from the house and back into the dark—anywhere but here. Not because I feared the danger inside. I feared what I'd do if she got hurt. I feared what I'd become if she didn't come back out.

I swallowed that impulse like I always did. Stuffed it down with all the other things I wanted and couldn't have.

She stopped and turned to me.

"I thought you couldn't come into people's homes. Like it was a vampire's weakness—like the sun—or something."

"No. It was just another one of Carrow's rules."

She scoffed. "You followed none of his rules. Why didn't you come into my home?"

"Because your father had a protection spell on your home, actually one larger than any other I've come across. It reached all the way to the trees, and I wasn't testing it."

She gave a soft smile before looking back at the door.

"It's probably spelled," I muttered as I shifted on my feet.

"Oh, I'm counting on it."

She placed her hand on the door and inhaled deeply as she concentrated. I knew that look all too well. Whatever feeling magic gave her, it must be similar to what I feel when I feed.

Gods, just looking at her turned me on. I loved how easy it was. How my mind went from murder to worship with a single glance. She could've burned me to ash and I'd still think she looked divine doing it. There was something wrong with me—I knew it. But knowing didn't stop the craving. I didn't want her. I needed her.

Her eyes shot open and the door blasted into the home,

splintering and knocking over glass. She stepped inside, scanning the room. I held my breath as I stepped in after her, half-expecting to be set on fire from the protection spell they had on the door, but nothing happened. Winnie took all of the magic.

She turned her head to a redheaded man who must have fallen out of his chair in the chaos, and his eyes widened.

My fists curled at my sides. That part, small and battered as it was, still screamed to pull her behind me. To shield her. Even though I knew she didn't need it. Even though I knew she'd hate me for trying.

"Miss me?" She waltzed through the room, picking up a glass that hadn't fallen, twirled it in her hand and then dropped it to the floor.

He shot a hand forward and muttered some words in another language but Winnie raised hers and seemed to grasp onto thin air. It was the same thing she had done the night she saved me from the witches.

She poked her lip out. "Oh come on, I thought you'd be smarter than that."

The man let out an agonizing scream as Winnie pulled her hand towards her and the man flew across the room until he was on his knees before her. A woman and another man ran out of a back room, the man holding a sword. I started to step forward and stop him, but before I could, Winnie glanced at them and the sword's metal melted in the man's hands.

The man screamed as he fell forward.

Gods alive, she was perfect. Dangerous. Terrifying. Every time she wielded her magic like that, like the world existed just to kneel at her feet, something primal in me howled for her.

Winnie crouched down in front of the redhead and smiled. "I warned you."

What was she talking about? When did she have a problem with him before?

"You've disrespected my brother. You're planning gods know what to take him down. Do you know what happened to the last person that hurt my family?" She leaned in. "I burned him alive just so I could hear his screams."

The man writhed under her invisible touch. "The two of you are not fit to lead the coven."

She scoffed, but before he could disrespect her more, I spoke. "Do you not realize that the only reason you are free to practice magic is because of her? Both of their sacrifices are the reason you are safe from persecution and yet you still try to fight them?"

The man turned to me. "Your Grace."

So he *did* know who I was.

"We will never be safe. Their line is the reason we can't go out into the night. They are the reason innocent people are hunted. It is time to end the lineage. Stop them, and we will be one step closer to stopping the vampires."

With that, something cracked.

He wanted her *dead*.

He wanted *her* dead.

My vision went red, not just from rage but from the part of me that saw only one solution: rip his throat out. Tear him limb from limb. I tasted blood. My own lip, split from how hard I bit down to keep from snarling. They had no idea. No idea who they were provoking.

But they did now.

The woman crouched next to the man with the most

wretched-smelling, burned hands let out a cry. "No."

She saw me looking at her and turned back to the injured man and continued whispering words as her hands hovered over his.

With my fangs bared, I said, "Do continue telling me on how you plan to *stop* vampires."

Winnie looked up at me with a sparkle in her eyes but she shook it off and turned back to the idiot nearly crying on the floor.

"I thought about killing you, but that's not enough for me. Because I have to assume you aren't the only one with these ill thoughts towards my brother." She patted him on the cheek. "I'd rather you be a walking warning to everyone else."

"Please no."

"You called me an abomination, looked down on my brother and me for what we lacked. But honestly, I think we are more powerful than anything you can fathom. I can take and take and take. Would you like to know what happens when I take *everything* from you?" Winnie gripped his throat and though I couldn't see what she was doing, the goosebumps on her arms told me all I needed to know.

He screamed so loudly that I wished for a moment I didn't have exceptional hearing. Winnie let go of him, and he slumped to the floor.

"You become *nothing*." She stood and adjusted her dress. "Let your accomplices know that if they don't back down, they will have an empty void just like you." She stopped at the door. "I wonder... when you have kids, will they lack a connection to magic like you?" She laughed. "I hope so."

We stepped outside into the night air. The salt still hung thick, the wind sharp as it curled around us like it knew we didn't belong here. She walked ahead of me, fire still in her steps, her jaw tight with leftover rage. The magic still clung to her like heat lightning, crackling beneath her skin. She was high on power, and she wore it well.

I caught up, and for a moment, we walked side by side. The air buzzed between us, heavy with things neither of us dared to say. My hand twitched. I could almost feel the press of her against me.

She glanced over, lips parted like she was about to say something. Her gaze dropped to my mouth and lingered. Every inch of me tightened in response. I clenched my jaw, forcing my thoughts back into the box I kept them locked in. But gods, she made it hard. Everything about her unraveled me.

"You held back," she said softly, a whisper in the wind.

"You asked me to."

Her steps slowed, just enough for me to feel it.

"That must've killed you," she added, the faintest trace of a smile playing at her lips.

I didn't answer. Couldn't. Because it had. Watching her handle it, watching her burn like the storm she was born to be, and standing in the shadows—silent—was agony.

But I'd do it again. For her. Always.

"They might tell everyone that you're a vampire."

"What are they going to do? Attack a castle of vampires? Attack you when they know you have an endless amount of magic from *said* vampires?"

She placed her hand on my arm to take us back and paused, looking up at me.

Her heart rate spiked. "August."

I shifted my expression, trying to hide every emotion I felt from her. "Take us back before my guards start looking for me."

"I'm hungry," Winnie muttered as we appeared in our chambers.

"I'm sure you are after the mess you made."

She rolled her eyes and tried to hide a smile.

You'd never realize it looking at her, but she loved to eat. She attacked a plate with the same intensity she brought to everything else. It used to catch me off guard. Now it just made me smile.

And I could use a distraction from those annoying feelings that were trying to come to the surface. I turned to open the door, already planning what food we could send for, and immediately regretted it.

Lavina stood just outside, arms crossed over her chest, her lips curved in that same cold, knowing smirk she always wore.

Of course she was here. Of all people.

Winnie stiffened beside me, and I could practically feel the wave of disdain roll off of her. Lavina's eyes flicked down and I followed her gaze to see mud on my boots.

"What were you two doing?" she asked. "It's not a good idea to go outside alone."

"I don't remember asking for your opinion," I said flatly.

She ignored me and looked up. "You shouldn't leave without your guards, brother. You know that."

"And you shouldn't still be walking around after what she did to you," I shot back.

Lavina's eyes darkened. She'd kept glorious distance between us since Winnie nearly killed her. And I preferred it that way.

"I was simply making sure no one was breaking the rules,"

she said sweetly, then turned to Winnie with a tilt of her head. "But I suppose you two know all about breaking things."

Winnie smiled and raised her hand. Fuck. I had to say something before Winnie decided to roast her right now.

"Go play court watchdog somewhere else," I muttered. "Before you say something you'll regret."

She stared for a moment longer. "I've planned dinner for tonight."

"Gods alive, Lavina! I thought we decided for the health of everyone that we weren't doing that anymore."

She shrugged. "I'm bored."

I almost denied her, but I felt a ripple of something sharp and electric coming off Winnie. Not dread. Not unease. Excitement.

Did she like the dinners? Did she enjoy watching my family claw at each other with veiled words and fake smiles? Or maybe she liked the tension. The danger of it. The chance to show she didn't flinch.

How twisted was that?

"Fine," I said through my teeth. If Winnie wanted dinner, she'd get dinner.

25

Bronwen

Dinner with the siblings hadn't happened in nearly two months, yet somehow it felt like no time had passed at all.

They slipped back into their roles with practiced ease. Lavina and Simon launched into the latest court gossip with theatrical flair, their voices weaving around each other like twin performers on a stage. Benedict sat in his usual place, silently focused on his plate, only glancing up to murmur a dry remark here and there when it suited him. Corwin's seat was empty, considering he was a pile of ashes in our hearth.

And then there was August.

He didn't say much. He rarely did in these settings unless provoked, but tonight he was... attentive. Watchful. His eyes—dark, piercing, and heavy with something I couldn't name—barely left me.

I tried not to squirm under his gaze, tried not to let the heat pooling in my stomach rise to my cheeks. But it was impossible to ignore. The way he watched me eat—like every movement of my hand, every bite of food, every flick of my tongue against my bottom lip, was something he wanted to memorize. Or devour.

My fork slowed halfway to my mouth. The memory of getting dressed together earlier flickered behind my eyes like a match being struck.

His hands had been on my hips the second my dress fell to the ground. And when his shirt came off, I lost my train of thought entirely. He'd backed me into the dressing table with a hunger that made my knees weak, the edge of the mirror digging into my spine as our mouths collided. It was reckless, frenzied—and if my stomach hadn't growled loud enough to almost embarrass me, we wouldn't have made it out of the room.

I'd whispered a promise against his throat—one I still fully intended to keep. I would make it up to him when we returned to our chambers tonight.

I caught the faintest smirk tugging at the corner of his mouth. He knew exactly what I was remembering. I turned back to my plate, ignoring the burn in my cheeks.

"I am beginning to worry about Corwin."

Lavina's voice sliced through the clinking of silverware and low laughter like a blade. My head snapped up, more at the absurdity of her words than anything else. Worry? About Corwin? *Now?*

I glanced at August, trying to turn my expression into something neutral.

He set down his glass with an almost lazy grace and gave Lavina a look as dry as dust. "No, you aren't. You care for nothing but yourself, Lavina."

She held his gaze for a moment before shrugging and turning back to Simon. "Do you remember Odin Draymoor?"

"The one who proposed to you decades ago, and when you

turned him down, he left?"

She nodded. "He's back. With someone else."

Simon leaned back in his chair, balancing it on two legs as he took a long sip from his goblet. "What's the problem? You didn't want him."

"No, but I want him to want me."

"You don't want that."

Lavina's eyes snapped to me. I didn't realize I'd said that out loud.

"What do you know about this? You married the one obsessed with you."

August let out a quiet laugh, dark and amused, like he found the idea more flattering than offensive.

I met Lavina's stare. "I was proposed to once too. And his obsession got him killed. By August."

August's head turned sharply toward me, eyes narrowing. "He *proposed* to you?"

I nodded. "Yes."

August didn't so much as flinch, but his voice came low and unbothered from beside me. "If I had known that, I would've killed him sooner."

I was starting to forget how much we used to keep from each other. I dropped my gaze before he could see me blush and fixed it on the untouched spread of desserts. Halston had gone all out tonight; weeks without nightly family dinners must have left him itching for something to orchestrate.

Chairs scraped against the stone floor as everyone began rising from the table, preparing to head to the great room. Lavina was already smoothing her skirts as she took Simon's arm, Benedict trailing behind them without a word. I pushed my chair back, but before I could stand fully, August's hand caught my wrist beneath the table.

"Not tonight," he said under his breath, eyes never leaving mine.

I blinked at him. "Why not?"

His lips curved. "Because you have a promise to keep."

* * *

The sheets were still tangled around our legs when I climbed back on top of him, both of us naked, sweat-slick and breathless. His hands slid up the backs of my thighs, thumbs digging into the soft skin as I sank down onto him again.

His head fell back against the pillows, lips parted, chest rising in sharp, shallow breaths. "Fuck, Winnie..."

I rolled my hips slowly, drawing a groan from deep in his chest. His hands tightened their grip, holding me still so he could thrust up into me with brutal precision.

"Ride me like you mean it," he growled, eyes dark and shining.

"I always mean it," I panted, bracing myself against his chest.

His hand came up to cup the side of my face, thumb brushing the corner of my mouth. "Look at you," he murmured. "Fucking beautiful like this."

It should have felt like a line. Maybe it was. But something twisted in my chest when he said it—something that made me move faster, made me lean into him more.

He sat up suddenly, our chests pressed together, his mouth dragging over my collarbone, then up to my jaw. "Don't stop," he whispered against my skin. "I need this."

So did I.

He didn't hesitate. His fangs sank into me with a sharp, aching bite that sent lightning through every nerve. The pain twisted with the pleasure until I couldn't tell them apart, until I was crying out and clutching his shoulders, riding him harder just to chase that edge. His body trembled beneath me, a deep, desperate growl rumbling in his chest as he drank. He always unraveled when he tasted me—when I let him lose control.

He pulled back before he took too much, lips slick with my blood, red eyes glazed. "You'll be the death of me," he rasped.

I smiled through ragged breaths. "Good."

Dark veins throbbed beneath his eyes. I skimmed them with my fingertips, feeling them pulse like a second heartbeat. He shuddered and drove into me to the hilt. I drew my hand down, and with the pad of my thumb I painted his mouth with my blood then dragged it along the cut of his cheek, the red stark against his porcelain skin. He went very still, eyes burning, as I leaned in and licked it clean, tongue following the path I'd made, tasting heat and iron and him. He broke then, a ragged noise blooming in his chest, and I caught it with my mouth, kissing him open until he was breathless.

It wasn't just about the sex anymore. Not really.

The moment shattered with the violent crash of the door slamming open.

My breath caught in my throat, the scream barely forming before August had already moved. In one fluid, instinctive motion, he threw me behind him, the blankets tangling around my legs as I hit the mattress.

He crouched low, every muscle coiled, his bare skin glowing in the low firelight, the predator beneath the king rising to the surface in an instant.

A young woman hit the stone floor, thrown into the room like garbage. Her body crumpled, tears streaking her face.

"I cannot get this one to calm down," Simon said casually, stepping into the room with blood-red eyes. "Either fix her or I drain her."

"Do not come into my room without permission," August snapped.

Simon bowed with mocking flair. "Well, excuse me, Your Highness. But considering how few servants we have right now, I figured you'd want the chance to fix this one before I lost my patience."

August stared at him for a long moment, chest still rising fast from what we'd been doing. Then he pushed off the bed, the air shifting around him as he stood. In a few quick steps, he crossed the room and crouched by the woman.

"What's the problem?"

She shot a fearful glance at Simon, then turned to August. A shriek ripped from her when she saw his eyes. "Vampires," she whispered as she scrabbled backward across the floor. "They're everywhere."

"You know you're only allowed to feed underground," August growled without looking up at Simon.

"I did—just forgot to clean up before I came back," Simon said with a careless shrug. His gaze slid between August and where my hand covered my neck. "So, what exactly would you call what you two were doing?"

"Simon," August warned.

"Fix her and I'll be out of your way."

August went to the woman who had backed herself against the wall and cupped her face gently, turning his head to glance at me. "Winnie. I need you to not freak out with what I'm about to do, okay? Can you do that?"

I nodded stiffly, unsettled by Simon's attention. He had never really bothered me before, but with the blood under my hand and the blanket wrapped around me, his eyes barely left me.

August turned back to the girl and locked eyes with her. "Calm down."

Instantly, her shoulders dropped and the panic melted off her face.

"Forget the vampires. Forget what you saw. Clean yourself up and get back to work."

She blinked, wiped her cheeks, stood, bowed... and walked calmly out of the room.

"Absolutely amazing as always, brother," Simon said, grinning.

"Get out."

Simon lifted a hand in lazy farewell and shut the door behind him. August stood and stared at me.

"What the fuck just happened?"

"I said not to freak out," August reminded.

"You just told that woman to calm down and she did. Like— completely."

"It wasn't the words," he said, climbing back onto the bed with me. "It was the look."

I backed away as he crawled closer. "You can make people do whatever you want... just by looking at them?"

He shrugged.

"Stop being so nonchalant about it! How do I know you've never done that to me before? How do I know that anything I've done around you—*for you*—was of my own free will?"

His gaze darkened—deepened—like a storm rolling in behind his eyes. The edges of the room fell away; candlelight guttered, sound thinned, and all the air seemed to funnel toward him. Heat rose off his skin in a faint glow. My heartbeat climbed to meet his, too loud, too eager. He was ruin and refuge in the same breath—something holy wearing something wicked—and I couldn't look anywhere else.

I wanted him. *Needed* him. The kind of need that emptied out reason and filled it with fire. I would have given him my throat, my pulse, the last of my stubborn pride. I would have lied, knelt, burned a kingdom to ash if he asked and then thanked him for the order. Let the world keep spinning; let it fall—I didn't care. There was only him.

A smile—slow, knowing—curved his lips. "You'd know," he said.

The words wrapped around my brain, silky and sharp, and then he blinked and the world snapped back into place. I gasped, stumbling as I pushed myself from the bed.

"What. The fuck. Was *that*?!"

"Compulsion," he said. "Like I said, I didn't use it on you. I would never use it on you."

"You could have stopped me from killing Carrow."

The words tumbled out before I fully processed what they meant. And when I did, it hit me like a punch to the chest.

He *could* have stopped me.

He'd watched me fall apart. Watched me break. Let me make the choice that nearly cost me everything—him included. My throat tightened, a flicker of betrayal sparked somewhere deep in my chest. But then again would I have been okay with him taking a choice from me?

No. I wouldn't have been able to forgive him if he manipulated me like that. It had to be my decision. Right or wrong, it needed to be mine.

Still, the weight of it lingered.

"But I didn't," he said quietly as he pulled me back into bed. "Even when you signed my death sentence."

His voice had barely settled in the air when his hand slipped beneath the blanket, fingers brushing the inside of my thigh. My breath hitched, and I hated how instinctively my legs parted for him.

I didn't stop him. Not at first.

His palm smoothed upward, teasingly close. I exhaled sharply, muscles tightening for all the wrong reasons. I shoved his hand away.

"The mood's gone," I said, not nearly nearly as firm as I wanted it to be.

He moved closer anyway, his breath brushing my jaw. "Come on, Winnie," he whispered, mouth almost against my ear. "I said I'd never use compulsion on you. Are you going to make me a liar now?"

The words sank into me like a hook. My body betrayed me first—leaning into him, my thighs tightening. That intoxicating heat swelled between us again, and any resistance I had left crumbled.

I gave in.

* * *

Later, I lay in bed with my head on his chest, tracing slow circles across the hard lines of his abdomen. His arm was draped around my back, the other hand sliding slowly through my hair in a rhythm that made it hard to think.

"Can other vampires do that?" I asked softly.

"No," he murmured as if he had no doubt that compulsion was still on my mind. "I'm the only one."

"Are there other gifts some have?"

"No. It's just me."

I tilted my head slightly, feeling his fingers pause briefly in my hair before moving again, gentler now.

"You're also stronger."

"Stronger than Carrow was in my father's body, too."

He didn't say it with pride—just quiet certainty. But it carried weight, and I could feel the truth in his voice. Not just strength, but something lonelier. The burden of being different, even among monsters.

"Why is that? Do you think it has to do with being the oldest?" I asked.

"Huh." August let out a breath that was almost a laugh, but not quite. "I guess it never came up."

"What are you talking about?"

"I'm the youngest of my siblings."

I pushed myself up, brows knitting. "What? Then why are you the one that's next in line?"

He looked up at the ceiling for a moment, as if sorting through old dust-covered memories. "Benedict is the oldest and was originally the heir. Then came Simon, Lavina, and Corwin. All by different mothers. All from Malachi, my father. Simon and Lavina were born only months apart—that's why they're so close. They were raised together. Benedict was already grown when they were born, and Corwin came a century after that. They were all born before Carrow took over my father's body."

"But you weren't," I said softly.

He nodded. "I was an accident. After Carrow took over Malachi's body, he got attached to a servant. She was quiet, obedient, exactly what he wanted. So he married her, thought she could play the part in his twisted little fantasy. For a while, she did."

"Lavina said she was marked."

He sighed. "Not by Carrow. He had another vampire mark her because he wanted to feed from her but had seen what could happen and didn't want any of the side effects. He locked up the other vampire to keep him from trying to find her after she was marked, but it didn't stop my mother from trying to get him out. She dreamt of him. Not dying by his hand but living a happy life with him. That was when Carrow decided to turn her."

Everyone had always been a pawn in Carrow's game.

And it was all so confusing. It always was. Carrow was a leech that attached himself to others and forced control. August said he was not his father. Maybe it wasn't his body, but it was his soul when August was conceived. It was easier to believe if I didn't think about it too hard.

"So you never got to know Malachi?"

He shook his head. "At first, I thought Carrow was my father. And in his own sick way, he was... *good* to me. Which only made things worse with my siblings. They went through the loss of our father. They had to watch Carrow wear his face. I didn't. I was a child when they were already adults—and they made me pay for it. Locked me in cells when no one was watching. Starved me. Made me feed off dead animals. All except Benedict. He kept his distance."

My stomach twisted. "How old were you when that stopped?"

"I was thirteen. I threw Corwin through a wall and had my hand in Lavina's chest, ready to rip her heart out, but Carrow stopped me. I shouldn't have been able to do that with them having hundreds of years on me. They should have been stronger than me. After that, my siblings kept their distance. And Carrow... he changed. I think he started to fear me."

August's voice dropped lower. "Then, one night, a servant spilled wine on me during dinner. I told him he would've been better off jumping off the balcony."

"And he did?"

"Yes. He ran straight for the railing. That's when I realized what I could do—what compulsion was."

"Gods," I breathed.

He nodded slowly. "And then Carrow grew obsessed. He saw how different I was. Declared me his heir. I think because I was conceived after he took over my father's body... it *changed* something. It made me something else. After that, there was no loving father. He only saw me as his next body. And when Carrow is obsessed, he turns wicked. Finding anything that brought me joy and taking it away just to try to break me. When he ran out of things, he took my mother away."

"Did he kill her?"

"I think so. I looked for her for years."

I wrapped my arm tighter around him. "I'm sorry."

"But none of it broke me. It only made my hatred grow more. And because of that little bit of fear he had for me, he let me be for centuries. Until he found you."

Memories flashed through my mind. My parents hanging. They were caught in the midst of all of it because of me. All

because of what I meant to August.
We had to stop Carrow.

26

Bronwen

"What is this one called?"

Out of the five tomes I'd flipped through today, I'd found drawings of a dozen or so swords, knives, and other blades that could've been it. Some Benedict had marked for further research. Others he'd dismissed with a shake of his head, like he could tell by instinct that they weren't the one. I didn't blame him. One of the entries said the blade was used to slice food and enchant it so that anyone who ate it would fall in love with you. Definitely not what we were looking for.

August leaned closer, close enough that I could feel the heat of him, his eyes scanning the page in silence. His brow furrowed as he concentrated on the language I couldn't understand.

"Blade of Aros," he read aloud.

The drawing showed a dark hilt with twisted, swirling designs, and a stone embedded in the center—black, with the faintest shimmer, like it was holding something back.

"Forged by the greatest bladesmith of his time with the help of a necromancing faerie," he read. "They created a stone that held the souls of every creature it was wielded on. Gifting the stone its souls, it gifts the holder the ability to lead armies of the dead under absolute control. But the balance is still not there—so every time the person summons an army, a price must be paid."

"That sounds promising," I muttered, glancing up at Benedict as he leaned in to take a look.

"It does," he said. "But I've never seen that one. And I'm not convinced it could actually transfer a soul."

He was always skeptical, but he still scribbled a note beside the page, just in case.

I flipped a few more pages until another blade caught my eye. It was a short blade as thin as a needle with an etching of a symbol.

"And this one?"

August let out a breath as he looked again. "Uniros. With one drop of blood drawn, you can make the person see anything you want them to see, but it only works for moments."

"That's not it," Benedict said.

I leaned back in the creaky wooden chair, rubbing my temples. "I despise this," I muttered. "I'm not made for sitting in a dusty room flipping through centuries-old tomes every single day. This isn't helping. This is exhausting."

August glanced up from his own pile, his expression sharpening. "You say that every day."

"Because I feel it every day," I snapped. "I'm not a scholar. I'm a witch who's used to actually doing something."

August's eyes narrowed. "You also say *that* every day."

"Because nothing changes!" I shot back. "We sit here for hours, digging through rot and dust, and for what? You're just using me—using what I am. That's all this has ever been, hasn't it? You needed help with research, and then I ended up in your bed, so now you get both."

Maybe it was that I was truly bored, or maybe it was because I felt like we hadn't gotten any closer to stopping Carrow and the clock was ticking. I could never admit it to him, but I was scared. Scared of Carrow coming back—and coming after me, but more importantly, scared of what it meant for August.

He stood slowly, the movement tight with frustration, rage simmering behind his eyes. "Need I remind you that I could have compelled you this entire time? I could have had you abandon your family and stay with me just to find the answers I needed, but I didn't. Can't you understand that? You always think my intentions with you are bad. Yes, I withheld things from you, and yes, I needed your help... but I never forced you." He turned sharply and moved toward the door.

"I thought you didn't want me out of your sight," I called after him.

He paused. "You're safe here with Benedict. No one else comes up to the archives."

And then he was gone, the door thudding shut behind him.

The room was silent except for the slow turning of pages and the steady scratching of Benedict's pen. I hadn't realized how loud August's presence was until it vanished.

Benedict's voice came softly, almost cautiously. "Augustus has never compelled you?"

I turned to him, shaking my head. "No."

He studied me for a beat, then asked, "If I may... why did you come here with him? Why would you put yourself in such a dangerous position?"

"We made a deal."

"A deal?"

If August trusted him enough to let him in on our plan, then surely he could know.

"Me for the freedom of witches."

He studied me for a moment. "That seems like a lot for one girl to have on her."

"Well, my father is—" I paused, feeling the familiar weight press on my chest, "*my brother* is the leader of the coven. It's worth it to me to know he and our descendants will be protected."

I expected him to ignore my answer and continue his work like he always did every time we had a conversation, but the rustle of parchment had gone still. I looked up.

Benedict was staring at me.

"What?"

"Those were your parents Carrow killed."

I nodded slowly.

He set his pen down, the scratch of ink on parchment falling still. "Well, that explains Augustus's actions."

I frowned. "I don't understand."

"He's reckless sometimes," he continued, "but not careless. Not when it comes to you. What he did that day—he didn't do it for appearance. He did it for you."

I sighed as I ran my hands through my hair. "Why must vampires always be so cryptic? What are you talking about?"

Benedict looked at me like I was the confusing one. "When he took their bodies down and buried them."

My hands started to shake.

"You didn't know."

There was no way he did that.

"How—how do you know that?"

"After it happened, we were sitting at dinner—one that Augustus was supposed to attend—but he wasn't there. Carrow didn't seem to care. Normally he would be furious if Augustus missed, but he was almost happy. But then Lavina mentioned that one of her latest meals couldn't stop talking about how a man with white hair took the witches down himself and ordered the Legion soldiers around. He had the soldiers burn the gallows while he carried the bodies past the town's gates. Carrow nearly killed us all when he heard that."

I sat frozen. The words barely registered.

He had the gallows burned. In daylight. He didn't do that for show. There was no advantage. No gain. He did it because he cared.

Because he *loved* me.

The realization hit so hard I could barely breathe. It hadn't all been strategy. It wasn't just manipulation and necessity. There were real feelings beneath it all—there always had been. I hadn't imagined it. I hadn't been a fool. He loved me.

And I'd broken it.

I didn't deserve him. Not after what I'd said. Not after what I accused him of.

And gods, what I would give just to have him look at me the way he used to. To feel that again—if only for a moment.

I ran through the castle, my footsteps echoing down the corridor as I turned sharply into the west wing. The heartbreak and guilt tangled in my chest like vines, tightening with every step. Pushing open the door to our chambers, I didn't stop until I stood in front of the tub where he soaked in silence.

"Leave us," I said, not looking at the servant by the door.

The servant hesitated, glancing toward August. He gave a nod, barely a movement, and the servant bowed and exited swiftly.

August pinched the bridge of his nose, not even glancing up. "Are you ready to kiss and make up?"

"You buried them."

He froze. "What?"

"You buried them," I repeated, the words strangled in my throat. "Why didn't you tell me?"

His eyes lifted to meet mine, confused but cautious. "Winnie—"

"You could've told me the day we came to the castle," I said, stepping closer, trembling. "But you didn't."

He stood from the bath and stepped out, water streaming off him as he wrapped a towel around his hips. "You're not making any sense."

"My parents, August!" I cried. "You buried them! Where did you bury them?"

His face shifted. He took a step forward, his arm lifting like he meant to reach for me, but I raised my hand and stepped back before he could touch me. My jaw tightened, and I swallowed hard, trying to keep it together.

"Take me there," I said. "Please."

The snow began to fall again, thin flakes spiraling down over the fresh-turned earth like some twisted kind of blessing. The ground, still soft from the first thaw, clung to my boots in damp clumps.

There were no markers. No headstones. Just two patches of uneven dirt, sunken slightly and dark with moisture. Graves, but only in the most technical sense. Anyone walking by might think it was just a patch of land that hadn't yet recovered from the winter.

They were tucked just outside of town, past the place where

everyone leaves their wagons for Market. Secluded. Hidden.

I didn't speak.

Didn't move.

August stood a few paces behind me, silent. I could feel his eyes on my back like a weight. The cold pressed in around me, but I barely noticed. My hands were clenched at my sides, fingers stiff from the cold and the tension that refused to ease. The kind of tension that didn't go away. That settled in my bones and stayed there.

"I will have them marked. So you can come back. Mourn them properly."

My eyes stayed fixed on the dirt. "How thoughtful."

He let out a long breath. "They're buried now. And the stage is gone. It's done."

"Done?" I laughed. The sound was brittle. "Nothing about this is done."

I turned toward him, not bothering to hide the venom in my voice. "You think this erases what happened?"

"No."

I had no one else to lash out at. No one to take the brunt of my anger. All I had was him.

"But it makes you feel better, doesn't it? Like cleaning up the blood absolves you."

He flinched, just barely. "That's not why I did it."

"No?" I took a step toward him. "Then why now? Why not then? When it mattered?" I shoved him, expecting him not to move. But he stumbled back a step, eyes still trained on the ground. It caught me off guard—how easily he let me push him. How he didn't even try to resist. For a second, I thought I saw guilt flicker in the downward tilt of his head, the way his shoulders sagged, like my words had landed exactly where

I wanted them to. But instead of satisfaction, all I felt was more rage. "Why didn't you try to stop him? You should have stopped him, August!"

Now he looked at me, and I forgot how to breathe. Tears shimmered in his eyes, and it caught me off guard. I had never seen him unravel like this before. He took a step closer, and I didn't move, too stunned by the sight of him.

"He sent some of his men to my home that day. They tortured me. Cut along my arms to drain me of my strength, drove stakes through my body, and left me barely alive on the floor. He knew that I would have tried to stop him if I had sensed what was happening." The next words came quieter. "He didn't give me a chance, Winnie."

The words struck like a blow.

Tortured. Drained. Left for dead.

I'd been so consumed by my pain, my rage, I'd never thought to ask what he'd suffered. It had been easier to blame him than to admit the truth: that he hadn't abandoned me. He'd been broken, too.

The day it happened, he was fighting his way through the crowd to get to me, pushing and clawing, desperation in every step. But his movements were sluggish, strained. His strength had been drained, his body still broken from what they'd done to him. I remembered the flash of white hair in the sea of people, the way he stumbled more than once. And now I understood why.

I looked away, the grave swimming slightly in my vision as the first real crack formed in the wall I'd built to keep him out. He hadn't known. He hadn't *let* it happen. He'd been a casualty too.

Not the same kind. Not nearly. But it twisted something in

me to realize I hadn't known the whole story either.

I turned to him. "I didn't know," I whispered.

"I tried to tell you, but your mind was far away."

I hesitated. The truth hovered just behind my teeth, sharp and dangerous. If I said it, there would be no taking it back. Would he hate me for it? Would he see me differently? My heart pounded as I weighed the silence between us.

But he deserved the truth.

"The night I came to you... my plan was to kill you."

His lips parted just slightly as if the words had struck him. "What?"

"I thought you had planned everything," I said quickly, the words tumbling from my mouth before I could stop them. "You told me it was all a game of seeing how far you could push me until I broke—and when I saw them hanging, I thought it was your final move. Your final attack."

I took a breath, but it didn't slow anything down. The words kept spilling out, desperate and raw. "But then I came to you that night and realized it wasn't you. You didn't do it. But I was already too far gone—too angry, too focused on revenge to back down. So I took your magic to stop you from stopping me. And now..."

I shook my head, tears burning behind my eyes. "It's all my fault. If I hadn't betrayed you, you would've stopped me and none of this would've happened. We wouldn't be racing toward the end of the world. I'm sorry. August, everything is my fault and—"

He cupped my face and wiped a tear that I didn't realize had fallen. "It doesn't matter now. None of it matters now."

But it did. It mattered more than anything. He pulled me in and kissed me. This kiss wasn't like the others. It wasn't built on lust or tension. It wasn't punishment or relief.

It was like he meant every inch of it.

And with it, every feeling I'd tried so hard to bury surged forward like a tidal wave. The truth rang louder than ever.

I was in love with August.

27

August

We walked in silence through town. The snow had already melted in patches along the edges, exposing dead grass and dark earth beneath, but the chill still clung to the air. I kept a few paces behind her—not to let her lead, but because I didn't trust myself to walk beside her yet. Not when my chest still ached with the weight of what I'd seen.

She hadn't cried at first. She never did. Winnie was too proud, too angry, too determined to be strong. But when she did... it undid something in me.

All this time, I thought pushing my feelings for her down was the only way to survive this. That distance would protect us both. That if I could just keep it physical—keep her angry—then maybe I could keep her alive.

But watching her break like that...

I realized too late that I hadn't protected anything. Least of all myself.

I loved her.

Gods, I loved her. And I was so fucking tired of pretending I didn't.

I let her hate me. Let her believe the worst about me. Because I thought that was easier than facing what I felt. I thought if she hated me, it would make things simpler.

It didn't.

It made everything worse.

Now, watching her walk down the street in silence, her arms wrapped tightly around herself, her head lowered against the cold, I knew I was done fighting it. All of it.

No more masks. No more distance. No more pretending.

I had spent so long trying to keep her at arm's length, and I hadn't even realized how empty that made me. But now... I couldn't go back to pretending. Not after today.

I'd fight for her now, even if I had to fight her for it.

I would let Winnie use her magic to take us back to the castle eventually, but right now, she looked like she needed this quiet walk—alone in her thoughts, surrounded by the silence she couldn't find anywhere else.

But the calm shattered when I saw Adar charging toward us.

"Bronwen!" he yelled.

She jumped like she'd seen a ghost. I stepped up next to her, ready. Though I didn't know for what.

She didn't look at me, just kept her eyes fixed ahead, wide and unfocused. Her voice came barely above a whisper. "He knows."

I frowned. "About the graves?"

She shook her head, breath catching. "About Bodaira."

Here we go.

28

Adar

They stood frozen, like statues caught mid-motion, as if they hadn't expected me to come. Or maybe they simply hadn't expected me to find out.

But I had.

Of course I had.

I was Father of the coven, and she'd gone behind my back like I was nothing.

The moment I heard what she'd done—how she went to Alden Gran in secret, confronted him without my knowledge, and stripped his connection to magic—I felt the foundation of everything Papa had built shake. That connection wasn't just his lifeline, it was his tie to the coven. And she severed it. On her own. Without counsel. Without me. If the others found out, it would spark panic, maybe even revolt. She knew that. And she did it anyway. Something in me broke.

And now, as I strode toward her, the fury burned hot and clean in my chest. She looked at me like she already knew what I was going to say. Like she knew she'd crossed a line she couldn't uncross.

August stepped slightly in front of her, but I didn't care about him. Not right now.

This was between me and Bronwen.

"I never expected you to do something like this!"

She opened her mouth to respond, but I raised my hand sharply, silencing her.

"No. That's a lie. I knew you were capable of something like this. You always act before you think! You're too impulsive, B! And this lunatic is not helping!"

August cut in. "I did not help her. I went with her, but I stayed back the entire time."

She turned to him, eyes flashing. "*Now* is the time you choose not to take up for me?"

He shrugged. "I told you he would react like this."

"I will not admit that you were right."

"Stop talking like I'm not standing right here! The coven is my responsibility—not yours."

August lifted an eyebrow. "Could've fooled me."

"You didn't do what needed to be done," she shot back.

"It's not your call to make."

"Why? Because I'm trapped in a castle? You may have taken the title because I couldn't, but it's just as much my right to make decisions."

"And you think that was the right call? They know he's a vampire now." My voice dropped. "What if they tell the coven? It took everything to keep the ones who helped us with Carrow from saying a word. What do you think happens if the whole coven finds out?"

August's eyes narrowed. "Maybe we should take this conversation somewhere more private." He gestured subtly to the crowd now pressing closer—faces pale, whispers rippling, some eyes wide with fear, others narrowed with curiosity. A few exchanged uneasy glances, edging closer to hear.

"No," I snapped, louder this time. "There's nothing left to talk about. You went too far."

A low murmur surged through the bystanders, a few stepping back as though afraid they might be caught in whatever was about to happen. The air grew tighter, the collective breath of the crowd holding steady as I turned sharply on my heel, fury still clawing at my chest. Her voice chased me.

"We'll talk more at breakfast, after you've calmed down."

I didn't stop walking. "If I even show up," I muttered under my breath.

* * *

Jonah and Darrin were already waiting for me at Darrin's house beyond the edge of town, the low flicker of candlelight making the small sitting room feel warmer than it was. Darrin's wife handed us each a steaming cup of tea before quietly excusing herself, leaving us alone with the ticking clock and the tension settling in.

I didn't sit. I couldn't.

Jonah leaned against the mantel like he owned the place, arms crossed and that too-eager gleam in his eyes. Darrin remained planted in his chair, silent and steady as always.

They didn't ask what happened. They didn't need to. Word had already made it this far considering the king and queen were spotted getting yelled at in the middle of town.

I was still burning.

Jonah looked at me and said flatly, "I know you're angry at her, but it had to be done."

I turned to him. "You're the one who told her, weren't you?"

"Yes. I knew she would handle it by any means necessary." Darrin sighed.

I paced in front of the hearth, hands clenched. "I don't want to lead through fear, Jonah. That's not what this was supposed to be."

"You don't get to choose," he said with a shrug. "Not with your gifts. If they think you're weak, they'll tear you down and I won't let that happen when there is something I can do about it."

I turned to him, the words sharp. "And what do they think now that my sister handled it for me?"

Darrin finally spoke. "They think it worked."

I blinked. "What do you mean, it worked?"

He looked up at me. "The others—the ones who were plotting to replace you—they came forward. They swore loyalty under a spellbinding oath. If they break it, they die."

The room fell quiet, save for the soft clink of cooling tea. I didn't know whether to feel relieved or sick.

"She's ruthless—but that's exactly what we needed right now," Jonah said.

Darrin placed his hand on my shoulder. "I admire that you're trying to lead like Henry did, but times have changed."

What he didn't say hung in the air between us.

You're different.

You don't have your own magic. You take. And people will not follow you because they love you. They will follow you because they're afraid.

29

Bronwen

His mouth crashed against mine the second we appeared in our chambers, and I let him. Let him drag me back, stumbling, until my spine hit the stone wall. His hands found my hips like they always did—demanding, bruising—and I answered with a bite to his bottom lip, earning a growl that vibrated straight down my spine.

"Look at me," he commanded.

He reached between us, undoing his belt with one hand while the other stayed tight on my waist, as if he thought I might vanish if he let go.

"Do you want this?" he asked, even though we both already knew the answer.

I nodded, breathless. "Yes."

"Do you want *me*?"

I did. I always had. And I knew what he was really asking. He was asking if I saw him, if I still *wanted* him despite everything. This was him trusting me with what little was left of himself.

And yes, gods, I did. I loved him so much it made my chest ache, like there was too much feeling inside me to fit in one body.

"Yes, August," I whispered.

He groaned, his mouth hovering near mine. "Always say my name like that." He turned me around, his chest to my back, breath hot against my neck as he pushed my dress up with slow, deliberate hands. "Keep your hands on the wall."

"Bossy," I muttered, but obeyed.

"I need you like this," he murmured against my ear.

When he entered me, it was rough, like it always was— but something in the rhythm slowed. Like he was trying to memorize me from the inside out.

His fingers tangled in mine, pinning them above my head as he thrust into me harder. "You feel that?" he rasped. "You're wrapped around me like you were made for this."

My legs trembled, but I didn't fall. He held me up—steady, unyielding, like I was something precious he refused to let slip away. The strength in his arms, the warmth of his body against mine, made me want to burn the image of him into my memory forever. His scent, the sound of his breath, the way his voice turned rough when he was close—it was all him, and I wanted to drown in it.

I let my head fall back against his shoulder, feeling the brush of his jaw against my temple, gasping as pleasure sparked low and hot in my belly. I wanted him in every way a person could want another. His body. His heart. His soul. The realization only made my voice shake when I whispered, "Don't stop."

"I'm not going anywhere," he growled, and in that moment, it didn't just sound like a promise—it sounded like forever.

His rhythm shifted, drawing out the tension that had been coiled in my belly. His hand slid down between my thighs, finding that aching spot that had been pulsing with need since the second he touched me. He circled it with his thumb, and I nearly cried out.

"That's it," he whispered. "Let go for me. I want to feel you unravel."

My hands scrabbled against the stone wall, trying to hold on as the pressure inside me built to a breaking point. Every thrust hit the exact place I needed him, every grind of his hand sent sparks flooding through my veins. My legs started to shake.

I shattered around him, biting down on my bottom lip to muffle the cry, stars bursting behind my eyes as he held me steady through it.

But he wasn't finished with me.

He scooped me into his arms like I weighed nothing, carrying me to the bed. His mouth never left my skin, pressing, nipping, claiming as he lowered me onto the mattress. I was still catching my breath when he shifted my hips and threw one of my legs over his shoulder, the stretch making me gasp.

August leaned in, kissing me again—slow, bruising, and full of heat—and thrust into me in a way that made my spine arch and my fingers claw the sheets.

"Look at me," he growled.

I did. And gods, the way he looked at me—like I was his world. Like he couldn't get enough. It was the kind of look I knew I'd carry with me for the rest of my life.

He kissed me again, deeper this time, and as my lips parted for him, he bit down. Hard. Not cruel, but claiming. Sharp enough that I tasted blood. A low groan tore from his chest, and he sucked the blood from my lip, slow and savoring, like it was the finest thing he'd ever tasted.

He gripped my hips tighter, pulling me flush against him,

and began to thrust again. The sounds of our bodies filled the room, and the burn in his eyes never left mine.

My breath hitched with every thrust, pleasure twisting through me again, raw and sharp and overwhelming. He kissed me again, swallowing my moans, then broke the kiss to murmur, "Let go for me again."

I shook my head, trembling.

His mouth brushed my ear. "Come on, baby, you can do it."

The words shattered what was left of my restraint. I broke with a helpless cry, the world going bright and breathless. His pace quickened, body taut with restraint that was quickly unraveling. I arched into him, fingers digging into his back. Then with one final thrust, he buried himself deep, groaning against my throat as he spilled inside me, shaking with the force of it.

* * *

The music pulsed around me, wild and untamed. Drums pounded like a heartbeat, and violins shrieked with a tempo that made the air itself vibrate. My dress shimmered beneath the candlelight, the hem brushing my ankles as I twirled, caught up in the frenzy of sound and movement. Laughter and shouts rose from the dancers around us, all swept into the chaotic rhythm of the night, bodies moving fast and fearless.

I looked up toward the stage where our thrones sat—where August always watched me. But tonight, it was empty.

Because he was here.

His hand caught mine, firm and warm, as he spun me again.

The corners of his mouth quirked in that maddening, knowing way, and for a moment, I forgot how to breathe. He wasn't watching from afar tonight.

He was dancing with me.

I laughed breathlessly, stumbling a little as he pulled me through the sea of bodies, the music spinning faster and louder around us.

"I don't know why you chose to live in town. This is amazing."

He caught me with an arm around my waist, steadying me. "I never had something worth staying for."

The way he looked at me then stole whatever breath I had left.

* * *

I woke slowly, the weight of sleep still thick in my limbs after we spent most of the night dancing. The bed was warm, the air around it cool. But something felt... off.

The other side of the bed was empty.

My eyes opened fully, and I listened. A faint sound in the washroom. He was in there.

I sat up, the sheet sliding down my bare skin, and let the silence stretch. It was rare to wake without him beside me. Rare to feel alone, even for a moment.

My feet hit the floor softly as I stood, brushing the tangled mess of hair from my face. I stretched slowly, my muscles still sore from the night before.

That's when I saw it.

Draped over the back of the cushioned chair across the room was a dress. Deep purple. Long-sleeved. Familiar.

Too familiar.

I went still.

Even from across the room, I recognized the stitching. The particular bend in the shape of the sleeves. The way the hem had been slightly uneven, not from carelessness, but because Mama had run out of the proper thread and refused to wait another day to finish it. I staggered forward a step. No. It couldn't be.

But it was.

I nearly fell to my knees as I crossed the room. My hand reached for it with a tremble I couldn't stop. Fingers brushing fabric. Soft. Worn in places. Real. I lifted the dress from the chair, clutching it to my chest.

My mother made this.

My breath shuddered as the weight of it sank into me. The past, the loss, the impossible tenderness of it being here—of it surviving. I thought I'd never see another one of her creations after finding our home burnt to ashes. Tears welled in my eyes before I could blink them away.

How did he find this?

The washroom door creaked open behind me. I heard his steps cross the floor. "I was hoping you'd find it."

I turned, the dress still clutched in my hands.

August stood there, steam curling faintly behind him from the room he'd just left. His white-blond hair was damp, pushed back from his face. Droplets traced the lines of his chest, catching on the ridges of muscle, making him look less like a man and more like something carved from divine hands.

A god, in every sense of the word.

But it was his expression that undid me. He lit up when he saw I was holding the dress, like the moment mattered as much to him as it did to me. Like he knew exactly what this meant.

"Where did you find this?"

He hesitated, then ran a hand through his damp hair. "When you visit your brother every week, I... go into town, too."

I blinked at him. "What?"

He gave a small, crooked smile. "No one recognized me with my hood on. Or if they did, they didn't dare say anything." He stepped closer. "I went to the stores and through the alleys. I asked anyone I recognized from Market if they had anything Odelia made. Most people said no. Said they burned the clothes she made after the executions—worried it was cursed, or spelled somehow. Superstition."

A muscle in his jaw flexed. "But a few hadn't. Some still had pieces hidden away. I gave them more coin than they'd ever see again in their lives. Enough that they couldn't refuse."

He turned and walked over to the armoire.

My breath caught as he pulled it open and began carefully lifting out more pieces—folded tunics, skirts, a patched jacket with a crooked button, all faded but intact.

"I know some of these are men's clothing," he said, "but I thought you'd like them anyway. Or maybe you could give them to Ad—"

I didn't let him finish.

I launched forward, the dress still in my hand, and wrapped my arms around his neck. I kissed him hard, fiercely, my tears still wet on my cheeks.

He caught me instantly, his arms locking around my waist like he'd been waiting for this—for me—to fall into him.

And I did.

* * *

I sat at the bakery, fingers curled tightly around a lukewarm cup of tea I hadn't even taken a sip of. The scent of fresh bread usually brought me a strange sense of comfort—of warmth and memory. But today it only made the minutes feel heavier, thicker.

Adar was never late. He was always here first, waiting at our usual table, already sipping something warm and pushing a small pastry in my direction before I even sat down. But now... the chair across from me remained stubbornly empty.

I tried not to fidget, yet my foot tapped beneath the table. Doubt crawled up my spine like cold fingers. What if he was still mad at me? Surely he was over it by now.

It was necessary.

But maybe I shouldn't tell him just how much I enjoyed doing it.

The coven was a sacrifice I had to make when I made the deal with August. I couldn't be the Mother they needed me to be when I was spending all of my time fighting for their freedom. I picked at the seam of my sleeve, suddenly aware of the fabric against my skin. My eyes drifted down, and I smiled faintly.

The dress I wore today was one August had given me that morning. It was a little big and definitely not the usual style I preferred—looser, more delicate in its stitching—but it didn't matter. Not when it was a piece of her. Of home.

The bell above the bakery door jingled and I glanced up.

Adar walked in, his expression unreadable as he scanned the room. But when his eyes found mine, he rolled them—just slightly—and I bit back a smile. He wasn't mad anymore. I could see it in the subtle twitch at the corner of his mouth, the way he walked toward me without hesitation.

"I thought you weren't coming."

He sat in the chair across from me. "I wanted to make you worry for a minute."

30

Bronwen

"The whore—no, that's not right. *Horse.* The horse... ran. Well, that was anticlimactic. I was a little more excited when I thought it said whore."

Benedict let out an audible huff. "I'll probably regret asking, but what are you doing?"

"August is trying to teach me how to read the old tongue. He wrote out some sentences for me to practice."

We'd spent the past few weeks working hard in the archives, trying to piece together anything useful. But truthfully, I knew I wasn't much help. Not when I couldn't read most of the tomes and was stuck staring at strange illustrations, trying to guess what any of it meant.

"Could you read them in your head? I'm trying to concentrate."

"I'll try," I muttered.

August had been gone for hours—off doing some mysterious, kingly thing he deemed too dangerous to bring me along for. And of course, the safest place for me in his eyes was here. With Benedict.

At first, I thought me having to be with him at all times was about my safety. But now I'd started to realize that he was just so obsessed with me and couldn't admit it.

And now? We were so far past that.

I flipped the page over and tried to focus again.

La... Lav... Lavina.

Ugh. Way to kill a mood.

Lavina is a... b... bi—"Bitch!" I burst out, grinning. "Ha! Lavina is a bitch. That's a good one."

Benedict slammed his book shut hard enough to make the table rattle.

"Why does he have you here?"

I blinked at him. "To help?"

"Is that what you're doing? *Helping*?"

"I—" I faltered. "I don't know. He said I needed to help."

Benedict leaned back in his chair, pinching the bridge of his nose. "I'm sorry. I'm just frustrated."

"You don't think I am?"

"It doesn't seem like it. You were more useful before the two of you started doing... whatever it is you're doing."

I didn't answer. Instead, I pushed the papers aside and stood from the table, the chair creaking as I walked away. My fingers drifted across the surface of the nearest shelf, trailing dust and the cool edges of relics I couldn't name. Bits of forgotten history that meant everything to someone once—and maybe nothing now.

Maybe that was what August and I were destined to become.

The silence pressed in.

Since August and I had found our way back to each other, I'd been living in a comfortable delusion. Letting myself feel safe and distracted. Like maybe this could be our life. Like we had more time than we actually did.

But we didn't.

We had less than two months.

Less than two months before the Blood Moon.

And the fear that had been buried under stolen moments and warm sheets began to bubble up again. I had lost too many things. I couldn't lose him, too.

I stopped in front of a cracked glass case and stared at the object inside without seeing it. My heart thudded harder.

"He can't come back," I said suddenly, turning to Benedict. "I didn't do what I did for nothing."

He looked up slowly, eyes narrowing. "What did you do?"

"I killed him." It was barely above a whisper. "I killed Carrow. I just didn't know he would take over August's body."

Before he could react, August burst through the doors, smiling from ear to ear.

"I have an idea. One that will get you out of the archives and one that might actually help us."

I quickly smoothed my expression. I didn't want him to see me worried when I knew he spent his nights restless. Tossing and turning from whatever nightmare he had conjured up. It wasn't me and the mark doing it. There hadn't been a day when he didn't feed on me for as long as I could remember. It was Carrow and the Blood Moon.

"And what would that be?" I asked as I plastered a smile on.

"Would you like to see the armory, Winnie?"

I didn't have to fake a smile when he said that.

We left the archives behind, the door groaning shut behind us as August led me down a corridor I hadn't been through before. The deeper we went, the quieter the castle became. This hall felt abandoned with its torches barely flickering.

He stopped at a heavy wooden door and pushed it open. The scent of oiled leather and cold steel filled my lungs as I stepped through and froze.

Weapons lined the walls. Blades of every shape and size, some polished to a mirror shine, others ancient and tarnished with age. Swords, axes, daggers, even staves and spears, all arranged in neat rows like an army waiting to be summoned. The collection stretched down the length of the room, enough to outfit the entire Legion.

And when I focused, I could hear the hum of magic inside some of them—soft and steady like a heartbeat, others sharp and erratic like a whispering scream.

"Gods," I whispered. "It's like a graveyard of wars." I turned to August and put my hands on my hips. "Why haven't you shown me this already? It's like a dream come true."

"I was too mad at you before."

I shoved him, not that he budged an inch.

"Benedict's been trying to match the blades we marked, but it's harder than expected. A lot of them look similar to the sketches we've got. I figured maybe you could sort through what's here—see which ones are humming with magic—and we'll narrow it down from there."

"I'll see what I can do."

I moved to the nearest wall, my fingers gliding over the hilts and blades, the metal cool beneath my skin. I paused at each one, feeling for the magic. Most were silent, but one made me stop. The magic curled around it like smoke, faint but undeniable.

I pulled it from the wall, surprised by the weight and how natural it felt in my grip. My pulse kicked up as I turned it in my hand. The blade glimmered faintly in the low light, etched with symbols I didn't recognize.

This one had a lot of power.

I turned around and pointed it at August. "This one."

In a blur, he was behind me, his chest pressing lightly to my back as he reached around to lower my hand with a firm grip.

"Let's not point magical blades at me when we don't know what they do," he said, his voice low near my ear. "Unless you're trying to get rid of me early."

I turned and smiled at him, letting it linger just long enough to make him narrow his eyes suspiciously before I walked away. I carried the blade over to the entrance and set it down carefully near the door.

Then I returned to the wall, ready to start again, fingers trailing over the next row of weapons. By the time I made it to the end of the first row—which must have held close to a hundred blades—I had found three more humming with magic. Some of the magic felt familiar. But others were foreign and strange, buzzing against my skin like static, pulling at the edges of my awareness in ways that made me uneasy.

We kept those separate from the others.

I started down the second row, slower now, the weight of the task settling into my bones. Then a sword caught my attention. The blade was long and elegant, forged of dark steel that reflected almost no light. Its hilt was wrapped in soft black leather, worn just enough to hint at use, and a single crimson jewel sat in the center of the crossguard. It looked regal, dangerous, and beautiful.

I reached for it and felt no magic. Just cold metal and perfect balance.

Still, I didn't put it back.

I stepped back from the wall and shifted the sword between my hands, letting the familiar motion of testing its weight ground me. I moved like I was preparing to spar, wrists rotating, feeling the way it moved through the air.

"Do you feel something in that one?"

"No," I said, still turning the sword slowly in my hands. "It's just... beautiful. The balance, the way it moves."

I glanced up and froze.

August had crossed the room without me noticing, grabbing a sword from the first row—one I had already deemed empty of magic. He turned it in his hands once, testing its weight with a flick of his wrist, before sliding into a fighting stance.

Then he tilted his chin and gave me that infuriating little smirk.

I just stood there, blinking at him. Shocked.

"What?" he asked.

I blinked again. "I didn't know you knew how to wield a blade."

"I've lived for centuries," he said with a lazy shrug. "You pick up more than a few skills when boredom is your most persistent companion. There are things I can do that would probably surprise you."

I smiled. "I can't wait to find out just how many surprises you're hiding."

He motioned me forward with a flick of his fingers. "Come on then. Remind me how you took down three Legion soldiers on your own."

I approached cautiously, tightening my grip on the hilt. Our swords met with a clean, sharp clang that echoed off the stone walls. I stepped back and swung again, testing his defense. He parried easily, his movements fluid, effortless.

We circled each other, our blades clashing again and again, the sound of steel ringing out between us. My breath came quicker, arms warming from the exertion as I twisted and ducked, trying to catch him off guard. He smirked at every failed attempt, clearly enjoying himself.

I feigned a left swing, then shifted my weight and came at him from the right. He blocked it just in time, and I caught a flicker of something serious in his eyes—like maybe he hadn't expected me to move that fast.

But then, just as I moved in again, ready to press my advantage, he vanished in a blink. He was behind me, his blade already lifted.

I spun, scowling. "That's cheating!"

He raised a brow. "It's not cheating; it's using my strengths."

I stomped my foot, half laughing, half annoyed. "Then I want fangs and speed too! That only seems fair."

His smirk faded, eyes locking on mine with an intensity that made my breath catch. "Would you really want that?"

I hesitated, the question catching me off guard. "I haven't really thought about it," I admitted. "But... I don't like the idea of aging while you stay flawlessly young. That doesn't exactly seem fair either."

He took a step back, raising his sword again. "I don't know," he said, the edge of a smile tugging at his lips, "I'm not sure I could handle eternity with your attitude."

31

August

Dinner had gone exactly as it always did: tense, drawn out, a chess match of veiled insults and subtle threats. And Winnie... she didn't just sit through it. She *thrived*.

She smiled at the cruelty. Tilted her head when someone tried to bait her. And when Lavina tried to jab at her with some cutting remark about manners or bloodlines or whatever bullshit she was stretching to be offended by—Winnie gave her a look that made the entire table fall silent.

Gods, it turned me on so badly I didn't even wait for dessert. I just stood up, took her by the wrist, and led her straight back to our chambers.

She didn't ask why. She already knew.

Even now, hours later, I was still drunk on the memory of it—of her. Of the way she didn't flinch. Of how she belonged there, at that table, in that world.

Mine.

"It is so weird to see you with your siblings."

That caught me off guard.

"Why?"

"Until recently, Adar and I had always been so close."

"You were raised a lot differently from me." *Understatement of the fucking century.*

She let out a soft giggle.

"What is it?"

There was a long pause before she answered. "Mama said we didn't learn to speak until we were about five, but it didn't bother our parents. They believed we were communicating with each other some other way because to us, we were the only thing that mattered."

I turned my head slightly to look at her, but she wasn't looking at me. Her gaze was fixed somewhere beyond the ceiling.

"Mama said that once, I was in the kitchen helping her cook dinner when I suddenly stopped, ran outside with a knife, and chased off this older boy who had pushed Adar down. She had no idea how I knew something had happened. Thought it was twin intuition." Her lips curled faintly. "It wasn't until breakfast a few months later that she came to the conclusion that we were speaking through our minds. We were arguing over something that morning—huffing, glaring across the table—until I finally threw an apple at his face. She said she just... knew."

I didn't speak, letting her keep going.

"I don't remember any of that. I don't remember being able to talk to him like that, but... I don't know. It was always nice hearing her tell the story. Like there was something special about us."

"Witches are odd things."

She shot me a glare, and I couldn't help the smile that tugged at my mouth.

"I'm just saying," I said, nudging her gently, "you two are already so unique that I wouldn't be surprised if there really was something... deeper. Something that tethered you together."

"I don't know," she whispered. "I wouldn't even know how to do that if I tried. But if I could do it now, I would have aggravated him until he got over what I did."

"How was he today?"

She didn't know it, but I had followed her to the bakery earlier, keeping my distance as she wove through the bustle of Market. Last week, she'd allowed me to walk her to breakfast, but the number of people in town for Market had pulled several into my path, stopping me to talk. I'd felt her irritation simmer with each interruption until she finally told me I couldn't walk beside her anymore. So I trailed behind at a careful distance, hood drawn low, my cloak swallowing me into the crowd.

The thought of being away from her, even for a few hours, made my chest ache and my skin feel restless, like some part of me was being tugged away.

"Oh, he was fine. He tried to be short with me again but it didn't take long for me to make him laugh."

"Well, I must have rubbed off on you."

She raised her head to look at me. "Excuse me?"

"You weren't really good with people when we met whereas *I* can charm anyone."

She cut her eyes at me. "You didn't charm me! You were just so aggravating that I finally gave up and took all of my frustrations out on you."

"Sexually?"

She shoved against my chest, but I caught her wrists and tugged her toward me, the tension between us sharp and heated. I kissed her before she could fire off another retort.

"As much as I'd love to see where this argument goes," I murmured against her mouth, "it's late, and we've got another thrilling day in the archives tomorrow."

She groaned. "Lucky me."

* * *

"We have looked through every tome here and found nothing that seems remotely close to what we are looking for." The words felt bitter on my tongue. I stood by the arched window, the last tome in my hand trembling with restraint. My grip tightened until the spine cracked. Then I let it fly across the room. It hit the far wall with a dull thud, pages scattering across the stone floor.

I'd been hiding it—my frustration, my impatience. Trying to stay composed, to stay strategic. But it was getting harder each day. We were running in circles, chasing dead ends in dusty pages, and I was sick of it. We needed to try something different. Something I'd already mentioned to Benedict countless times.

"We need answers."

Benedict didn't even flinch. He was too used to my temper by now. "No," he said flatly, cutting me off like he always did when the idea came up. "Doing that is too risky."

"Doing what?" Winnie asked. She was perched on the edge of the long table. She had been so calm today, but her fingers twitching told me she was just as worried as I was.

Benedict's hesitation was brief, but telling. He didn't like this idea. He worried word of what we were doing would get out. But we were out of options now.

"He wants to question someone who knows exactly what happens," he muttered.

"Halston," I cut in.

Benedict nodded once. "Yes. But he would die before betraying Carrow."

"Not after Winnie gets her hands on him."

I glanced at her, the corner of her mouth twitching from what I said. Benedict looked between the two of us with open wariness.

"And after you get your information?" he asked, tone low. "He will come after you. He won't let it go."

"Not if we kill him."

The words left Winnie's mouth in a quiet breath, but they slammed through me like a thunderclap. I turned fully to face her, and gods help me, I smiled.

She really was terrifying. And I adored her for it.

Benedict's voice dragged me back to strategy. "How do you expect to get him without raising suspicion? He's either downstairs or with a handful of servants at all times."

"I'll do it," Winnie said before I could offer myself up.

"No," I snapped. "He's paranoid. Always has been. If he senses even a sliver of threat, he'll lash out. He won't hesitate to kill you."

Winnie stood from the table and crossed the room, her chin lifted in defiance. "He won't suspect anything. All I need is to get a hand on him. Once I do, we'll be gone before even you high-sensing vampires could notice."

Benedict muttered a curse under his breath but nodded. He knew he was outnumbered with two crazies in the room. "Fine.

Bring him here. Just make sure you land in a dark corner so he doesn't burst into flames before we can question him."

She nodded once. Then she looked at me, amusement dancing across her expression. "I need you to bite me first."

32

Bronwen

I walked down the steps with my hand covering the open wound on my neck, praying that I wouldn't come across a vampire before I got to Halston. I kept reminding myself—over and over—that the only real risk was running into Lavina or Simon, since the others remained deep underground.

And even they weren't stupid enough to mess with me anymore.

August nearly snapped the chair arm in two when I told him I planned to walk through the castle alone, blood dripping down my neck. But once he heard the full plan, he knew I was right. There wasn't a better way to get close to Halston.

I slowed my pace as I neared the dining hall. A sharp voice barked out orders beyond the heavy doors, the clank of dishes echoing behind it. Good. He was right where we expected him to be.

I grabbed the large door and began to ease it open.

"Where are the silver for—" Halston turned and froze when he saw me.

I stumbled into the room, catching myself on the nearest

chair, breathing heavily, as if I could barely stay upright. It had to be believable.

His face drained of color. "What happened?"

"Augustus. He lost cont—" I paused for a breath, eyes darting around like I couldn't focus. "He lost control and took too much."

"Oh, dear." He straightened, his eyes narrowing. "Well, you shouldn't be in here. Not like this."

"He said he was done with me!" I let tears fall as I took another weak step toward him.

The servants moved around us like ghosts, setting dishes, saying nothing. Either they were compelled or were simply pretending like nothing was happening.

Halston's mouth curled. "Of course he was. He always tires of his toys eventually." He moved closer, slowly, deliberately. "Do you think anyone will protect you in this castle? You smell like temptation, and not everyone has Augustus's self-control."

He threw up a hand as if swatting away a nuisance. "I'm sure he'd like to finish what he started. Please find your way back to him."

"No." I locked eyes with him and tried to mimic the blank glaze I'd seen on the servant August compelled in front of me. "He said to go to the great room. He wants a show tonight—to share his queen." I swallowed hard. "Please. Take me there."

Halston let out a slow, twisted laugh. "Augustus really hasn't changed. Always playing games he doesn't finish."

His hand reached out, fingers tightening around my arm in a grip that bruised. The moment he touched me, I grabbed hold of him and pulled. The dining hall vanished in a blink. The air thickened with dust and parchment as the archives formed around us.

I let go.

He stumbled, disoriented—and August was already there. He plunged a stake into Halston's chest, just shy of his heart.

August dragged him to a chair and chained him down, the metal biting into his wrists as he gasped for breath. His struggles only seemed to amuse August. Then, with a glance that promised nothing good, August reached for the table and snatched up a blade. That's when I saw it—a pile of jagged wood slivers, an assortment of blades, and a long iron rod, its edges rough and splintered like he'd ripped apart a shelf with his bare hands to forge it. He'd been busy while I was gone.

August used the blade to cut into him—deep, precise gashes over his arms, legs, and neck. Slivers of wood followed each slice, wedged into place to stop the wounds from closing. Blood pooled beneath him.

"Augustus, what is this?" Halston winced, the sound of his strained laugh catching in his throat.

August leaned in close, wildness burning in his eyes. Anger and satisfaction twisted together on his face. "I used your methods."

My stomach turned. Halston had been the one who tortured August while my parents were being hunted. I wanted to kill him right then—every part of me screamed for it—but we needed him alive for now.

His eyes flicked over August. A slow, twisted smile spread across his face, as if he recognized the predator before him and welcomed it. "And to what do I owe this pleasure?"

"We're looking for something. And you're going to help us find it."

"Oh, am I?" Halston trembled as he barely held his head up.

"And what might that be?"

"The spelled blade used to transfer Carrow's soul."

Halston's expression shifted. "I will tell you no such thing."

August shrugged. "I was hoping you'd say that."

He moved like a shadow, smooth and silent, picking up the long iron rod from the table. Without hesitation, he plunged the tip into the cut on Halston's thigh. The vampire screamed, arching against his restraints.

"That one was for every time you laid a hand on me," August said quietly.

He leaned close and whispered something I couldn't hear, then drove the rod into Halston's abdomen. Halston howled. Benedict stood at the edge of the room, unmoving. He looked paler, as though he was forcing himself not to turn away. His hands were clenched behind his back, and his gaze didn't quite meet mine.

August grabbed Halston's jaw, forcing his head up. "Where is it?"

Halston's voice was shredded with pain. "I'll never—"

Another strike. A blade this time, dragged with exacting control across Halston's clavicle. Blood spilled. A splatter hit the stone beside my foot.

I should have been disgusted. I should have looked away.

But I didn't.

Watching August unravel him thread by thread was... intoxicating. This wasn't madness. Or maybe it was—but it was beautiful. There was a darkness in him that answered the one in me, and every time I thought I'd seen the worst of it, I only found more to want.

I stepped closer, silently, my gaze tracing the curve of his mouth as he smiled, Halston's blood smeared across his jaw and soaking his sleeves, dripping from his hands. It wasn't just a smile—it was the expression of a predator savoring his kill while Halston begged. Not for mercy—just for breath. Every day, I saw more of what he truly was.

And I liked it.

"It is the Blade of Aros." Halston's voice broke through the trance I was in.

I had heard that before. It was one of the things that led us to a dead end.

August's gaze cut to Benedict, a silent order in his eyes. Benedict flinched and began rifling through the nearest stack of tomes with quick, deliberate movements until he found the right page. He passed it over without a word, and I stepped in beside them, leaning close enough to see.

August had been teaching me to read in the old tongue, but I was still learning. I couldn't make out the entire passage, but I recognized two words—army and dead.

The one that controls the dead.

"Where is it?" August asked Benedict.

He shook his head. "I thought it was still in Alentara."

We all turned to Halston. Even through the pain, he smiled.

"This isn't working," Benedict snapped.

August turned to him, blood splattered across his face, and smiled like a demon himself. "I knew it wouldn't. It was fun, though."

Benedict took a half-step backward, then stopped, his discomfort obvious now. "Well? What are you going to do? The name of the blade means nothing if we don't know where it is."

Before August answered, I spoke.

"We could get Adar to bring truth serum."

Benedict looked at me like I had just said the most absurd thing imaginable. "*Truth* serum?"

"Yes, truth serum."

"No. That won't work," August mumbled as he stared at Halston.

"Why not? It worked on you."

That made him pause. He finally turned to face me, the fire dimming slightly in his gaze. "No, Winnie. It didn't."

The words hit me harder than I expected.

"You lied," I whispered.

He lied back then—when I thought I was watching his truth spill out under the serum's influence. When I believed, even for a second, that he had no choice in what he told us.

But he did. He'd let us think the drug worked. He'd played along. Perfectly.

And now I had no idea what part of that night had been real, or if any of it had. I should have been furious. But instead, I felt that familiar, unwelcome thrill spread through my chest like wildfire. Because it wasn't just that he had fooled all of us—it was that he had chosen to. Controlled it. Played the game better than anyone else in the room.

"No, I told you the truth, but I knew if I told you it didn't work, you wouldn't have believed me."

That only made it worse. Or better. I couldn't tell. I didn't know which part of me was louder anymore—the girl who had once wanted to be good, or the woman who couldn't stop being drawn to the monster.

"You manipulate everything." I couldn't help but smile as I shook my head. "Even when you're bleeding out, even when you're caged, you're still pulling strings."

His gaze flickered with amusement. "And you like it."

"You don't know what I like."

"Don't I?"

We were standing too close now. The room seemed to tilt around us, heat and blood and magic threading the air between us like wire. It was too much. But before I could say another word, Halston let out a low groan from behind him. A twitch of life he hadn't earned.

August's jaw tensed. He stepped back, the moment shattered. "Right," he said. "Back to work."

He leaned forward, his wild eyes locked on Halston's as he gripped the arms of the chair. "Last chance to tell me where it is," he said.

Halston spat in August's face.

August didn't flinch. He just smiled, slow and cold, and wiped the blood and spit from his cheek with the back of his hand. He stood and walked out of the room. I glanced at Benedict, searching for some hint of where August had gone. He only shrugged.

But August wasn't gone long. And when he returned, he wasn't alone.

A woman trailed behind him, her chestnut-brown hair tangled and her face streaked with tears. At first, I didn't recognize her. But when Halston sucked in a breath like he'd been stabbed again, I remembered—the woman he danced with at the parties. The one he whispered to in the corners, touching her hand like it meant something.

"Do not bring her into this," Halston rasped.

August didn't answer. He took her by the wrist and dragged her farther into the room. Each step she took brought a new scream as her skin began to blister under the faint sunlight pouring through the high windows.

"Tell me where it is," August said again.

Halston's entire body was shaking. "It's under your throne. In the great room."

Benedict was gone. Halston glanced between the two of us and for the first time, I saw something more human in the monster than I had ever seen. Benedict stepped into the room again with something wrapped in cloth. He pulled it out to reveal a silver dagger with a black jewel and carvings on the hilt.

August's eyes lit up, as if he finally saw the end. He glanced back at Halston, his grip on the woman tightening as if daring Halston to breathe wrong. "You're not lying, are you?"

"No. That is what is used to bring Carrow back. Please just let her go."

August stared at him for a moment before he nodded.

"Okay." August gave her the gentlest push—like it meant nothing at all. The sunlight caught her instantly. One step, and she erupted into flames. Halston screamed like his soul was being ripped apart. Benedict recoiled, slamming his back into the wall, horror carved into every line of his face. The fire devoured her completely, and when there was nothing left, it vanished too. No embers. No smoke. Not even the scent of ash. As if she had been erased.

August turned to me and shrugged. "Can't have witnesses."

I didn't need him to say it. I stepped forward, locking eyes with Halston one last time. The strong will he once had was gone—his body broken, his mind shattered. I grabbed his arm with one hand, feeling the thrum of his power beneath my grip, and summoned his magic. My other hand rose, fingers curling in the air as I willed his heart to tear free and come to me.

He didn't scream this time.

33

Bronwen

"Now what?" Benedict stepped from the shadows, his hands trembling slightly as he handed August the blade.

August turned it over in his hands, his eyes narrowing before running his thumb slowly over the hilt. "We have to destroy it," he said as though the decision had already rooted itself deep inside him.

August didn't hesitate. He turned to me and held it out.

The blade was cold in my hands, the metal humming like it was alive. I turned it slowly, the black jewel set into the hilt catching the low light, refracting it in a strange, sickly pattern. The carvings were ancient, but I could feel the spellwork beneath each line as if it was just created. It pulsed. Like a second heartbeat, thudding faintly in my palm.

"The jewel almost seems alive," I muttered, unable to tear my eyes away. I knew we had read about it, but all of the information I had learned in the past few months meshed together.

Benedict answered. "There isn't much about it in our records. But it's said to control the dead. The wielder feeds it souls, and in return, the blade can raise an army from the grave."

"Feeds it souls," I repeated, my stomach twisting. The stone felt alive because it *was* alive in a sense. A world created to hold souls, but I wondered what inside it hungered for souls.

I looked up at August. He was watching me too closely, like he already knew what I was thinking.

"She spelled it," I said slowly, "to hold his soul. And when someone sacrifices another soul to it, that's when he moves—he leaves the blade and inhabits the body." I glanced down at the stone again. "I think he is in there."

August's jaw tightened.

"If I take the magic from it," I continued, "it will be useless. And there will be no way for him to take your body. This little world will be destroyed, and he will never be able to come back."

August didn't say anything, but his eyes shone brightly. We were finally at the end.

I wrapped my hand around the hilt. The moment my fingers closed over it, a jolt of energy raced through me. My knees nearly buckled. I steadied myself, exhaled slowly, and shut my eyes. The magic came like a tide.

Dark, hungry, violent.

Whispers poured into my mind—thousands of voices, all speaking at once, crawling over each other. A scraping sound filled my ears, like claws dragging across stone. Then something sharper surged through my hand. A cold spike of pain drove up my arm, curling through my chest, coiling around my ribs. It found my lungs and squeezed.

I gasped—but no air came.

I dropped the blade as the world tilted and the floor rushed toward me. But I didn't hit it. Arms caught me—strong, steady, smelling of cedar and smoke.

August.

I tried to open my eyes. Tried to speak. But there was no strength left. Only the sound of his voice, soft and low, murmuring something I couldn't understand. His hand brushed the hair from my face.

Then there was nothing but darkness. But even there, I could still feel him holding on to me.

And I didn't want to let go.

I was running. The ground beneath my feet was scorched black, cracked open like a wound. The sky above churned red and gray, clouds moving like smoke. Twisted trees clawed toward the heavens with skeletal branches. Something screamed in the distance—a high, keening sound that made my blood turn to ice.

I didn't know where I was going, only that I had to run. That if I stopped, I wouldn't make it out.

Shadows moved between the broken trees—monsters, grotesque and disfigured. One turned as I passed. Its face was half-melted, its eyes glowing with hunger. Beside it, people staggered like puppets with strings cut, their limbs stiff and jerking. Not quite dead, not quite alive.

One locked eyes with me—milky white, soulless. Its mouth opened, and in a voice that sounded both ancient and broken, it said, "It comes at a price. It always comes at a price."

I stumbled back, heart racing, and turned to run again.

Through fog, through rot, through the broken remnants of a world that felt cursed.

Then I saw him.

Carrow.

He stood in the path ahead, but something was off. His posture uncertain, his face twisted in confusion—as if he had never seen me before. That's when it hit me.

It wasn't Carrow. Not the one who hunted me. Not the one who planned to take August's body.

It was Malachi. The last soul Carrow had ripped from their body so he could make it his own.

Oh gods.

I was in the stone.

I turned, trying to escape before he could speak, but a hand grabbed my wrist—firm, cold. I spun around and slammed into a figure with brown hair, grayish skin, and ears that tapered into sharp points. His eyes were the color of ash, and they narrowed at me.

"What are you doing here?" he asked, teeth bared.

And I knew. This—this was Carrow. Not the shell he wore. Not the polished image he used to control others. This was what he truly looked like.

And I had just stepped into his world.

His grip tightened like a vice as I thrashed in his grasp, his cold fingers digging into my skin. Panic rose sharp and fast in my chest.

"What are the two of you trying to do?" he hissed, voice guttural and laced with something inhuman.

I shoved at his chest, but it was like trying to move stone. "Let me go! Let me go!" I screamed.

"Let me go!" I screamed as my vision darkened. I gasped as the air rushed to my lungs. My eyes flew open, my heart still racing, breath shallow. I was no longer in the cursed place, no longer in Carrow's twisted world.

I was in our room. In our bed.

August's arms were wrapped tightly around me, grounding me. One of his hands was threaded gently through my hair, the other pressed protectively to my waist.

"Winnie," he murmured. "You're okay. It's me. I've got you."

"What happened? Where is the blade?"

"Benedict locked it away."

"Did it work? Did we stop him?"

He hesitated. "I don't think so."

I opened my mouth to respond, but the moment I tried to push myself upright, a jarring, unnatural sensation shot through my left hand. I froze.

Black veins curled and twisted up my hand and forearm, pulsing beneath the surface of my skin like something alive. They were raised—protruding—and the skin around them felt tight, wrong.

I stared at it, heart sinking, throat dry. "August... what is this?"

His face was tight with worry, but he didn't hesitate. "It's the magic from the stone. It fought back when you tried to take it. The room went dark and it seemed to swallow your soul before letting you back out."

I looked down at my hand again. "So I failed," I whispered. The words tasted like ash.

"No," he said immediately, but the tension in his jaw betrayed him. "You didn't fail. You tried. You fought it harder than anyone else ever could have. But... it didn't let go."

I shook my head slowly. The chill that had crept over me since waking tightened in my chest. "I couldn't destroy it."

August leaned forward, brushing a strand of hair from my cheek. "You survived it. That means something. We'll figure out the rest." He kissed my cheek. "We still have time."

I wasn't sure if that was true. But I wanted to believe him. Gods, I needed to believe him.

*　*　*

Days bled together.

More searching. More sleepless nights hunched over old tomes and scrolls, chasing threads that unraveled as quickly as we touched them. The dark veins in my arm remained—constant, aching, a reminder of what I'd failed to do.

August had gone to speak with Varric—the mad one who mumbled things that made no sense. He said he'd go alone. Said I needed rest.

But when he came back, hours later, I could tell.

He stood as he always did, tall, composed, jaw set in that unyielding way. But his eyes had given up pretending. They were heavy, holding the weight of whatever he'd heard. I didn't ask what Varric said. I just sat beside him and laced my fingers through his.

That night, the castle was quieter than usual. No servants bustling past our door. No echoing footsteps in the halls.

He lit a fire, the low orange glow flickering against his pale skin, and I curled near it, pulling my knees in. A moment later, he settled behind me, his legs stretched out, pulling me between them like I might break apart if he didn't hold me together.

"You should sleep," he murmured against my hair.

"I can't," I whispered back.

His lips brushed my shoulder, and when I turned toward him, he was looking at me like I was something sacred. His hand traced the curve of my jaw, down to my collarbone.

"You're still trembling," he said softly.

"You're still pretending you're okay."

His mouth found mine—soft at first, familiar. Then deeper, like each breath fed something hungrier between us. His hands slid beneath my shift. "You've ruined me, Winnie," he breathed against my neck.

I ran my hands through his hair. "Isn't that what you wanted?"

He lifted me into his lap, our foreheads touching, breaths mingling. "Tell me what you need," he rasped.

"You. Just you."

He laid me back on the rug before the fire. His hands undressed me with unhurried reverence, his mouth following. When he finally pushed into me, our gasps tangled. He moved slowly, brushing hair from my face, watching me like he was memorizing each moment.

"You are my reason," he said, voice breaking.

"Don't stop," I begged.

"Never."

And he didn't.

We moved together like we'd always been meant to, a rhythm that felt older than us both. My name on his lips, his on mine. When it was over, we stayed tangled on the rug, skin damp, hearts pounding as one. We didn't say the words. We didn't have to.

It was in the way his hand kept tracing the line of my spine.

In the way I gripped his wrist, unwilling to let him go.

In the way we held each other long after the embers cooled,

as if letting go might break the fragile world we'd built in that moment.

as if letting go might break the fragile world we'd built in that moment.

34

August

She was still asleep.

The low embers in the hearth cast a faint orange glow across her bare skin, illuminating the curve of her back, the hollow of her throat, the soft rise and fall of her chest. Her dark hair was spread out, wild and tangled from my fingers. I didn't dare move.

I just stared.

Memorizing her. Every freckle. Every lash.

The way her lips parted like she was breathing out a final word. My hand hovered above her shoulder, aching to touch, to trace the heat of her skin, but I stayed still—like if I moved too fast, she might disappear.

She was here. She had chosen to stay.

Gods, what was I doing?

I should've let her go a long time ago. I told myself over and over again that keeping her close was about protection. That it was about stopping Carrow. But now, watching her like this, I couldn't pretend anymore. She wasn't just the key to ending this.

She was everything.

I let my fingers trail down her spine. She shifted slightly, sighing in her sleep. Her voice echoed in my mind—*You. Just you.* She hadn't said it like a demand. She'd said it like a truth, as if it had always been me.

And I knew then I couldn't keep being selfish.

Carefully, I lifted the edge of the blanket, exposing her left arm. The veins were still there—dark, raised, like something poisonous burned into her flesh. She'd tried to act like it didn't bother her, but I'd seen the way her fingers twitched when she thought no one was watching. The way her gaze lingered on it like she was trying to convince herself she was the same.

But she wasn't. And she was trying to bear it alone.

* * *

The great hall shimmered with candlelight, flames kept high in the chandeliers and far from reach, casting golden halos over the marble floor. Music echoed faintly against the vaulted ceiling, delicate and slow.

She was in my arms, her gloved hand resting lightly against my chest, her other tucked into mine as I guided her across the floor. The dress she wore was deep crimson, fitted perfectly to her figure, every curve and line made to ruin me. But it was the gloves that held my attention—elegant silk, elbow-length, and hiding the dark veins beneath.

She'd insisted on them, brushing off my concern with a smile that didn't quite reach her eyes.

But she was still the most beautiful thing in the room. In

any room.

"Look at you," I murmured as I dipped my head, lips brushing her temple. "Everyone's staring, you know. Can't blame them. You look like a goddess."

She rolled her eyes, but the smile tugging at the corner of her mouth betrayed her.

"Don't do that. Don't act like you don't know it," I whispered against her ear. "That dress, those gloves, your lips—*fuck*, Winnie. You could bring a man to his knees with a look."

Her gaze flicked up to mine, amusement dancing there.

"I should be worried," I said, letting my thumb brush over her gloved fingers. "Every man in this room wants you."

"But I'm with you," she said simply.

And gods, that undid me.

"Say that again," I breathed.

She leaned in. "I'm with you."

I pulled her closer as we turned in another slow circle, unwilling to let the moment go.

"I hope you know," I murmured, "I've never wanted anything the way I want you."

The sun was beginning to rise by the time we slipped away from the great room. The halls were quiet now—most of the castle descending into the hush of daylight, where vampires tucked themselves behind thick doors and shuttered windows.

But not us.

I walked beside her slowly, our fingers laced, stealing glances at her when she wasn't looking. I was obsessed with every inch of her.

The second our chamber door shut, I pressed her against it, my hands on her hips, my mouth on her neck.

"August," she breathed, but her hands pulled me closer.

I kissed along her jaw, her throat, the bare skin above her dress. I didn't stop until I'd guided her to the bed. I peeled the gloves from her arms with slow care, kissing her palms, her wrists, the veins she tried to hide.

She was the only thing that mattered to me. And I needed her to know it.

"Winnie," I whispered against her shoulder, lips brushing her skin. "I need to tell you something."

She blinked slowly, eyes heavy with affection and heat. "What? Do you love me or something?"

The words hit like a blade between the ribs. My breath left me. My chest ached.

"I love you," I said. "But that word—it's not enough. It doesn't explain how I feel well enough. I need something that tells you that every waking moment I have is spent thinking about you, wanting you, aching to be near you. And at night, when I used to dream of you killing me, I didn't mind— because the last thing I saw before I died was you."

Her lips parted, but I kept going.

"All I care about is you. There is nothing else. Just you. And because there isn't a word that means all of that, all I can say is this: I love you. I love you so much it hurts."

I watched her swallow, tears building slowly in her eyes. And I kissed them away before they could fall. My own eyes burned. I blinked fast, but it didn't stop the sting. My voice broke when I spoke again.

"And because I love you," I said hoarsely, "you have to leave."

"What?" She drew back, blinking at me like I'd just struck her. "No! I'm not going to leave you. We are going to fight this until the last second."

I shook my head, every part of me screaming to take it back. To pull her close and never let her go. But I couldn't be selfish any longer.

"There may be nothing we can do, but I will not stop trying to find a way to stop it." I couldn't tell her what Varric said. "But you—you have to get as far from here as you can. Get Adar and run. Go to another kingdom and hide from Carrow. I may not be able to save myself, but I will not let him have you."

She grabbed my arms, her fingers digging into my skin. "They can't do this to you if you're not here. We can run together."

"The blood in my veins puts a target on my back. They would never stop hunting me. But you—at least without me—you have a chance."

"I will not leave you," she said fiercely. "I'd rather die with you than spend the rest of my life running without you."

"I've been selfish with you since the moment I met you," I whispered. "I should never have forced you to come here."

She stared up at me, her entire body shaking. "You know you can't make me do anything. I was angry, but I came because I wanted to. Because I wanted to be with you."

I brushed my fingers down her cheek, memorizing the shape of her. Even if I still found a way to stop this, she'd never forgive me for what I was about to do. But I would carry her hatred forever if it meant she was safe.

"Still, I should've never given you that option. I should've let you go, because I knew what could happen. I knew what it might cost."

I kissed her forehead, then looked into her eyes and did the only thing that might save her.

"I will not be selfish with you anymore."

She felt it instantly—the shift in my voice, the pull of the command.

Her body went rigid. "August, no—"

"I love you, Winnie," I said, the compulsion settling deep inside her.

"August!"

"Get Adar and never stop running."

35

Bronwen

The market was alive with sound. Merchants shouted in a language I only half-understood, selling fruits the color of fire, silk scarves that rippled like water in the wind, and spices that burned my nose even as they enticed me. The sun beat down overhead, a harsh and brilliant contrast to the cold we'd left behind in Joveryn. Here, everything was dust and gold and heat. Sweat clung to my back beneath the loose cotton dress I wore, and my dark waves were pulled up in a messy knot to keep my neck cool.

Adar and I moved slowly between the stalls, pretending to be unhurried. Blending in. We'd been doing that for weeks now—moving from one place to the next, never staying long, always looking over our shoulders. Seranthia, tucked between the sea and stretches of shimmering desert, had so far proven safe. But I never felt truly safe.

Adar bartered with a vendor in a shaded stall. I stood beside him with a basket of fruit resting against my hip, the sun glinting off the gold ring still tied to the string around my neck.

It had been a month. A month since August compelled me to leave.

To never stop running.

And that's exactly what we'd been doing. We'd slip into some sun-bleached, dusty little town far from Joveryn, and Adar would try to tell me we were safe now. But somewhere deep in my bones was something screaming that I couldn't stop. That the second I let myself believe in safety, something would find us.

August thought he was protecting me, and maybe he was. Maybe if I'd stayed, I would be dead by now. But the knowledge didn't make the betrayal hurt less.

He didn't ask. He took the choice from me like he said he'd never do.

And yet, even now—sweating under this foreign sun, dressed in stolen clothes, surrounded by strangers—I missed him. I missed the way he looked at me like I was the only thing that mattered. I missed his temper, his hands, his voice in the dark.

But missing him didn't change anything. The Blood Moon was coming soon, and I could feel the magic in my arm buzzing with warning.

Had he already found a way to stop Carrow and was searching for me to bring me home? I doubted it.

I was just praying for a miracle. A way for him to stop Carrow so he could come to me and I could punch him in the face. And then kiss him.

I hated him for sending me away, and I hated myself more for still loving him.

And that I never told him.

Adar called my name, jolting me out of my thoughts. He was waving me over to another stall, where a woman with silver-streaked hair offered woven shawls dyed in shades of crimson and cobalt. I pasted on a smile and walked toward him, heart aching with every step.

I stepped up to the booth and smiled at the young girl standing behind the table with her mother. "I love the shades of green you have."

"They just came in from Joveryn," the young girl said shyly.

"Yes, I am so glad our northern neighbor is having fairer weather now. We missed trading with them these last few months," the mother said as she rested her hand on the girl's shoulder.

"How much for this one?" I asked, my fingers brushing over the deep emerald green fabric, feeling the cool, smooth weave beneath my touch.

Her eyes flicked from the cloth to my face, appraising. "Two coins."

"You should charge more," I said, tilting my head as I held the fabric up to the light.

She smiled, the fine lines at the corners of her eyes deepening. "A discount for you. It matches your eyes so well it's like it was meant for you."

I let out a small laugh, tucking a stray curl behind my ear, and reached into the pouch at my hip to pay her. She pressed the fabric into my hands with a warm nod.

"Thank you," I said, folding the fabric carefully and tucking it under my arm as we stepped away from the booth. The air shifted, hotter now that we were leaving the shade, and the market's noise softened into the background hum of distant voices and clinking coins.

"You okay?" Adar asked as we reached the edge of the market, his gaze flicking sideways to study me. "You looked... somewhere else."

I adjusted the basket on my hip and let my eyes wander over the sandy street ahead. "Just tired," I murmured, forcing my tone light, though my fingers tightened around the fabric as if it could anchor me.

He didn't believe me. I could see it in the way his brows pinched slightly. But he didn't push. We kept walking.

A group of children ran past us, laughing. For a second, I almost smiled. Then I caught sight of a man watching me from the other side of the street—too still, too focused. My stomach dropped. But then he turned, revealing a weathered face and a toothy grin as he called out to someone in the distance.

Not a threat. Not this time.

Adar stepped closer, his shoulder brushing mine. "We're safe here," he said under his breath. "You can relax."

I nodded, trying my best to give him a reassuring smile as I wrapped my new scarf around my head. "It doesn't help that our eyes aren't easily forgettable, though. If someone did want to come after us and mentioned twins with glowing green eyes, they would have people pointing in our direction."

Adar tilted his head in thought.

The street opened up to a sun-bleached cliff edge with a low stone wall built along it. Beyond, the ocean shimmered under the relentless heat. Adar leaned back against the wall, arms braced on either side, his gaze flicking between me and the view.

He shot me a sidelong look, a faint crease forming between his brows. "I hope you're not always going to be this jumpy," he teased, though there was a flicker of worry beneath his words.

I set the basket on the ledge. "He compelled me to never stop running, Adar. My mind is constantly screaming *run, run, run.* When I'm lying down at night, I feel like I'm going to be sick because I'm not doing what he told me to do. That compulsion doesn't go away." I arched a brow at him. "And unfortunately for you, he included your name in his command—so congrats, you're stuck running for the rest of your life, too."

Adar huffed a laugh under his breath. "Yeah, well, at least I make running look good," he shot back, his tone dripping with smugness.

I rolled my eyes and turned my head away from him with a sharp exhale, choosing to stare out at the horizon instead. The silence that followed stretched between us, filled only by the distant crash of waves.

A warm breeze swept over us, carrying the smell of fresh-baked pastries—sweet, buttery, and so rich it nearly made my knees give out. The craving hit me so hard my mouth flooded instantly, and the rest of the world seemed to blur for a moment.

"Will you go find where that is coming from and get me some?" I asked, the words sharper than I meant, still prickling from our argument. I crossed my arms and glared at the horizon, then forced myself to soften my expression and tilt my head toward him with an exaggerated pair of puppy-dog eyes. "Please?"

He pushed off the wall with a nod, the corner of his mouth twitching like he found my sudden change in tactics amusing. "Sure."

I looked out at the ocean, my stomach turning at the memory

of it. The boat ride here had been a nightmare—every lurch and roll sent me clutching Adar's arm like my life depended on it.

Because it had.

One hard wave would've tossed me overboard, and I knew I wouldn't have lasted long in the water.

When I'd gone to Adar the day August compelled me to leave, it was as if he'd been waiting for me, prepared. Like he'd known this was how it would end. I didn't tell Adar just how close I had gotten to August, but I felt like he knew. He never said as much, though. I think he could see I was already barely holding it together without him adding his opinion. We'd stopped by Jonah's on the way out so Adar could hand over his title of "Father" and complete control of the coven to him. Another thing that felt a little too smooth, like they'd already talked it through.

It gnawed at me that Adar had done that. Passing on the title of Father wasn't something you could just take back. It was a permanent surrender of everything our family had built. Even if, by some miracle, we made it back to Joveryn, there would be no reclaiming it. And the way he'd handed it over so decisively told me he didn't believe we ever would.

Someone cleared their throat.

"Please tell me they had grape—" The rest snagged in my throat as my gaze locked on a pair of dark, unblinking eyes. Benedict stood a few paces away, his tall frame casting a long shadow across the sun-bleached ground. His black hair was wind-tossed, his jaw shadowed with stubble, and the set of his mouth was tight, unreadable.

"Benedict?" His name came out broken.

A thousand thoughts crashed through me, all of them

slamming back to August. Had he sent Benedict? And if so, why wasn't he here himself? Was he hurt? Safe? I was angry at him for what he'd done, but if this meant I could go back to him, none of that mattered.

"I'm sorry, Bronwen," Benedict said, and there was something final in his tone that made my skin prickle.

"What?" The word was barely out before he was behind me, a cloth pressing hard over my mouth and nose. A sharp, sweet scent flooded my senses. I clawed at his arm, feeling magic hum beneath his skin, but my strength bled away before I could pull.

36

Bronwen

I woke to the feeling of lead in my veins. Heavy. Cold. Paralyzing. Every limb felt like it had been filled with stone. My head throbbed, each heartbeat a deep, aching pulse behind my eyes. My mouth was dry—so dry it felt cracked—and my tongue tasted like iron. A sickly pressure coiled around my chest, making every breath feel like I was inhaling smoke.

I tried to move—tried to open my eyes—but even that was a battle. My lashes stuck together. My body didn't feel like my own.

The world was dark. Blindingly so.

Panic surged in my chest as I jerked against unseen restraints. My hands were tied tightly behind my back, the coarse rope digging into my skin with every small movement. Something rough and musty covered my face, trapping the scent of damp cloth and earth. The same type of rope that held my hands together was wrapped around my mouth.

I shifted my weight and tried to use my shoulder to push myself up. My legs trembled, sluggish and uncooperative, and I collapsed onto my side. I inched forward, dragging myself along the ground, but the ropes dug deeper, biting into raw skin. Somewhere in the distance, a twig snapped.

"We have a surprise for you."

The voice came muffled, warped through the fabric, but close. Too close. My heart pounded in my ears. My breath came fast and shallow, dampening the gag as I tried to calm the rising tide of fear.

Footsteps crunched across leaves and twigs, growing louder. Closer. Then rough hands clamped down on my arms hard enough to bruise, yanking me forward without care. I was hauled across uneven ground, my body jolting with each jagged root and jutting stone I struck. My knees scraped raw against dirt and rock, the chill of the forest floor seeping through my clothes like ice. One of them let out a low, cruel laugh, the sound dripping with amusement at my helpless struggle, before jerking me harder just to hear me gasp.

"No." It was a whisper—broken, horrified. It wasn't mine.

Chains rattled somewhere close, the sound jagged in the still air.

A rough shove sent me forward, the impact jolting up my spine. Fingers like iron clamped down on my shoulders, forcing me to stay there, grinding me into the cold earth. I could hear their laughter above me—low, cruel, and full of amusement at how easily they could keep me there, broken and kneeling.

Before I could lift my head, the bag was ripped from over it. Fog hugged the forest floor in curling tendrils. The smell of ash and damp soil filled my nose, thick enough to choke on. I pushed myself up off the ground as best I could, head pounding.

A scream tore through the stillness, sharp and raw, ripping

through the night like something wounded beyond saving. It echoed through the woods, shuddering in my bones, a sound that didn't belong to me.

"No!"

My eyes darted toward the sound—

August.

The sight of him stole the breath from my lungs. He was bound in chains, his body restrained by thick iron cuffs that bit into his skin and wrapped tight around his wrists and throat. The vampires holding him stood tense, muscles straining as they gripped the chains, their eyes fixed warily on him like they knew how dangerous he was even restrained. Moonlight filtered through the branches above, striping his pale, furious face in silver. His bare chest heaved, and his lips were peeled back over his fangs, a low, feral growl vibrating from somewhere deep in his chest.

There were several vampires in the clearing—more than I'd realized at first. Some I recognized from the parties at the castle, faces that had once been masked by polite smiles and jeweled goblets. Others were strangers, their features sharp and unreadable, watching with the stillness of predators who didn't need to blink.

"Let her go! I am your king, and I command it!" His voice cracked with something deeper than fury—anguish sharpened into a threat. His whole body coiled with brutal intent, veins bulging as he lunged forward, yanking against the iron so violently the chains shrieked in protest. The metal bit deep into his wrists, tearing skin, blood slicking the cuffs, but still he strained forward like he could rip through steel by will alone.

He roared again, the sound raw, guttural, and edged with

desperation, barely human. "Do you hear me? Let her GO!"

One of the vampires staggered from the force of his pull, boots skidding in the dirt. The others dug in harder, shoulders braced, planting their feet like anchors to keep from being dragged toward him.

August twisted like a storm given shape—snarling, eyes wild, the whites glaring around his irises. Every muscle was wound tight, vibrating with the need to destroy. He didn't care who saw. He didn't care what shattered in the process.

This wasn't just desperation.

This was a man coming apart at the seams, fury spilling out of him like it could burn the forest to the ground.

They held him.

Barely.

"Let her go! That is an order!"

He looked feral—dangerous and unhinged, a creature poised to tear the world apart the second those chains failed.

My heart was pounding so violently it hurt. I tried to scream for him, but the gag turned it into a muffled, broken sound.

One of the vampires stepped toward him, calm in the face of his fury. "We are to protect the bloodline."

August's brow furrowed. "What? She isn't a part of the bloodline. She—"

He froze.

His gaze turned to me. Not just to my face—but lower. His eyes dropped to my stomach. His face went still.

"No," he whispered. "What have I done?"

He heard something I couldn't. Knew something I didn't.

"Winnie," he whispered, "Winnie..." He frantically looked between my face and my stomach.

And then I realized what he heard.

Another heartbeat.

It beat beneath my skin like a secret I'd never meant to carry, loud enough for him to hear, loud enough to break him.

August staggered as if the truth had slammed into him with more force than any chain could deliver. His lips parted, but no sound emerged—only the faint hitch of a breath that seemed to hollow him out from the inside. His eyes stayed locked on my stomach, wide, stricken, as if the world had narrowed to that one truth.

Hot tears blurred my vision, spilling down my cheeks. I thrashed against the gag, desperate to speak—to tell him, to deny it, to confirm it—but the ropes bit into my wrists and the words died in my throat.

"Your sacrifice for the rest of us is greatly appreciated," one of them said.

They spoke to August as they uncovered the dagger, but he didn't so much as glance away from me.

"Forgive me, Winnie," he whispered, the words frayed and trembling.

I tried to crawl toward him, dragging my knees through the dirt until they burned, but my bound hands kept me from going far. Each inch forward was agony—my shoulders screaming, wrists raw from the rope, breath tearing from my lungs. I had to stop this. I had to get to him before they did it. My pulse roared in my ears, drowning out everything else.

"Close your eyes."

I froze mid-crawl, my chest heaving. August had stopped fighting. Why wasn't he fighting them? He promised he wouldn't stop!

The full moon reached its peak, casting pale light over everything, silvering the chains and the blade glinting in the dark.

"It's time," one of the vampires said.

"Please," August said again, softer this time, almost pleading. "Close your eyes, baby."

The desperation in his voice scraped at something deep inside me, warring with every instinct I had to keep my eyes open, to fight, to not give up. I didn't want to. I wanted to see him, to hold on until the last second. But the way he said it—like it was the only thing he needed from me—broke me. My lashes lowered, and I squeezed them shut.

It didn't stop me from hearing the dagger pierce his flesh. It didn't stop the way my heart felt like it was being torn out of my chest. A groan slipped from his throat and then... nothing. No cry. Just silence and the weight of my world ending. My mark burned—throbbed—and then went quiet.

I opened my eyes.

August was bent forward as the vampires unhooked and unwound the chains, letting them fall from his body like they no longer dared hold him. He turned slightly, and the moonlight caught on the jeweled dagger buried deep in his chest, making it gleam like something proud of what it had done.

I held my breath, refusing to believe what I was seeing. Maybe it didn't work. Maybe he fought it off somehow.

He reached for the hilt, fingers curling around it with slow, deliberate certainty, as though savoring the feel. Then, with one unhurried pull, he drew the blade free, the sound of metal sliding against flesh whispering through the clearing.

He straightened to his full height, and when he turned to face me—

"Oh!" His laugh was sharp, delighted, inhuman. "What a

wonderful welcome back gift!"

He closed the distance between us, each step slow and savoring. My pulse spiked. No. *No, no, no.* I tried to kick myself backward, heels digging into the dirt, but the ropes and the ground fought me at every inch. My mind was a frantic snarl of thoughts—run, fight, scream—but my body refused to obey. He was still coming, shadow stretching over me.

He crouched in front of me, studying me like a prize. "We are going to have a marvelous time."

Then he stood again and flexed his fingers, watching the way the joints moved with an almost reverent fascination. He turned his hands over slowly, palms up, then down, inspecting each one like a man trying on a new suit and marveling at the perfect, stolen fit. His gaze roamed down to his arms, his legs, his chest—assessing, claiming. Then he stretched, like someone waking from a long sleep inside another's bones and finding them exactly to his liking.

"This body," he purred. "So strong. So perfectly broken in."

He dragged his hand over his chest where the wound had been, fingers tracing the edges of the fresh, scarred symbol burned into the skin—twisted and sharp, etched in the same cruel language carved into the blade's hilt. When August looked up again, the light in his eyes was wrong. Too bright. Too eager. And whoever was behind them wasn't August.

It wasn't just the way he spoke.

It was the way he smiled—with joy, not cruelty. The pure, victorious joy of having taken what he wanted.

August was gone.

And Carrow was here.

37

Bronwen

It had been a week. I thought. There were no windows. No lights. Sometimes no sound. Time had twisted strangely in there—stretching, curling in on itself. I had only known I was still alive because someone kept shoving bread and water under the door.

I had expected to die on the spot. I waited for him to drain me. Snap my neck. Crush me beneath his boot. But instead, he told them to lock me away.

I thought I had started to lose myself after the third day. My thoughts had looped endlessly. Was it really Carrow? Could August still have been in there, buried beneath the weight of someone else's soul?

I tugged at the metal gloves encasing my hands until my wrists ached. They'd knocked me out again after the ritual, and when I woke in this cell, the gloves were already locked in place—heavy as shackles, their cold bite digging into my skin. They weren't meant for comfort; they were meant to prevent me from pulling magic.

But magic wasn't the only weapon I had. I would make every

creature in this cursed castle pay—if I could just get out of this room, get my hands on anything sharp or heavy enough to use. Surely Carrow wouldn't leave me here forever. If he'd wanted me dead, he would have ended me the moment he saw me.

Sometimes I wondered if he was trying to drive me mad before he killed me. Papa's words replayed—*Darkness will consume you.* Was this the darkness he meant? At least Adar wasn't with me. I wondered what he thought when he couldn't find me after Benedict had taken me. I just prayed he was safe.

The door groaned open, and I shielded my eyes as candle-light spilled into the darkness. I braced myself for the usual shove of bread and water, but instead the light kept moving closer.

When my vision adjusted, I saw him—and my stomach twisted. Benedict.

"Get away from me," I bit out, my voice so hoarse it hardly sounded like mine.

He stepped toward me, and I scrambled back until my shoulders hit the cold wall, my pulse pounding.

"Bronwen." He lifted a hand as if he meant no harm.

"I am going to kill you," I said, meaning every word.

"I'm sorry, but I had no other choice." He took a breath, as if steadying himself for confession. "Once I found out who you were—what you did to Carrow—I couldn't let you go."

He shifted his weight, glancing briefly toward the door. "If Carrow returned and found out you were here, he'd punish us all. All I've ever wanted was to leave this place, to make a life of my own, but I was never given any freedom. I was kept on a shelf as his backup plan." His gaze flicked back to me, sharp with something between guilt and resolve. "And now—with this, with you—I hope he'll reward me with freedom."

I said nothing. No matter what reason he had, it wasn't enough.

"Benedict." August's voice filled the room, and for one heartbeat, a fragile peace bloomed in me—familiar, aching, and almost enough to make me believe it was really him.

But then it shattered.

He was gone.

August was gone. And the truth of it hit like a blade between my ribs. The man before me wore his face, his voice, his body—everything I loved—but there was nothing behind those eyes that belonged to him anymore.

It was like watching a ghost wear his skin, and every instinct screamed to reach for him even as my stomach turned. My chest tightened until it hurt, a raw mix of grief, rage, and disbelief. I wanted to cry, to scream, to tear him away from whatever darkness had taken him—but I was frozen, pinned by the horror of knowing he would never look at me the same way again.

And still... his body stood before me.

Benedict quickly dropped his gaze, head bowed in submission. "I will leave you."

"No, I may need your assistance in a moment."

August—*Carrow*—crouched in front of me, dropping down so quickly it startled me. His eyes lit up with something wild, and he leaned in, grinning as though he'd just unwrapped a long-awaited gift.

"A baby!" he exclaimed, the words bursting out of him with an almost giddy excitement.

I covered my stomach with my hand, the instinct protective and fierce, even as my pulse thundered in my ears.

He gave a low chuckle. "It was so thoughtful of the two of you to continue my line for me. Poetic, really. August—so noble, so tortured—unknowingly creating the vessel for his own replacement." He leaned in closer until I could feel the cold echo of his breath, and the scent of blood hit me hard. "I've had quite the dilemma these past few days. You see, I *despise* witches. Filthy, conniving little things." He let the silence stretch until it felt heavy in my chest. "Do I really want my next body to be some twisted fusion of a witch and a vampire?"

I drew my legs up to shield my belly, but it wouldn't matter.

"Normally, the answer would be no. But then you killed me, Bronwen. You reached inside and pulled the magic out with your bare hands. I haven't seen anything that divine since the world shifted. That power... that fire... that rage. It was *exquisite.*"

He glanced down at his arms, flexing his fingers, admiring the stolen form like a fine robe. "Augustus's body is a marvel. Stronger than I anticipated. But your child?" He smiled. "A baby born from the two of you? I could carve empires from its bones. Can you imagine what I could become?" Then his tone dropped. "But can I risk keeping you alive long enough to give it to me? That's where my dilemma lies."

He reached up and brushed my hair from my face. I tried to swat him away, but he grabbed my wrists and examined the glove. "Ah, yes. How do you like these? I considered cutting your hands off, but then I'd risk you bleeding out before I decided what to do with you."

I ripped my hand away. "Don't hurt the baby," I whispered.

He tilted his head. "I won't, if you make a deal with me."

I stayed silent. Because if I spoke, I might scream. And if

I screamed, I knew he'd hurt me just to hear what I sounded like broken.

"I will let you continue the pregnancy," he said, his hand lifting to trace a mockingly gentle line down my cheek before gripping my jaw just a little too hard, "but while you do, you will be the obedient little wife I want you to be." His smile widened, predatory and sure of itself. "Do as I say, and no harm will come to the child."

I stiffened, heat rising in my chest. "Why don't you just compel me to be what you want me to be?" I spat the words, the taste of them bitter.

He tilted his head as though amused. "That would have made this all so much easier…" He shifted slightly, his face angling toward my ear. His breath ghosted across my skin, sending a shiver down my spine. "But it seems compulsion was linked to Augustus's soul, not his body, and I am unable to do it." He drew back just enough to meet my gaze again, his eyes glinting with cold amusement. "But I do not need compulsion with you. You will do as I say."

My hands curled into fists inside the gloves. "I am going to make you pay."

"Do not push me, witch," he hissed. "I have no need for you or that baby. I am already teetering on killing you where you sit. You push me one step further, and I will rip it from your body."

The cold certainty in his tone turned my stomach. I knew he wasn't bluffing. I had no protection here—nothing to stop him if he decided to follow through. For now, there was only one choice: endure and bide my time until I could find a way to escape.

His expression shifted, dark amusement curling into something hungrier. His gaze dragged slowly over me before he leaned in. "Being my wife also means letting me feed whenever I want to. And I have been craving you since I got into this body." He paused there, as if savoring the thought, his lips curling in a slow, knowing smile. "It's as if his needs have been left in this body. His cravings."

A cold wave of dread crawled up my spine. My stomach tightened and bile burned the back of my throat. The thought of Carrow's mouth on my skin, using August's body to take from me what was never his, twisted something deep inside. I remembered what it had felt like when August fed from me—how it had been possessive, electric, almost reverent. This would be nothing like that. This would be theft, defilement, a reminder that the man I loved was gone and all that remained was a monster wearing him like a disguise.

He traced a finger slowly over my neck. "Augustus's mark is still there," he murmured, a hint of curiosity in his tone, "and I am hoping that means I will not experience any of the effects."

I wanted to fight, to spit in his face, but I could feel the walls closing in. All I could do was try not to show him how much it would destroy me.

"Benedict," he called over his shoulder. "I am not exactly sure if I have full control over Augustus's tendencies and cravings yet, so I may need you to pull me off of her."

He gripped the back of my head suddenly, fingers tangling painfully in my hair and yanking until my scalp screamed. The shock of it forced a gasp from my throat, sharp and unbidden, and he seemed to savor the sound before his lips curled into that cold smile again. "I am going to bite you now."

He moved fast, too fast, slamming me back against the stone.

His mouth was on my neck before I could twist away. The bite came without warning, teeth driving into flesh with no care, no restraint. It wasn't like before. There was no warmth. No gentleness. No flicker of connection.

With August, I had felt consumed—but safe. Claimed. Desired.

But this—this was desecration.

Pain ripped through my shoulder, radiating down my spine. My body screamed to get away, to fight, but he was too strong. I pushed at him, clawed at his chest with my gloved hands, but he only drank deeper, greedier.

It was August's mouth, but it wasn't him.

It was Carrow. Using what he'd stolen. Enjoying the horror of it.

Tears burned my eyes. Not from pain. But from grief.

"Carrow," Benedict said, but Carrow ignored him as I squirmed under his grip.

My eyelids grew heavy, the room tilting as exhaustion crept in, my body fighting to stay awake even as every heartbeat made me weaker.

"Carrow!" Benedict barked again, and in that haze, he ripped him off me.

Carrow fell back with a dark, breathless laugh and wiped his mouth. I slumped against the wall, breath tearing in and out of me in shallow, desperate pulls, every muscle trembling from the drain. "I do not know how Augustus managed to keep control with you. That is going to take some practice."

He rose to his feet in one fluid motion, tapping Benedict sharply on the shoulder as he passed. Benedict flinched, looking horrified, but kept his eyes on me. "Bring her some food to get her strength up. She is needed in the great room in a few hours."

38

Bronwen

I rested my hand on the growing curve of my belly. Everyone talked around me, mostly ignoring me until they asked small questions as if it were the most normal thing in the world for me to be here with Carrow inhabiting the body of the man I loved most.

The routine was set now. During the day, I was locked in that same cold, damp room Carrow had thrown me into all those months ago. But as soon as the moon rose, the servants would come. They would bathe me in silence, dress me like a doll in the gown that had been chosen for that night, then lead me to dinner.

Lavina, Simon, and Benedict would already be waiting, seated as though nothing had changed. They barely acknowledged my presence unless it suited them. I wasn't a prisoner. I was a spectacle. A living display of Carrow's control.

After dinner, we descended to the great room, where laughter and music filled the air. Vampires danced and drank and played their games beneath the flickering candlelight. I sat beside Carrow—beside August's body—and tried to survive the night.

Lavina took to draping herself across him whenever she could, fawning like a dutiful daughter, performing loyalty while reveling in the fact that her brother was gone. I watched her hands touch him, heard her laugh too loudly at his jokes, and imagined killing her each night.

Some evenings, I let my mind wander, let myself pretend it was still August beside me. That his hand on mine meant something. That the heat in his gaze was for me—not for what I carried.

But it never lasted long.

When the sun threatened the edge of the sky, the illusion shattered completely. Carrow would lead me back to his chambers like I was his prize. He would bite a new place each time—never enough to kill me, but enough to bring me close. He would touch me in ways I wished I could erase from my memory. I would squeeze my eyes shut and scream silently for Adar, praying for a miracle. It was silly to believe that there was a small piece of me tethered to my brother, but it was the only hope I held on to.

I still wore the gloves. At that point, I thought my skin might have fused to them and they'd never come off. No one left me alone with so much as a fork. But I was too tired, too heavy, too hollow to do much damage even if they had.

Some nights, I wondered if I would even survive the birth.

Carrow said nothing of what would happen after. But I knew. I could feel it in his gaze, in the way he watched me now—not as a person, but as a vessel. I would give him what he wanted, and then he would decide what I was worth.

Maybe he would keep me—to breed more children. More vessels. Maybe he would let Lavina drain me for sport. Maybe he'd smile as he ordered someone else to carve me open.

I didn't know which fate was worse.

But nothing compared to the agony of seeing August's face twisted in cruelty. Of hearing his voice speak words that didn't belong to him. Of watching his hands—the hands that once held me so gently—become instruments of pain.

It had started to warp the memories I had of him, no matter how hard I fought to keep his presence alive.

"Eat, darling," Carrow said smoothly beside me, the words slicing through the fog I hadn't realized I'd sunk into. "You'll need your strength."

I blinked, fingers tightening on the edge of the tablecloth. The low hum of conversation around the table continued, but his words pressed into my skull like a hand against the back of my neck.

He didn't look at me when he said it, just raised his glass lazily and took a sip, the corner of his mouth twitching into something that might've been a smile—if it hadn't been so razor-edged.

My stomach turned. The food on my plate looked foreign. Cold. I hadn't touched it.

Carrow finally turned his head toward me, those too-familiar eyes glinting with something sharp. "You wouldn't want to pass out halfway through. That wouldn't be very entertaining."

Across the table, Lavina laughed like he'd told a joke, and someone clinked their glass.

But I couldn't hear them anymore.

All I could hear was my heart pounding and the child shifting restlessly beneath my skin—as if it knew, too. I forced myself to lift each bite to my lips, not because I had any appetite, but because the tiny life inside me demanded it. Every swallow was a silent promise—it was all for the baby now, every ounce of strength I had left.

* * *

When I woke again, I was back in the cell.

At least, I thought I was awake. The stone beneath me was real enough, cold against my skin, but everything else felt... different. Too quiet. Too still. My body felt like it was floating just above the floor, tethered only by breath.

Then I saw them.

A forge blazed ahead, heat rippling through the haze like a desert mirage. Shadows danced across the far wall, tall and strange. Figures moved within the firelight.

A swordsmith poured molten metal into a mold, his movements efficient, practiced. He couldn't have looked older than twenty-five—if he were aging at all. His skin bore a faint golden glow, and his features were sharp in the way only the immortals could be—cheekbones that could cut glass, a narrow jaw dusted with ash, and slightly pointed ears that poked through soot-darkened curls.

He was fae.

He wore a leather apron stained with centuries of work, and his arms, though lean, moved with a strength that seemed effortless. Even his stillness carried weight—like he belonged to the forge more than he ever had to the forests or palaces of his kind. This was a craftsman, not a warrior, but his creations would outlive kings.

The blade hissed in its mold. Behind him, another artisan carved the hilt with precision, and the chanting of the two witches began to weave into the very air, their eyes fixed on a black stone resting at the center of the table as if drawing its power.

My gaze followed the black stone as the air seemed to thicken; the sword rose from the mold as if unseen hands bore its weight. I could only watch as each component drifted together—the hilt meeting the blade, the fit seamless, as though the weapon had always existed in this form.

The women's chanting grew louder, more urgent. The stone bled shadow now, spreading into the blade as if feeding it. As if binding itself to the steel.

Realization struck me.

The Blade of Aros.

A weapon forged to command armies of the dead, stealing one soul at a time until none remained. I felt the weight of witnessing its creation, my chest tight with dread. *What was I doing here?*

"Come, Carrow," the swordsmith said as the witches' chanting tapered off, the last syllables echoing in the charged air. The newly-forged blade drifted until it settled itself on the table.

I turned my head slowly, the heat of the forge prickling my skin, realizing I was witnessing a memory like the countless ones I had of August.

"Carrow!" the swordsmith barked, impatience sharpening his tone.

My gaze swept the room again, heart lurching hard as the truth hit me like a fist—I hadn't merely been pulled into a memory. I was inside it. Inside *him*.

I was Carrow.

I was seeing through his eyes.

I looked down at the soot-covered hands, the rough fabric clinging to a younger, leaner body, the forge smoke in my lungs—it was all his. And he had been here. At the blade's beginning.

After Carrow took August's body, the nightmares had stopped—but the mark August left remained. I used to hope it might protect me, ward Carrow off from claiming me. But it hadn't. Not truly.

This was something else. Something deeper.

I could feel myself inside him—Carrow. His thoughts didn't block mine, and my instincts guided his body. I could move, I could breathe, but it was as if my spirit had been draped in his skin. This memory hadn't been summoned. It had been given.

I stood, legs moving before I fully commanded them, and stepped toward them

"This has to work," the fae who carved the designs muttered desperately, more to himself than anyone else.

"It will," the swordsmith answered. "It will raise armies from the dead. We will take Alentara from the creatures and finally be able to live in peace."

"It is done," the older witch murmured. "The ancestors have spoken. Our magic always comes at a price. To keep its strength to create armies, souls must be sacrificed."

The lead witch turned toward me—toward *him*—her eyes narrowing with a subtle disdain, as if she were barely tolerating his presence. There was no warmth in her gaze—only calculation, and the faintest sneer that said she saw right through him. Like he was lesser. Temporary. Useful, but beneath her.

"Give this to your master."

My—*his*—hands trembled as they reached for it. When our fingers closed around the hilt, the world went white.

When it came back, I wasn't in the forge anymore.

I was still in Carrow's body—but now I stood at the edge of a forest, hidden in the shadows of towering trees. From the cover of the tree line, I looked down onto an open battlefield, the earth below a canvas of carnage. The pale, swirling sky cast a dull sheen over the blood-slicked terrain. The air reeked of ash and rot.

Bodies lay strewn across the ground, a grotesque quilt of death. Most of them were fae—fallen warriors in fractured armor, their weapons still clutched in lifeless hands as if refusing to surrender even in death. Among them lay a scattering of creatures, but only a few; the rest prowled over the fallen, feasting without hesitation.

They were nightmares pulled from the oldest, darkest pages of ancient tomes. Winged beasts with bone-covered faces crouched on crooked perches, screeching with hunger. Serpentine horrors, their hides slick with gore, glided through the carnage on rows of hooked claws, black eyes glittering like polished stones. Wolves that walked upright tore at the remains, their massive jaws snapping and their muzzles dripping crimson, howling in twisted victory.

"It's time."

I turned slowly to see a fae I hadn't realized was standing back with me.

His rust-colored hair was braided down his back, streaked with soot and blood. His skin, sun-warmed and golden, gleamed beneath plates of silver-dulled armor etched with ancient sigils. Even from a distance, there was power in the way he stood—still, calm, as though all this death were nothing new to him.

In his hand, he held a blade. *The* blade.

This was Aros.

He lifted his gaze, scanning the torn landscape with a grim expression—no triumph, no fear. Just understanding. Then, with both hands, he plunged the blade into the blood-soaked earth.

The ground pulsed.

And the dead rose.

All around him, corpses jerked to life—not mindlessly, not like puppets, but with purpose. The dead fae and creatures alike. They turned, not toward Aros, but toward the creatures that had slaughtered them.

The monsters shrieked as the risen dead launched their assault. Some beasts were cleaved down instantly, others turned and fled. The air filled with the clash of steel, the howl of magic, the roar of vengeance.

I watched as the battlefield shifted, the chaos twisting into something far more dangerous.

This was absolute control.

39

Bronwen

The child grew heavy inside me, stretching skin and space until there was almost nothing left for me to call my own. The days blurred together—meals and parties, eyes tracking my every movement, Carrow whispering soft threats against my belly like bedtime stories.

But the visions never stopped.

They came without warning—sometimes in sleep, sometimes in the middle of a sentence, leaving me gasping like I'd been pulled through time itself.

In one, I saw Aros, regal and radiant, standing tall as fae warriors knelt before him. One by one, he called them forward—not to reward them, but to sacrifice them. Each soul fed into the blade like kindling. And each time, the magic darkened. I could see it in the steel. In the stone. In the sky above, which turned redder with every offering.

Another vision came in firelight—Carrow, still young, still a servant, watching from the shadows with wide, hungry eyes. Not at the magic or the blade, but at the way they looked at Aros.

Carrow soaked in every moment of it.

I saw him older—maybe only a decade had passed, or maybe hundreds of years. The buildings, the language, and the fashion changed around them, but he had stopped aging. Still in servant's clothes, but no longer watching. He was acting. I watched his hands steal into Aros's tent under cover of night. I saw the blade in his hands.

He didn't hesitate as he drove it into Aros's chest.

And for the first time, he looked alive. But a witch stood in the shadows. She stepped forward as if summoned by the act, her eyes glowing gold. "You will die within a year."

That was the price.

He had traded immortality for power.

In the most recent vision, I saw him in Joveryn still clinging to the last threads of mortality. He moved through the town like a shadow, but he watched her.

She practiced magic in the woods, always alone. She screamed into the night, into the wind, at a family that didn't understand her. Her disdain festered like a wound. He waited. Stalked. Learned her schedule, her weaknesses, her loneliness.

And then he offered her something in return.

Power.

Her name was lost to time now, but I saw her clearly— emerald eyes, ivory skin, thick curls as black as night, hands that shook when she touched the blade for the first time.

My ancestor.

She helped him create the spell. She poured her magic into it. She believed him, and together, they created the vampires and shifted the world.

Now, I sat curled in the corner of my cell, my arms wrapped

protectively around the weight of my belly. My back pressed to the cold stone wall, and I let my eyes slip shut, trying to block out the ache that throbbed low in my spine.

"Your grandparents would have loved you," I whispered. "Your grandmother would have cooked you the best food, and your grandfather would have let you pet the horses. And your father... he would have spoiled you so much." A tear fell down my cheek. "We would have argued about it nonstop, I'm sure. But I wish I could have seen the two of you together. He deserves to be here. To see how much you'd love him. How much *I* love him."

I had to get us out of here. Mama said I used to speak to Adar in my mind. August believed it was true. So I breathed slowly and tried to find Adar.

I pictured his face. Not just his features, but the feel of him. The way he always smelled like old paper and pine. The steadiness in his eyes when the world around us cracked. I remembered the sound of his laugh, the quiet cadence of his voice when he corrected me as we sparred. I pulled all of it close, like string I could wind through my fingers.

Please.

My breath hitched. *Please, Adar. If you can hear me—*

The first pain came like lightning, a white-hot spear ripping through my core.

It tore through me, sharp and brutal, yanking the air from my lungs and cutting off the thought with a scream I couldn't hold back. I doubled over, clutching my belly as a second wave followed, even more vicious than the first, leaving my vision spotted and my breath ragged.

No. No, not now.

I wasn't ready. I wasn't strong enough. I needed more

time—just a little more time. But the baby had made its choice, indifferent to my pleading.

My time was up.

The cell door crashed open with a sound that rattled the walls. Servants rushed in as if they'd been told I would break tonight. Maybe they had. Maybe he'd known before I did. I tried to resist, to brace myself against the pain long enough to fight back, but my legs had given out hours ago. They lifted me from the floor like I weighed nothing, my limbs dangling uselessly as they carried me down the narrow corridor. One of them murmured, "Careful, careful—she's too far along."

I barely registered where we went. Just the change in air. The cold stone gave way to soft lantern light and the faint scent of lavender and something iron-rich. The room they brought me was one I had never seen before. It felt too clean. Too prepared. A basin steamed in the corner. Herbs smoldered in a clay dish. The air was too warm.

They laid me on a bed that creaked under my weight, and another wave of pain struck so hard I thought my vision had fractured. A woman stepped forward through the haze—older, lined with time, but her hands didn't shake.

But it was Carrow who drew the eye.

He stood just beyond the ring of light, unmoving. I could feel his presence more than I could see it—something heavy pressing into the air. He hadn't blinked once. I felt his gaze through every contraction, cold and exacting, more invasive than the hands pressing against my skin. He watched my stomach like it was a vessel of gold being pried open. Not for me. Not for life. For what was inside.

Hands clasped behind his back as if in reverence. But it wasn't reverence. It was restraint. Barely.

His eyes burned into my belly.

"Do not let my son die," he said simply.

The *son.*

The healer didn't look at him. Just gave a small, cold nod before pressing a hand to my stomach. Her fingers were warm and firm. "Breathe," she said.

I tried, but the pain came. And it didn't stop.

Time dissolved. I didn't know if hours passed or minutes. I couldn't see. I couldn't think. I could barely remember who I was. There was only pain, and the memory of August's touch in the moments before we'd created this life. That was what I held on to.

I pushed with what strength I could find, each contraction wrenching a groan from deep in my chest. Sweat soaked my hairline, my hands gripping the sheets until my knuckles ached. The healer's voice cut through the haze, sharp but steady, urging me on. I wanted to stop, to curl away from the pain, but her tone left no room for disobedience.

I faded in and out—sweat-soaked and trembling. The healer barked commands I couldn't understand. Someone dabbed my forehead with a cloth. My heart stuttered more than once. But I didn't beg. Not even when I thought I was going to die.

And then—

A sound.

For a second, I thought I was hallucinating, that my own voice was echoing back at me—broken, reshaped, and unrecognizable. But then it came again, cutting through the haze.

A cry. A *baby's* cry.

My baby's cry.

My chest felt as if it cracked wide open. The tidal wave of sound washed away the pain, and none of it mattered anymore.

The only thing that existed in that moment was that sound.

"It's a girl, Your Grace," someone said, the words seeming to float through the air.

A girl. A beautiful, perfect girl.

Mine.

I tried to lift my head. Everything ached. My chest felt like it was caved in. But I *had* to see her.

"No!" Carrow's scream tore through the room like a curse.

I forced my head up from the pillow, blinking through tears and blood and light. "Let me hold her."

The healer turned to me, but Carrow was already moving.

He crossed the room in seconds and snatched the baby from the healer's arms. Not with care. Not with awe.

With fury.

"Give her to me," I gasped, one arm lifting despite the fire in my side.

I tried to push myself up, but my arms shook and gave out. My body wouldn't move the way I needed it to—not fast enough. Tears spilled freely now, hot and blinding.

She was mine. She was mine, and he was taking her away.

"Please." My voice cracked. "She's mine."

He stepped back, holding her as if she were a spoiled meal. His face was twisted in something worse than rage—disgust.

"Give her to me."

He turned fully to face me. "I have no use for a girl."

* * *

Days passed.

I didn't know how many. No one came other than a servant to give me food, but I refused to eat.

I curled around the emptiness in my body and stared at the wall, my arms wrapped tight around myself as if that could replace what had been taken. My daughter. My child. Ripped from me before I even held her.

I didn't cry anymore. I couldn't. My tears had dried. My throat had cracked. My heart had shattered and left nothing in its place.

He hadn't come back.

I thought maybe he'd left me to rot. That maybe this was the end after all.

Then the door creaked open. Carrow stepped in, perfectly composed, as if he hadn't stolen my baby.

"Where is she?" My voice sounded foreign. I hadn't heard it in days.

His eyes swept over me, and he smiled.

"I've decided," he said casually. "I want to try again."

My blood went cold.

He stepped closer. "I can't stop thinking about it. The idea of a half-witch, half-vampire vessel. It's too... intriguing. Too *perfect* to waste."

I stared up at him, hollow and shaking. "I would rather die."

His smile faded.

He crouched in front of me, close enough that I could smell the copper on his breath. "Then I'll force-feed you if I have to," he whispered. "I've done worse for less."

I tried to shove him away, but my arms barely lifted. My strength was gone. He grabbed me by the throat and shoved me back against the wall with a sudden violence that knocked the air from my lungs.

"You will rest," he hissed, "and when you're healed enough, I'll be back to try again."

He let go, and I crumpled. I couldn't stay here. He couldn't touch me again. I had to do something. *Anything.*

I closed my eyes and pictured my brother again.

40

Bronwen

*Adar. Adar. Adar. Adar. Adar. Adar. Adar. Adar. Adar. Adar. Adar.
Adar. Adar. Adar. Adar. Adar. Adar. Adar. Adar. Adar. Adar. Adar.
Adar. Adar. Adar. Adar. Adar. Adar. Adar. Adar. Adar. Adar. Adar.
Adar. Adar. Adar. Adar. Adar. Adar. Adar. Adar. Adar. Adar. Adar.
Adar. Adar. Adar. Adar. Adar. Adar. Adar. Adar. Adar. Adar. Adar.
Adar. Adar. Adar. Adar. Adar. Adar. Adar. Adar. Adar. Adar. Adar.
Adar. Adar. Adar. Adar. Adar. Adar. Adar. Adar. Adar. Adar. Adar.
Adar. Adar. Adar. Adar. Adar. Adar. Adar. Adar. Adar. Adar. Adar.
Adar. Adar. Adar. Adar. Adar. Adar. Adar. Adar. Adar. Adar. Adar.
Adar. Adar. Adar. Adar. Adar. Adar. Adar. Adar. Adar. Adar. Adar.
Adar. Adar. Adar. Adar. Adar. Adar. Adar. Adar. Adar. Adar. Adar.
Adar. Adar. Adar. Adar. Adar. Adar. Adar. Adar. Adar. Adar. Adar.
Adar. Adar. Adar. Adar. Adar. Adar. Adar. Adar. Adar. Adar. Adar.
Adar. Adar. Adar. Adar. Adar. Adar. Adar. Adar. Adar. Adar. Adar.
Adar. Adar. Adar. Adar. Adar. Adar. Adar. Adar. Adar. Adar. Adar.
Adar. Adar. Adar. Adar. Adar. Adar. Adar. Adar. Adar. Adar. Adar.
Adar. Adar. Adar. Adar. Adar. Adar. Adar. Adar. Adar. Adar. Adar.
Adar. Adar. Adar. Adar. Adar. Adar. Adar. Adar. Adar. Adar. Adar.
Adar. Adar. Adar. Adar. Adar. Adar. Adar. Adar. Adar. Adar. Adar.*

*Adar. Adar. Adar. Adar. Adar. Adar. Adar. Adar. Adar. Adar. Adar.
Adar. Adar. Adar. Adar. Adar. Adar. Adar. Adar. Adar. Adar. Adar.
Adar. Adar. Adar. Adar. Adar. Adar. Adar. Adar. Adar. Adar. Adar.
Adar. Adar. Adar. Adar. Adar. Adar. Adar. Adar. Adar. Adar. Adar.
Adar. Adar. Adar. Adar. Adar. Adar. Adar. Adar. Adar. Adar. Adar.
Adar. Adar. Adar. Adar. Adar. Adar. Adar. Adar. Adar. Adar. Adar.
Adar. Adar. Adar. Adar. Adar. Adar. Adar. Adar. Adar. Adar. Adar.
Adar. Adar. Adar. Adar. Adar. Adar. Adar. Adar. Adar. Adar. Adar.
Adar. Adar. Adar. Adar. Adar. Adar. Adar. Adar. Adar. Adar. Adar.
Adar. Adar. Adar. Adar. Adar. Adar. Adar. Adar. Adar. Adar. Adar.
Adar. Adar. Adar. Adar. Adar. Adar. Adar. Adar. Adar. Adar. Adar.
Adar. Adar. Adar. Adar. Adar. Adar. Adar. Adar. Adar. Adar. Adar.
Adar. Adar. Adar. Adar. Adar. Adar. Adar. Adar. Adar. Adar. Adar.
Adar. Adar. Adar. Adar. Adar. Adar. Adar. Adar. Adar. Adar. Adar.
Adar. Adar. Adar. Adar. Adar. Adar. Adar. Adar. Adar. Adar. Adar.
Adar. Adar. Adar. Adar. Adar. Adar. Adar. Adar. Adar. Adar. Adar.
Adar. Adar. Adar. Adar. Adar. Adar. Adar. Adar. Adar. Adar. Adar.
Adar. Adar. Adar. Adar. Adar. Adar. Adar. Adar. Adar. Adar. Adar.
Adar. Adar. Adar. Adar. Adar. Adar. Adar. Adar. Adar. Adar. Adar.
Adar. Adar. Adar. Adar. Adar. Adar. Adar. Adar. Adar. Adar. Adar.
Adar. Adar. Adar. Adar. Adar. Adar. Adar. Adar. Adar. Adar. Adar.
Adar. Adar. Adar. Adar. Adar. Adar. Adar. Adar. Adar. Adar. Adar.
Adar. Adar. Adar. Adar. Adar. Break Her Heart. Adar. Adar. Adar. Adar.
Adar. Adar. Adar. Adar. Adar. Adar. Adar. Adar. Adar. Adar. Adar.
Adar. Adar. Adar. Adar. Adar. Adar. Adar. Adar. Adar. Adar. Adar.
Adar. Adar. Adar. Adar. Adar. Adar. Adar. Adar. Adar. Adar. Adar.
Adar. Adar. Adar. Adar. Adar. Adar. Adar. Adar. Adar. Adar. Adar.*

Adar. Adar. Adar. Adar. Adar. Adar. Adar. Adar. Adar. Adar. Adar.
Adar. Adar. Adar. Adar. Adar. Adar. Adar. Adar. Adar. Adar. Adar.
Adar. Adar. Adar. Adar. Adar. Adar. Adar. Adar. Adar. Adar. Adar.
Adar. Adar. Adar. Adar. Adar. Adar. Adar. Adar. Adar. Adar. Adar.
Adar. Adar. Adar. Adar. Adar. Adar. Adar. Adar. Adar. Adar. Adar.
Adar. Adar. Adar. Adar. Adar. Adar. Adar. Adar. Adar. Adar. Adar.
Adar. Adar. Adar. Adar. Adar. Adar. Adar. Adar. Adar. Adar. Adar.
Adar. Adar. Adar. Adar. Adar. Adar. Adar. Adar. Adar. Adar. Adar.
Adar. Adar. Adar. Adar. Adar. Adar. Adar. Adar. Adar. Adar. Adar.
Adar. Adar. Adar. Adar. Adar. Adar. Adar. Adar. Adar. Adar. Adar.
Adar. Adar. Adar. Adar. Adar. Adar. Adar. Adar. Adar. Adar. Adar.
Adar. Adar. Adar. Adar. Adar. Adar. Adar. Adar. Adar. Adar. Adar.
Adar. Adar. Adar. Adar. Adar. Adar. Adar. Adar. Adar. Adar. Adar.
Adar. Adar. Adar. Adar. Adar. Adar. Adar. Adar. Adar. Adar. Adar.
Adar. Adar. Adar. Adar. Adar. Adar. Adar. Adar. Adar. Adar. Adar.
Adar. Adar. Adar. Adar. Adar. Adar. Adar. Adar. Adar. Adar. Adar.
Adar. Adar. Adar. Adar. Adar. Adar. Adar. Adar. Adar. Adar. Adar.
Adar. Adar. Adar. Adar. Adar. Adar. Adar. Adar. Adar. Adar. Adar.
Adar. Adar. Adar. Adar. Adar. Adar. Adar. Adar. Adar. Adar. Adar.
Adar. Adar. Adar. Adar. Adar. Adar. Adar. Adar. Adar. Adar. Adar.
Adar. Adar. Adar. Adar. Adar. Adar. Adar. Adar. Adar. Adar. Adar.
Adar. Adar. Adar. Adar. Adar. Adar. Adar. Adar. Adar. Adar. Adar.
Adar. Adar. Adar. Adar. Adar. Adar. Adar. Adar. Adar. Adar. Adar.
Adar. Adar. Adar. Adar. Adar. Adar. Adar. Adar. Adar. Adar. Adar.
Adar. Adar. Adar. Adar. Adar. Adar. Adar. Adar. Adar. Adar. Adar.
Adar. Adar. Adar. Adar. Adar. Adar. Adar. Adar. Adar. Adar. Adar.
Adar. Adar. Adar. Adar. Adar. Adar. Adar. Adar. Adar. Adar. Adar.
Adar. Adar. Adar. Adar. Adar. Adar. Adar. Adar. Adar. Adar. Adar.

Adar. Adar.

41

Adar

Snow had started to fall again as we prepared for another winter. I shoved the cabin door open with my shoulder, arms full of firewood, and kicked it closed behind me. The wind clawed at the frame before it shut. I dropped the wood with a sigh near the hearth, shaking the cold out of my coat.

The fire had burned down to low embers. I knelt and began stacking the wood, the movement automatic. My hands were rough, calloused, nails blackened from work that never seemed to end. My beard had grown thick and uneven, scratching at my jaw, and I hadn't bothered trimming it in weeks. Food was harder to stomach than the silence, and most days I forced down only enough to keep moving. The hollows beneath my cheekbones deepened, but I ignored them.

I kept this place livable—barely. Fixed the leaks in the roof, patched the cracks in the stone, chopped and hauled enough firewood to make it through the cold. It was better than doing nothing. Better than listening to the silence.

After the market, I hadn't gone north again. I stayed in the south, rooted in a place that felt more like exile than refuge.

I didn't try to reach the coven. I didn't send word to anyone. What would I say? That I'd lost her? That I stood by while the last person who mattered was taken from me?

No. Instead, I buried myself in this little house and shut out the rest of the world, pretending the walls could keep the truth out.

I tried not to think about that day, but it seared my memory like a brand that would never fade. She'd sent me off for something too sweet—the way she liked it, always indulgent. I'd only been gone a few minutes, the kind of absence that should have meant nothing. When I came back, she was gone, the basket she had been carrying toppled over onto the ground.

I ran through every alley and every stall, shoving past vendors, knocking over baskets of fruit, screaming her name until my voice cracked raw. My chest ached, lungs tearing with each breath, but I didn't stop. Desperation drove me, but under it all was the gnawing certainty that it was my fault she was gone. If I hadn't left her for something as foolish as a sweet, if I had stayed at her side like I should have, none of it would have happened. I was ready to rip the town apart beam by beam, stone by stone, until I found her. My throat was raw from shouting, and still I ran, driven by panic and the guilt that weighed heavier than my own bones. And at last, I did.

August had her pressed against a wall, his fangs in her neck, draining her while she went limp in his arms. I saw red. I didn't see the tenderness, didn't see the restraint. I saw a predator finishing the kill. And worse, I saw myself too late to stop it.

It had all been a game. He'd hunted her like prey and taken her from me just because he had grown bored in his miserable immortal life. Or maybe the Blood Moon had passed and we just didn't realize it. And it was Carrow who killed her.

I didn't protect her. I should have been there. I should have never left. I didn't protect our parents, and now I had failed her too. She was all I had left, and I had abandoned her for a moment of carelessness. That truth gutted me deeper than any blade.

Then—

"Adar."

I froze. The logs slipped from my hands and clattered across the floorboards, the sound too loud in the silence. My chest constricted as I whipped around, breath caught, scanning the cabin. Empty. The fire hissed low, shadows clawing at the walls.

My heart hammered so hard I thought it might break my ribs. I swallowed, throat dry, and forced myself toward the window. My boots scraped against the rough wood. I pressed a palm to the frosted pane and looked out. Woods. Snow. Stillness. No one. Nothing.

Then it came again.

Adar. It was a whisper inside my mind. Soft as breath, but so real it prickled the hairs along my arms.

My pulse thundered. I staggered back from the glass, chest heaving. Had her spirit come to me? Was I losing my grip, slipping into madness after too many nights alone? I squeezed my eyes shut, fists clenched, trying to steady myself. But the sound of her voice lingered, curling through my mind until I could almost feel her there with me.

Adar. Adar. Adar. Adar.

I slammed my hands over my ears, trying to shut it out, nails digging into my scalp as if I could claw the sound away. My whole body shook with the force of it.

"Stop!" I screamed, the word tearing out of me like it might drive the whisper from my skull.

Then memories hit me so forcibly that I fell to my knees. They weren't mine—but I felt them like they were. I saw her inside that wretched castle, dressed in finery and fire, fighting with every part of herself to survive. I watched her stare August down with eyes that never wavered, and then, I saw her fall in love with him. And he fell just as hard. I saw the way he looked at her, the way he softened, the way he bled for her in ways no one else could see. He was good to her—gentler than I thought him capable of being—and for a time, she was safe in his arms.

And then they ran out of time.

I saw us running, spending our nights under the stars when we couldn't find shelter. I saw that wretched day at the market and watched myself step away from her. Except I didn't watch her death through her eyes. Because she didn't die that day. She was taken. It was all an illusion to think she died. To keep me from coming after her.

I felt her fear when they drove the blade into his heart and everything changed. When August vanished in an instant and Carrow's soul stepped into his skin like it had always belonged there. One heartbeat, he loved her. The next, he was a monster wearing his face. The cruelty. The manipulation. The beatings. The way he twisted her spirit until she barely recognized herself. I saw her become smaller, quieter—except for the moments she burned. When she refused to break.

I watched her belly grow, heavy with the life they created, watched how she held on to that child as if it were the only thing anchoring her. And then I saw it—the birth. The screams. The blood. The way she fought, and the way it was all ripped from her in one final, cruel stroke.

Her baby. Her daughter.

Stolen.

I screamed her name until my throat tore raw, but it wasn't enough—nothing was ever enough. The sound broke against the silence, swallowed whole by her absence.

I collapsed to my knees in the firelight, chest heaving, heart splitting open as her pain surged through me like a tidal wave I could never outrun. Tears blurred my vision, and a low, strangled moan clawed from my chest as guilt devoured me. I hadn't protected her. I hadn't saved her. And the weight of that truth pressed down on me until I could hardly breathe.

Adar. The whisper came again.

She was calling for me. Somehow she had tethered her mind to mine, her presence brushing against the edges of my thoughts like a fragile thread of light in the dark.

I opened my mouth to speak but quickly closed it, my breath shaking in my chest, terrified that even whispering might snap the connection.

B? I thought, the word trembling as I sent it out to her.

Adar? I–I'm not going crazy, am I?

Her voice, even echoing inside my mind, was faint and frayed. It carried none of the fierce certainty, none of the relentless fire that had always defined my sister. Hearing her like that twisted my stomach with dread.

Bronwen? I breathed her name inside my mind, the sound cracking with disbelief. My throat tightened as I forced the thought out. *Is it really you?*

Then an image of a dark room lit only by shadows, its stone walls damp, and a heavy door barred from the outside flashed through my mind. The air felt suffocating, a prison meant to break her.

Come get me. The words landed like a plea, threaded with desperation that hollowed out my chest.

42

Bronwen

Curled in the farthest corner of the cell, my back pressed to the cold stone wall. The only light came from a single slit in the ceiling high above, casting pale gray shadows that never changed. I'd lost track of how many days had passed since I'd reached out to Adar. Since I'd pulled on that frayed, forgotten thread in my mind and found him.

I didn't even know how I had done it. I just knew that I had screamed inside my head so loudly that somehow, he'd heard me. Since then, he had spoken to me now and then. Small reassurances. A whisper in the dark when I needed it most. *I'm coming.*

I held on to those words like lifelines, replaying them when the silence stretched too long, when the pain threatened to consume me. He said he was working on getting magic. That he couldn't get to me yet, not without it.

I understood. But gods, it was getting harder to wait.

Because it wasn't just fear that kept me curled up in this place. It was grief—deep and hollow and unrelenting.

My baby was gone.

I didn't know what Carrow had done with her. Had he killed her? Hidden her away? Was she crying somewhere, scared and alone? Or worse—was she with him?

That loss clawed at me more viciously than the hunger or the cold or the silence ever could. It was the kind of pain that rooted itself in my bones, that stole the breath from my lungs when I tried to sleep. Some nights, I felt the flutter of phantom kicks low in my belly, cruel echoes of a life I never got to hold. I would jolt awake clutching at myself, desperate to find her still there, only to be met with hollow silence and emptiness.

Every time footsteps echoed outside the door, I flinched. Every time the lock scraped open and a tray was shoved inside, I held my breath.

Not yet, I told myself. *But soon.*

I refused to let myself think of anything else.

Just *soon.*

Carrow hadn't come to me yet. That was the one grace the gods seemed to have gifted me with.

Until I felt the air shift.

There was no sound. No footsteps. Just a rush of pressure, like the room exhaled all at once. I shielded my eyes as a flicker of light sparked, blinding in the gloom. Spots burst behind my lids as I squinted into the sudden glow, heart thundering.

When my eyes adjusted, I saw him standing there, a small ball of fire glowing in his hand, casting shifting shadows across the stone walls and chasing the darkness back. The light flickered against the hollows of his face as my heart stuttered.

Adar.

He crouched before me, and I barely recognized him. His face was thinner, cheekbones sharp where they hadn't been before. Shadows bruised the skin beneath his eyes, and a rough scruff covered his jaw as if he hadn't had the time or will to shave. He looked unkempt, worn down, as if every day I'd been locked away had carved itself into him too. His eyes were wide with panic and relief all at once.

He reached for me gently, arms wrapping around my small, curled frame like I was something breakable.

"B," he breathed, tucking his chin into the top of my head. "Gods, I found you."

I wanted to cry. I wanted to fall apart in his arms, but I couldn't. I had no tears left. Only the silence and the weight of everything I had lost. I clung to him anyway.

"I didn't know if you'd really come," I whispered.

He pulled back enough to look at me. "You found me first, remember? You never stopped fighting. I just had to catch up."

His hands trembled as they touched my arms, as if he didn't believe I was real.

"You look like hell," he said softly.

"Thanks," I rasped. "Did you bring anything for that?"

His gaze dropped to my hands, to the ugly metal gloves still fused to my skin. He reached out slowly, fingers brushing the edge of one as if testing its resistance. Then he tugged, gentle but firm.

"Don't," I said. "It's no use. My skin's probably grown around them by now. It would take a lot of magic to get them off without tearing my hands apart in the process."

He froze, eyes meeting mine. The guilt in them made my chest ache. "I didn't know they hurt like that."

"They don't. Not anymore," I lied. "Or maybe I've just stopped noticing. That's the same thing, right?"

He smiled for a second. Just a second. "We're going to get far away from here. But first—B, I need you to hold on. I only have enough magic to take us part of the way. Once we're clear, I'll get more. I promise."

"No."

He froze. "What do you mean no? We have to get out of here before anyone finds out."

The easiest way out would be to go with Adar now and run. But I'd let my heart overpower my head for too long. And it had done nothing for me.

I needed to finish what I was born to do. Put an end to the person who had taken everything from me.

"Bring me a vampire."

43

Bronwen

Adar didn't try to change my mind. He just looked at me, and something in his eyes shifted. He knew he couldn't sway me. Not now.

I closed my eyes and sent the image into his mind. A place where I knew one vampire would be alone. Always alone.

Adar nodded once, jaw tight, and vanished before my eyes with a soft snap of pressure in the air. And I waited, hands clenched into fists, every nerve in my body bracing for what was to come.

I blinked—Adar was back, with Benedict slumped unconscious in his arms. Adar let out a breath, his chest heaving as he flexed his fingers, magic still crackling faintly around them.

"What—?" Benedict gasped, stirring as he hit the floor. His eyes locked on mine. "Bronwen."

I didn't answer.

Adar looked at me. "What now?"

I couldn't tell him. But if I did, he might have tried to stop me.

"Give me a blade."

He hesitated for a fraction of a second, then reached beneath his coat and passed me a dagger, handle-first.

Benedict moved to rise, but Adar's hand clamped down on his shoulder, forcing him still. I stepped forward, the blade steady in my grip. I didn't ask permission. I didn't explain. I just sliced a clean, precise line across Benedict's forearm. Blood welled immediately.

And I brought it to my mouth.

The taste of Benedict's blood hit my tongue, warm and metallic, and magic sparked through my limbs like wildfire.

"B!" Adar's voice cracked with panic as he lunged forward.

But I was already moving. I turned the blade inward, pressed it against my sternum, and drove it in before he could stop me.

I woke with a sharp gasp, air flooding into my lungs like I'd been drowning. My back arched off the floor and I flailed for a moment, unsure if I was alive or trapped in some other twisted dream.

Then I stilled. The dark cell was suddenly clearer than I'd ever seen it—every crack in the stone, every speck of dust floating through the air. The distant drip of water sounded like it was beside me. I could hear things—tiny things—like the scraping of rats in the walls, the flutter of moth wings in the light slit above. And something else.

I could hear a heartbeat.

I turned my head slowly and my nostrils flared as Adar's scent hit me like a wave—earthy, warm, tinged with fear.

And underneath it, his blood.

It was intoxicating. Rich, alive, calling to something deeper than instinct—something primal and starving. My throat burned with need. My teeth ached.

I could smell him. I could feel him. Every beat of his heart thundered through me like a drum summoning a forgotten hunger.

I was a vampire.

Benedict slumped on the floor, his skin still pallid but slowly regaining color—signs of life inching back into him. Adar must have drained him of everything he had. Good. He would need every scrap of magic he could muster to get us as far as I intended to go.

"B." Adar dropped beside me, his hand pressed to his chest. His breaths were uneven, and though he tried to mask the pain, I could see it clearly now—his pain and mine, mirrored in his expression. The moment our eyes met, I felt it. The horror, the disbelief, the weight of what I had done. "What did you do?"

"I'm putting an end to this."

Maybe it was reckless. Maybe it was the last desperate act of someone with nothing left to lose. But it was the only path forward I could see. I didn't care what it would cost me—not if it meant destroying the monster who'd taken everything.

Even if I never felt the warmth of a fire again and the sun forever burns me. Even if this hunger would hollow me out until nothing remained but a shell of who I used to be. Even if I would be driven closer to the insanity I saw August fight every day.

The hunger was growing.

I turned my head toward Adar. His heartbeat still pounded in my ears, his scent flooding my senses. The thought of sinking my teeth into him surged, violent and hot, and my chest ached with the war between hunger and love. He had come for me, risked his life, and yet my body screamed to devour him. I shook my head hard, tears burning as I forced the craving down.

I would never hurt him. Never bite him.

I clenched my jaw and forced myself to look away. I would find another way to feed. He had already given me enough.

"You have to leave," I said through gritted teeth.

He reached for me, and I jerked back.

"I am not leaving you again."

I closed my eyes as I tried to focus on the smell of the cell and not Adar. "I will meet you at the gate. You can't be here for what I am about to do."

Adar hesitated. I felt it ripple through him—the conflict, the disbelief. But I knew he could feel me too: the wall of fury and resolve that would not budge.

His jaw clenched. "What about him?"

I followed his gaze to Benedict, still slumped on the floor. My stomach twisted, but all I saw now was betrayal. Memories of his betrayal burned hot and sharp—how he had come for me and delivered me straight into Carrow's hands. Rage and grief tangled in my chest.

"Burn him."

* * *

I lay sprawled on the cold stone floor, my limbs limp, every nerve still screaming from the transformation, my skull pounding with a single, relentless command to feed. Footsteps echoed beyond the cell door—measured, deliberate, heavy, as though each one was meant to remind me of what was coming.

I forced myself not to move, though my body trembled. I already knew who it was.

The hunger inside me stirred again, clawing at my insides. I clenched my teeth and kept my eyes closed. They were red. I knew they were red.

I didn't want him to see me like this. Not yet.

The door flew open with a heavy slam that echoed through the stone chamber. I flinched but didn't move, keeping my eyes shut, my breathing shallow.

"Is my dear wife asleep?" he drawled, amusement laced in every syllable.

Still, I didn't move.

He crouched in front of me, his presence thick and dark, pressing in all around me like smoke seeping into my lungs. His hand trailed slowly up my bare leg, pausing at my knee before his mouth latched onto my thigh. Fangs pierced my skin—sharp, possessive, certain he still owned me.

But I smiled as my eyes snapped open.

The sound he made was a wet gurgle, his hands clawing for his throat. His arms went slack, his body toppling backward, confusion flooding his gaze.

Vampire blood was poison to other vampires.

I sat up and hummed as I looked down at my hands. The ugly metal gloves still clung to my skin—too tight, fused with pain and time. I flexed my fingers and slowly began to tug at the edge of one. It resisted at first, the edges catching against raw, tender skin. Then it gave way with a sickening pull. Skin tore. Blood welled.

But the pain faded almost instantly, replaced by a strange tingling warmth. I watched, breath caught, as the skin began to stitch itself back together, slow but sure.

I pulled off the second glove. More flesh came with it. More blood. But again, it healed.

I stared at my bare hands, flexing them slowly. The skin was pink and new, but stronger. The black veins still curled up my left arm, stark against my skin—a mark of what we had failed to do.

I straddled him and cradled his face, desperate for one more glimpse of the man I had once loved. My chest ached with the want to believe I could find him again, but that man was gone.

"Where is my baby?"

Carrow tried to speak, but nothing came out.

I patted his cheek. "Come on, I know you can do it. Tell me where she is."

A sinister smile twisted his lips. "D-d—" he choked, the vampire blood still eating away at his control. "Dead."

Rage ignited in my chest, raw and wild. My hands shook as I pressed one flat against his ribs. He didn't even have time to blink before I plunged my hand into his chest. Flesh gave way. Bone cracked. My fingers closed around the thrumming organ that had once belonged to the man I trusted.

His eyes widened, a choked sound escaping his lips.

I felt nothing but fire.

"This is for her. And him. And every fucking thing you've taken from me."

His eyes shifted into something softer and closer to fear. "No—it's me. I'm still here."

I hesitated, just for a second.

"It's me, Bronwen." His voice cracked like something

human, something buried.

My grip on his heart tightened, fingers digging into the muscle. "He didn't call me Bronwen."

His expression twisted with anger, but before he could say another word, I rose from the floor with his heart clenched in my fist.

Epilogue

Bronwen stepped through the hall slowly, intending at first to head straight to the great room, but her feet betrayed her. They carried her up several flights of stairs, through the corridor, and halted before the door she'd seen Lavina slip into countless times.

Lavina sat at her dressing table, brushing her hair. The moment the door opened, her gaze caught Bronwen's in the mirror.

"Does Carrow know his pet is out?" she mocked.

Bronwen didn't answer.

Lavina turned, the brush slipping from her fingers and clattering to the floor as her eyes dropped lower.

"What did you do?" Her voice was tight with disbelief.

Bronwen followed her gaze.

Carrow's heart pulsed in her palm—slow, sluggish beats that hadn't quite stopped. She didn't even remember bringing it with her. She didn't remember *not* bringing it either.

Lavina stood abruptly, panic flickering in her eyes, but she was too slow.

Bronwen was already there, closing the distance with predatory speed. Her hand drove into Lavina's chest with a wet crack, twisting deep until her breath rattled and her skin turned a sickly shade of gray. Lavina's mouth opened in a soundless cry, eyes wide with horror as her knees buckled.

Bronwen shoved her back, letting her crumple lifelessly to the floor.

A rustle broke the silence from the bed. Simon stirred beneath the tangled sheets, unaware. Disgust burned through Bronwen as she took in the sight—of course he was here, with her. It made too much sense. The bile rose in her throat at the thought of their intimacy, but she refused to let it slow her. She crossed the room in a heartbeat, looming over the bed. He blinked awake just in time to see her shadow fall across him, confusion etched across his face. It was the last thing he saw before she drove her hand down, ending him before he could even scream.

Bronwen looked down at the torn slip she still wore, crusted with dried blood and things she didn't want to name. A ripple of distaste passed through her—not shame, not now, but something close to awareness. The thin fabric clung uncomfortably to her skin, stiff with what it carried, and she felt the weight of it as though it were chains.

She raised her gaze, teeth pressing into her lip. The heart in her fist pulsed sluggishly, and she could feel its rhythm against her palm, as if it mocked her.

She turned from the bed and walked toward Lavina's armoire, pulling it open with one hand while the other still clutched the heart. The heavy doors groaned, revealing rows of indulgences.

Silks, velvets, lace. She'd always had expensive taste. Bronwen thumbed through the garments until she found something beautiful—dramatic and dark, something fit for a queen. She pulled it free and held it up against herself, the fabric rich and heavy compared to the ruined slip. She slipped it on, the fabric whispering against her skin, smoothing over her shoulders as if claiming her. For a moment, she simply stood there, breathing, feeling the change in herself as much as in the gown.

Then she turned to the mirror.

Red eyes stared back at her. She let out a laugh—something that sounded strangely familiar.

She didn't flinch.

Her hand lifted almost lazily, smoothing her hair as if nothing about this moment were extraordinary, tucking a stray strand behind her ear with deliberate calm. The gesture felt mocking, defiant.

She stepped back out into the corridor, shoulders squared, breath steady, vision sharp as glass. Carrow's—no, *August's*—heart was still beating softly in her grasp, its sluggish rhythm a quiet reminder of what she had done, and what she would never return from.

A gasp broke the silence.

A servant stood at the end of the hall, a tray trembling in her hands, her eyes wide with horror. She turned to run.

But instinct surged faster than thought.

Bronwen was on her in a blink, knocking the tray to the ground as she pinned her to the wall. Her scent wrapped around Bronwen—sweet, ripe, alive. The pulse in her throat beat like a drum, calling to the monster that had rooted itself deep inside Bronwen.

Her teeth sank into her neck, and everything else disappeared.

The first taste was fire and silk—warmth that spread like sunlight through frozen veins. It filled her, lit her from the inside, chased away the lingering cold of death. The shock of it nearly made her knees buckle, a desperate sound rumbling from her throat as if she couldn't get enough fast enough.

The servant writhed for only a second before falling still.

Bronwen drank deeply, each swallow flooding her with power, every drop stitching together the pieces of herself she thought she had lost.

When she finally tore her mouth away, the servant's body slumped heavily in her arms. She lowered her to the floor almost tenderly, though her hands still trembled. She wiped her mouth with the back of her hand, smearing blood across her lips. The copper tang lingered on her tongue, rich and sweet, making her shiver.

It was intoxicating. It was *everything.*

She was no longer a witch forced to borrow scraps of power. Now, she was something far greater.

A strange lightness settled in her chest—not joy, not exactly. But something like it. Contentment, maybe. Clarity. Like the sharp edges of grief had dulled just enough to breathe around them. Some things that once clawed at her mind now felt distant, inconsequential.

She adjusted her grip, shifting the weight in her hand without thought. It wasn't until she glanced down that she realized she was *still* holding August's heart. Somehow, she hadn't let go. Couldn't let go.

She wiped the last trace of blood from her chin and began to hum. It was an old tune. One her mother used to sing while sewing late into the night. The sound echoed through the corridor as she descended the stairs with a lightness that felt unnatural but welcome.

She smiled to herself, the great room calling to her like a stage waiting for its final act.

As she stepped through the grand doors, the music faltered.

A haunting silence rippled across the room. All eyes turned. Gasps scattered like broken glass as vampires froze mid-dance, mid-sip, mid-sentence.

She didn't look at them.

The hem of her gown whispered over the marble as she glided forward. She ascended the steps to the thrones. At the top, she paused, letting her gaze sweep over the empty chairs—theirs. His. Hers. She moved to August's throne and ran her fingers along the armrest, then the underside until she felt something odd. A small stone, just slightly raised.

She pressed it.

With a soft click, the back panel slid open, and she reached in without hesitation. Her hand closed around a familiar hilt, but she no longer felt the hum of the dark power that called to her before. She pulled the Blade of Aros free, the steel gleaming like shadow and moonlight.

"Idiot," she muttered under her breath, lips curling at the edge.

If they didn't have the dagger, they couldn't let Carrow's soul out again.

She stood back up to see everyone staring at her from below. "Don't mind me."

Some of the guards exchanged uneasy glances, their eyes flicking from her face to the heart in her hand. She followed their gaze, blinking as if surprised to still be holding it.

"Why haven't you let it go, Bronwen?" She didn't mean to say it out loud.

But she couldn't. Her fingers were locked around it, as if her body had made the decision for her.

The guards shifted, subtly moving to block the stairs that led back down. She stared at them a beat too long, then turned to the edge of the platform. She blew out a breath and stepped off.

There was no rush of fear, no twist of panic. Just a smooth descent, her body moving like it had always known how to fall without consequence.

"That was easier than I expected," she murmured to herself.

In a blur, she slipped through the crowd and out of the room, leaving silence and fear in her wake.

"Get her!" someone finally yelled.

So she ran.

Her bare feet hit the stone floor, silent and swift. The weight of the blade and the heart didn't slow her. If anything, they steadied her. She burst through the front doors of the castle, the night air sharp and cool on her skin. A thousand stars blinked down at her as she sprinted down the long road toward the gate that led to town.

Behind her, the guards shouted to each other. Orders barked, boots slamming against the ground. She didn't stop until she spotted Adar pacing in the shadows near the gates, his hands raking through his hair as panic etched deep lines into his face.

He turned toward her, eyes widening at the sight of her clutching both a heart and a blade. Whatever words he had died in his throat. There wasn't time for explanations. Soon, they'd be overrun.

Bronwen didn't hesitate. She thought of the place she'd seen in one of the old tomes and shoved the image into Adar's mind.

His eyes went wide, his mouth falling open. "What the fuck is that?" He nearly stumbled back, shaking his head.

"Take us there," she commanded.

Adar threw up his hands. "That looks more dangerous than where we are now!"

"Just do it, Adar." Her words snapped like a whip, daring him to argue again.

Something in her voice silenced him. He swallowed hard, shoulders rigid, then reached for her hand as if it were the only thing keeping him steady.

They collapsed onto the ground, swallowed by darkness—save for the eerie glow of a vibrant, shimmering pool nearby. Strange howls and distant screams echoed through the void. Adar scrambled to his feet and reached for Bronwen, but before his hand could find hers, something cold and unseen coiled around them both, slamming them hard against the earth.

A boy-like creature stood before them. He couldn't have been more than thirteen, with wild black hair, pale skin, and a slim, gangly frame. But what made him more than a boy—something not quite human—were his pitch-black eyes, pointed ears, and the inky clouds that floated around him like living shadows.

He was fae. Or something close enough to be worse.

"Who are you?" The question rang with quiet command. Despite his youthful appearance, he radiated authority as he looked down at the intruders bound in black mist, forced to kneel before him.

Adar glanced at his sister, but she said nothing.

"We—we are humans seeking refuge. We mean no harm."

The fae's black eyes bore into Adar, sending a chill down his spine. Something slithered through his mind, invasive and cold. The boy was in his head, searching, unraveling truth from lie.

"You lie to me. You are no human. You are a witch—but not like any I have known."

He turned his gaze to Bronwen, who made no effort to resist the magic that held her. A strange calm washed through her as her eyes met his, a fleeting peace she hadn't felt in what felt like forever. Despite the weight of the black mist and blood on her, she smiled softly at the boy, as though simply looking at him eased something inside her.

In an instant, the boy released her. She crumpled to the ground.

"You are... I do not know what you are. I have seen nothing like you before."

The boy's gaze dropped to the heart and blade cradled in her hands. His eyes flared with sudden alarm, the shadows around him tightening.

"You are from Joveryn. How do you have such a blade?"

Bronwen's gaze flicked down to the dagger, then rose to meet the boy's eyes once more. She didn't speak. There was no point—he could pluck the answers straight from her thoughts.

He looked between them again, the truth unraveling itself in his mind. And for the first time in nearly a decade, the lonely boy felt something stir inside him—connection, belonging.

He wasn't about to let that slip away.

"You will come to my castle."

And as she followed the fae boy through the darkness of the forest, a rare calm settled inside Bronwen. For the first time in so long, she felt at peace. Yet she also knew one thing to be true.

Darkness had consumed her.

And she had brought her brother with her.